····· RAILROAD ·····

To Ralph,

Thank you for the support.
Enjoy the book.

Peter Howe

by Peter Howe

Melvoy's Railroad

Copyright © 2018 by Peter Howe

Cover Illustrations and Book Design by Heartisan Creations.

All rights reserved. This book or any portion thereof may not be reproduced or used in any manner whatsoever without the express written permission of the owner, except for the use of brief quotations in a book review.

Printed by CreateSpace, An Amazon.com Company
CreateSpace, Charleston SC

First Printing, 2018

ISBN-13: 978-1544985398
ISBN-10: 1544985398

ALSO BY THIS AUTHOR

Peter Howe has other books that are currently available on Amazon and other online book sellers. These include:

The Game Changer: A Collection of Poetry (2015)

Confront the Raven (2016)

More coming in the years ahead!

DEDICATIONS

I would like to dedicate this book, first to every person who dares to dream of a future where we can rise above our current mindset. I also wanted to dedicate this book to my mother and sister who are extremely supportive and I love so much. I also want to dedicate this book to my friends Stephen, Stacey and Fran who I often told about this book and were encouraging with every update. Also, my cousin Steven, the older brother I never had. I would also like to dedicate this book to my friends Steve, Rob and Chris the guys who make me glad when it's Monday. My friend Ben, who has been there with me helping me get my name out there at various events and was also encouraging during much of the process of writing this novel. Dave and Sarah, who were very encouraging but also agreed to be early reviewers for the book. My long list of co-workers both current and former who have been encouraging and welcoming with every update. Finally, I would like to dedicate this book to everyone who reads it start to finish and understands not just why I wrote it, but why I had to write it.

This book was edited by my mother Debbie Howe.

I would also like to thank Jennifer from Heartisan Creations for her hard work and determination in assisting me with the interior formatting and exterior cover design for this book.

CHAPTERS

1 : HUMBLE BEGINNINGS 3

2 : YOU THINK YOU'RE TOUGH 9

3 : THE LAST STOP UNTIL VIETNAM 14

4 : VIETNAM, ROUND ONE 17

5 : IMMATURE LOVE 24

6 : VIETNAM, ROUND TWO 27

7 : THE SIXTIES ARE OVER, MY LIFE HAS BEGUN 32

8 : THE FORMER ENEMY 35

9 : LOVE & MARRIAGE 38

10 : BECOMING A MAN 44

11 : VIETNAM, ROUND THREE 51

12 : WALKING IN DIFFERENT SHOES 54

13 : SERGEANT & FATHER 59

14 : 1975, DISCO & DEUTSCHLAND 63

15 : HOME BITTERSWEET HOME 68

16 : THE KILLJOY RETURNS 74

17 : BIG SKY, BIGGER PROBLEMS 79

18 : THERE'S SOMETHING ABOUT TEXAS 84

19 : SECOND LIEUTENANT, FIRST PRIORITY 92

20 : THE COLLISION 97

21 : BETTER OFF WITHOUT THEM 107

22 : THE NEW DECADE 113

23 : DECORATION, DIVORCE & DESPAIR 116

24 : I GOTTA GET OUT OF THIS PLACE, IF IT'S THE LAST THING I EVER DO.. 125

25 : GO AHEAD, MAKE MY DAY 127

26 : THE FIRST SPARKS... 134

27 : BILLY'S WORDS 138

28 : THE HAPPIEST PLACE ON EARTH 141

29 : RE-ELECTION, REJECTION, REFLECTION.......... 148

30 : INTOLERABLE & INEVITABLE............................. 155

31 : CHURCH BELLS RING.. 160

32 : IT'S TIME TO CHANGE COURSE 166

33 : WHAT I WAS WAITING FOR...SORT OF................ 173

34 : PANAMA!... 179

35 : I LEFT A DANGEROUS COUNTRY FOR THIS?....... 183

36 : MAKE A DEAL, BREAK A DEAL 193

37 : IT DIDN'T HAVE TO BE THAT WAY 199

38 : I TOOK THE LEAP, THEY TOOK THE PLUNGE...... 206

39 : LOVE (& HATE) ARE IN THE AIR! 217

40 : 1989: A PANAMANIAN ODYSSEY........................ 225

41 : NOT ALL BOMBS ARE DROPPED BY ENEMIES 235

vii

CHAPTERS

42 : FALLING THROUGH OUR FINGERS 244

43 : TWO BATTLES 247

44 : THE RAILROAD BEGINS 251

45 : THE STRUGGLE 257

46 : THE LOSS 267

47 : POINT OF NO RETURN 272

48 : TOO LATE? 280

49 : SAVING THE DAY 288

50 : THE ENEMIES WITHIN MY WALLS 293

51 : LIGHTNING CRASHES 304

52 : I HATE THE 1990S 310

53 : THE MAN COMES AROUND 317

54 : A DEAL WITH THE DEVIL 323

55 : YOU CAN'T SPELL MINNESOTA WITHOUT MINE . 330

56 : IT ALL COMES CRASHING DOWN 337

57 : WHY AM I STILL HERE? 350

58 : GOODBYE CIA 358

59 : WHERE IS HOME? 363

60 : UNFINISHED BUSINESS 368

61 : LIKE ME? 373

62 : THE LONG ROAD TO RECOVERY 379

63 : MIRACLE OR MASSACRE? 382

64 : GETTING THROUGH THE STORM 390

65 : NOT THIS TIME 395

66 : A NEW HOPE 401

67 : BACK FROM PRISON 404

68 : MORE TROUBLE ON THE HORIZON 410

69 : STOP THE FUTURE, I WANT TO GET OFF! 414

70 : THE MANCHURIAN CANDIDATE 418

71 : MAKING NIXON LOOK GOOD 421

72 : THE COLD WAR BECOMES HOT 425

73 : WHAT IS & NEVER SHOULD HAVE BEEN 428

MELVOYS RAILROAD

by Peter Howe

CHAPTER 1

★

HUMBLE BEGINNINGS

My name is Charles Melvoy and it is hard to believe that I turned seventy-three years old today. Where did all that time go? Where did that grey hair come from? I don't know, it just crept up on me. In any event, I hope you can learn from my life. I am writing this knowing it won't paint me in a good light but I am willing to take whatever grief comes from it. After everything that has happened, I don't want it all to be in vain.

I was born in Ann Arbor Michigan on July 17, 1949. I was the oldest of three children with a younger sister Cathy who was born on May 20, 1951 and the youngest was Billy, born on October 3, 1954. I was the good son who wanted to be like my father, my sister Cathy wanted to be like my mother.

My brother Billy was the troublemaker of the family, and usually if something happened, it was Billy, and maybe being the youngest, he wanted attention. One time that comes to mind, was when he was six and he got on top of the kitchen table and started swinging back and forth on the chandelier. I came downstairs just as he had started and I told him to get down. He said, "No this is fun."

No sooner did he say that than the chandelier came loose and he let go, with it hanging half-broken out of the ceiling. When our mother came home a few minutes later from the corner store, she was surprised and we both got in trouble. Billy got in trouble for swinging on the chandelier and me for not watching him more closely, for the twenty minutes she had stepped out. There are other stories like that but that is the one that comes to mind.

We grew up in a nice house, in a decent neighbourhood, and my childhood was pretty normal and like most boys I looked for a model of manhood. In many ways, I idolized my father so I always tried hard in school, and wanted him to be proud of me, he taught me what being a man was in the traditional sense. If my mother and father wanted me to watch Billy, I tried to keep an eye on him, which was usually easier said than done. Other than those incidents, we all got along pretty well on a day-to-day basis. Every summer, my father, Billy and I would go for fishing trips where he would tell us about the old days before they had supermarkets. Billy usually was trying to compete with me to see who could catch the bigger fish, and I usually won but he surprised me a time or two.

Like many kids I tried a few different sports and played them for different reasons. However, as time went on I grew to like football, because you could run, tackle and do it without having to learn how to skate. I remember one time when Billy was really young, I was trying to teach him how to tackle. I remember telling him to charge at me, but he would always slow down because he was scared of the impact. So, one day, I started teasing him until he got mad enough to charge at me and he actually knocked me back a step.

Even though he occasionally caused trouble and he was five years younger, I always wanted to look out for him and show him how to do things. I got that from my parents- my father and mother always took time to teach us things.

I remember sometimes on the news, they would have a story about the President of the United States and when I was a child that President was Dwight D. Eisenhower. My father admired him a great deal and used to say, "I worked for him."

I would ask, "You did?"

He said, "Exactly, I was a soldier and he was the five-star general and supreme commander. Charlie, that man is the President of the United States, and you always respect the President of the United States, and if he ever comes to town, you had better salute."

I responded, "I will Dad."

A little later on, Presidents Kennedy and Johnson didn't get as much of his admiration, but he still respected that they were the Presidents and people like Robert McNamara, the Secretary of Defense under Kennedy and Johnson, always came across as a brilliant man who was determined to win.

Most of my childhood I saw things like that on the old black and white television – good and bad, us and them, black and white – everything seemed so simple. Back then the idea of what a man and woman were supposed to be, were far more defined, so I didn't teach Cathy sports stuff. She would play with her dolls or want to learn how to make cupcakes or cookies from my mother.

I remember one Christmas I think I was nine, Cathy, Billy and I all agreed that whoever woke up first, we would wake up the other two so we could get our presents. As luck would have it, Cathy woke up first, and she woke us up and we came downstairs and were so excited to see our presents that we didn't realize it was 5:30 am. We started yelling with excitement when my father came down and said, "Go back to bed, we'll call you at 7:00, your presents can wait until then."

Of course we didn't sleep, how could we? It was Christmas morning, eventually 7:00 am came around, and we came downstairs and got to play with our presents. It seemed like such a good plan at the time, so we decided to apply this rule to Easter and future Christmases but we remembered to wait until 7:00, so we wouldn't get our father mad at us.

So, we weren't really close, but we did things together and looked out for each other. I remember back when Billy was in kindergarten, and two kids who were in grade two started picking on him. One day my friend Greg and I were walking through the playground when we saw these two kids shoving him. I immediately leapt into action and told them that he was my brother and they had better back off, and they did and while that wasn't the only time I helped Billy, it was one of the ones that I remember most vividly, partially because of how quickly they scurried away. Back then in the late 1950s and early 1960s people didn't take stuff like that too seriously, it was just accepted as the norm.

I remember one time in grade five, this kid in grade seven beat me up and took my lunch money, but I don't remember the kid's name. My father asked me what happened and I told him, then my father told me something that I never forgot, "Charlie, the kid was older than you, you were scared and you hesitated. Next time don't hesitate, when you are standing toe to toe with an enemy, you charge forward, if I hesitated at the moment of truth, I wouldn't be here right now."

So, a few days later, I'm pretty sure it was a Friday, he tried to take my money again but this time when we started throwing fists, I took a few shots, but I cleaned his clock. He expected me to be scared like last time, but this time I was intense, I was fierce, I was a man. When I got home my mother fretted over my bruises, but my father asked me what happened, so I told him, he patted me on the back and said, "Good job, kid."

It was a really proud moment. After that, for the next few years, everyone at school respected me and knew I wouldn't take any guff from anybody.

A key time in my life was high school, when I eventually became one of the top guys on the football team, because I was very reliable and always worked really hard. Coach Lennox used to tell me, "Charlie if all those guys practiced as hard as you did, I would have bought the trophy polish already."

On the field, I followed my father's advice, not to hesitate and it worked every time. The only time I can remember that it didn't work completely, was one day when there was one guy who was built like a wall. I tried to tackle through the guy, I went down and he went back three or four steps. All the guys were amazed that I even tried that and that I had knocked him back several steps. A few of them couldn't help but ask me why I tried to do that and I told them, "Charlie Melvoy fears nobody."

My senior year was very exciting, with a pretty good football team. I remember we were winning quite a bit and there was talk about our team winning the regional championships. I remember the captain, the assistant captain, Tony and I called a meeting with all of the guys saying that we had all better step up, because we had two more games to win if we were going to get into the regional championship. We all tried to get the guys inspired to step up, although it may not have been as good as those speeches in movies, but it seemed to work. We won the first game and we were very excited for the next one.

Unfortunately, that day it seemed like the rest of the guys had two left feet, although I played as hard as I ever had and we were tied with the other team going into the fourth quarter. I remember that scoreboard showing "17-17" with one of those touchdowns being mine in the second quarter which had earned me quite a few comments of "atta boy."

Coach Lennox told us not to give up and that if we played this quarter and give it one hundred and fifty percent, then we would go to the championship game, where we would win the trophy we had worked for all season. Unfortunately, one bad throw, an interception and two good plays by the other team and we were down by a touchdown, which was when the other guys basically gave up. When that buzzer went off, I knew that I had given it everything I had, but my teammates didn't care as much as I did. As disappointed as I was, I came off that field and my father put his hand on my shoulder and said, "Hey Charlie, don't get down on yourself. I know you played your best, you know you played your best, you have nothing to be ashamed of. The ones who should be ashamed are those bums who started dragging their feet."

He finished by saying, "Son, I'm proud of you."

Despite that encouragement, I felt upset that we didn't finish victorious. It was like the season would always be one game away from being finished and it bothered me for a long time.

Those years changed me despite that one bad game, and I gained even more confidence and more importantly I eventually found out who I wanted to be as an adult. I decided this from my history classes, where I was taught about the wars of the past, and those heroic men who fought the British for freedom. During the revolutionary war that gave birth to America, and how I wanted to fight for my country as my forefathers did, and all I needed was a cause. The cause of course was red, my cause became fighting communism. I was in high school in the mid 1960's where we heard fairly often about those Russians and what they could do, and how they were trying to spread communism across the world. Ever since grade one, they had told us about how to duck and cover under our desks, which looking back was ridiculous. If nuclear weapons had hit us, those desks would have been like a piece of paper in a raging inferno.

Getting back on topic, 1776 was the year our forefathers stood up to the British Empire, and all of those soldiers who died for our freedom, whom I really looked up to. By that point, I also knew about World War II and how Hitler tried to take over the world and how all of those soldiers died fighting the Nazis. I was inspired by their sacrifice, their courage and after everything they had done for us, I wasn't going to let the Iron Curtain take it away.

The summer of 1967, I turned eighteen and I had a fun summer with my friends – working, going to a few bars, that type of stuff. I told my friend Anthony how I wanted to go into the army, and he was scared for me. He was telling me about how I might get killed like his older cousin, but I told him I wasn't afraid of that, and I was prepared to fight and die for my country. Best of all, when I returned home I would have a free ticket to college if I wanted it. But his concerns did make me hesitate, and for a couple months after high school, I worked full time in the local grocery store where I went from bagging groceries for a few months to becoming the assistant supervisor.

Finally, the day came when I knew I had to stand up and fulfill my life's purpose. In October of 1967, I went to my parents and told them that I wanted to join the army and help America fight in Vietnam. I will never forget the smile that came across my father's face as his eyes lit up with pride, because he had been a veteran himself fighting in Italy in World War II. He had told me all these stories about his first trip to Italy, followed by his second deployment that ended just before the end of the war. Perhaps he felt like I was following in his footsteps, or maybe he was glad that I had heard what he told me over and over again, about how the Viet Cong invading South Vietnam was like Hitler invading Poland. In either case, he was thrilled but my mother wasn't very happy.

She loved all of her children so much, that she didn't want to see anything happen to any of us. My father and mother argued about it a lot, but I don't remember how long. I just remember my mother seeing the body bags on the news and being afraid that one day I would come home in one. Eventually, she gave in and gave me her blessing. Although I thought that I had it all figured out, in retrospect I was an eighteen-year-old kid, what the hell did I know?

I found out that the start of training would be in January, and in a way I was relieved because I knew my mother would want one more Christmas with me before I left. During the next couple of months, I saw how polarizing this war was, and a majority of the people told me I was doing the right thing and being a true blue American for joining in. The smaller group told me that it was an unnecessary war, it was murder and the other stuff that I basically ignored, because I just dismissed it as pot smoking hippie garbage. I thought that they may not love America enough to fight for it, as much as I did.

It was a great Christmas, and I remember the notepad I was given by my mother so I could write to her once I was over there because she wanted to hear from me often. Just after New Year's Day my father took me ice fishing where he asked me if I really knew what I was getting into. I told him exactly what I thought, how I was taught how to be a man from a real man, and that I would be fine. He seemed skeptical but supportive, perhaps he was torn between his pride and concern, and since it was only a week or so away, the reality of my decision was hitting him.

The worst memory I have was leaving Billy, who by this point he was thirteen and he and I got into a big argument. He said, "You have been kissing Dad's ass your whole life and now it's going to get you killed."

I responded saying, "I am fighting the commies so you can have rights and you can have a future."

His response was, "That's why I hate this family. Mom and Dad don't want children, they want robots that just repeat what they say, I'm my own man. I'm not going to do everything just because Mom and Dad want me to, I'm not going to be a Charliebot like you."

I called him an ungrateful brat, and suddenly my mother heard us arguing and she split us up. She tried to tell me that he was upset that I was leaving and was too young to deal with it. I looked at her and said, "He should be old enough to respect what people do for him."

He and I barely spoke another word to each other after that, and there was a very bitter parting. At the time, all I saw was him being an ungrateful brat, the kid who all of us especially me looked out for, the kid who was being told how to be a man and who wasn't thankful for it at all.

CHAPTER 2
★
YOU THINK YOU'RE TOUGH

On a Saturday in January 1968, my father drove me to Norfolk, Virginia to their training camp, and during those two days, he and I had quite the discussion. During it he told me not to talk back to the instructor, answer everything with, "Sir, 'your answer' and sir."

He really stressed that it would be one of the most difficult things I would ever do in my life. He told me some of the stories from when he was in the army during his time in Italy. There were some quiet times too. As we drove those hundreds of miles where I saw all of those people in those towns and fields, so full of life and so bright with the sun shining off the snow, that it just filled me with pride to know that this wonderful place was my country. Just as we pulled up to the camp, my father and I shook hands and he told me, "I'm proud of you son."

I greeted a few of the people who were nearby and I remember a few of the people I attended the camp with, and their names were Ross, Phil, Jim, Sid and Mark. In the case of Mark, I eventually got to know him too well. On Sunday evening, I found my barrack and I knew tomorrow would be a challenge unlike any other, but despite all the warnings, despite all the hard work I put in football practice, nothing could prepare me for this.

That Monday morning, they woke us up at 6:00 am as they would every morning from then on, and told us to see the barber and that we had better be back by 8:00 am or there would be hell to pay. I had short hair already but feeling the trimmer go across my scalp was simultaneously relaxing and scary. I kept trying to remind myself that I was tough, and I needed to remember that I was Charlie Melvoy and Charlie Melvoy fears nobody.

My bunkmate was named Ross, who was a good guy and he and I talked for a few moments. Then the Drill Sergeant Miller walked in, we soon realized why he earned the nickname Miller the Killer. He got in everyone's face and asked various versions of, "What makes you think you can make it in this army?"

These also included some versions of, "Who the hell are you, you look like shit."

These comments could be anything to cut us down and it wasn't personal – everyone got yelled at. Basically, in this stage there is no right answer, and there are only wrong, more wrong, and very, very wrong. I was proud of what I had accomplished in high school, and I was young and boy did I say something stupid. He got to me after tearing into a few other guys and said, "What makes you think you can make it in my army, dirt bag?"

I responded, "Sir, because I'm tough sir."

By saying that, I was inviting him to kick my ass. He responded, "You think you're tough? Did your mommy tell you that?"

I responded, "Sir, no I played high school football, sir."

I immediately regretted saying it, what a fool I was. He responded, "You played high school football? Well this ain't a game sweetheart, there are no cheerleaders, there are no time outs and when the Viet Cong come at you, they aren't coming to take a ball, they're coming to take your head!"

During that speech, his face got closer and closer and his voice got louder and louder. "Do you still think you're tough?"

I responded in a less proud voice, "Sir, yes sir."

Boy was I asking for it. He said, "Prove it. Drop and give me twenty."

I did the twenty push-ups, as I had done many times before during football practice. He ordered me to do another twenty, and although I managed to do it, I was getting tired as my arms began to tremble. Then he ordered me to do another twenty, where in I collapsed part way through but he ordered me to keep going until I finished, even though I was exhausted. My back hurt, my arms hurt and according to Ross, my face was beet red. Miller stared me directly in my eyes and said, "You are going to have be a lot tougher than that, if you expect to wear that uniform in combat."

He then moved on to get in the faces of the other guys so he could tear them down one by one. The reason why what I said was so stupid was that it put a target right between my eyes for Miller to make an example out of me. When you enlist into the army, they tear you down, and if you have pride or you think you are special they will rip it out of you by any means necessary.

Now it was the winter, and we went out running through the snow, although winters in Virginia weren't as bad as those I had experienced in Michigan. Those first few days I became friends with Ross and usually additional tasks are assigned to you and your bunkmate, so we knew we had to work together to survive. If you were assigned chores and they didn't get done and done well, you were in trouble. For the first two or three weeks of training whenever Miller walked in, one of the first things he would do is walk up to me and say, "Drop and give me twenty."

Then before he left, he would tell me to do another twenty, thirty or whatever he felt like that day. Sometimes when we were doing those long marches, he would tell me that I had to carry one of the guys the last hundred yards. After doing that once or twice, I was ordered to carry Phil. The first time carrying Phil was so hard, you have to understand Phil was six feet and five inches tall, well over two hundred pounds, and thankfully less dense than the guy who was built like a wall who I ran into on the football field. Phil was the biggest and naturally heaviest guy in the group. I collapsed part way but Miller kept yelling and telling me that tough guys don't quit. Any guy with any sense knew from my example that you did not screw with Miller the Killer.

Phil's specialty was hand-to-hand combat, a lot of the other soldiers still had the intimidation of the larger guy, which was the intimidation that my father taught me not to have. When we did the hand-to-hand combat sparring sessions, I fought with everything I had and even though he won, I always had an impressive showing. If Miller told you "not bad" that was the closest thing to a compliment you were ever going to hear. Because of how hard I fought and the fact that I kept carrying Phil over and over, Phil both pitied and respected me and told me that he would look out for me if I needed it.

As beat up and exhausted as I was doing everything else and doing these extra tasks, including a few that I probably forgot, I noticed that I was getting stronger and that I was pushing beyond what I thought my limits were. After those two or three weeks, Miller laid off because I hadn't quit, I was doing what was demanded. The other big reason was that there were other guys that had done things to piss him off, whether it was not cleaning up like they were supposed to, talking out of turn, their uniform not looking right or whatever. Eventually Charlie Melvoy was not the designated whipping boy anymore, which made me feel so relieved.

One thing you need to understand is that during those first few weeks my muscles ached worse than they ever had before. I would be asleep and suddenly one of my calf muscles would knot up and I would wake up in such pain that I was struggling to breathe. Some guys just couldn't handle it and quit, with Miller being less than flattering about anyone who did.

About halfway through I felt like I was turning the corner, as I was hearing a few more of those "not bads" from Miller, but once again, that's as close to a compliment as you were going to get. I remember writing a letter to my father telling him about what I had survived and as I wrote that letter, I wanted more than anything to see my parents again and have that warm family reunion moment. Unfortunately, nothing in the military is warm; there is cold, there is hot, but there is no warm.

One thing I hadn't mentioned up until this point was that the guys not only were afraid of Miller, but they were kind of nervous around Sid. The odd guy would catch him looking at them in the shower, and a lot of guys were scared and were worried he might be queer. You have to understand back then, people weren't as open about it. In 1968, being queer or gay was illegal so if anything like that happened it was kept very quiet. You would get rumors every once in a while, but you wouldn't have people coming out in public saying "Yay I'm gay" and have people welcoming them with open arms. In 1968, that was unthinkable.

Ross was the pretty boy of the group, with blonde hair, and good looks, so Sid began to spend a lot of time talking to him. The story as I know it was that Sid had been following Ross a little bit, and he began to cling to him. Apparently at one moment, Sid said something about Ross having great lips. Ross apparently told Sid to stay away from him and that he did not want to be part of any of that stuff. Well pretty soon, word spread around about this and all the sudden Mark decided to take it upon himself to drive Sid out of the platoon by any means necessary.

So, the next day when all of us were in the shower, Mark waited for Sid's eventual looking around and suddenly Mark called everyone's attention to it. Before we knew it, people were throwing soaps at him and the term "faggot" was used over and over again. Then Mark got right in his face and said, "If you don't get your queer ass out of here by lights out, we will beat your lights out, got it you fucking faggot?"

Sid was really hurt, and he did quit before lights out and we never saw him again, and we tried to forget that he existed. Honestly, Mark wasn't kidding and who knows what would have happened to Sid if he had stayed. I guess we will never know and maybe it is better that way.

So, there were five of us who became friends, Phil "the hill", Ross, Jim, Mark and myself. Mark bunked with Jim so he would tag along and that was how he became part of our group. During those last couple of weeks, the five of us became our own group and the other people knew that if you screwed with one of us, you were screwing with all of us. We began to talk about how we were going to kick so much ass once we got to Vietnam. We were going to take all of those commie Viet Cong soldiers and either wipe them out, or have them screaming back to their mothers.

Finally, the day came, when all of those people that couldn't cut it left and those who remained were going to be judged, and we were so excited when all five of us made it. It was then announced where we were going, and before we knew it, we were U.S. Soldiers about to defend the world from the Commies and to show the Soviets how powerful our country was. The last thing Miller said to me was, "Melvoy, when you said you were tough, I thought you were full of shit, but you busted your ass and now you are, so when you get to Vietnam, give 'em hell."

I proudly responded, "Sir, thank you sir."

It had been eight weeks, and it was now a Saturday in March, and the next group of soldiers was coming in on Monday, as we had. That night our group said our temporary goodbyes and knew that we would be seeing each other again when we shipped out on May 4th.

CHAPTER 3
★
THE LAST STOP UNTIL VIETNAM

Those two months were more or less a repeat of the same things, people around town either knew I was in basic training and I was going to Vietnam or they thought I had fallen off the edge of the earth. There was a lot of people saying how amazed they were that I was willing to take on this challenge, and almost everyone over forty was calling me a fine young man.

Things at home were tense, even though my mother and Cathy had made peace with my decision and my father couldn't be prouder, Billy and I had an uncomfortable tension. Since I left, he and his friend at school were listening to all these hippie ideals going around. One of his friends had an older brother who was one of these hippies, I saw him a couple times and it looked like he hadn't washed his long hair in weeks. My father was getting into arguments with Billy about how he didn't like who he was hanging around with. It always ended the same, with my father telling him to respect his father and tradition. Billy would say something to him to get him even angrier, my father would tell him that he was going to send him to the military academy if he didn't change his tune. This usually ended with Billy leaving the table or the room saying how angry he was at our family. I would try to confront him about it but my mother would always grab me by the wrist, and shake her head no, because she didn't want this to get any uglier than it already was.

This tension had been building since I signed up for the army and of all the times for it to happen, it all boiled over during our Easter dinner. We were all called to be there, and Billy rolled his eyes about being there, but he sat down. My mother was really trying to uphold our family tradition. Our grandmother on my mother's side was there as well as the extended family. The tradition always was that my father, since my mother's father had passed away years earlier, would bow his head, to lead the saying of grace, as well as cutting the turkey.

As soon as the blessing was finished, Billy rolled his eyes again, and I reluctantly kept quiet trying to keep the peace. Before long, some of the cousins and uncles were congratulating me and talking to me about how great I was doing and how I was a patriot. Billy was bristling with every passing moment, and although I should have pulled him aside and talked to him, I was so focused on everyone's praise at that moment. My father was basking in the glory, with a bright smile on his face, and the statement came up, "Yeah, he's a chip off the old block."

Uncle Roy, who we didn't get to see very often and lived just outside of Des Moines, was there and was completely unaware of our family conflict. Just as I was enjoying all of this praise, Uncle Roy turned to my brother Billy and said, "So Billy, in just a few years you will be eighteen and you can join the military just like your brother."

Billy got upset and said, "Why, why is it so important in this family? Why does everyone have to be part of the military industrial complex?"

I was annoyed and said, "Billy, knock it off."

Then it all exploded, "Oh, that's right if I don't have Dad's opinion, I don't have an opinion! Well fuck you!"

My father stood up and in a very angry voice said, "I've had it with your language and your disrespect young man. You are going to respect your father, your family and your country, just like your brother."

Billy got up, slammed his chair and ran for the door while screaming, "Everything's about Charlie!"

My father went after him, but as I got up, he told me to stay. So I stayed and spoke to my other relatives while Cathy comforted my mother who was crying in the kitchen because her big family dinner, that she took so much pride in, was ruined.

About an hour later, my father came home with Billy nowhere in sight, and I asked what happened but he didn't say, so I followed him to his den. Finally, he told me what happened.

"You know that filthy hippie that Billy and his friends have been hanging around with? Well he went to some place where a whole bunch of them were living just on the outskirts of town, they told me that they weren't going to let me hurt Billy's free spirit."

His disgust as he said this was obvious. "So, I am going to let him stay in that dirty place for one night and if he isn't back here tomorrow morning by 10:00 am, with the biggest apology he has ever given, I am going to call the police and bring him back here. Then I will drop him off at the military academy immediately."

He continued as he paced back and forth, "What is going on with these kids, they have no respect and they are all about this flower power bullshit, no son of mine is going to be some filthy, unemployed, disrespectful, pot smoking hippie."

I asked my father if it was my fault, "Maybe Billy is jealous of everyone making such a big deal about me."

My father assured me, that if anything I was a great person for Billy to look up to, but that Billy needed a kick in the ass. The next day, Billy didn't come home and just as my father said at 10:01 am, he called the cops to go get his son. They brought him home before 11:00 am and my father shoved a suitcase into his arms and said, "Get in the car, there is a military academy northwest of Grand Rapids, they will make you a man."

The last thing I saw was a look on Billy's face that could kill.

The next few weeks were very uncomfortable and the truth was that Billy was gone and would be until the middle of June. I began to re-focus on my mission, going to Vietnam to fight the communists from taking over South Vietnam and in the process, showing the Communists America's strength. I was looking forward to seeing all of my friends from basic training again, because it would be almost a nice escape from the tension at home.

Things were starting to get back to a feeling of normal, until one day we got a phone call from the military academy. Billy had somehow escaped and run away, and although he may have been a troublemaker he wasn't dumb. They had no idea where he was, and from the best they could tell, he had escaped from the barracks, climbed the fence and ran to the nearest dirt road. They believed that he may have hitch-hiked from there.

My father was left in a state of disbelief, my mother and sister were heartbroken and I had to leave for Vietnam in a couple days. I said my farewell, although I was reluctant to leave but I had already signed up, so at this point I didn't have a choice. My mother once again became scared because she didn't want to lose two sons, but I promised her I would be back in six months at the end of my deployment, and I would be back in time for Thanksgiving and Christmas.

As my father drove me to the military base where I would be leaving from, he shook my hand and promised me that he was going to find Billy and that by the time I came home everything would be all right. I left conflicted, feeling like I had a war to fight but feeling like that the people at home needed me too.

CHAPTER 4
★
VIETNAM, ROUND ONE

I said hello to everyone as we got on the plane heading over to Vietnam, and they began telling us about what had been going on with the Viet Cong (who will be referred to from this point onward as the VC). They were holding their ground and we were there to not only stop any possible advancement but to drive them back. A few people mentioned that just looking at Phil "the hill" should send them running and we all had a good laugh. When you are in a war zone, you need whatever fun and joy you can find.

During the first few days that we got there, there wasn't much action, but there was a lot of telling us this or that. Telling us what certain procedures were, what areas were safe and which areas weren't and so on. We got about a week in, when we were called to fight off a VC attack on one of our bases to the west.

As we got there our training and recent practice kicked in, and we began shooting. What was hard to deal with about this how much more noise there was, things were happening faster and it was harder to process everything that was going on. At one point Ross had managed to shoot a barrel of oil that exploded and eventually the invading soldiers were either killed or retreated. We eventually came across the two enemy soldiers who had been behind the oil barrel, one was dead and the other squirming and quietly letting out breaths in pain. We looked on, somewhat shocked at the charred flesh and being not quite sure what to do.

Mark looked at us and said, "Hey guys watch this."

He proceeded to kick the soldier in the ribs. Jim immediately spoke up and told Mark to stop, Mark ignored him and did it again, but Mark did stop when Phil grabbed him by the shoulder and said, "That's enough."

That was when the Platoon Sergeant came by and said, "Quit playing around, one of you put him out of his misery and let's keep moving."

We looked at each other for a moment, then I stepped forward and aimed my gun at his head. He had this look on his face as if he was bracing for the impact, but still I had never killed a man before.

If I had killed anyone, it was during the shooting earlier from some distance away, but looking directly into the eyes of the person you are killing makes it a lot harder. The first kill is always the hardest, I hesitated again, when Mark said, "Today, Charlie."

I pulled the trigger the sound was sudden but filled the air and then I began to walk away. Ross spoke to me for a few minutes on the way back about how I did the right thing and not to worry about it. He knew how hard the first kill was and wanted to make sure I wasn't going to be deterred.

Over the next few weeks I began to notice how good we were all getting along, we also began to see that there was no shortage of VC soldiers. Killing a few here and there adds up, but no matter how many got picked off, there was always more on the way. It also didn't help that some of these took place in a jungle area and it was hard to know whether you were fighting two or ten.

During those first couple months, I received a few letters from my mother and father, telling me they hadn't been able to find Billy, but they weren't giving up. Cathy had a boyfriend that my parents approved of, and I was happy for her. As I look back at these letters now, I realize just how much they meant to me at the time.

The five of us were fairly lucky; most of us didn't have any serious injuries and were faring okay in the everyday grind of the tour. In a strange way, it was still fun, talking with your friends, going out on adventures, having a few close calls, and stories that were fun to tell and hear about. One of those stories were we went into one of the safe towns and walked into the local bar. We had talked about meeting some of the local girls, who were so different from the girls of our respective hometowns.

One day, Jim began talking to this one girl when her boyfriend and two other guys walked in, and told us to get away from his girlfriend. Jim rolled his eyes and said, "Okay, didn't know."

He began to order another drink when the guy told us to get lost and that he didn't want to see Americans in his bar. Phil stood up and asked him why, and this guy spouted off about how "Americans just take what they please and don't care about Vietnam."

That was when I stepped forward and got in this guy's face saying that we were there protecting their country, and that they should be glad we were there or they would have to face the North Vietnamese alone. The tension was enormous, and I don't know whether the guy owned the bar or whether he was just some blow-hard throwing his weight around. Just as we began to go to the bar to order drinks, he grabbed the back of my shirt and threw me backwards into a small table. By the time I got back up, Phil was throwing one guy over the bar, Ross and Jim were keeping everyone else back and Mark was the beating the troublemaker with a stool, in fact he was beating him bloody. I didn't see what happened to the other guy. Finally, Phil and I told Mark to stop and he reluctantly did, but that guy was a bloody mess. He was probably going to have to go to the hospital after that. After that I pulled Mark aside and asked him what the deal was, then he responded by saying, "He picked a fight, when you pick a fight with a U.S. Soldier, you deserve whatever you get."

At the time, it sounded like the right answer. Afterwards, Phil told me about what happened during that brief period that I was down on the floor, he also reminded me of what he had said to me during training – that he always had my back.

Unfortunately, the good times don't last forever and whatever fun I was having stopped one day in October, when a few of us were sent on a mission. There had been a rumour that a couple dozen VCs had just come into a village nearby and a few of us, along with a Vietnamese translator, went to check it out. We were told that the village was in a minor valley and that we could look at it from a safe distance. The village was just outside of a larger town that had been ruined by the fighting some time ago. There were five of us on this mission – Mark, myself, two other guys whose names I can't remember, and the translator.

As we got closer and looked from a distance from behind a hill, the village had several huts most likely built for the refugees from the larger town that had been destroyed. As we looked, we noticed that there was probably a dozen VC Soldiers, which made us immediately decide to retreat and inform the Sergeant. Unfortunately, one of them had spotted us and began shooting. I told Mark to crawl to the jeep as the shooting started and call for help.

Within seconds our translator was shot, as the remaining three of us were shooting, and thankfully Mark came back with some more weapons from the jeep. Now we had some major firepower, but despite this they shot one of the other guys in the chest. We had probably killed three or four of them, when I noticed that there were children were being rushed into a particular hut by two of the soldiers. Then we got the automatic weapons and that turned the tide, and then unfortunately things took a bad turn. Mark grabbed the rocket launcher and asked if there were any others. The other guy that hadn't been shot told him about the two that were in the hut that had the children in it. Mark began to aim it when I asked him what he was doing and his response was, "Now or ten years from now, what's the difference?"

I told him to stop and that there was no need for this. Just as it seemed like he was getting annoyed at me, he asked me to look over and to see if that truck was ours. I grabbed the binoculars and could see the U.S. Markings on it, and when I turned around and saw him aiming and then firing the rocket at the hut containing the children and two VC soldiers. It was a large explosion, and that was when I lost it and he and I began fighting right there. This guy had just killed dozens of children, which made me so angry that I lost it on him.

We were fairly evenly matched for the brief moment that we were exchanging punches and were trying to overpower each other. Before either one of us could get a serious advantage over the other, the Sergeant and other soldiers got out of the truck and ordered the guys to pull us apart. We had messed each other up pretty good, with bruises, blood, black eyes and my nose got knocked a little bit to the right and had to be re-set.

The Sergeant demanded that we explain what happened, so I told him my side, Mark proceeded to claim that the only reason he did it, was to get the two VCs that were inside. I knew better though. Eventually the Lieutenant demanded that we shake hands and put this behind us. The Sergeant later pulled me aside and told me, "Look Charlie, sometimes there is collateral damage and you just have to accept it and move on. The important thing is the VC lost some more territory and another dozen soldiers."

Over the next few days Mark and I were angry at each other, and although he may have fooled other people I knew what he had done. A few days after this, an unarmed Korean man came into our camp and showed us a picture he had taken of numerous weapons in an abandoned building in the destroyed larger town that I mentioned earlier. In his broken English, he had told us about how the VC were planning a major assault. He knew that they were gone now and that if we went in, we could seize their weapons.

The Major and Lieutenants went into the room to decide how to proceed. They came out some time later and decided that we would move out and go there. So the Major agreed that they would send numerous soldiers into that building as well as the other nearby buildings just in case there were others.

We were separated into groups, and the Sergeant was worried about Mark and I fighting again so he split us into different groups. Our entire company was out on this mission and the Sergeant didn't want infighting to screw it up. They were fairly certain this could prevent a major raid and weaken the VCs from gaining any new territory.

As we drove to the buildings, the orange sun was setting. I volunteered to be one of the people in one of the trucks watching our backs with my rifle. I was split between being excited thinking about raiding all of those weapons from the VC and stopping a major attack before it could begin, and the thought that we might get killed if this raid was poorly timed. We went into the buildings looking around for any soldiers or any signs of explosives. As we were going up the stairs we kept looking, when all of the sudden we got all the way up to the top floor and saw there was nothing. Jim and Phil were with me when all of a sudden we got a message on the army radio, saying that we had been double crossed and that the VC were surrounding the buildings. The guy who had come with us was a kamikaze who had killed himself as soon as he knew the game was up. We looked outside the significant holes in the walls and saw all of the VC with the buildings surrounded.

As we began to wonder about what to do, they had an interpreter with a megaphone who began to talk to us as we were spread out in the three buildings. "Attention Americans, you invade Vietnam, you try to rule us like the French before you, now you not only kill men, you killed twenty-three children. We have you outnumbered, these rocket launchers are aimed at your buildings, just like the rockets you fired at Vietnam's children. Either come out unarmed and your death will be quick. Or we blow up those buildings and burn you alive. You have three minutes to decide your fate."

One of the other soldiers looking out the other windows, saw the rocket launcher aimed at our building, and we began to frantically decide what we would do. Phil immediately came up to me and gave me a big hug, and said, "Tell my Mom and Dad back in Bethlehem Pennsylvania that I'm sorry."

I wasn't sure what he was going to do, that was when he pulled out of the kit eight grenades and began attaching them to himself. I grabbed his arm and told him not to, but he told me it had to be done. He put a grenade in each hand so he had six on him, everyone agreed to pull the pins at once as he prepared to jump. Preparing to grab one of the pins knowing it would kill a friend was painful, and I barely found the will to do it. Just as the man with the megaphone yelled one minute, Phil threw himself through the open hole in the side of the building. Phil began to throw them as he fell and I never saw how many, but within a few seconds there was absolute chaos and explosions breaking out, and I knew that Phil "the hill" was dead.

We then went to the windows and began opening fire, not only did Phil take out the rocket launcher aimed at our building, he took out the launcher aimed at the building to our left. The one rocket launcher still took out the other building. As we all opened fire, we knew that we might not make it out alive. During the fighting, I was shot in my right kneecap and went down. It was one of the most painful things I had ever experienced, that hot lead not only burned but actually smashed into my knee. It's hard to find the words but amazingly after several more minutes of fighting and several more people dying, we finally won. There were three people in our group left standing and two more injured on the ground like I was. Jim helped carry me down so we could get out of there.

The officers overseeing our region of the conflict came the next day to investigate what had happened. The few healthy soldiers left in our company had told them the story. As I was helped out of the infirmary, I went to see if anyone else had survived and I saw one man who was in a coma, another who was in a wheelchair and I saw others too. As I became more and more sad and angry, that was when I saw Mark and my blood began boil, I didn't care that he had stubs where his right arm and left hand were. I began yelling, "You son of a bitch, you're the reason for all of this! You killed those kids and now Phil's dead, Ross is dead, the Sergeant's dead, and most of our company is dead!"

That was when the nurses began to pull me away and insisted that I calm down.

Jim came to me later that day and asked how I was feeling, and so I told him how pissed off I was. I was told that I would be shipping back home early with a purple heart and that with a little bit of surgery and rehab at the military hospital, I would be as good as new soon enough.

Before I left two promises were made. The first was a promise to myself that I would issue my personal condolences to Phil's family. He had literally died for us, so it was the least I could do. The second was a promise to the military officials not to talk about what had happened. If anyone asked, just to say that there was some fighting and I got hit.

The day they came to take us home, I saw Mark being helped into another chopper headed for home and I thought about how that was too good for him. He deserved to be in the ground instead of all those other guys. My right knee still was in pain and I had to take various painkillers while they were going to ship me home a few weeks early.

When I came home, my father and mother picked me up and were so glad to have me back. Shortly after we went home, I insisted that someone drive me to Pennsylvania. I couldn't drive because my right knee was still hurt and I was told not to put weight on it, by both the military and civilian doctors. After a week, my old friend Tony finally agreed to make the trip.

Finally, we got there and when Phil's father answered the door, I began to tremble as I knew it would be hard to talk to these people about their son's death. I skipped certain details, but I told them about the grenades and him throwing himself out the hole in the wall but most of all his last words. His mother thanked me for coming and his father shook my hand. As Tony and I drove home that day he asked me, "What are you going to do now?"

I looked at him and said, "I don't know."

CHAPTER 5

★

IMMATURE LOVE

My father was a foreman on a loading dock and told me that he would be willing to help me find a job at the loading dock, and that I would probably fit right in once my leg was healed. I had to wait a couple of weeks but I got the surgery needed to take the bullet out of my leg. I was told that I would need about three months of healing and rehab until my leg would be all right again. The problem was that when I wasn't at physiotherapy I was home which was very boring for me after being so active in the military. There weren't a thousand channels on the TV or the Internet back then as there is now.

I began to notice my father drinking more than he used to and on a typical weeknight he used to have one or possibly two beers. After I had returned, he'd had four or five beers. Every time that I tried to ask about Billy, either my mother or father would change the subject. When you have nothing to do for hours, you end up fixating on things. I worked hard on my physiotherapy because I wanted to get better and do something else and hated just sitting around. The other thing was, I wanted to be able to corner my father and finally find out what happened with Billy.

One night as my knee was almost back to normal, I finally sat down with my father to talk about Billy. It had been two months and they were pretending that he didn't exist. Sure, I thought that he had been ungrateful and disrespectful but he was still part of our family.

Eventually, I got my father to tell me that Billy had intentionally run away from the military school. Billy had told the instructors at the school that he was going to escape and it was only a matter of time before that happened. Apparently, while Billy was at the hippie's house, he had made some deal with a couple of them to wait outside of the place until he could escape. The guys who did it, apparently took him across the state line and to who knows where. I could tell that it really bothered my father that Billy, his son, hated him so much he would rather run away with strangers than stay with his family. Unfortunately, my father was still in denial about his drinking and I didn't realize at the time how serious alcoholism was then and now.

24

15 or 16 yrs old.

I met Cathy's boyfriend, his name was Jason who seemed like a good guy, and he was a bartender at the time who seemed to have all the ambition in the world. Jason, Tony and I went out to a bar in Detroit one night a few weeks before Christmas. While I was there I saw a beautiful woman, with hair shining like golden strands, teeth whiter than the snow outside and eyes a beautiful blue like the ocean. Her name was Lisa, and she was such a sweetheart. I began to speak to her, although I was nervous but did a really good job of hiding it.

Somehow, I was more scared of saying something wrong to this beautiful woman then I was of getting blown up by the VC. We agreed to meet again, and we began to date. Being with her was intoxicating, but I was very split about where I wanted to be.

As winter once again became spring part of me wanted to go back to Vietnam in order to fight those VC soldiers, which had become my life's purpose. Part of me wanted to stay there with Lisa, who at that time I was sure was the love of my life. I truly felt like I was being torn in half.

There were two things driving me back to Vietnam. First was the job, which wasn't a hard job but it did seem boring and predictable. At first I liked how calm it was, but after a while it became boring and repetitive. I got along well enough with the guys but it just felt like I was in a rut. As the summer began, I was getting very tired of this ordinary feeling, and not to mention I was determined to win that war and the war wasn't over yet. Every time I heard about it, I would think to myself, "They need me, I need to go back there."

The other thing that was happening was that I was considering whether to propose to Lisa. Even though she and I had been dating for only five to six months, I thought it was true love. One night she and I started talking about our future, and I started talking about us having a more traditional marriage where I would go to work and she would stay home. She really wanted to be a teacher and was actually going to teacher's college. She and I had a big argument, where she told me that she loved children but she didn't want to just stay at home, she wanted to have a career.

Finally, she and I broke up because I thought that she didn't want me to be a real man. I had believed up until that point, that a woman only works if the husband couldn't provide and if a man can't provide then he was failing his job of being the man of the house, the breadwinner. At the time, I believed that scenario far too much to be willing to let my future wife work. She broke up with me saying that she wanted to be a teacher and she wanted her own career.

Once she and I broke up, I had no reason to stay in Michigan and

Melvoy's Railroad

1969

I decided that I was so tired of this town. I was tired of the boring job, I was tired of the awkward life at home where we knew Billy was gone and we kept trying to not talk about it. I was also tired of all the news about the growing hippie movement, including Woodstock, which happened that year. I just had to get away from it all, so July 12th, I shipped back out ready for Vietnam and ready to unleash all of my frustrations on the enemy.

CHAPTER 6

★

VIETNAM, ROUND TWO

This time was very different. The first reason was because within a few days I realized that I had chosen to spend my twentieth birthday in a war zone, which most people wouldn't call a happy birthday, but it suited me well. The bigger thing that happened was I met a few new people, particularly Reggie Kenny and a man who became a big part of my life named Lieutenant McLachlin. It all came to a head when our platoon was assembled, with about twenty or twenty-five guys. Lieutenant McLachlin sent one of the Sergeants to get three guys: Reggie, a guy named John, and myself. Lieutenant McLachlin asked us if we knew why we were called, but none of us knew, even though I was trying to figure out what I had done wrong.

McLachlin said, "I got screwed with the rookie platoon, you three are the only ones with previous experience outside of my Sergeants."

He came up to Reggie and said, "You have done three rounds here and this will be your fourth, you are a Private First Class, with an outstanding record."

He went up to John and said, "You've done this once before and according to the reports you did a good job."

He then came to me and even though I had seen the last two guys get complimented, I was still bracing for some berating. McLachlin said, "You had one round here, and are apparently very eager to take on responsibility. You were awarded a purple heart as a result of an ambush that killed most of your company."

He then took a step back to look at all of us and said, "I don't want anyone in my platoon to be killed by inexperience. We need all the soldiers we can get and keep. So, you three have an extra responsibility and I expect you along with the Sergeants, to keep the rookies in line. Do you understand?"

We immediately responded, "Sir, yes sir."

He then said, "We're done here, head to your bunks."

As we walked back, John kept to himself, and I eventually found out that he wasn't interested in mentoring anybody, so it became the job of Reggie and myself. The first question I asked him was, "Have you ever

Melvoy's Railroad

been told that before?"

Reggie told me, "No, most Sergeants just assume everything. I think he will be one of the easier ones to deal with."

Reggie and I became friends because we had a mutual respect for the other. He had been really lucky, and had successfully avoided serious injury during his three deployments to Vietnam. I was amazed at how he did it, in view of the fact that many people I knew couldn't handle training, let alone being so involved in the battle. He told me, "You just focus on the mission as best you can, keep yourself aware, and you can avoid a lot of trouble."

I was impressed, but at the same time he was impressed with me because I had been seriously injured. He told me that he had seen men die but never more than five or ten at a time. He had trouble imagining the massacre that killed most of my company and the courage that I must have to come back after witnessing all of that carnage.

I was always very interested in becoming better and gaining more respect and it was during my conversations with him that I learned how to earn the rank of Private First Class. It became a new goal for me to strive towards and it reminded me that even though I had to obey orders now, one day I could be giving them. In fact, I was unofficially allowed to give orders to the new guys, so I began to see myself becoming an authority figure. My father had become a Private First Class shortly before the end of World War II. The idea of reaching the same heights as he had was a new force to drive me, besides all the frustration I incurred back home.

As time went on, I went out every day and the killing of the VC got easier and easier. It got to the point, where I began to wonder how I could go a week without taking out one of them. Every time I saw them, I saw the bastards who killed my company. I saw the bastards who killed Ross and who Phil died trying to save us from. In those uniforms, I saw everything that I hated.

At the same time, I had to switch gears often and keep some of the rookies from getting themselves killed. I remember one time when these two rookies saw a small building and they were about to head towards it. I looked and saw movement through the side window and ordered them to stand back. They asked why and then I told them to get down and out came five VC soldiers. We had to fire at them from behind a wall. Had they have gone into that building they would have been ambushed and killed for sure. Instead, we took a couple of them out, and a few more of our guys got the drop on them and in the process, we got one of their walkie talkies which gave us a clue about what their next move was going to be.

It was after that when Lieutenant McLachlin and I began to become close. I guess he saw me as someone who could one day take his place, or at least someone he knew he could rely on. When someone is barking orders at you, you often forget that they sometimes have their bosses barking orders at them. Not many things are more reassuring to a military officer of any rank than to know that there are people with you – above you, below you etc. – that you know you can rely on. I became one of those guys for Lieutenant McLachlin as well as for Reggie.

One day Reggie and I went to the local bar, where we each picked up a cute Vietnamese girl. If I had still been with Lisa, my ex-girlfriend, I would have felt guilty, but since I was single, I didn't care. After we got intimate with these girls, he and I went back to the bar to celebrate and relax, then Reggie asked me a question – a question that surprised me. "What do you think is going to happen when the VC runs out of troops and we finally win this war?"

That was the strangest thing about this war. I assumed that our victory was inevitable, but I had heard for the last year and a half since Walter Cronkite gave up, that it couldn't be won. The only answer I could think to give at the time was, "Well the Soviets would be a lot more careful with screwing with us."

Reggie said, "Here, here."

We had a couple cigarettes and thought about what would happen next.

My most vivid memory from this time period was dealing with some of the Privates, with two of them being killed, and blame starting to be thrown around regarding who was at fault. It was about six weeks before the end of the tour when the conflict boiled over between these cliques that had formed within the company. Both Reggie and I had mentioned to the Sergeants and Lieutenant McLachlin that this could turn into something serious.

One night after lights out, a few of the Privates got up and began assaulting the guy who they thought had let the other two Privates die. As I woke up and realized what was going on, his friends had woken up and a fight had broken out. I had grabbed a baton and headed over to break this fight up. What I didn't realize was that the Sergeants had heard the commotion, were on their way and had heard my entire speech after I split them up. I said something very close to, "I have had it with you assholes, we are fighting an enemy, we have Gooks with guns trying to kill us every fucking day, we don't need to fight each other."

I then turned to the guys who had started it. "Look, I know you're pissed off about losing friends, I have been there, I have had to tell the parents of my dead friend how he died. If you are pissed off, pick up your damn gun and aim it at the VC cocksuckers who shot him. I'm not going to do push-ups because you can't get along. Now man up, put this behind you, or so help me God, I will kick somebody's ass."

I let out a loud breath, and let out all that anger had been built up for a couple weeks, which had boiled over. (I know that some of you may have been uncomfortable with the Gooks comment and I regret it now, but back then people weren't so politically correct, and that term got used a lot in the barracks.) Getting back on topic, the Sergeants basically told all the guys to get their asses back to bed, and not start anymore bullshit.

The next morning, Lieutenant McLachlin and the Sergeants came out and said that they weren't going to tolerate this bullshit, so he ordered all of us to do fifty push-ups each. That was difficult, but then they came up to me and said they wanted to speak to me in private. Lieutenant McLachlin asked me, "What the hell happened last night?"

After I told him, he looked at his Sergeants and then looked back at me and asked, "If you could do last night over again, what would you do differently?"

I paused, having no idea what the right answer was supposed to be, so I just said, "I would have done the same thing, put those guys in their place and remind them of what they are here to do."

Lieutenant McLachlin, asked me to go back to the barracks and he would call me back later. So I went back performing the usual chores, but I couldn't help but feel a little nervous. I had come to respect Lieutenant McLachlin and didn't want to disappoint him. When I was called back into Lieutenant McLachlin's office, he told me that because of the balls I showed jumping into that fray, the authority I showed taking control of it, and the responsibility I showed getting the right message into their heads, he was promoting me early to Private First Class. What a moment it was. As the Lieutenant and the Sergeants shook my hand, I had not felt this much pride since my days in high school football when I scored a touchdown and Coach Lennox would tell me what a great job I was doing. This was the most I had ever missed my family at home and I knew that this would be the time when my family would be so proud of me. I wrote a letter, telling them I would be home in mid-January and about my early promotion.

I got congratulations from Reggie and he took me out to celebrate. He and I promised to stay in touch and that he and I would have each other's backs going forward. I remember my last conversation with Lieutenant McLachlin when he pulled me aside and said that he had bet $50 that one day I would become Lieutenant Melvoy. That statement meant the world to me. If he was that confident in my abilities then he saw something special and I remembered that for a very long time.

I said, "Sir, thank you sir."

I was ready to go home, because I had missed Christmas at home, missed my family and by the time the six months had gone by, I had forgotten why I left my home. I would enjoy and needed having a little time off to rest so I could return to the fray.

CHAPTER 7

THE SIXTIES ARE OVER, MY LIFE HAS BEGUN

I returned home in the middle of January 1970, and the night after I got home, my parents threw a party for me at the house to celebrate my promotion. My mother came up to me, almost in tears, and told me, "You have no idea what this means to your father, I haven't seen him this happy in months."

I was enjoying being at home that night my father gave me a present, which I still have on my dresser today. It was a framed picture of me in my uniform and at the bottom of the frame was a Bible quote from 2nd Timothy 1:7, "For God did not give us a spirit of timidity, but a spirit of power, of love and of self-discipline." My father told me that I had grown to embody that spirit and that he couldn't be prouder of me. I was so proud of what I had accomplished and was so glad to have the time to really embrace it, but the only question left was what was my next step in life?

I decided that I wanted to help the military effort, so I applied for a job to be a recruiter for the next few months. The current recruiters began to tell me how to sell young people, on how they can get to college, help their country, develop character and how to find which one of those things will appeal to which people. I began to wonder if I was misleading them, but I realized that we needed to get more men over there and they would find out what it was like soon enough. I had to recruit as many men as I could.

As time went on, I did successfully recruit some men in different shopping malls. Sometimes I had people coming up to me and getting in my face about being a tool of imperialism or some other similar accusation. These were the very hippies and "intellectuals" that I came to despise as time had gone on. Sometimes the arguments got very heated, and I remember telling them that they couldn't lace up my boots, and they were too lazy to do the hard work needed to protect America. I was disgusted by these people, who were usually college students going to or coming from their classes, thinking that they were so informed. But in reality they had no idea what was going on in Vietnam, but I did. I had seen it, felt it and fought it. So for the next few months recruiting was my work and that was my battle.

The other fresh start that I got was in my love life. My last girlfriend had been Lisa and a few one-night stands with Vietnamese women. I wasn't sure where to even look until one day my friend Tony said that his girlfriend Rebecca had a single friend and would like to arrange a double date for me. Of all days it was on Valentine's Day, which just so happened to be a Saturday that year. I remember asking him who she was, he said that her name was Veronica and if I just showed the old Charlie Melvoy confidence that I had in high school, I would charm the skirt off her.

We met for dinner at a place that Tony knew in Detroit and I got there a few minutes before everyone else, and my pulse began to race as I tried to figure out what to tell and what not to. I kept trying to remind myself what Tony was saying about turning on the confidence that I had and I would be fine.

Then she arrived, and I kissed her hand, and I knew old tricks from movies still worked back then. I was stunned by the beauty I saw. Her hair was a hazel brown and shorter, but not too short, and looked like she was a combination of a few different movie actresses. As we got talking I realized that she was far more of a match for me than Lisa was. Veronica wanted to be a mother, she loved men in uniform, and really liked a take charge kind of guy. We all had a great time, and by the time the night was over, Veronica gave me her number, kissed me on the cheek and said she hoped to see me again.

After I got home, I was smitten but there was something about her that I truly loved. It took me a little while to figure out that I loved how innocent she was. I had been to hell and back, and after arguing with hippies during the day, I came home to a broken home at night. Here she was this untouched innocent girl that knew how to help me forget about any troubles I had. As our relationship progressed, I realized that I had one thing to do, which meant I had to keep Charlie Melvoy the soldier and Charlie Melvoy the civilian as separate people. She was becoming the purest thing in my life and I didn't want any of those horrible things in the world to ever come anywhere near her.

When I introduced her to my parents, my mother and father both overwhelmingly approved, and especially when Veronica asked my mother about her recipes, it made my mother so happy. My sister also approved, but she didn't really say too much.

After my three-month assignment ended I had a choice to make, do I go back to Vietnam, or do I go somewhere else? I had only been dating Veronica for two months, how would I move my career forward and become a Sergeant without having to leave her?

Chapter 7 : The Sixties Are Over, My Life Has Begun

The decision was made to send me to Japan for a tour, which was surprising, because the war in Vietnam wasn't going well and I surely thought that they would need me there. Instead whoever was making the decisions was sending me to Japan. I had thought that we won this war, but what I didn't know was that there were still some guys trying to fight Americans, even though we had been rebuilding their country for the last twenty-five years. Although I was going to be deployed there, I was a little concerned, but it was going to be safer than Vietnam and it would help put Veronica's mind at ease.

I will never forget the last few days before I left, because it was the Memorial Day weekend in May. There under the stars she and I made love for the first time, I couldn't have been happier, and I knew after that weekend that she would wait for me. I was going to come back even better than before. In fact, after I came back, I assumed she and I were probably going to get married.

CHAPTER 8
★
THE FORMER ENEMY

I remember the last conversation I had with my father before my tour in Japan, when he put his hands on my shoulders and said that even though he didn't fight the Japanese, he fought the Germans and Italians. The line that I remember vividly was, "I guess they weren't lucky enough to dodge fighting a Melvoy after all."

After which we both let out a good laugh and then he and I went for drinks at the legion. My mother was less supportive as she began asking why I kept going back into combat. I guess she expected me to be more like my father in the fact that you do a tour or two, you come home, settle down, raise a family etc. My mother, God bless her, didn't understand that the war my father fought ended, but the war that I was fighting against communism wasn't over by a long shot. Maybe one day it would be over and I would find a spot in civilian life, but for the time being I was a committed soldier who wasn't walking away until the job was done.

This tour was very different from what I experienced in Vietnam. What I saw wasn't jungle and blown up buildings with a war zone. I saw a society that was looking more like our own, which in a way baffled me because I was over there to protect against attacks on Americans. We had spent billions over the previous twenty-five years rebuilding their country and giving these people a standard of living that the Communists had forgotten was possible. There were certain parts of the Japanese culture that I found charming, for example, I loved the fact that the Japanese culture had a strong history of respect for their elders. It was refreshing as opposed to what I had experienced the previous couple of years in the U.S. All of that rhetoric like "don't trust anyone over thirty", "free love" and other expressions were tiresome and I was glad to be in a place that didn't seem to be infected with it.

Looking back one of the reasons why it angered me so much was that I still hated the hippies that had taken my brother from me. No one over thirty I knew had kidnapped anyone and it's easy to have free love when you steal it. I didn't like some of the other Japanese customs, like eating with chopsticks, the language bothered me and I always had the suspicious feeling that they were bashing us in their language.

One of the few people I came to know and appreciate was Mr. Sugimori. He was a slender man in his fifties and, unlike others, he used to bow to us every day when we were standing guard. He appreciated us, but we would go through town now and then and get dirty looks from the people. You got the sense that they were uncomfortable with us there, even though we had rebuilt their country. We could have left them with their piles of rubble but we helped them get back on their feet.

However unlike in Vietnam, where their dislike of us was much more obvious, like the bar fights I mentioned earlier, the Japanese seemed far more reserved and unwilling to start any trouble. After a while I just felt uncomfortable, there was very little real fighting, basically we were glorified security guards. They didn't like us there, but didn't have the nerve to say it to our faces. I grew weary of that very quickly and after a while, I began to wonder if this even counted as combat. I would have probably had more fighting as a cop in Ann Arbor. The good news was this did count, and I didn't have to be there forever.

The thing that surprised me the most about my trip to Japan however wasn't the culture difference, or the Japanese people's dirty looks. This trip kept reminding me of Billy and how on one hand their culture was more demanding of respect than ours was and maybe that's what happened to Billy. Also, how their subtle disrespect felt like Billy's, in the way they didn't appreciate who helped them rebuild and give them the modern economy that they were functioning with. Tokyo was actually resembling New York City with all the business and all the people, all the rushing. They had all that because of our efforts to get them back on their feet.

About a month before returning home, I got a letter from Veronica who said that she missed me so much and really wanted me to be home for Christmas. My letter back assured her that I would be back just after Thanksgiving and I asked her to save me some turkey. I still have that letter, even though the paper and writing has faded, re-reading it makes the memory as clear as day.

The only person over there who I developed any kind of friendship with in those months was Mr. Sugimori. We started off talking about the weather, and then we talked about our respective families. I never mentioned Billy to him and for some reason he and I just started to become friends. Considering all of the bad things I had heard about the Japanese growing up, I was surprised to meet one that I enjoyed talking to so much.

Shortly before leaving Japan I had a discussion with Mr. Sugimori about just random things, although he spoke English pretty well, his accent became distracting once in a while. I asked him about the dirty looks that I kept getting and I asked him when they would realize what the U.S. had done for them. His response was far from what I was expecting and I expected complete agreement. He said, "Charlie, you need to remember their looks come from what happened in 1945, not what you are doing now. War brings out worst in all of us, and even the memory can make a man act like animal. Time heal all wounds but some wounds are so deep, they need a very long time."

I didn't know what to say to that, so I just shrugged it off with, "Whatever you say, Mr. Sugimori."

I didn't understand what he meant, although I certainly do now. At the time, I didn't understand not just because of his imperfect English, but because I didn't understand how dirty looks were anything like men acting like animals or war bringing out the worst in people, because I saw it as bringing out my courage and my best. I didn't say it to him but I thought to myself, "If he wanted to see an animal, I should have introduced him to Mark, a bastard that killed kids."

I left Japan, a place with weird food and weird ways but a place where I rarely felt like my life was in danger. I felt as strong and tough as ever, and that gave me the utmost confidence to propose to Veronica when I finally returned home.

CHAPTER 9

★

LOVE & MARRIAGE

[handwritten: TIME LINE]

I came back as 1970 was coming to an end and I found out that my sister Cathy was getting married and they eventually would on May 8, 1971. During my absence, my mother and Veronica had become friends, and my mother almost saw her as a second daughter. My mother began hinting to me that she and I should get married, have children and of course that was the plan.

However, with my sister getting married, I didn't want to have two big weddings at the same time. It would have just been too much at once for everybody. Besides Cathy had always been really reserved and unlike me, who had my moments in football or the promotion in the army, she never really had great moments. Cathy deserved to have a moment of her own, where I would be the background for once. So I decided I would propose right after Cathy's wedding, and after all if I had to wait until August to get married, so be it. Of course, things don't always go as planned, you will find out why later.

I found a job working with the military going back to recruiting, which I knew would be another stable few months and from there, I didn't know. While I was figuring that out, things between Veronica and myself were going really well, she was in love with me and I was in love with her. *[handwritten: 1971]* We had as perfect a Valentine's Day that year as I could have imagined, as I pulled out every romantic cliché I could think of. We ate at the same restaurant as we did on our first date, we went to a couple of the places we went to on our other dates, and the only reason we didn't return to the place where we first made love was the February temperature in Michigan – that level of cold would have killed the mood – but otherwise it was perfect. Those few months felt great, because my mother was happy, my father was happy, I was happy, Cathy was happy, Veronica was happy, and everything was excellent

The month of March was when things flew off the handle. I remember because by the time Easter came around things were really tense. I guess Easter was not a good holiday for our family anymore. It started during March because whenever the subject of Billy came up, everyone tried to change the subject. Tony had told Veronica that I had a younger brother and she kept asking me as well as my mother what had happened and why Billy was nowhere to be found. Unfortunately, this led to a big fight that almost broke us up, when things became tense. It really bothered her that I wouldn't tell her and as much as my mother liked her, she would get annoyed whenever Veronica tried to find out from her what happened to Billy. So that was the one way that my family didn't like her, because we were public with our successes and private with our family's failures. That was the way we thought, and a lot of people back then thought the same way. If that had happened in today's era and someone had posted that news on Facebook, Twitter or some other public forum on the Internet, my parents would have been absolutely mortified.

Unfortunately, things blew up one night, when my father's car was in the shop and he asked me to pick him up from work. As I picked him up he seemed irritable. I didn't know what he was mad about, although I had not only gotten there on time but I was there ten minutes early. All he seemed to say was that he wished more people in this world would mind their own damn business. I didn't know what he was talking about but I will get to that story later.

Just as we got home my mother was yelling at Cathy, and the first thing we heard when we walked in the door was, "I didn't raise you to be a harlot."

My father's eyes lit up wondering what was going on and my mother told him that Cathy was pregnant. My father started yelling like a madman. I forget the exact words but it was close to, "Goddamn it Cathy, you couldn't control yourself until May? You better hope he doesn't dump you right now, because who will buy the cow if they get the milk for free? Don't you have more respect for yourself or this family? Imagine what the neighbours will say if they find out what you did?"

Cathy was in tears and she must have felt horrible about herself. I should have stepped in, but truth be told, at that time, I kind of agreed and I was also more or less in shock. My father ordered her upstairs and out of his sight. He then turned to me and said, "You had better keep your mouth shut about this. That girl of yours is always asking about Billy, so the last thing we need is her finding out about this, so keep your damn mouth shut!"

I simply responded, "Yes sir."

He grabbed a plate and threw it and as it smashed on the wall, I began to see that things weren't as great as I thought they had been. My mother was also in tears as she cried on my shoulder. I expected her to say something about Cathy, but instead she was blaming herself and she said something like, "I've been a terrible mother."

All I could do was hug her and tell her that she was a great Mom and I knew she loved us. The Billy issue was on the tip of our tongues, even though it had been three years, and I couldn't stop wondering what was going to happen for Easter this year? I cringed at the thought, and couldn't fathom what was going to happen if this news came out.

The next few weeks were some of the tensest weeks of my life up to that point. I couldn't believe what had happened. At first, I didn't even know what to say to Cathy. I remember asking her if Jason knew and what was happening. She said that he knew and that he was going to do the right thing, go through with the marriage and just tell everyone the baby came early.

By this time Jason had been promoted to bar manager and was making good money. If she was going to get pregnant before marriage, this was the best possible time and circumstances. Truth be told, even if they found out the morning before the wedding, my parents would have reacted very similarly. The biggest problem was that she was scared that our father didn't love her anymore, that she was one more toe over the line from him kicking her out into the street. I told her to just keep it quiet and eventually this whole thing would blow over.

Then I found out that my father's car was in the shop, I initially thought it was something like engine trouble, but what I didn't know was that he had backed his car into a post and broken a tail light which was strange because that wasn't like him. He always went the speed limit, was always telling me the importance of having a spare tire, and road flares for anything that might go wrong. When he was teaching me how to drive, he once gave me a ten-minute lecture about how dangerous it is not to check your blind spot. He was one of the most careful drivers you would ever meet in your life.

I overheard him on the phone, which made me wonder how it could have happened, and the roads hadn't been icy in a few weeks. As all of this began to build up, I remember Easter happening, when we had all the uncles and cousins here. Jason was there with Cathy, and my parents couldn't help but give him very disapproving looks like they knew what he did. It was really uncomfortable, although Veronica was as sweet as anyone could be, she wasn't so naïve that she couldn't see that something was seriously wrong.

After dinner was finished, we went into the TV room, where Veronica asked to speak to me in private. "Charlie, what's going on with your family? You can cut the tension with a knife."

I tried to brush it off as if they just weren't feeling talkative, but we had been together enough that she could see right through that lie.

"Why can't you tell me what's going on?" *Timid?*

I tried to say something about how it's complicated and it's best to leave it alone. She grabbed her coat and began to leave, saying, "If you can't tell me the truth, and if you don't love me enough to tell me the truth, then maybe we shouldn't be together."

This of course was the worst possible situation for me, my father walked in just as she was saying that, and by this point he had been hitting one of his special occasion liquors and began to go off. "Maybe you should mind your own damn business, and stop asking about people you're never going to meet, like Billy, that damn delinquent."

She looked very confused and said, "I wasn't asking about Billy."

He proceeded to go off about how he's getting tired of seeing her around all the time and that if she expects to have a husband, she needed to "keep her big yap shut."

This angered her so much she stormed out. My mother showed up part way into this rant and tried to tell my father to calm down and to get some rest. He proceeded to go off on her about him working hard every day and if she kept her eyes on Cathy, she wouldn't have gotten herself into this situation. By this point, he was starting to slur his words, and I knew he was on the verge of exposing Cathy's secret to the rest of the family. I tried to say to him that he had said enough, but he proceeded to get in my face about how this isn't the army, and he was my father and would always outrank me. I had never talked back to him before, but now I was close. Finally my mother had managed to pull him upstairs, as he was muttering about how no one respects him and does what they're supposed to do anymore.

The rest of the family had probably put the pieces together and realized Cathy was pregnant, which left her speechless and didn't even want to look anyone in the eye. I had to go after Veronica and try to make things right with her. The thought of losing her was overwhelming.

I attempted to gracefully bow out and thankfully in the military, they teach you to think quickly on your feet. I told the rest of the family that I had promised Veronica that I would spend some time with her family as well.

I got in my car and went looking for her; I caught her as she was turning onto the street that she lived on. I pulled over and asked to speak to her but she was in tears and told me to leave her alone. She turned around to me and asked me why I wouldn't tell her things and why I hadn't proposed to her yet. I asked her to get in the car and as she sat in the car I told her everything that had happened within my family. I told her about Billy leaving, my father drinking more, Cathy's pregnancy and all of that stuff. She was so shocked, that she was almost overwhelmed by all of it, and explained to me that her family was nicer and didn't seem to have these problems. I also told her that there were two reasons why I hadn't told her these things. The first reason was that my family had sworn me to secrecy and the second reason was that she was the purest, most innocent thing in my life and I wanted to protect her from these things.

I then told her about the fact that I was planning to propose after Cathy's wedding. Her eyes were already wide but that brought a smile to her face. She forgave me for everything, and as we were hugging in my car, I knew that I never wanted to be without her and that I needed to buy her a ring. However, I also knew that I needed to keep her away from my family until things settled down.

For the first time in a long time, I had lied to my parents and Cathy. They didn't know that I had told Veronica everything, and she had agreed to keep all of it secret.

However, the next few weeks were really rough. First my father had a close call with his car almost hitting someone, this was very strange and I began to try to keep an eye on him as the wedding date got nearer. For some reason, that Easter night replayed in my head over and over and after seeing how overwhelmed Veronica was by the news of my sister being pregnant, I decided that there was no way she could ever handle the things I had seen. How would she handle children being blown up, the other cruelties of Miller the Killer and all of the other things that soldiers had to confront?

As the wedding date drew closer and closer, as I thought more and more about getting married myself, I made a promise to myself. I would never tell her about anything that happened in uniform. It would be like Las Vegas, what happened there would stay there.

Cathy and Jason's wedding came, and despite everything that happened to Cathy they still had a lovely day. Right after the minister said, "I now pronounce you husband and wife, you may now kiss the bride."

I saw the biggest smile on her face that I had ever seen. During the party afterwards, my father was getting really drunk and my mother left early with him. Despite that uncomfortable situation, just as planned the next day in the early afternoon, I went to Veronica's house, and got down on one knee and proposed to her. I had told her a month earlier that I was going to propose, but seeing that ring herself, made it real and she must have said yes ten or twelve times. I was about to become a husband, and we went about setting the date for August 21st – I couldn't have been more excited.

Those next few months were the best and worst simultaneously. The thought of finally getting married was exciting, however the problems with my father were becoming harder to ignore. In the summer he came home early one day because he had been sent home for supposedly drinking on the job. To say he was angry was an understatement and began to weave this story about how they were trying to kick out all the old guys, so that they could bring in their children, nephews etc.

All of us could plainly see that there was a problem, but you didn't talk back to my father, as he was as hardheaded as anyone I ever met. My sister began to show, as in her stomach was becoming more pronounced and of course the whispers started, people were asking, "If she got married in May, why would she be showing in June?"

When we were talking about Veronica's and my wedding everything seemed great, but other things around us definitely weren't so great. The one thing I have always said about Cathy's husband Jason was that he was loyal, and always stood up for her. You will find out later why I said was and not is.

As we reached the last few weeks before my wedding, things were both exciting and scary, as we were getting ready to take the next step in our lives. We were getting ready to take some big leaps forward and I knew that I wanted to start a family with Veronica, because I had no doubt she would make a great mother. I had always had my mother and father and in the army, I always had other people to rely on, but now if you become a father you are the head of a household. It is really hard to know that the buck stops with you and you have to take the leadership role. I wasn't completely sure if I was ready for it, but I knew that I had to try.

Tony was my best man, as he was always my good friend and the one who introduced me to Veronica in the first place, and who else would be better. As she came down the aisle, in that brief moment everything seemed perfect. The family problems, and the war, all melted away as this beautiful woman came closer and closer with every passing second. I will never forget the moment when we kissed and it was perfect. At this brief moment, everything was wonderful. August 21, 1971 will always stand as one of the greatest days of my life, and one of a few days where I wish time could have stopped. I wouldn't have changed the tiniest detail, and thankfully the reception afterwards went very well and my father controlled his drinking. The food was wonderful, and in my speech I remember telling everyone, "Someday I hope everyone has a day that is as great and perfect as the one I am having now."

Fifty-one years later I feel that way again. I hope everyone has a day like that in their lives at least once and that was one of mine.

CHAPTER 10
★
BECOMING A MAN

While we were planning for the wedding, Veronica and I had to decide where we were going to live, and where I would work. Staying in Ann Arbor was out of the question, because there was nothing steady in the military there and we couldn't stay very long with her parents. Due to the tension at home, I wanted to keep her a safe distance from my parents for the near future.

I made some calls and I got a job running the loading dock at a military base in Ohio because of my previous experience. Part of the reason I got this deal, was that during the summer I contacted Lieutenant McLachlin who I hadn't spoken to in months. We had a great chat and pretty soon he told me that he would see what he could do to help me out. By early June I was officially signed up, to move into military housing. I would get three days off for my wedding, which was the day before, the day of, and the day after. Whenever I heard about these people who go to Europe for two weeks for their honeymoon, I wondered if they knew how lucky they were.

I actually moved in to the military housing in early July, but Veronica couldn't move in until after we were married. After seeing my parent's reaction to Cathy's news, I didn't want to further provoke their wrath. Pretty soon I got a reputation among my superiors for doing good work, following orders well and being very reliable.

By the time the fourth week of August came around, Veronica actually moved into the housing with me. People were telling her that she had a real good man. It was hard being away from her during July and the first two weeks of August but I knew that I would have to get through it.

I became good friends with a guy named Nick, who was actually planning to go into the air force in a year or two but wanted some ground experience first. He was so glad when I showed up, and we became great friends right away. He actually began to tell me about his cousin Brian who had been captured and interrogated by the Viet Cong and how bad that situation had messed him up. It made my own nightmares seem like nothing by comparison, as I was pretty good at ignoring the nightmares once I woke up. It was amazing to hear of someone who had lost much more than I had at the hands of the VC.

The hardest part of the experience, before Veronica showed up, was knowing that she was waiting for me back in Ann Arbor. I was so tired of that town by 1971. I was twenty-two years old and I wanted a different life, a life with a strong purpose, and the one I had dedicated myself to years earlier. Once Veronica got there, I was faced with a different challenge, and felt like I had to be two different people. I had to be switched on in military mode almost everywhere, and once I was home I had to turn it off and be the husband. Trust me when I tell you that you can't be in military mode with your wife, because I had heard about other guys who had made that mistake and their wives would take exception to it.

I continued getting great reviews from my superiors for my hard work, initiative and the leadership I had started showing. Within a couple months, I was showing the characteristics of a Sergeant, harsh but fair. I had actually gotten in one guy's face about him screwing up, when the Sergeant walked in and when I told the Sergeant what the guy had done, the Sergeant pulled me behind closed doors and told me that I was overstepping my boundaries, but otherwise I was completely correct.

I knew then that my next goal was to become a Sergeant and get as high in the military as possible. Maybe one day I would get to inform the President of military policy, obviously, Nixon would be long gone before that day would arrive, but it was becoming my dream. I thought to myself, "How exciting would it be to have a private meeting with the President of the United States of America to discuss policy? How exciting would it be for the President of the United States of America, the most important man in the world, to agree with a proposal I thought of?" That was the dream, that was a goal, although one that would have to wait for a long time.

Speaking of dreams, or in this case nightmares, my mother's nightmare was becoming reality. By the time the fall came around, my father had been fired for being passed out drunk at work. This was stunning because it wasn't like he only got that job a week ago, he had been hired by that company when my mother and father got married in 1947. He had worked at that warehouse as long as I had been alive. This was so different from what I knew about who he was, and as the weeks went by he found another job, but about a month later he lost that one because he was still drinking. My parents, especially my mother had always been great at saving money, so they had savings and she was so scared of those savings disappearing without my father's income. This was compounded by the fact that the cost of everything went up so much in the 1970s.

My mother was so scared that she asked Cathy and I for help. Cathy let Jason handle the household finances, so he and I made a decision that we would alternate sending my mother some money; he would send her some one week, and I would on the next week. I could tell that this was bothering Veronica, not that we were going without or anything, but she was bothered by the fact that my father was dropping the ball.

For a few months, I was in denial, and thought that he would straighten himself out, find a new job and everything would be just fine. At the same time, with every two weeks that went by I began to wonder why my father hadn't straightened himself out yet. It wasn't turning out so well, my father spent a good chunk of Christmas dinner ranting about "those bastards firing me a week before Christmas."

No one wanted to say anything, but I was seeing more and more that the man who had raised me was disappearing. The one who had told me to never blame other people when I screw up, the man who had told us to take such pride in being our best, was being replaced by an addict. The man I knew would not have been saying these things, but would have been so happy to see his first granddaughter Cynthia who had been born on December 14th. Instead all that he was talking about was himself and what he was angry about.

As 1972 started, a lot of things were happening, and Veronica and I were starting to think about having children, while hearing through the grapevine about Cathy trying to adjust to the new life of being a mother. Her adjustments included the struggles of being woken up in the middle of the night by crying and all that stuff. I think that is why Veronica wanted to wait for a while to learn from Cathy's experience before she committed herself to it.

Things took a turn for the worse in February when my father found out about my mother taking Jason's and my money. He was livid, and so angry with her that she was asking people for handouts and undercutting him as a man. I didn't know what we were going to do, so I decided that I would call Jason the next evening and talk about it.

The following morning, I woke up extra early to clear the snow from the walkway, but when I came back Veronica was really upset because my father had called her. During that call he told her that if I didn't show up to his house Friday night that he would come here and kick my ass. She was scared and I couldn't believe that my father was that angry and that he actually wanted to fight me. I called Jason, but Cathy picked up, so I told Jason and Cathy that if our father called, don't agree to anything, I knew that I had to deal with this.

That was on Thursday, and I did something that I never thought I would do. I called Lieutenant McLachlin and told him some of what had happened and asked him what I should do. I usually didn't bring up family matters to people in the military but this was different and because he had taken on the role of a second father, I felt like I could trust him. His response was that my father isn't mad at me, he's mad at himself and that once I stare him right in the face, he will back down and come to his senses. It sounded like a good plan, so I told Veronica that I was going straight there after work on Friday night. I even called my mother that morning to tell her to let him know that I was coming. Veronica gave me the most heartfelt kiss she ever had and told me that she loved me and that she would be praying that everything would be okay.

The drive back to Ann Arbor took almost four hours with the snow, and I braced myself for something that I had never thought would happen – the possibility of me having to fight my own father. This was the man I grew up respecting, almost idolizing, the standard of what a man should be, now he had fallen and was blaming me for him failing to live up to his responsibilities. I kept asking myself what I should say, how I should say it, where is the line between telling the truth and crossing the line?

As I began to see those familiar Ann Arbor streets, I began to feel like I was re-entering combat, but without that familiar feeling of a rifle in my hands. It was past 10 pm when I pulled onto our street as the snow continued to fall. As I pulled into the driveway and got out of the car, I took a deep breath and knew that the next few minutes might be the hardest of my life, hoping that Lieutenant McLachlin would be right.

As I approached the door, my father came out looking as stern as ever, "Well, look at the big shot, rather than taking care of his own wife, he thinks he needs to take care of mine."

I became more annoyed, "Well someone has to, you've gone from being Mr. Barry Melvoy to Mr. Jack Daniels."

He came down the stairs to face me as I stood on the front lawn. He responded with his breath visible in the winter air, "Who the hell do you think you are? I raised you and taught you everything you know, you wouldn't be anything if it wasn't for me."

As he had come down the stairs I was still several feet away from him, trying to keep out of arms reach. "I haven't forgotten that. You have forgotten what you taught me and you need to get yourself together for everyone's sake. You're not the man who raised me. Barry Melvoy was a man of dignity who would never blame other people because he dropped the ball."

Remember that line I was scared of crossing? That short speech was the moment I crossed it, my mother was inside looking out the window with her hand was over her mouth as if she was holding her breath. He took a swing at me and shouted, "I'll drop you!"

I tried to take him down to subdue him but in the process he hit me a few times, breaking my nose in the process and he wrestled his way back up as I was trying to hold him down. He kicked me in the knee as I went down, then he laid into me a couple times, and that was when I knew I couldn't hold back any more and I began throwing fists back. I couldn't be in the defensive mode anymore. Just like he taught me, charge forward, show no fear and you will be victorious. I threw some fists back at him as he and I continued to exchange blows. The pain barely registered because at that moment your adrenaline kicks in and all you can think about is taking this guy down to save your life. The fight wasn't even that long, but in that moment time ceased to exist and all I knew was my father and I beating the hell out of each other.

Finally, as we fought we had gone towards my car parked in the driveway. I swung him around and he went head first into my driver's seat window. I punched him twice, and I punched him one more time across the jaw for the knockout. My hand was sprained by that last shot. The shot connected and as bad as it hurt it was a relief because I knew he wasn't getting up. As I looked down at my unconscious father, I looked at the shattered window, and felt the blood coming down my nose and face. I looked at our front lawn with the red blood scattered across the white snow and looked at all the neighbours who were watching from a distance and realized that our family truly had been broken.

The next morning, I was bailed out of jail by Jason, who had come over and smoothed everything out with the neighbours. My father wouldn't have pressed charges even if I had thrown the first punch. My mugshot showed a man who had been through the ringer.

My father spent the night in the hospital getting a few stitches and I got whatever care they could afford in the jail since the police assumed I was the aggressor because I was the younger man who had beaten up the older guy.

Jason took the bull by the horns and came up with a solution. To direct our father to Alcoholics Anonymous. He apparently knew people who knew people who had gone to those meetings and it had helped them. At this point I would have told my father to join the circus if it would fix this situation.

My mother called the minister, who had become the minister of our church two years earlier, to help us with an intervention. I wasn't sure if God and the Devil working together could have gotten my father to see that he needed help, but he had been such a proud man all of his life. As he came home from the hospital we were all waiting there. It was tense to say the least, as my father began to put up his defenses to what was being said. My mother finally spoke up in a way that I hadn't ever heard from her. "Barry Melvoy, this has gone too far! Look at you, you have bruises all over, two missing teeth, no job, and you have embarrassed us in front of the neighbours in a worse way than our daughter's pregnancy ever could have. I can't take this any longer, Barry Melvoy, either get help… or get out!"

By this point she was in tears, ran into their bedroom and slammed the door. In nearly twenty-four years of marriage, my mother had never threatened to leave. My father looked around at everyone else, and he looked at me and asked if I was happy now. I responded saying that I wish he could just get help, and return to being the man I respected, rather than who I fought last night. I specifically said, "I don't regret what I did last night because you were out of control, and you wouldn't stop so I knocked you out."

Cathy looked at him and said, "My daughter needs a grandfather, a real grandfather."

The minister looked at him and said "Barry, if you look around this room, there are several people in it who love you and want you to get better. Please get help, as it says in the good book 'pride goeth before a fall.' Last night was your fall, please abandon your pride before you fall further."

He paused as if the realization hit him like a ton of bricks and his eyes lit up with the realization of what was going on and he blurted out, "God Damn It!"

As I was told he went into his bedroom and told my mother that he would do whatever it took to make things right with her. My parents didn't like divorce and saw divorced people as people who failed, so the thought of becoming one of them was one of the things that drove my father to get help. He began going to A.A. meetings the following week and his recovery from alcoholism began.

As I drove back that night, with a black eye, a broken nose that had been re-set but a little crooked, plenty of bruises, and a hand that was hurt and would hurt for a week or so, I went back thinking that anything I do in my life from this moment onward would have to be easy compared to the ordeal I had just been through.

As I returned home, Veronica was horrified to see what happened. My face told the whole story.

I tried to lighten the mood by saying, "You should see the other guy."

She wasn't laughing at my joke as she tried to tend to the wounds. I assured her that my father was finally getting the help he needed and I guess that I cracked open his hard head. As I went to bed that night, I began to wonder how much of this I should tell the guys on base and also if this would be the start of a better time in our family. I had faced one of my greatest fears. I had fought through it and we were getting to the light at the end of the tunnel. While I had stopped feeling like a boy a long time ago, I was now beyond any shred of any lingering doubt, a man.

CHAPTER 11
★
VIETNAM, ROUND THREE

The next couple of months saw my father regularly attend his A.A. meetings and begin to get his life back on track. I got the message in April that there was going to be one more troop surge in Vietnam and I was going to be deployed in July, along with others. It was hard to imagine going back to Vietnam one more time, and Veronica was still making peace with it, although she was relieved that she wasn't pregnant because she didn't want to raise a child by herself. Also unlike Cathy, we were not living near her parents or mine who could help us. Eventually she accepted my deployment, and she told me that when I came back, she and I would start having the child that we begun talking about in the last several months.

Before my re-deployment, I had several talks with Lieutenant McLachlin about what was happening and he informed me that the fighting was winding down slowly in Vietnam. So now was as good a time as any to get some hard experience to go towards my promotion. He had actually just been promoted to Major, and he began to tell me what I needed to do in Vietnam to be promoted to Sergeant. This was an exciting opportunity, to not only make more money, but to begin calling the shots. I could then get a position as a Drill Sergeant and train people as I had been, with the possibilities filling my head.

The week before I left was wonderful, Veronica couldn't have been better and by the time I was packing my things to leave, she gave me a kiss and the tightest hug she had ever given. During the flight I began to replay in my head all the advice that Major McLachlin had given in terms of how to get my promotion to Sergeant.

I hadn't been in combat for a while, so I was a little rusty, but it came back pretty quickly. Within the first three weeks, I was in the aircraft shooting the VC or suspected VC. I remember not just taking orders but giving them to the new guys who had never been in combat. My commanding officers the Sergeants and Lieutenant took notice of my efforts.

One of the most vivid memories was of one of the guys who I was talking to, whose name was Charlie too. He was from New Jersey and we began to be friends, and became known jokingly as the Charlie Company. Unfortunately, that friendship didn't last very long, not because of a personal problem but because of his death. The worst part was that I was there, and I actually saw the bullet go into his head, the blood just spilled out and the blank expression on his face before his body collapsed in an awkward heap. My sadness quickly turned into anger and I just let the bullets fly out in retaliation during the remainder of the battle.

We drove back the VC soldiers we were fighting and I remember hearing one of the guys say to the Sergeant, "Charlie's dead," and the Sergeant asking if it was the other Charlie's last name or mine. I showed up before the other Private could answer and told him. It had never been clearer, or more bluntly shown how close I was to getting killed. That experience was the epitome of the old phrase "it could have been me."

Whenever I sent letters home to Veronica I did a lot of editing and events like the other Charlie's death I didn't mention, I tried to only focus on the positives. I wanted to keep this dark place from my family back in Ann Arbor, and definitely not tell Veronica about a place that is so associated with death, danger, sadness and anger. When you have someone in your life that you love with all your heart, you don't want all of that to get anywhere close to her. It's the same reason I told her to stay home when I went to confront my father.

I still have a faded scar on my forehead from one night when I was having a very vivid nightmare, basically I just remember the VC surrounding me and no matter how fast I ran they kept gaining on me. Finally, I ended up in some room, vaguely like the loading dock at the base, when I saw them coming through the loading dock door by the hundreds. As I panicked, I fell out of my top bunk and scraped my head on the bedpost on the way down. To say it was a shock would be an understatement.

Even though the first time in Vietnam was the most shocking and the one that saw the most death among my brothers in arms, this time made me resent Vietnam so much more. I had a beautiful wife waiting for me at home, and I had to deal with these Communist bastards that just never went away. They just kept coming and coming and coming.

The one bright spot was that eventually, Major McLachlin's advice came through and on November 17th, I became a Sergeant in the United States Military. This was a tremendous honour for me. How many people don't have the guts to sign up, how many fail basic training, how many leave after being a Private and how many never even prove themselves as an authority figure? I was now a Sergeant, if only

Miller the Killer could see me now.

Although the promotion did rekindle my will to fight, by the time New Year's came around, I just wanted to go home and was counting down the days. When you hear guns and explosions almost every day, it becomes hard to enjoy the sound of fireworks. Every time one goes off, you look around to make sure that no one is dead. Those last few days at the beginning of 1973, began to feel like an eternity, as much as I loved the military and as much as I wanted to beat the VC, by this point it was looking like a stalemate was inevitable. That situation angered me so much, because I felt like the United States wasn't able to really put their best effort into it. I remember thinking that if the full effort was put in like during World War II, they wouldn't have been able to take it. If we had dropped the A-bomb on Hanoi, they would have surrendered so fast and the other Charlie would be alive and so many more Americans wouldn't have given up on their country.

The 1970's was becoming a very cynical decade for a lot of people. Of course, we couldn't drop the A-bomb because Russia was watching their back, and all I could think was, if the U.S. and only the U.S. had the bomb, the world would be such a better place. Everyone would know not to screw with us and those Communist regimes would be scared to sneeze, let alone take over anywhere else.

As I left Vietnam, I was relieved but also somewhat bitter, when you go into war you don't imagine a bitter stalemate that everyone wants to forget. You don't imagine people counting casualties and saying, "How many more unnecessary deaths must there be?" You don't imagine musicians coming out of the woodwork telling the world that what you are fighting for isn't worth it. You imagine what happened at the end of World Wars I & II, the victory, celebration, respect, parades in the street, and a prosperous time that follows not long after.

When I signed up, what I saw was not in the brochure. As I got on that plane to head home, I felt somewhat empty as if we didn't finish the job, like that football game that my team lost, but much, much worse. It burned me from the inside and I carried that disappointment and frustration around for years and years.

CHAPTER 12

WALKING IN DIFFERENT SHOES

After coming home, I had to try to pick up where I left off as if nothing had happened. How do you tell your wife that you have seen hundreds of people die? I never knew the answer to that and I still don't. After a few weeks, we made a few big decisions. First, we were going to have a child, but before that I would become a Drill Sergeant, so that I would have plenty to do here in the States getting the next generation of soldiers ready. I had already built up my confidence to where I could get in some young guy's face and put him back in line if he was full of himself or not doing what he was supposed to do. Obviously, there is more to it than that, but you cannot be a Drill Sergeant with a quiet humble voice.

So, while I was still thinking about what went wrong with Vietnam, I was able to push it to the back of my mind and focus on some of the positives. My father had not had a drink in months, he had gone back to his old job and things seemed to be on course with him and my mother. Things were also going well with Jason and Cathy, who had just bought a share of the bar that he was managing and they were opening up two locations, and if things kept going this way for him, he and Cathy would have plenty of money. As the spring came Cathy was pregnant again and to say that my parents reacted better would be an understatement. I was going to be an uncle for a second time.

Finally, as April came around, we realized that we were going to have to move to Maryland. The upside was that this training was not like recruit training because it was far less physical and far more mental. As the twelve weeks went by, they made it crystal clear that as a Drill Sergeant I had to be as harsh as possible in order to make sure that those men going through basic training knew that if they started trouble it would be hell. I was able to bring Veronica with me to the military barracks here she took up hobbies like knitting and sewing to help her pass the time.

The most vivid memory I have of that training was one guy asking me something by addressing me as Charlie, and the instructor pulled me aside immediately and told me something I never forgot.

"Look, if you are going to be an authority figure, you can't have anyone calling you Charlie. That is a civilian name that doesn't command the respect a Drill Sergeant needs to command. You need to be Sergeant Melvoy everywhere, and even if some punk tries to call you Charlie, you always demand that they call you Sergeant Melvoy. Furthermore, even with civilians, demand that they call you Sergeant Melvoy, Mr. Melvoy, or at the very least Charles. Charlie is name that belongs to a kid, not a Sergeant in the military, so from now on you need to be Sergeant Charles Melvoy, do you understand?"

I told him I understood and from that moment onward, no one would call me Charlie again without me correcting them on the spot. Most people adjusted fairly quickly, although it took Tony almost a year to stop calling me Charlie and to start calling me Charles.

As we practiced dealing with the new crop, before I knew it I was yelling in a guy's face, telling him to drop and give me twenty. I was becoming this strange mix of my father, Coach Lennox and Miller the Killer.

The day that I graduated was yet another proud day, and Veronica made me one of the best chocolate cakes she ever made. We then made the decision that we would stop putting it off and we would start a family of our own. I had waited more than long enough to be the father that I knew that I could be, because after all I had learned from the best.

I remember after the twelve weeks were over, I was going to be assigned to a recruit training center in Illinois, and this August was going to be first day of recruit training. I was going to take this bunch of maggots and turn them into soldiers and eventually I would be recognized for building the best soldiers around. That Monday in August, I walked in exactly as they told me, with an intense stone face, and even though they don't know what you're thinking, they know it's serious.

I remember those days really well. I had to get up in the faces of these young guys and break them down and rebuild them. I had a few troublemakers. Let me explain it, if someone is screwing around and not taking this seriously, you have to get them on the right track. If you screw around on the battlefield, you might be dead or you might let one of your own die. So, if these guys think this is playtime, it's my job to scream in their face until they realize playtime is over.

I began that first walk down the hallway, with all of those guys lined up, when one of the guys made a fart noise as I walked by and I could tell who made it. I got in that guy's face, "What the hell are you doing maggot?"

He began to say, "I'm just kidding."

I cut him off immediately, "This ain't some bar where you can drink your face off like some dumb ass, you are going to be in combat someday, and if you do that in combat, the enemy will be laughing at you for being goddamn stupid, and getting yourself killed."

I came up to another guy and I asked him, "What's your name, punk?"

He responded with a smirk on his face, "Sir, the Incredible Mr. Higgins, sir."

My eyes lit up, as this guy was asking to get his ass kicked even worse than I did a few years earlier, "Oh you're incredible Higgins, we'll see about that, you look like shit to me."

He then made it worse by saying, "You must be blind."

That was the moment when I got right in his face and said, "You want to prove something, you want to prove to something to me? Take your boots off right now!"

He looked at me confused and I kept on him, "Did I stutter? I said take your goddamn boots off right now!"

He did it, and I followed by saying, "Now Mr. Big Shot, stick your arms out with your palms face up!"

He was very confused, when I put one boot in each hand. "Now here is what is going to happen. You are going to hold those arms up, and if I hear those boots drop or if I see you in any position besides this one, everyone in this room will have to drop and give me thirty push-ups. So, everyone here, you better hope that Mr. Higgins is as special as he thinks he is."

I proceeded to get into the face of the next guy waiting for the boots to drop, which I knew wouldn't take long. I had done this exercise and I remembered how hard it was especially the first time. I also knew that if he knew everyone was watching him and would be mad at him when he failed, he would be a lot more likely to keep his mouth shut and take orders. You're not supposed to hit anyone but there are always ways to make sure that the smart-asses know that you are in charge and that they definitely are not. I could hear the whispers of the guys trying to push him not to drop them, but soon I heard them drop. He was shaking his arms, clearly having no clue how hard it would be within a minute.

I walked up to him, "Well the incredible Mr. Higgins let all of you down, so everyone get on your faces, drop and give me thirty push ups!"

When they were done I said, "Remember, no man is bigger than the United States Army, if I didn't learn that I would have died on the battlefield a long time ago. If you think it's over ladies, guess what – this is only the beginning!"

You had to make examples out of people. I remember Mr. Higgins quitting not long after that, and whether he quit because of the exercise or whether the other guys drove him out, either way it wasn't my problem.

After that the rest of the guys had seen how things worked and most of them got their act together. I remember every once in a while, if someone wasn't doing their jobs properly, I would point to their boots and say, "Are you bored? Do you need to do some strength training?"

They would hold up their boots as I would continue, "No matter how tough you think I am, this is Sunday school compared to what you will see on the battlefield. I have seen men die and I have killed them, I took a bullet in the knee and I went back for more. If you aren't tough enough to handle that and keep going, then you don't deserve to be in this army and you don't deserve to wear that uniform. I will be back when I damn well feel like it and you better not let those boots drop!"

The strangest part of this whole experience was being this harsh and going home to the house next to the barracks and being someone else. Remember the name "Miller the Killer," now in uniform between lights on and lights out I became "Melvoy the Killjoy."

When I went home I crawled into bed with my wife and became a loving husband. It is a very hard feeling to be so split; I managed to do it for a while, even though it wasn't easy. As the weeks went by, I noticed that I was embracing my new job as the Sergeant more and more.

These guys were learning as I had learned and were making sure not to make the same mistakes more than once. As I looked at those guys, I wondered which ones would one day be part of the army that would finally take down the Soviet Union and if I did my job right, they would be ready, willing and able to. As graduation day approached, some of them didn't make it, which happens every time, but the ones that did knew their job inside and out. I was still more appreciative than Miller. I actually began to tell a few of them "good job" if I saw something done very well. If you get complimented in the military, then you must have earned it, because there are no smiley face stickers or concern about anyone's self-esteem. When the day finally came, I was proud that I had taught these guys well, and I felt a little like a proud father.

I remember the speech I gave to them before they left, as they were sitting on the grass in a semicircle, as I stood at attention looking back and forth at all of them. "Former President John F. Kennedy said, 'ask not what your country can do for you, ask what you can do for your country,' and he was damn right. I am looking right now at a group of men who are real Americans, who were willing to give more than take and were willing to go through the hell of basic training to get themselves ready. I know what you went through and I went through it myself. Mark my words, the day will come when you will be needed, the day will come when the bugle will call and when that day comes, remember every damn thing I taught you and fight with everything you have. Do you understand?"

They unanimously responded, "Sir, yes sir."

I responded and they all began to leave, "Dismissed."

CHAPTER 13

★

SERGEANT & FATHER

After the first set of men shipped out, the next set was going to be arriving, this time they were less troublesome, and I remember one guy, when I asked him why he was here, he said he had joined to be "the greatest American soldier of all time."

When someone has delusions of grandeur like that, you have to break them down and show them how hard it is. So, I took a page out of Miller's book and found the skinniest guy in that group and I made this guy carry him back and forth on his shoulders across the length of the barracks. After the first round, he was winded, and by the time he was partway through the third one, he gave up.

That was when I got in his face and said, "Before you start telling everybody how great you are, you better have what it takes to back it up, because if you or anyone of these maggots tries to bullshit me, I will call you out on it."

Notice I chose the smallest guy who was probably about one hundred and forty pounds, and not the guy who was over two hundred pounds. If this guy hated me, I can only imagine what he would have to put up with if Miller was the Drill Sergeant. Of course, there was the odd issue of guys not doing their chores, or being sloppy holding their weapons, but that is just simple stuff, and you straighten them out and they become fine soldiers.

The second group arrived in late October, and were settling into the usual routine, and when some guys couldn't handle it, other guys stepped up. I remember one guy who seemed nervous and he had a lisp. I began imitating it and pointing out that if he is nervous he had "better get over it" and fix the way he talks. Looking back, it may have been insensitive, but that is how things were – we mould you a certain way, and you had better fit into that mould.

One night shortly before Thanksgiving, I came home and Veronica was at the stove making me a late snack before I went to bed. She made the greatest mashed potatoes in the world. She said that she had something important to tell me. I rolled my eyes expecting some complaint from my mother about not being able to make it to her house for Thanksgiving this year. Unfortunately, Veronica misunderstood it and it turned into an argument.

The next morning before I had to go wake up the new recruits, she took my hand and said, "I went to the doctor – I'm pregnant!"

I was overflowing with pride, we had a big hug and kiss, and for the first time since our wedding, I was consumed with joy. The next few days were so hard because being the same harsh person you have to be as a Drill Sergeant is very difficult, when you have such wonderful news that makes you so happy. Of course, she had morning sickness, and I just wish that I had more time to help her through it, but being a Drill Sergeant was very demanding work.

Thankfully the eight weeks ended just before Christmas and the newest set of recruits weren't coming until mid-January. We went to my parents' house for Christmas, and this one was much happier than the one previous. We were talking about little Cynthia who was now a year old. My father had been sober for about nine months and the fact that a new little grandchild was now on the way, was very exciting. It actually felt more like the holidays that we used to have, when we were happy, talking, joking, which was really, really nice. I hadn't seen my mother this happy in years and my father was pretty much back to his usual self, the man's man that had raised me. I remember before we left, Jason mentioned to me how much better my father was doing and that he was impressed. Cathy was so proud of little Cynthia, and she had actually trained Cynthia to salute when I came in. She was at that age where you can begin to teach them things. It made for an adorable picture that I still have to this very day.

As 1974 began, I was becoming a proficient Drill Sergeant and was getting very good reviews from my superiors. The hard part about the beginning of the year, besides hearing about Watergate ad nauseam, was that as Veronica's pregnancy continued she needed more help. Even though Cathy had given birth to her first son Connor on September 15, 1973, and had told Veronica what pregnancy was like, nothing can prepare you for it. I tried to figure out more ways to help her, but after a while it became a fruitless effort. There were some days when she wasn't happy with me, so it was hard to know how much of her annoyance was my fault and how much of it was her hormones.

This situation became more difficult when I found out that I had been transferred to West Virginia and moving while having a pregnant wife is not an easy task. She wasn't happy for those few weeks to say the least, but we made the move.

I was refining my technique as a Drill Sergeant and I knew that pretty soon we would be the proud parents of a beautiful child and that the child would have great older cousins like Cynthia and Connor.

Not too long before the move, was my father's milestone of one year without drinking, and to say that he was proud of this was an understatement. I remember wishing that I could be there in Michigan to go out to dinner with them to celebrate, but I had a job to do and a move to prepare for.

The last couple months of Veronica's pregnancy were very hard for her, it was difficult for her to walk, she felt tired a lot and she was reaching the point where she just wanted to have that baby now. By the time July came around it became a running gag, I would ask, "How are you doing, honey?"

She would respond, "Still pregnant and big as a house."

On July 28th, only eleven days after my own birthday, the day arrived. I was there in the delivery room encouraging her. I probably sounded like Coach Lennox saying, "Just keep pushing," and, "Come on, you can do it."

Finally, the baby was born and when the doctor handed that beautiful baby girl to us, it was the moment that made all of the last nine months worth it. As I looked at that child, such humble innocence, such sweetness to see something so pure and so good, I knew that I would never see the world, or my place in it, the same way again. We eventually agreed to name our daughter after Veronica's aunt who had died when Veronica was eleven, which is not the type of suggestion you say no to. That was the story of our first child, Jackie Melvoy.

The next few months gave me a new perspective, because when you have a baby, you start to see the world differently. The feeling I had was the feeling that I needed to protect my wife from the enemy, and was now multiplied by ten with that perfect little child. It gave me a new focus, and made me push the recruits even harder so that they would fight those Communists that much harder.

As the next few months went by, I knew they were calling me Melvoy the Killjoy, but I didn't care. We were going to make the best soldiers to take down the Communists, so that by the time my daughter was all grown up, this Cold War would just be a memory.

I remember one guy who I got in the face of, he tried to get out of trouble by saying, "Sir, I'm doing my best, sir."

I responded like this, "Really? You're doing your best? You can't climb over this obstacle in twenty goddamn seconds, instead of the ten it should take, and you are doing your best. If the soldiers of the past were as sloppy as you, England would still be taxing us without representation, or maybe we'd be hailing Hitler. Let me tell you something, we aren't going to put those Communist bastards down by moving slower than molasses. You got that maggot?"

He stood there stunned, realizing that I knew he wasn't really doing his best and that if he was going to be a soldier, he would have to step up a hell of a lot more than he had been.

Another very vivid memory I have from that year, was having Major McLachlin come one day to observe how I trained and come over for dinner that night. He saw how I was training the soldiers, I saw him taking notes, at the end of the day he and I went back to my house for dinner, and on the way he told me what he saw.

"Melvoy, you have great intensity, they know not to mess with you and they seem very obedient, but one thing you need to remember to do in the later stages is make sure that they can think for themselves when no one is around. When you are in the middle of combat, you need to be able to make your own decisions in the blink of an eye. That's one of the reasons why I admired what you did when I promoted you to Private First Class. You didn't need to be told anything, and you stepped up on your own."

I remembered that and that might have been one of the best pieces of advice that I was ever given by a Commanding Officer about being one. That night he met Veronica and saw our baby Jackie, and was really happy for me. He had become so much more than just a Commanding Officer, he was becoming a second father, considering the alcohol problems that my real father had, and it was nice to have another one whom I could turn to.

Before he left that night, he and I had a talk in the basement, and he told me something really big. "Melvoy, let me tell you something, one day when those Communists finally surrender, guys like you and me will be called heroes. History will talk about how we conquered the biggest most lethal enemy this country ever had despite all the doubters, despite how Vietnam ended. In the end, America will be victorious and if you ever have a son, he will be proud to follow in your footsteps."

I responded, "I sure hope so."

He added one more thing, "Melvoy, any shmuck can sharpen himself a blade, a lot of guys can get a gun and fire it, but nuclear weapons require resources that a lot of the world doesn't have. When America finally beats the Soviets, nobody else will even be in our league and the world will be a lot safer with us keeping watch."

Major McLachlin was very optimistic, and believed that just as much as I did, that regarding Vietnam, we lost the battle, but in the grand scheme of things, it was only a matter of time before we would win the war. Looking back on that talk now, it's amazing how someone's predictions can be so right and so wrong at the same time.

CHAPTER 14

★

1975, DISCO & DEUTSCHLAND

One thing that stands out to me about this time was how little free time I had. I had almost forgotten how little time Veronica and I had to ourselves. We would be lucky to get an hour to ourselves without either the baby waking up, or just being tired from the day.

Eventually this began to strain our marriage, and she began to feel trapped in her own house and that the spontaneity was all but gone in our relationship. So eventually she dragged me out to a disco club for a night of dancing, and thankfully one of the other wives from the base, who she had become friends with, agreed to watch Jackie. It was so weird to me, to be going out dancing and having a drink or two. It was weird and so different from what my life had been for the last few years. We tried to go out other nights but schedules conflicted and we only got one or two more nights like that.

I could tell that it was bothering her, life on the base was boring and there wasn't a whole lot on TV at the time. There wasn't the thousands of channels there are now, or the Internet for that matter. She didn't like West Virginia, and I never found out why, but she just didn't feel comfortable there, and perhaps she was just tired of living on military bases. Eventually she got a very different change of scenery than either of us expected. We found out that in April I was being re-deployed to Germany. I didn't like the idea because I imagined it would be like my deployment in Japan, with death stares from the former enemy. However, this time I would be a Sergeant rather than a Private First Class and I thought that explaining this to Veronica was going to be quite the task.

To my surprise there wasn't really an argument, but it was more of a roll of the eyes. I tried to tell her how nice it would be, and that it would be a great change of pace.

She just said, "Fine honey, whatever you want."

I can't tell you how much I wish that I had dealt with these problems then, at the time I just thought she would get over it soon enough. You'll see how that turned out later on.

Shortly before we left I had a talk with my father and things were going well, and he was celebrating two years of sobriety and had gotten himself back on track. When I told him that I was going to Germany he jokingly said, "Making sure we didn't miss one right?"

We both had a good laugh and he made me promise to be there for Thanksgiving this year.

"Of course," I told him.

Before we hung up he said, "I wish I could see you more, but I know you're doing well and I'm proud of you."

By now, it was the end of April, we were about to go to Germany, and I had noticed that Veronica had gotten up earlier in the day and had vomited. We went to the doctor's and we found out that she was pregnant again. I was thrilled, although she seemed torn but forced a smile anyway. Looking back I realize that I wasn't really interested in her problems and just assumed that she would be fine. Eventually, we would be back, she would have the child in eight to nine months, and I would be earning my way to Lieutenant and everything would be just great, or so I thought.

We arrived at the airport in Berlin, the first few days felt like a new adventure and were greeted by the person picking up all the soldiers at the airport. As we drove from Berlin to the base it was so strange hearing about the wall that divided the country and how some people were risking their lives to sneak across it. Veronica actually asked when the wall was built and the driver said it was built in the early 1960's to stop people on the Communist side from coming over. I looked at that wall, the way that I would look at the gates of hell, behind that was a terrible place where people suffered and the ones who maintained it were demons working for the Devil himself.

I remember asking the driver, "How long do you think the wall is going to stay up?"

He responded, "With the way things are between Soviets and their allies and the Americans and their allies, I will probably be long dead before that wall comes down."

Just as we approached the base, Veronica began to ask about what there was to do in Berlin or other parts of Western Germany. I immediately cut her off and said, "I don't want you going around this city alone or with Jackie, you should stay on the base where it's safe."

The driver interrupted, "Actually West Germany is a relatively safe area, in some places it's safer than areas in America."

She gave me a look that was pure disapproval and frustration.

We began to settle into our roles after the first week and a half, and she began having morning sickness again, but because of the hours I would work, she often dealt with this alone. Not to mention dealing with Jackie, Veronica must have had the patience of Job. I remember one day I came home early to pick up a report that I had written last night and when I walked by Jackie and she actually said, "Da-da."

Veronica and I were stunned that she had just said her first word. It was a blissful moment, it is amazing how forgetting a report and going back to get it can give you such a sweet moment.

One thing that they don't tell you when you get promoted is that while you get to give orders and you do get more authority, you also get more paperwork. It's a little bit tedious filling out performance reviews for the four people under your command. I had my eye on being promoted to staff Sergeant. For those of you that don't know, Sergeants have authority in combat over four men called a Fire Team whereas staff Sergeants have authority over nine men called Rifle Squads.

My hard work was paying off and my superiors were recognizing my effort, believe it or not but it was in the later portions of that trip when I was informed that the staff Sergeant who was leading a firing squad had been in an accident and was being sent home and they decided that I was ready. I was so excited that I was moving up the ladder again, and I was determined to get as high up as I could, perhaps even one day become a General. In some ways, I admired Eisenhower and his story, I admired that he made it to the top of military and helped lead the military to victory. After I got the promotion, I called Major McLachlin who was very happy for me and began to tell me that I only had a little bit further to go before I would be a Lieutenant. Then one day I could be where he was, I could be Major Melvoy, which of course had a good ring to it.

Germany as a country was very different, it was brighter and sunnier than Michigan and they really loved their beer and chocolate. For her birthday that year I bought Veronica a box of German chocolate and it blew her away. The thing that amazed me most was how many of the people there had just accepted the big wall that split their country in half. I couldn't imagine a giant wall cutting Michigan in half and knowing that Detroit was on the other side.

The other thing that amazed me was that they actually had this love/hate relationship with their Nazi history. On one hand, there was an unbelievable amount of death, destruction and shame, but on the other hand, Hitler did do some things to help Germany such as build the Autobahn, which is still in operation today. It was a very different environment than Japan and while it wasn't enormously different from the United States, it was different enough that some days you woke up and wondered about the strange quirks of this country. Not to mention, they were speaking in German a lot and when people are talking in some other language, you can't help but wonder if they are talking about you. While I did learn some German while I was over there, I always ended up speaking slowly to the point where a conversation of any real length in that language would have been a waste of time.

The actual base was similar to an American one back home but it was a bit of an odd experience. One of the events that I remember really well, was two guys who began to get into a fight about some woman they had met in a bar. The thing that made this incident memorable was that one of the guys threw a punch and the other guy dodged it and the guy who threw the punch hit a metal pipe and broke his hand. I gave those guys quite a speech about how you have a job to do and you shouldn't be fighting over which one of you is going to get laid from some easy woman. The other thing I pointed out was to be more aware of their surroundings.

"You and your enemy are not fighting in a void. There are things around you that can either harm you or help you win, in this case Muhammad Ali here (joke intended) wasn't paying attention and punched a solid lead pipe and broke his damn hand."

Sometimes little teaching moments like that pop up and it is important to remind guys of those simple things like being aware of your surroundings.

The craziest thing about being the authority figure is that sometimes you forget to take your own advice. I wasn't taking into account how hard it was for Veronica to look after Jackie while being pregnant. I was thinking way too much about myself and other problems. One of those other problems was told to me during a phone call, I think it was around Labour Day that year. When it turned out that the loading dock that my father was working at was being shut down. Apparently, the company was being bought and their assets were being merged and the dock that he had worked at for so many years of his life was closing sometime in November.

At first, I didn't say anything to Veronica and eventually we got into an argument where she felt like we were growing apart. At first, I had chalked it up to her hormones, and when I suggested that it might be her hormones talking, it didn't go over well to say the least. Eventually she found out about my father being laid off and I told her that we might have to give my mother money again and that I didn't know how my father would react.

This shut down Veronica's objections for a while because she saw how this was a big problem not just for me, but also for my side of the family. Between Veronica's pregnancy and the issues with my father being laid off, I decided that we would stay at my parent's house for three months, once the tour in Germany was over, and in that way I could help my father and my mother could help Veronica.

We left Germany around Halloween and she was now almost seven months pregnant and I began to wonder about whether it would be a boy or a girl. That last month I would talk to my mother and father, but what I didn't fully realize was that the way they were talking was sounding vaguely like they had been a few years ago, when his drinking was so out of control that he was unemployed. He had been trying to find other work, but there aren't a lot of loading docks in Ann Arbor, so his searching for any different jobs became a struggle as well.

There are a couple things I remember doing before we left Germany. I remember calling Tony and asking him if I could bring something home for him. Tony was German on his mother's side and I thought that he would appreciate something from there. I brought back a couple bottles of German liquor that I didn't think that we had back at home. The other thing I remember not long before we left, was taking a drive on the Autobahn, and as much as I enjoyed driving faster than I normally could, it was so strange to think that I was driving on the road that Hitler built.

CHAPTER 15

HOME BITTERSWEET HOME

Coming home was a nice change of pace and when they say there is no place like home, it is so true. Home is the place that you know best, you are the most familiar with and home is where the people who care about you are. Cathy had given birth to another son on April 27th named Marco. Veronica mentioned that in a few years all of those little children, Cynthia, Connor, Marco, Jackie and our next child could grow up to be a really close-knit group of cousins. Jason and his business partner were doing very well for themselves, and they now had three locations for his sports bar called Game Night. The first two locations were making money but their third one was struggling a bit, however he had confidence that things would pick up with the Super Bowl, hockey season, etc.

That was the good news, but the bad news was that when we came back to Michigan, my father was down to his last week at work and he hadn't found anything else. My father didn't have any college education, he had experience but he was also over fifty years old, and it's not easy to find a new job when people see you as over the hill. He had turned fifty-one earlier in 1975 and was really, really upset about the situation, and he began to go on rants about "these damn college kids, read a bunch of numbers and say, 'let's fire some people' and don't give a damn about loyalty."

While I couldn't disagree, it was beginning to sound like the way he talked before and I knew that if my father was going to stay on track, I might need to keep my eye on him. I explained to my mother that Veronica and I were going to be around for the next few months and that I was hoping she would help look after Veronica and I would keep an eye on him. She agreed and must have told me ten times how glad she was to have me back and how glad she was to get to spend time with her granddaughter.

The problems started on Friday, the last day the loading dock would be open and the other guys were going out to the bar to drink to commemorate the closing. Eventually they convinced him to go with them to the bar. My father usually got home around 5:45 maybe 6:00

pm, but once 7:00 passed my mother got worried. We didn't have cell phones back then, so getting in touch with someone was a lot more difficult. I began to get worried as well, and eventually I began calling around to the numbers in our address book.

Eventually, around 8:15 pm we got a call from one of his co-workers who said that they were at a bar downtown and that he had drank over a dozen shots of whiskey and had passed out. I thought that this was going to be a disaster especially if my mother found out, so I lied, it wasn't easy, but I lied. I told my mother that his car had broken down and that he had gotten it towed and was at a mechanics garage needing to be picked up. So, I went to pick him up, when I got there two of his friends were trying to get him on his feet, as he was muttering, "I'm fine, I went three years without drinking, and I have a few and you guys are all worried, so back off."

I came up to him and told him that he needed to come home and that my mother was worried, then he started to get angry asking who I was to give him orders. After all I was staying in his house. I was overcome with dread at the thought of having to fight him again, so I tried to go the food route and managed to convince him to come home because she was cooking him a steak. That actually worked and as we began to drive back home, he began to pass out again, and I began trying to figure out who could bring home his car without letting the cat out of the bag. Before I could come up with an answer to that question, he began to grab his stomach and say, "Oh no."

Then he began to lower the window on his side as quickly as he could while he vomited out the window. I pulled off to the side of the road so he could finish, as I looked in disgust at the chunks of food on the side of my car. He had been doing so well, and he hadn't had a drink since March of 1972 and now this happened. So we eventually came home, and I proceeded to tell him that we weren't going to tell my mother because we don't want her to worry. So I told him to go upstairs as quick as he could, get changed, drink some water and try to stick to the story.

What I didn't realize was that my plan had been ruined before we even got home because one of our neighbours had been at that bar and had come over and told her. As we got there, she had already packed some of his clothes and as we walked in she shoved the suitcase into his chest and told him that she would not go through this again. I believe her exact words were, "Come back sober or don't come back at all."

She was so mad at him that she totally forgot that I had lied to her, but getting away with a lie was the last thing on my mind at that point.

I drove him to a motel and I assured him that we would straighten all of this out in the morning. He was getting drowsy from all the liquor and by the time we got there he was almost passed out. I helped him into his room as he mumbled and I left him a note on the nightstand in the room. As I got him into bed and placed a bucket right next to it, I took a step back and saw the man that I had looked up to so much, now fallen and pathetic and if we didn't fix this there was no telling how far it could go.

After I left the room I called Jason and asked if I could pick him up so we could get my father's car from the bar. He was going to be free soon so I picked him up at one of the Game Night locations, where they were pretty busy between basketball, hockey and football so I guess it was always Game Night. As we drove to my father's work to pick up his car, Jason and I had a long talk about what we were going to do, and decided do make sure my father went to another A.A. meeting immediately. His meetings had been Tuesday night, but we couldn't wait that long.

Finally, we came home, and I was very anxious and couldn't stop wondering, "How are we going to keep this family from completely falling apart?"

Later that night when we were alone, Veronica asked me what we were going to do. I said that if she tried to talk to my mother and I got my father back on the wagon, everything would be fine. Even though she was seven months pregnant, when her family was in need, Veronica was ready to step up.

The next morning I went to the motel. I still had the key from last night and when I opened the door, he wasn't in the bed, and the light was on in the bathroom. I went into the bathroom, bracing myself to see something terrible. As I turned the corner, I saw my father sitting there on the floor with vomit in the toilet and some of it on the floor. He looked terrible, like he had been drained of all of his strength. He had this look in his eyes that I had never seen before, like his life was over.

I sat on the edge of the tub and we talked, and I told him that we were going to get him back on track. He was truly scared that his marriage was over. I assured him that Veronica and I would work night and day to fix this. So I pulled him back up and I told him that he was going to an A.A. meeting today, and this was the beginning of a long stretch of time without drinking. He got cleaned up, and we had some breakfast, but he didn't feel like eating much.

We got him to the meeting for noon, and I wanted to make sure he went through with it, but the organizer said the meeting was for members only. So I was forced to listen from outside the door, and it sounded like he stood up and told everyone what had happened. In the middle of telling everyone what happened, he actually broke down crying saying that he had screwed everything up, that he was a failure of a man and that he had let everybody down. I was absolutely stunned to hear him say this. You have to understand that my father didn't cry and if he ever did, he never let anyone see it, much less a group of strangers. So hearing him talk this openly and be so vulnerable was really hard to listen to. I never told him that I heard what he said, and as far as he knew I sat outside and read the newspaper.

After the meeting, he and I went out for lunch and he turned the conversation around. He didn't want to talk about himself anymore, but only asked me what I was going to do. I told him I didn't know, but I was excited about Veronica having another baby and the doctor had estimated her due date for January. My father and I hadn't had this close of a conversation in years, talking about what we were looking forward to. I told him my plan to get as high up in the military as possible; how one day I might even be a General, like Eisenhower.

Eventually, the conversation worked its way back to the issue of his drinking. We decided that he would stay in the motel one more night and then we would go to church together. It seemed like a good idea, so I came home, thinking that selling this idea to my mother would be easy, but I was wrong.

She talked about how embarrassed she had been since his drinking had been going on. She still had the picture in her dresser drawer of the blood in the snow taken by the police from the night that he and I fought and how it reminded her of what his drinking had done to her family. I told her that I was going to take him to the A.A. meetings until he gets sober again. She was still unconvinced and I didn't know what to do. Problems are always so much bigger when the people involved are so close to you.

The next day I brought my father to church and I remember wishing the minister would have been doing a forgiveness sermon, but he was talking about prayer and dedication. My mother still didn't want to talk to my father and my father's fear of his marriage being over began to overwhelm him. You have to remember that his generation didn't divorce, because divorce was a sign of incredible failure and shame, but the truth was he didn't know how to handle it.

Thankfully around the time of Thanksgiving, Veronica finally got through to my mother and she agreed to take my father back. I had been watching him like a hawk, and he had not had a drink since that Friday night. Thanksgiving was tense, but at least we were becoming a family again, and I couldn't stand to see the pain my father was in, to see him so emotionally vulnerable. It was so different from what he had been when I was young. Sometimes part of growing up is the unfortunate realization that the people you look up to aren't quite what you thought they were. This time around my father had to look for new work, the unfortunate irony was that while Jason would have hired him in a minute, Jason owned a bar which would have been a strong temptation and one that we were afraid he wouldn't be able to resist. Thankfully, they had their savings, as well as Cathy's support and mine if they needed it, so we knew that they would find something else eventually as long as he stayed on the wagon.

The next few weeks after Thanksgiving were much better and even though there was still some tension, it was a lot lighter and you could actually ignore it. Meanwhile, Veronica was going to have a baby soon, we weren't sure exactly when but we were holding our breaths knowing it would be soon. I still have the photo from that Christmas, where everyone looks so happy, with Jackie's hand up in front of her face as if she was trying to hide from the camera. That picture brings a tear to my eye seeing her as she was.

During December, I must have made dozens of phone calls trying to arrange where I would be once my vacation time was done in early March. The last thing I wanted was to be too far away from my family during this time, so I was lobbying for somewhere in Michigan but apparently it wasn't in the cards. The best I could get was a position returning as a Drill Sergeant outside of Fort Wayne, Indiana. At least that way, if there was an emergency I could drive there in a matter of hours. If I had been put in Hawaii and there was an emergency, I don't know what I would have done.

My father managed to get a new position lined up in Flint, which was a longer drive, but it was a union job and with his experience at the loading dock, he was hired and would be making more money. So he found out that he would start in February, and as a result those weeks waiting in January felt like an eternity for him. Things however were getting better and the disaster was beginning to turn into a very unpleasant memory.

However, without question the highlight of this time was the birth of our second child, my first son, Randall Philip Melvoy. The middle name was in reference to Phil "the hill," which seemed like the right thing to do, to honour such a brave man. I remember being there in the delivery room, and we didn't know in advance whether it would be a boy or a girl. The fact was, I was hoping for a boy, so that I could take him to ball games, take him fishing, teach him football, baseball, and all that great stuff. When it finally happened, we were thrilled and just like July 28, 1974 when Jackie was born, I was so happy on January 22, 1976 when my son was born. Needless to say, those few months between November 1975 and February 1976 were stressful but we got through it.

I remember those first few weeks of having Randall, Jackie was so amazed to see this little person and it was so touching to see the two of them together. Today, people take pictures all the time of everything, back then pictures took a lot more effort. I still have the pictures of our children from when they were little and they are worth a thousand times their weight in gold. I remember Veronica being nervous and unsure about moving to Fort Wayne, Indiana, but I told her we had to, and that everything would be fine. I knew she was uneasy about it, and I knew that she didn't like leaving Michigan again, but I assumed that she would adapt and everything would be perfectly fine.

CHAPTER 16
★
THE KILLJOY RETURNS

The return to being a Drill Sergeant was a little bit of fun, as I had a fresh crop of maggots to turn into soldiers. I was able to take my frustration and direct it at the screw-ups in this group. One of the things I remember about going back to Indiana was this guy who reminded me so much of Mark. I saw how savage he was during the hand to hand combat and his mannerisms were a dead ringer for Mark, though the hardest part was that he was doing everything that was being asked of him. There was nothing I could really say, unless he laid a hand on somebody outside of practice so there was nothing I could do. I struggled with that for a little while, but I didn't know who I could talk to. I just had to watch and wonder what crop of kids this bastard would blow up if given the opportunity. The hardest part was that we needed trained killers who knew how to follow the rules and wouldn't hesitate when the trigger needed to be pulled. I could tell this guy wouldn't, and in a strange way, I wanted some of the other candidates to be more like him.

Of course, I had some smart-asses and pretty soon they learned to keep their mouths shut, and every once in a while, I would give them a little bit of my past, so they knew what they were in for. Most of these guys had only seen war in movies and sometimes the closest thing they had done to fighting was wrestling their brother in the backyard. I remember seeing the shocked looks on some of their faces when I began to describe seeing the bullet going through the other Charlie's head. I remember saying "I knew him, he was a friend, I saw him get his god-damned brains blown out when a bullet went into his head. Trust me when I tell you that if you get queasy at the sight of blood and guts you will get chewed up and spit out like a two-cent piece of gum. So, you better toughen up real quick, got that Mary-Anne?"

By the time I got through with them they weren't going to be naïve enough to think that this was going to be a G-rated movie. I was back to being Melvoy the Killjoy pretty quickly, but the strangest thing was, I actually took pride in that name, because in a way I had learned from a tough hard ass and most guys had learned from tough hard ass guys. If you are a Drill Sergeant and they think you are fun, you are doing your job wrong and I always remembered that.

The thing that stood out most about going to Indiana was that when I was at work, it felt like a second home, but when I wasn't working, I felt strange and it took a little while for me to get used to it. Veronica was now at home with two children under two years old, and she began to talk about trying to do more fun stuff like going out to dinner or going dancing but it always seemed like there was something in the way. Maybe the weather was bad, or one of the kids would be sick, but the romantic night that Veronica hoped for was always not as important as what was happening and it was always going to happen "another time."

There was a week before the end of the second group of recruits from Indiana, when we found out that her Aunt Judy had passed away from a stroke. Veronica had loved Aunt Judy but hadn't seen her in years, but unfortunately someone had to stay with the children and I told her that she couldn't go to the funeral. That made her so upset, but all I could think about was how I wanted someone to make dinner when I got home after a hard day. I was also thinking about how if someone called I would need her to take messages. I was thinking about how the trip might be hard for the kids to handle. I was thinking about nearly everyone except her, she eventually conceded and agreed that she would call her cousins with her condolences.

That was in July, and she didn't say much about it for a while, and then I committed one of the mortal sins of a marriage. I was so busy talking to my parents and training the newest set of recruits, that I forgot our fifth anniversary. Even though there are bigger anniversaries than that one, it was the biggest one we'd had up to that point.

That was a hard day. She seemed so happy that morning but when I came home, there was no dinner and she told me she would remember to cook when I remember. Then she went into the bedroom and closed the door.

It took me almost fifteen minutes to remember that it was our anniversary; when you are in combat and you feel like you are being attacked, you are supposed to counter attack. In combat that can save your life, in marriage, it's suicide. I told her that she should have reminded me and that she knows how busy I am. I then tried to ask her why she didn't appreciate the effort that I was putting in. She opened the bedroom door in tears, saying, "Yeah, you put in so much effort for everyone else, except me. Everyone matters so much to you except your own wife."

She slammed the door in my face and blocked the door. I told her to open the door but she wouldn't. I started banging on the door and began to order her to open the door. I said, "I have fought in wars for you, I have slept with one eye open in Vietnam for you."

She responded by yelling back, "Then sleeping on the couch will be easy."

I then looked over and saw Jackie; she was two years old and looked really scared, and as innocent as she could. With those big innocent eyes, she asked, "Daddy, why are you and Mommy angry?"

I told Jackie it was nothing and everything will be fine tomorrow, and I told her to go to bed. I sat there on the couch and I began to wonder what was going on with my marriage. I didn't fall asleep until 3:00 am that night and I had to wake up at 5:00 am. If the recruits are up at 6:00 you need to be ready to get them out of their bunks so they can hit the ground running.

When I went in for the day's training I was in the worst mood I had ever been in because I was tired and really pissed off. That day even Miller "the Killer" would have told me to cut them some slack.

That day I showed them absolutely no mercy. I walked in that morning and told them to get their shit together, I had no time for anything and if they screwed with me this would be the worst day of their lives. I don't remember everything, but a few of the things that really stood out were things like one guy's bed wasn't made and I snapped at him and made him do sixty push-ups. Another guy was running a little slow and I kicked him in the ass and told him that he had better hurry up or else. That day I pushed them until they were drenched in sweat and one of them came to me and asked to please back off.

I didn't show him any respect, I yelled at him right in the face and said, "You lazy maggot, you won't be able to ask the enemy to take it easy on you! If you ever get captured by the Russians, they will throw you in Siberia and give you so much shit that you will be begging to be back here. So shut the fuck up and keep going!"

The fact that it was a really hot day didn't help things. They were drenched in sweat, breathing heavier than they ever had and by the end of the day the guys who were exhausted were carrying the guys who were almost dead.

Right before dinner I told them, "If I hear one peep out of you cocksuckers, you will get more of what you got today and worse!"

Five guys with potential quit within the next twelve hours. Everyone makes mistakes but that day I drove away five guys who were decent soldier material and I'm sure everyone else who stayed was tempted to walk out that door. When I came home that night, I was still mad and so was Veronica. All we did was talk to the children and try to avoid looking at each other. I slept on the couch again, although I had a better night's sleep, it still wasn't enough and I woke up feeling rotten.

The next day I was feeling more levelheaded despite how rotten I felt and realizing I went too far yesterday. However, Drill Sergeants are never ever supposed to apologize, because they have to be an absolute authority to those guys going through training. So the best thing I could do was cover my tracks while at the same time assuring the guys that what they got yesterday was not going to be the new norm. "Listen up ladies, those of you who are looking around wondering where the other ladies went, they couldn't hack it and ran away and I say good riddance. Combat is not a routine job, you don't know what crazy shit you are going to get, and what you got yesterday was a surprise pile of shit. If you think that you can't handle that ever happening again, then get your asses out of my platoon. Am I clear?"

They responded, "Sir, yes sir."

I was hoping with that speech, the guys would think that I had simply thrown that in their way for them to conquer it and that now that they knew the worst of training was over.

When I got home that night, Veronica had sent the kids to her new friend Beth's for the night, because she didn't want them to hear us arguing. She told me that things needed to change, and I told her that in a couple years things would be a lot easier. She asked me why, and I suddenly realized that I didn't really have a plan, I had to make up a lie. I told her that once I became a Lieutenant my hours wouldn't be as long and I would be able to manage my own schedule more. I even told her that we would have more time for us and that I would start putting in a lot more effort, I told her a mix of what she wanted to hear and something to buy me some time. The amazing thing is that it actually worked, and she believed me and we made up. I was so happy to get things back to the way I wanted them.

The next month I was trying to find out how long it would be until I became a Lieutenant and I found out that it would be at least another little while. I assured her that Major McLachlin was giving me the best advice possible to speed up the process. It is so much easier to endure something when you think that it's going to end soon, as opposed to having no idea if it will ever end.

While all of this was going on, I was wondering in the back of my mind if my father was keeping on the wagon. Fort Wayne, Indiana was far enough away that if something happened I could drive back to Ann Arbor. I found out later on that we were going to be moving to Montana. Taking that into account we would be even further away, so

I wanted to put my mind at ease that things were going to be fine at home before we went even further across the country. I spoke to my father first who explained how he was enjoying the new job, he was making more money and he was enjoying working with the people in Flint. Call it paranoia, but I then decided to speak to my mother who said that things had been going along well enough and he seemed to be back to his usual self and verified his statement about being in a better place.

This may have sounded paranoid but the other thing that you have to keep in mind is that the same fall that we moved to Montana, Cathy had three kids and Jason and his business partner were now running four locations of Game Night. So, they were both really busy and if things fell apart between my mother and father again, there wouldn't be anyone to help to put things back together. By the process of elimination the responsibility seemed to fall onto me.

As we got into that moving van with little Jackie and Randy, preparing to move some place new and different, I just saw it as a new challenge, but the kids were nervous. Jackie was two years old, which is old enough to ask questions, but not always old enough to understand the answers.

I remember her asking, "What if I don't like Motana?"

Veronica did a great job assuring her though, and we were able to move everything forward. The two things I remember thinking as we drove there was how beautiful all of the wide-open space was, with parts of it looking like a picturesque postcard. The other thing I remember thinking was how nervous Veronica looked. I remember thinking that after a few days she would settle in and everything would be fine. You would think a soldier who had seen and done everything I had by that point, wouldn't be naïve, but in some ways, I still was.

CHAPTER 17

BIG SKY, BIGGER PROBLEMS

The first little bit of time in Montana was great. It was still decently warm out, with wide, open space, and it seemed like there was a cool breeze blowing most of the time. I wasn't a Drill Sergeant at this base, I was just a staff Sergeant and administrator. Shortly after I got there, I found out that I was first in line to be moved up to Sergeant First Class. I was getting closer and closer to the rank of Lieutenant, and what a proud day that would be. I had remembered the words of Major McLachlin when he said that he was betting that I would be a Lieutenant someday.

They call Montana big sky country, which is an accurate description, and it felt like a new adventure and I was enjoying the scenery. Also, on my first few trips into town, it seemed like people were more friendly and respectful not just of the military, but in general. So, it didn't take me too long to warm up to Montana, but Veronica however saw things differently.

We hadn't been out dancing together in a dance club since the spring of 1975 and disco was not big in Montana, not even in their biggest city, Helena. The people in the community seemed much more interested in country music, which Veronica only liked once in a while. The other thing to keep in mind is that because it was such a small and close-knit group, she couldn't help but feel like an outsider. I don't know why I remember her name, but Grace Appleton was apparently the alpha female on the residential part of the base and was apparently a gossiper. That characteristic turned Veronica right off, and she felt like there was no place for her there. Every day I got a little bit more used to it but Veronica would hate it a little bit more.

I remember a phone call I had in the fall of 1976 from Major McLachlin, where he was telling me about how he wished we had just bombed North Vietnam like we did to Japan. He was afraid that America was losing its guts and will to fight. He had become very aware of the situation in Cambodia, and he was disgusted about how nothing was being done. He saw America's unwillingness to intervene as a sign of weakness, and told me something that made sense at the time, but now I see differently. He told me that Russia had lured us into fighting the Koreans and the Vietnamese so we would have all of the fight out of us when they decided to strike. The Cambodians were the test to see if we had had enough and that we were failing that test if we don't show the Russians that we still had plenty of fight left, and then we would be sending them a subtle white flag. This stayed with me for quite some time, and just like in high school, Charlie Melvoy feared nobody and neither should America.

The day-to-day actions were easier and I was doing more administrative work, paperwork, the odd phone call, etc. It was different and it felt easier than being a Drill Sergeant because when you are a Drill Sergeant you have to be cranked up for numerous consecutive hours, whereas sitting at a desk doing paperwork felt very easy by comparison. I made sure to jump on any opportunity to show that I was a team player and ready to take on any task. My strategy paid off beautifully when the day came in mid-December, frost was on the ground and I was informed of my promotion to Sergeant First Class, and of course you can't just dance around yelling "woo-hoo."

Obviously, I gave the standard, "Sir thank you sir."

That night when I came home, things were happy because I was also not working as late and I had more time at home, which made things a little bit easier for Veronica.

Unfortunately, this positive new status quo was ruined by a one week trip that happened in the New Year. The United States and Canadian armies were having a conference to talk about North American security. I was selected with some other people to meet up at a military base outside of Edmonton, Alberta. Veronica hated the thought of being left alone with the kids for a whole week and thought the trip was optional. The truth was I had only been to Canada a couple of times in the summer as a boy and had no interest in going there in the winter.

The trip itself was interesting, we talked a lot about dealing with things such as insurgents and air attacks. When you start realizing all of the tools that we had at our disposal such as radio, phone, it made me think about how glad I was that we had this technology. If the Russians had this and we didn't, we would be either dead or red. The nights were fun and there was a local pub where we could go in the evenings and I would hear all about how things were done in Canada. Canadians were so similar to us but it was interesting to see how they seemed to have a different ethic than we did. They still saw the Soviets as a threat, but they were challenging them to hockey games, rather than fighting for the actual world. I remained professional, but inside I just found this to be such a strange country, nice but strange.

As the conference came to an end, I came home with pages and pages of notes. When I got home Veronica was trying to be nice, but I could tell she had that mad tone of voice. I tried to make it up to her by taking her out the night of Valentine's Day, which at first went perfectly, bringing out candy and chocolates. The candle lit restaurant was the icing on the cake, and of course I complimented her on how beautiful she was, so everything was going great. Unfortunately, the wonderful evening came to a crashing halt, when we went to pick up our kids from one of the other homes on the base.

Jackie asked a question, "Mommy, what's a bitch?"

I immediately snapped and told Jackie never to say that word again, and she began to get upset and began to cry. Veronica asked her where she heard that and Jackie said, "Mrs. Morris said you were a –"

I cut her off and said, "Don't say it, we get the point."

The night was completely ruined, and we later found out that Grace Appleton and Natalie Morris were friends and they were badmouthing Veronica with our children there. Not only did this ruin Valentine's Day, but it also strengthened Veronica's growing hatred of Montana. The worst part was that I worked with Natalie's husband Carl, and we got along pretty well, so this basically threw a monkey wrench into our working friendship.

The next day I spoke to the First Lieutenant on the base and said that I wanted to sort this out immediately, so Sergeant Appleton and Private Morris were called in to discuss the incident. I remember telling the Lieutenant what happened and Morris' story was that he had been called by someone to help fix the guy's truck because one of the parts was ordered late. It had to be ready for the next day and he passed Grace as he was leaving but he didn't know about this and had no part of it. I wasn't sure whether or not to believe him.

Sergeant Appleton's answer was far less apologetic, "Look Melvoy, I have no problem with you, you command well and I respect you and your service record. The problem is your wife; ever since she came here she just complained and complained and complained. My wife shouldn't have said it in front of your kid, but she didn't say anything that wasn't true."

That was when I got angry and told him that if he wanted to say anything else about my wife, I'll be happy to respond outside. The Lieutenant was trying to calm things down, when Morris spoke up, "Melvoy, she doesn't fit in here."

I took exception, "Tell me something Private, did you ever even go into combat? I went to Vietnam three times and I earned a purple heart. What do you have besides a lack of respect?"

The Lieutenant knew that this wasn't going to get better, so he immediately ordered all of us to stand down.

He looked at them and told them, "Tell your wives that loose lips sink ships, and to shut their pie holes before they cause any more problems."

He then turned to me and said, "Melvoy, I don't think this is going to work, so I am going to make some phone calls and get you and your family transferred somewhere else. It should take two to three weeks, so between now and then I expect all of you to show the utmost professionalism. Are we clear?"

We all responded, "Sir, yes sir."

I left knowing that the next few weeks would be unpleasant and filled with awkward silence between these men and me, who I previously thought of as my work friends.

When I came home that night, I pulled Veronica aside and told her that we were getting transferred in two to three weeks. She was ecstatic, she put her arms around me, and kissed me on the cheek and the lips over and over while saying, "Thank you, thank you, I love you so much."

It took me a moment to realize that she thought that I had arranged that on purpose and I decided just to go with it. At the time, I figured "when you are in the dog house, get out any way you can, as fast as you can."

Soon we found out we were getting transferred to Fort Worth, Texas in March. This was great because it was not only going to be warmer, but Texas had a lot more people and there would be more for Veronica to do. On top of it all, we were getting there before things could get much worse on the current base.

The day before we left, someone posted a note on our door that said, "You're leaving? Good Riddance!"

Veronica almost never swore, but when she saw that note, she blurted out, "I hate this fucking place."

I was in a rush so I just told her to calm down and to remember that we were leaving tomorrow and that Texas was going to be nicer, warmer, and they probably had more to do there. I rushed off to work, where most of the guys were pleasant enough wishing me luck. I realized that I was going to miss this place. Which seemed so nice at first, but that changed pretty quickly. I just had to hope that Fort Worth, Texas would be better.

That drive to Fort Worth was long but worth every bit of it. I remember that it started to rain that day as we went through Wyoming. I remember looking at all of those vast fields of crops, and the beautiful sun shining across the fields. Of course, I had seen farms before, but never so many of them. Beyond that, I remember stopping in a hotel for the night in Colorado. Driving through those mountains, seeing all of those roads winding around and the occasional elevation sign reminding you why your ears were popping. It was a great drive and it was just two days where all I had to think about was getting there. I refused to let myself worry about anything else.

Just before we crossed into Texas, we pulled off at a gas station in a small area of Oklahoma that was just north of Texas' northern border. I remember making small talk with one of the attendants, and he noticed that I had an accent, although it sounded to me like he did. He asked me where I was from and I responded that I just came from Montana but was originally from Michigan. He then asked where I was going and I told him that I was on my way to Fort Worth. He looked at me with a straight face and said, "Michigan, you'll probably be alright. If you was from California or New York, there might be problems."

I was a little puzzled and asked him what he meant, he responded, "Things are different down here, and some of them west coast and northern folk don't understand that."

I thanked him for his time and went on the road again. I had been to Canada, Vietnam, Japan and Germany, how different could Texas be?

CHAPTER 18

THERE'S SOMETHING ABOUT TEXAS

One of the first things I noticed about Texas is that they had almost as much state pride as national pride, and maybe even more so. If I counted five American flags there would be between and three and four Texas State flags, and there were so many of both, it was sometimes hard to keep track of them all. As we pulled up to Fort Worth, the sun was out it was as if we had traveled forward in time about four weeks to spring. We were greeted at the base with salutes, and pretty soon we were shown our new base housing. It was pretty nice and Veronica was just thrilled to have a fresh start somewhere else. I remember meeting one Private who began asking me questions like, "Did you ever serve in combat? Do you have any special recognitions?"

By the time I told him the truth, which was that I had been deployed overseas five times, once in Germany, once in Japan, three times in Vietnam and I had earned a purple heart, he was just about to ask me for my autograph.

I told him the simple truth, which was to be proud of your military service, but never be so proud that you think you're special. That day I really taught that kid something important and I can only hope he remembered that. At first, things on the military base were just standard operating procedure; there wasn't any glaring difference between this and other bases I had served on. Paperwork still needed to get done, chores still needed to be assigned, so it seemed to be business as usual.

Over the next few months, I tried to settle in to this new place, and the weather was hot and sunny quite a bit. Like in Montana, there seemed to be a lot of respect for the military especially in Fort Worth, but the thing that really stunned me was the undercurrent of racial tension that existed. I actually saw that the white and black soldiers would almost never talk to each other, except when absolutely necessary. You have to understand that back then racism was more blatant, but in the south, it was a real hot button issue for almost everyone. To the best of my recollection, things got tense between some of the black soldiers and some of the white soldiers.

One day in particular, things boiled over as a brawl broke out between some of the white and black soldiers. They may have hated each other, but by the time it was over they all hated me more. I broke it up and let them have it. "Listen up ladies, I don't give a good god damn what colour your skin is, I care about what colour your flag is, what colour your uniform is, and what colour your eyes are, because I don't want anybody smoking pot. I will not tolerate this bullshit on this base, so here is what is going to happen. I am going to be up all night, running you fuckers ragged and by the time it's over you will be too tired to hate anybody."

I did exactly that and I stayed up running them ragged until midnight. This would have nearly killed a civilian, but they were soldiers and I knew they would survive. However, it was late by the end and thankfully there was a good supply of coffee on the base. By the time midnight came around, I told them all to shake hands and that if they ever pulled this again, it would be a lot worse.

While I don't regret what I did that night, I regret the results that came about accidentally. By the time I came home to bed, Veronica was asleep and I knew that if everything went right tonight, I wouldn't have to do that again. The next morning not only was I tired, I got a hell of a surprise from Veronica who was mad that I had been out so late. She wondered why I hadn't called to tell her I would be out so late. I asked her why she was so upset and she said that she was already overwhelmed with Jackie and Randall and now… I suddenly realized with that pause and the look on her face, that she was pregnant again. I was a mix of stunned and thrilled at the news that I was now going to have three beautiful children. Veronica, was now more worried because she thought that I was drifting away again. I told her that I was getting close to being a Lieutenant and things would be easier then. She began to have her doubts, but I still assured her that everything was going to be great. The good news was that the women on the base were more welcoming of her than they had been in Montana and I told her to feel free to ask them for more help.

I was late getting to the base that morning because of that discussion which was bad enough, but then I got ambushed by Lieutenant Keith, asking me what the hell I did last night. "I got eight soldiers who can barely move today because you ran them until god damn midnight. Why did you do that?"

I responded that they got into a fight and I punished them accordingly. Lieutenant Keith started hinting that I should have been punishing the black soldiers worse because "they usually start these things."

I stood my ground and told him that since I didn't know who

started what, I had to punish all of them severely enough, that all of them would know not to start more trouble. He backed off a little bit and told me that if this ever happens again, I need to make sure he deals out the punishment, not me. This bothered me, but he was my superior officer and at the end of the day until I hear otherwise from someone higher up than him, I had better follow his orders.

When I got home that night, Veronica was feeling a little bit better, but was still worried about how she was going to manage three children. Unlike in Montana, she became good friends with a woman named Gloria, Lieutenant Keith's wife, who was about ten years older than her and had some kids of her own. In some ways Gloria became a little bit of a mentor to Veronica, which was similar to the way Major McLachlin had become a mentor to myself.

I remember Father's Day that year. Jackie was about to turn three, Randall was a year old and Veronica, Gloria, Lieutenant Keith and I were having a dinner at their home. Keith had come from Alabama, so to me it sounded like he had an accent and vice versa. It was a great time, we talked about this and that, and although he and I had had a strong disagreement about the earlier issue, we got along great. One of the things he told me that night after having a few drinks, was that if there is one good thing about the Democrats being in office, it means that they won't be sending us off to war for a while and he could just relax and wait for his pension.

That bothered me a lot, because I figured that I would eventually retire, but hated the idea of signing up to something and leaving before it was done. It was that same uncomfortable feeling I had back when I was in the high school semi-finals football game, the feeling of disappointment and loss; that feeling that I felt five-fold when I was leaving Vietnam, without the victory and leaving with loss. It seemed like he had almost resigned himself to the idea that whatever happens, will happen and as long as he makes out with his money, he's fine.
I looked at my kids playing tag with his kids in the backyard and I realized I never wanted my kids to think of me the way that I was thinking of him at this moment. I remembered that instance for a very long time.

As the summer took hold, I got a taste of how hot things were in Texas. Michigan summers were one thing, but Texas summers were something else. If the guys on the base were doing nothing, they would be sweating tons, so it would look to the untrained eye like they were working their asses off. Those few months were pretty standard. Lieutenant Keith and I gained more of a mutual respect, even if what he said when he was drinking indicated otherwise.

When I came home one day, I saw Veronica just as upset as she could be. Almost in tears, I asked her what was wrong and she told me that she was at Wal-Mart earlier and lost Jackie for about twenty minutes. What happened was Jackie had decided to play hide and seek without telling Veronica. She eventually came out from wherever she was hiding because she was hungry and Veronica nearly died of embarrassment when the announcement was made across the store. "Mrs. Melvoy please come to the customer service area, we found your daughter. I repeat, Mrs. Melvoy please come to the customer service area, we found your daughter."

Unfortunately, I responded poorly to this, asking Veronica what she was doing, rather than making sure our daughter was safe. She got defensive and the whole thing turned into a big fight.

She didn't understand the stress that I went through at my job and I didn't take her job very seriously at the time. Eventually we more or less agreed to disagree about whose fault it was and that she would try harder to keep her eye on the ball.

During this time, other things seemed to be going quite well. My father was back to his normal self, and had been clean and sober for a year and a half. His job at the auto parts plant in Flint was going reasonably well, Jason's business with Game Night restaurants was going very well and he was about to open his fifth location, which would be his first outside of Michigan. To top it all off, we found out at the beginning of the fall that Cathy was pregnant again and was going to have her fourth child. So things seemed to be rolling along well enough, but unfortunately, things weren't as good as I thought. Veronica began to talk to me less and began spending a lot more time talking to her friend Gloria. At first, I was fine with this because it meant that I didn't have to worry about too much else. I could just come home have a brief conversation, eat dinner, and watch TV. What a perfect combination – everything a man wants, right?

Thanksgiving on the base was great, and several different women came together to put together an enormous feast for all the families. I remember telling Veronica to contribute her mashed potatoes, as I was sure they would be the best. She agreed and that Thanksgiving I couldn't have been happier and as an added bonus, I found out that I was about to be promoted to Lieutenant in a few months, barring any issues of misconduct that is.

Veronica and I went home for two weeks for Christmas and New Year's, which was a great welcome home. This was the first time that I began to notice the commercialization of Christmas and the change of our culture. Jason and Cathy had bought their kids a bunch of stuff for

Christmas. They must have spent $30 or $40 on each one of their kids, which was a lot of money back then. I didn't understand it, but their oldest daughter Cynthia got this big Barbie doll set with accessories and all sorts of stuff. I knew that Jason was doing well and his Game Night locations were doing well, but I was surprised that he had so much money to spend. Our gifts when I was little were simple and cheap, maybe a small toy and a bit of chocolate.

I remember asking Jason why he was spoiling his kids so badly and he and I got into an argument about it. He was telling me that we should be providing as good a life for our kids as we could. I believed that if you give kids too much they never learned to work for anything and will think everything falls out of the sky. I was convinced that if they kept this up, Cynthia, Connor, Marco, and the next child would grow up to be those kids who Veronica would tell me about who have a temper tantrum in the grocery store. She told me time and again about those times the kids would be screaming at the top of their lungs because the parent wasn't buying them the candy they wanted.

Eventually Cathy and Veronica got us to change the subject and we moved onto other topics, such as my upcoming promotion to Lieutenant. I didn't know exactly when it was happening but I knew that it was close. I was even more puzzled by all the gift giving, when I heard about Jason saying that he is trying to be careful because of the loan he took out to build the newest location, as well as paying off the others. I remember thinking to myself, "If you need money, why are you spending so much money on Christmas?"

But I kept my mouth shut just to keep the peace. That continued to bother me, wondering why Jason and Cathy were spending so much. The part that worried me the most, was that if we had more Christmases like this, my kids would start complaining about not getting as many gifts as them. We got back to Texas just after New Year's. I had to get back to business and began to wonder if all of that money was going to cause problems for them down the road.

The next month was difficult, and it seemed like Veronica was annoyed all the time because by this point, she was eight months pregnant and was dealing with two other kids. We must have gotten into arguments every other day and I tried to just chalk this up to her hormones and that everything would be fine once the baby was born.

Those two weeks before she had the baby were hectic, because I received the news that I had been waiting for. I was going to be a Second Lieutenant in the army base outside of San Diego. I was excited and Veronica and I got into a big argument because she was rolling her eyes at the thought of us moving again. I told her that this was what we had been waiting for – sunshine, beaches, more money, and more time to spend at home. I had worked so hard for our family in order to provide all of that to her and the kids. I kept rhetorically asking myself, "How come she didn't realize how hard it is for me to take such a senior position on the base?"

The tension built up to such a degree that she said she didn't even want me in the delivery room, but eventually she let me in though, so I didn't miss it. She gave birth to our youngest son Matthew, which strangely enough happened on Groundhog's Day on February 2, 1978.

We would be moving in mid-March and I began to try to suppress her complaints when she tried to tell me about how hard it was. I started telling her that my mother raised three kids and plenty of other women raised a lot more than three kids, while their husbands worked, and she just had to forge ahead and keep doing as well as she had been. She conceded that she would eventually get used to three children and that eventually things would get easier, especially with the kids going to school.

This placated her for a little while, and she gave me the line, "I guess you're right."

Eventually we got ready for the move, and Lieutenant Keith and I had one last talk before I left. I remember him telling me something that really stuck with me. He said, "Melvoy, you are one of the most driven people I have ever seen in my life, there aren't many with your work ethic. I hope we can have a beer together someday down the line."

We saluted and I left to get ready to pack for California. I pondered that for a few days. I once again rhetorically asked myself, "Imagine if everyone in our army was as driven as me, how successful would we be? How much harder could we have fought? How many more victories would we have?"

The winter that year was pretty mild, at least compared to the winters that we had in Michigan. As we loaded up the car, I remember looking for Veronica and asking her where she went to, and as it turned out, she had left to say goodbye to Gloria. We bickered about the fact that we had to leave and get on the highway before the rush hour traffic started.

We hopped in our car, and I still remember Veronica looking behind from the passenger seat and taking a picture of Jackie, Randall and Matthew all in the back seat. The drive to San Diego was difficult, Jackie was three and a half and Randall had just turned two and they started yelling in the back seat. I told them to stop. I gave them one final warning and when they didn't stop, I remember pulling off at the side of the road to spank them both. I remember their yelling becoming crying, I remember telling them to be quiet or it would happen again. They slowly quieted down while whimpering in the process. If they had been older I would have told them the old line, "This hurts me more than this hurts you," but I didn't think they would have understood it. I had never spanked them before, because Jackie and Randall were usually much better behaved and usually stopped the first time I told them to.

This led to more bickering with Veronica who thought that they were too young for that type of punishment. I responded that you have to start young or they will grow up to be spoiled brats. I remember saying, "Trust me, if Jason and Cathy don't start getting hard on their kids, they will wake up one day with kids that cause trouble and they won't know what happened. You have to be tough on kids, like my father was on me."

Her response was, "Just because your father did something, doesn't mean you have to. He's made a lot of mistakes and..."

I cut her off right there and said that she was crossing the line. He was my father, I loved him and he had worked very hard the last few years to straighten himself out and I didn't want to hear another word about it. Little else was said and several hours were spent in tense uncomfortable silence.

We started talking again as we were deciding where to pull off to sleep for the night. We said as little as possible but we eventually agreed to find somewhere near Phoenix. Since it was hard to find other places, the idea of there being a motel in a major city was a safe bet. We started talking again that night about the fact that we both should take this move as an opportunity for a fresh start, and to try to leave the past behind and be a better husband and wife. At the time I said okay, other than needing to spend a little more time with the kids, I didn't think I was really doing anything wrong. I just said sure expecting her to change her tune and it seemed like we made up, but the issues were still there.

We got up the next morning and went out for breakfast and then were on the road to San Diego and the new military base where I would be a Second Lieutenant. I remember as we crossed the state line into California, that we were getting closer and closer to our destination. I remember thinking about how close we were to Hollywood and how it would make for a nice vacation to drive a short distance and see the landmarks. I also couldn't help but think about how much better things were going to get as my rank climbed closer to the top of the military. I was twenty-eight years old and the military was my life. I had dedicated ten years to it if you included basic training. I had seen the world, both the good and the bad, I had a family, a stable career, and things seemed to be going great.

All that time on the road made me remember something that Major McLachlin had told me long ago. After we got into our new home, I grabbed the phone and made the long-distance call to Major McLachlin's base and I said, "Hello Major McLachlin, how are you doing?"

He responded, "Good, Melvoy, how are you?"

I responded by saying, "I have just been transferred to the base outside of San Diego and when you come to visit, I expect you to bring a housewarming present."

He was perplexed, "Housewarming present, when did you start wanting those?"

I cleverly responded, "Well I figured you will be able to afford one now that you won that $50 bet about me becoming a Lieutenant one day."

There was a short pause on the phone, we started laughing and he proceeded to congratulate me and mentioned what a great set-up that was. This was the greatest news to him and I remember how happy I was to tell him about it. By the time the conversation was over it was almost 11:00 pm, and I knew that tomorrow I had to introduce myself as the new Second Lieutenant at this base and show everyone that if I gave an order, they had better listen to it.

CHAPTER 19

SECOND LIEUTENANT, FIRST PRIORITY

When we got to California, Veronica and I had made promises to be a better husband and wife. The problem was that within a couple weeks I was back into old habits, working later than usual, taking on extra responsibility at work and not spending enough time at home. This became the new norm and by the time May had come around, that was the standard. Excelling as a Lieutenant became my first priority and everything else came second. I remember one time my old friend Tony called to see how we were doing and we hadn't spoken to each other in almost a year. Within five minutes, I kept looking at my watch wondering how quickly I could end the conversation.

Being a Lieutenant had its own challenges. I now had to sort out the types of conflicts that I had gotten involved in back in Montana. I remember that there were two guys who had gotten into a fistfight over allegations that one guy slept with the other guy's wife. I remember calling the guys into my office and the story was simple. One guy said that his wife told him that she had cheated on him with another guy and had named this other guy. Meanwhile the accused said that he never touched her and wouldn't screw around with another man's wife. I had to remember my training about how to deal with the situation but started with figuring out if the allegations were true. I told the accused Private to prepare his log and to have people ready to verify where he was. The plan was simple, if he did fool around, transfer him before the jealous husband kills him, and if he didn't, then prove it and get them to shake hands and move on.

Eventually after the married man asked his wife where and when it happened her answers got vague and were more focused on the idea of "he was better than you." It soon became clear that she didn't cheat or at least not with whom she said she did. She just wanted to drive him crazy by making him think she cheated.

I got the two guys to shake hands and that was the end of it. Eventually rumours spread about the whole incident and the woman was ostracized from the base and picked up her bags and left. Thankfully they didn't have any kids together, but I told him exactly what

I thought, "Good riddance, you're better off without a manipulative witch like that."

One of the strangest things that happened during my time as Lieutenant was that I would start hearing stories from the local guys that were not that different from mine. Stories about how they had cousins, brothers, friends or others who had been lured into the hippie mindset, which was still around but didn't have the tidal wave of momentum that it had back in the 1960s. California was a much more liberal state, even back then and the things that happened in California eventually went through the rest of the country. For example, just a few years earlier, Ronald Reagan was the Governor of California, and eventually became President of the United States.

I remember the first big earthquake we were in, was a four-point-four on the Richter scale and quite frankly, when I came home Veronica was talking about how scared the kids were because they hadn't experienced anything like that. Also, Jackie wasn't even four years old, and Randall and Matthew were even younger. This lead to the first big argument Veronica and I had after we arrived in California. She was now scared to stay there, especially when she heard about the possibility of a ten on the Richter scale, also all the disaster movies that had come out in the last couple years that she was hearing about, probably weren't helping. Eventually I talked her down and told her she would get used to them and that it was a small price to pay for all of this beautiful sunshine. She reluctantly accepted this, but I could tell she was still upset and I assumed she would just get over it. You can probably see the pattern now that I wish I had seen at the time.

I got the message that on March 30, 1978 Cathy had her fourth child, which was another daughter they named Melina. Our family had built up a lot in the last several years and before we knew it, whenever we were talking about the kids to my father and mother, we started referring to them as the Grandchildren. I remember at one point, my father jokingly saying that if we keep having kids, pretty soon the minister would think that we were turning Catholic. Back then Protestants and Catholics didn't get along as well, so making jokes about each other was commonplace. The truth was if I had asked for more children, I think Veronica would have gone off the deep end. I was happy with three kids and those three kids were already giving Veronica all that she could handle.

As the summer took hold, I had less of the manual labour to do, because the higher up you get in the military structure, the less dirty work you have to do. We were an hour away from Los Angeles, which was a place with movie stars, landmarks, famous restaurants and other

Melvoy's Railroad

tourist stops. Veronica must have asked me a few dozen times to take a day trip with her and the children to see the Hollywood Hills, and the Stars on the Walk of Fame, but I was always too busy. I always had reports to write, meetings to attend, training to supervise, etc. She eventually cornered me into going with them to see the sights one afternoon in August. The date on the picture says August 19, 1978 with all of us there smiling in front of the Hollywood sign, which still makes me smile to this very day.

The most incredible part of that summer was the end. I couldn't believe it when Jackie was having her fourth birthday, but it really hit me hard the following September when she was going to her first day of Junior Kindergarten. I saw her little pink backpack and felt shocked that she was already going off to school. It wasn't grade school, but still my little girl was going to school. As you might imagine every once in a while, I would get to look at her drawings that she would bring home, those little stick figures with block shirts and big smiles which was a reminder of what she was being protected from. Her pictures had no war, had no family fighting, drugs or anything else that adults had to deal with. In an odd way, they were a reassuring symbol that we were doing our job.

Veronica had mostly been isolated and only talking to military mothers and military families, they seemed to be more like traditional families. Once Jackie started going to school, she slowly began getting to talk to other mothers who were less traditional. It didn't happen all at once, and for Halloween she was excited about taking the kids around the base to trick or treat at the different houses. However as 1978 became 1979, she was becoming less and less satisfied with being Mrs. Charles Melvoy. All of the promises I had made a couple of years earlier about things being better and having more time to help her when I was a Lieutenant, were now being exposed.

I didn't really see this at the time, and I was too busy focusing on bigger things such as working my way up to First Lieutenant. I was talking about where the next battle with the Communists would be, and how the military should use the media to get people past what came to be known as Vietnam Syndrome. For those of you that don't know what that is, allow me to explain: Vietnam Syndrome was the public belief that the United States should not enter into a war ever again unless a quick guaranteed victory was assured. I remember one of the guys talking about the night Walter Kronkite said that he believed that Vietnam would end in a bitter stalemate and how that was the beginning of the end. When that broadcast was done in the late 1960's Walter Kronkite was a very reputable news anchor believed to be as trustworthy as they came. People trusted the media back then and they especially trusted him, and to put it simply, when Walter Kronkite spoke, America listened.

With the Carter Administration came talk about the country running out of energy and Jimmy Carter's pleas to the public to save energy and to push for legislation that would reduce consumption. I grew to despise Jimmy Carter, at first it just seemed so silly to have a President telling everyone about the sacrifices they needed to make, rather than telling the country about the great lives they should be leading. The people of Russia didn't have our quality of life, and now the President was telling us that we should have less. That idea didn't work for me, and it didn't work for a lot of people who didn't buy what Jimmy Carter was trying to sell.

When you spend so much time thinking about that as well as all of the day-to-day stuff, pretty soon other things like my marriage got lost in the shuffle. Throw in all the stuff that Veronica was starting to hear from all of these California women and pretty soon she started complaining a little more, and a little more. By Christmas 1978 she was wondering why I didn't buy her the things she wanted. I told her that I didn't know what she wanted which was why I bought her a cheese grater, which didn't work so well. We didn't spend that Christmas with any of the family because I didn't want to risk putting my kids in contact with the spoiling going on with Cathy's kids. Then Veronica started in about why we weren't going anywhere, and not even to see my family or hers. She started asking if we were on a military base or Alcatraz.

As the New Year of 1979 began, the arguing between us was getting out of control. We must have argued every single day until I gave in and decided to meet her part way. We would find a house outside of the military base and I would drive to the base. Thankfully by this point I had saved a pretty penny or two and we were able to buy a good-sized house in San Diego that wasn't too far away from the base. We were even able to keep Jackie going to the same school. I thought that was the end of the problems, but of course I was wrong. Veronica and I were growing apart, but I was so focused on other things, that I missed it entirely. We also agreed to do Easter dinner on Saturday at my parent's house, and Sunday at her parent's house. It was also during this time I set my sights on becoming a First Lieutenant, which I knew I would achieve eventually barring any unforeseen circumstances.

It was spring and the weather was warming up, not that it got that cold in southern California. Veronica and I had worked out our issues, or so I thought, and moved into our new house on May 1st. I actually thought that the house we were buying was the house we were going to live in for the rest of our lives. I thought it would be a place that I would call home until my last days, and I thought that the family of Charles and Veronica Melvoy was on its way up. Of course, I thought this because I was a Second Lieutenant in the military nearing promotion, a husband of a beautiful wife and father of a daughter and two sons. I had been to Vietnam, Germany and Japan, I had seen men, women, and children die right in front of me but I had persevered. I thought there was nothing that life could throw at me that I couldn't handle and triumph over. I had fought my own father in the front yard, and what could possibly be harder than that? Well as you can probably guess, there were a lot of things I didn't see coming and that summer in 1979, I was in for one of the biggest shocks that I would ever receive in my life.

CHAPTER 20
★
THE COLLISION

It was Sunday June 3, 1979; there were clouds overhead and the night before, the weatherman said there was going to be heavy rainfall and a thunderstorm later in the day. We had just come back from church, and the sermon that day was about the miracles of faith. I remember the minister saying, "Do not underestimate the power of faith, if the faith of one man can move mountains, the faith of billions could move the entire world."

Not long after we got home and finished eating lunch, I had a call from the minister of my parent's church in Ann Arbor, asking me how I was doing and wondering if I was doing anything that day. I jokingly mentioned the one-liner I heard earlier at my church and he responded, "I should use that one someday."

As the conversation shifted, he began asking me about what I was doing that day, and I told him we didn't have anything planned and he said, "Good, good."

I thought it was very odd when the phone call ended, because it just came out of nowhere.

I told Veronica keep the kids from making noise because I needed some peace and quiet, so I could read my book in the den in silence. It was about half an hour later when I heard the doorbell and I assumed that Veronica would get it. Roughly a minute or so later, she walked into the den and said that there was someone here to see me. I asked who, and she said, "I think it's better if he tells you."

As we were walking to the door I asked, "Is it Major McLachlin?"

She responded, "I don't think so."

She was really nervous, I finally came to the door and saw a man about an inch shorter than me, with a trimmed beard and thick, longer hair that stretched down to the base of his neck. I didn't recognize him at first, and he said, "Charlie, it's been a long time."

I paused, still unsure to whom I was talking. "I'm sorry I don't recognize you, have we met?"

He said, "It's been a long time, I guess I really look different. I'm your brother Billy."

The shock hit me like a tidal wave and I dropped the book I was reading.

I was speechless, as I had never expected to see him again. He had disappeared off the face of the earth eleven years ago, and to our family he was presumed dead. All of a sudden I was overwhelmed with shock, anger, relief, and I don't know how many other thoughts.

Veronica suddenly spoke up, "Well come in, it looks like it's going to rain. Do you want anything to drink?"

Billy said, "Thank you, water or juice would be fine."

By the time he got settled on the couch, I had gathered some of my thoughts. Veronica began to talk about how good it was to finally meet him and began to tell him about our three kids, and Billy responded by saying, "That's wonderful, I would love to meet them."

I spoke up with the angry thoughts coming to the forefront. "Veronica, take the kids out, I don't want them to hear this."

She reluctantly said, "He's your brother who you haven't seen in years, there's no reason to be upset."

I got angrier and said, "The hell there isn't!"

She then said, "Fine, you want to get mad at someone you haven't seen in ten years then okay, I'll take the kids out and you can have at it."

She called upstairs for the kids to come down, as Billy and I remained in tense silence. She told them they were going out for ice cream, which of course made them happy as she rushed them out the door.

As soon as the door closed, I sat down in my chair and stared at him, the more I stared the more I began to see my brother's facial features, and the more I thought of him the angrier I became. "Where the hell have you been all these years? Now you finally come and find me, what you do you want – money? Is your dope dealer about to break your legs?"

Billy was nervous and said, "This isn't about money. This is about family, I want to reconnect with all of you."

I was barely able to think, all I had was anger. "Oh, isn't that nice, you want your family back. Well tell me then brother, if you wanted to be a part of our family so damn bad why did you run away in the first place? You hurt our mother, you hurt our father, you hurt Cathy and you hurt me, the guy who looked out for you more than anyone else. You traded us in for a bunch of hippies who didn't give a damn if you fried your damn brains out."

By this point I was standing and yelling and he was trying to calm me down saying over and over again, "Let me explain, calm down."

I finished by saying, "Everyone thought you were dead. You didn't write, you didn't call, you just let all of us think you were gone forever!"

I sat back down, looked at him and said, "Now the Prodigal Son returns, what do you want, money?"

He reluctantly began to speak, "Charlie, this isn't about money. I told you this is about family. I ran away because I thought Dad was trying to crush who I was and turn me into you, and the truth is you and I were very different people."

I interrupted saying, "Oh, you got that right."

I could tell he was getting annoyed and in a way, I almost wanted to provoke him, I almost wanted an excuse to fight him. He continued, "Charlie –"

I cut him off, saying, "My name is Charles, Lieutenant Charles Melvoy."

He took a deep breath and said, "Fine, Charles, I ran away because I wanted my own life. I don't regret what I wanted, I regret how it happened and what happened."

I interrupted again, "You don't even know what happened, you weren't there when our father had his drinking problems, you weren't there when he relapsed, you weren't there. When I was fighting for our country in Vietnam, where were you, passing a joint? Have you ever seen men die in front of you?"

This was when his restraint fell through and he began yelling back, "Yes I did! I was taken across the state line by a few of the guys who helped me escape. We were wanderers for weeks, until we eventually found our way onto a commune north of here. I lived there for a couple of years trying to follow their rules and in the process, I watched a few guys overdose on drugs and die! I walked out of there when I was seventeen and made a decision to turn my life around. I took my GED, worked my way through college and now I am getting ready to open up my own psychiatrist's office in Sacramento! I don't want your money or anyone else's, I just want to reunite with the family that I have missed for the last eleven years and have been scared to connect with because I knew that Dad would react the way you are reacting now!"

By this point, he and I were eye to eye and were both getting close to coming to blows. I looked at him with such rage, "Oh, I'm glad everything turned out okay for you, but you can't just abandon us for eleven years and then waltz back in here and pretend everything is okay."

Billy looked at me and I saw a look in his eyes of pure defiance as he said, "I'm sorry about the way everything happened, but I want to reunite with the family. If you can't accept that I am sincere, fine. I'm flying to Detroit on Thursday, and then I am going back to Ann Arbor to reunite with our family. You can come with me and help the situation, or you can just hold onto that anger until it destroys you from the inside."

The tension was so thick that you could have cut it with a knife. I responded, "I don't give a damn where you go on Thursday. The only thing I care about is whether or not you are going to get out of my house yourself or whether I will have to throw you out bodily."

He began to leave but he stopped at the edge of the door and looked back, "Charles, if you can find it in yourself to forgive me and once again be my brother, I will be in room 314 at the Holiday Inn in San Diego."

He closed the door as he went out to his faded blue car and drove away. I just remember being so upset that I actually threw a family picture we had taken the previous Christmas, which smashed on the wall.

I just remember being so upset at the nerve of this guy to abandon us for eleven years and then expect me to drop my career so he can use me as a human shield when our father sees him. Eventually the kids came home, and as expected Veronica told the kids to wash up and asked Jackie to help Matthew. She asked me what happened, and when I told her what happened, she and I began to argue as she was actually trying to defend him, saying that from the sounds of it, he had grown up and that this was our chance to catch up on lost time

I remember saying, "If I abandoned our family for eleven years, would you be happy to see me again? I don't think so Veronica."

She finally said something that really surprised me, "Charles, stop thinking about yourself and start thinking about your mother; you said yourself, she thinks he's dead. I can tell you that as a mother, if I thought that one of my children was dead, I would give my soul to get them back."

I paused, as all I could think about was how I felt and how they would be so angry with him for leaving. She continued, "Charles, go with him back to Ann Arbor. Please do it for your mother."

I said, "Veronica, here's what you don't get. He's just going to leave again and I'm not going to be part of my mother's heart getting broken again. People don't change, he was selfish then and he's selfish now."

I stormed off in anger that my own wife wasn't on my side but taking his side. I stewed about the situation for the rest of the day, just focusing on what an ungrateful brat Billy was and how he abandoned our family and wasn't there when we needed him most.

Before the day ended I called Major McLachlin and after he told me about his impending promotion, I asked him what I should do. I told him the whole story and Major McLachlin suggested that I go with Billy, not to approve but rather to make sure he's not trying to con our parents for money or something else. I considered that advice as I thought about what Veronica said about how badly she would want her family back if she lost them. I then replayed the whole day in my head and I realized that the minister from Ann Arbor must have known about this. That was why he called out of the blue, and how Billy found out where I was and knew that I would be home. So the next day during my lunch break, I called the church to speak to the minister, and after waiting a few minutes he came on the line and I asked him what he was doing and why he helped Billy get in contact with me.

The minister went on to talk about how he heard Billy tell him how he felt and how he had wanted to get his family together and how much it hurt him every holiday. After I told the minister how suspicious I was, he responded with, "You may be right and you should not leave yourself too vulnerable, but I think that a man who knows that anger awaits him but is willing to face it anyway, is someone who is probably sincere and at least deserves a chance."

I finally realized that he had a point, and I had to tell my superiors about taking over a week off with only a couple days notice. Thankfully, when I told them that it was a family emergency and I had to fly back to Michigan, they accepted that. On Tuesday night, I told Veronica that she and the kids were staying out of this, as things could get ugly, and I drove to the Holiday Inn in San Diego.

I went to Room 314, knocked on the door, and Billy answered. "Charlie."

I immediately interrupted him, "I told you my name is…"

He then interrupted me, "Sorry, Charles, I am really glad you changed your mind."

I responded, "Somewhat, I still think that you were an ungrateful brat for abandoning us and I still suspect that you have some ulterior motive, but you are my brother and I'm willing to give you a chance to prove me wrong."

He then proceeded to say that he was going to fly to Detroit on Thursday, meet with Cathy and Jason that night and then bring us all together at our parents' on Friday. In the back of my mind I kept waiting for the speech that begins with, "I just need this."

I told him that I was going to be watching him and if he were here to leech money or anything else, I would kick his ass across the border to Canada.

Billy looked at me and said, "Charlie." He stopped himself, "Charles, look, I want this for all of us, I just want my family back. I'm sorry that you still can't see that, but I wonder how much of that is me and how much of that is your projection?"

I asked him what the hell he was talking about and he started to give me psychobabble about how people project their feelings onto others and stuff like that and he lost me in less than ten seconds.

We flew out on Thursday, and saying goodbye to my kids for a week was going to be tough but I knew this was going to be very hard, but it had to be done. It was so surreal, and I knew that this man was my brother but it almost had not sunk in that Billy was alive and sitting the row ahead of me on the airplane. Somehow it still seemed like a stranger was sitting there.

Right after we got to the airport, I called Cathy and I asked her what she was doing and she told me that Jason was working and that she and the babysitter were looking after the kids. I told her to stay home because I would be over there soon with a big surprise. Billy was hoping that she would be willing to go over to our parent's house so we could all be together.

We went over to Cathy's house that evening, I was driving the rental car with Billy in the passenger seat and this was when we actually began being able to have small talk. I told him that I was glad that he turned his life around and was doing something positive. He thanked me and said that he appreciated the fact that I was giving him a chance.

We finally reached Cathy's house around 8:00 pm, and I was hoping that she would be able to handle the shock. Eventually, as we pulled up to Cathy's large house (much larger by the standards of the time), in the wealthy part of Lansing, Billy mentioned that he was happy that Cathy was doing so well. I told him to stay in the car because I wanted to brace her for the shock, Billy agreed, and I got out.

Cathy has always been a very gentle person, and fainted at the sight of blood until she was twenty-one. I knocked on the door and she answered with a grin from ear to ear and she asked what was going on that I had to be so secretive about. Somehow this was harder for me to talk about, than the death of Phil "the hill" ten years earlier. I mumbled slightly, took a deep breath and said, "That surprise I told you about, is in the car. Billy is alive, he's well and wants to reconnect with the family."

Her eyes rolled back in her head and I caught her as she fainted and lowered her down, Billy came out of the car immediately upon seeing her falling. As she began to get her bearings, she saw Billy and I standing over her asking if she was okay. She began to stare at Billy and with complete disbelief she said, "That's Billy, he's so old. He has a beard and long hair."

We eventually got her into her kitchen as she was trying to comprehend what had just happened, and looking back, I should have given her way more warning than I did.

Once the shock began to wear off, she asked Billy what happened to him and he told her roughly the same story he told me. I was surprised that she was so quick to throw her arms around him, with tears in her eyes and say that she was so glad that he was okay. I didn't want her to go after him with a butcher knife, but how could she just let him off the hook like that? I guess that was Cathy, always, soft, gentle, and too good for her own good. Things took a small downturn when she asked if he needed anything and I stopped it right there, "No you aren't giving him anything, you're handling him with kid gloves and he's – how old are you?"

Billy looked at me with annoyance, "Twenty-four."

I then turned to Cathy, "Yeah twenty-four, he's not a kid anymore."

There was a silence, followed by Billy saying, "I wasn't going to take anything except a glass of water. I'm glad Cathy is still capable of forgiveness."

As you might imagine, he was getting on my nerves and I was probably getting on his just as much.

That night, Cathy insisted that we stay at her house, and she gave Billy the guest room and I slept on the couch. I remember thinking how unfair that was, "After everything I've done for this family, he gets the guest room and I get the couch?"

I was disgusted, but in a way I began to look forward to tomorrow, because Cathy may let him off the hook, but I was sure my father wouldn't. I knew that Barry Melvoy would give Billy the tongue-lashing of a lifetime and all I had to do was stand there and make sure it didn't come to blows.

The next morning Cathy called our parent's house to tell them that we were coming over with a big surprise and that she had better have the camera ready. Cathy was once again smiling from ear to ear and almost had an extra twinkle in her eye. While Billy was in the shower, I asked her why she seemed so happy, and she said that she was so glad to have our family be whole again. She was looking forward to Christmases and other events with the whole family together. She actually told me about how she prayed to God after Billy ran away, and prayed that he would bring us together again but after a few months she thought that maybe God had said "no."

She could now tell her children with certainty that miracles do happen, and I could have thrown up at such sentimental hogwash. I told her that before any pictures get taken, our father was going to tear

Billy apart and that it had been a long time coming. She tried to tell me that it wasn't going to be like that, and it was going to be something right out of a movie. I remember thinking, "She's been watching too many of those Disney fairy tale cartoon movies."

As we drove closer and closer to the house, we knew that our father would be home between 6:00 and 6:30 pm because of the drive home from the factory in Flint. As we got closer I almost began to look forward to hearing my father rip this guy apart, this person who abandoned our family, sure we were going to let him back in, but not let him off easy. We got there just a few minutes before and when we told our mother the news of Billy's return, her eyes nearly popped out of her head. As she looked at him and began to see those familiar features underneath his beard, she threw her arms around him and began muttering things like, "I'm so glad you're okay, I thought I would never see you again."

I expected this, as my mother was always the soft and gentle one and Cathy got that from her. When we got in the house, she asked what he was doing and he began to tell her about his studies to be a psychiatrist.

Suddenly we heard the noise of our father's car pulling into the driveway and I took a step back, ready to watch justice unfold, the firm hand of justice. Our mother got Billy to sit down at the kitchen table as our father walked in and seeing all of us, was wondering what was going on. Our mother walked up to him and told him that at long last our family is whole again and she called Billy in. As Billy walked in, I saw the hesitation as he probably figured that our father would react the same way that I did. At first my father was speechless, and wasn't sure what to think, he then began to get teary eyed as he looked at all of us and threw his arms around Billy and started gushing sentiment. My jaw nearly hit the floor, and I believe his exact words were, "I am so glad you are okay, I thought I had lost you."

He looked at Billy and asked him how long he was in town for and Billy told him that he was free for a couple weeks and all of a sudden my father was transformed. He was asking my mother to cook a feast worthy of Christmas because they had so much catching up to do, and that they should go fishing. Suddenly my father turned to me and asked me to go with them. I told them that I only had until Sunday, so he said, "Let's go tomorrow, it will be like old times. I haven't been on that lake in a long time."

I was in a situation where I felt like I couldn't say no, because when you see your father that happy, it's really hard to bring him down. That night everything was about Billy; Cathy, my father, and mother were hanging on his every word. Before I knew it, my father and Billy were bonding. I felt like I woke up in the Twilight Zone, as if my father had been replaced with someone else, he looked like him, he sounded like him, where was the man putting his foot down? I was quiet during dinner because I was trying to comprehend what I was hearing, and trying to understand what was happening to all of these people.

Later that night, Billy wanted to go out for a walk, which was a red flag, being that it was 10:30 at night in Ann Arbor, where was he really going? So, I followed him from a distance, although Cathy didn't want me to, but I insisted and eventually he went to the local park where he sat down on one of the swings. From a distance I could see him reaching into his coat, and that was when I marched towards him expecting it to be booze or a joint.

As I got within three feet of him, I blurted out, "Alright you junkie, what are you doing?"

He turned around in surprise and confusion, but he wasn't holding drugs, he was holding a pen and a small journal. He asked with confusion, "Charles, what are you doing here?"

I responded, "Never mind that, what the hell are you writing there?"

He responded saying that it was his journal and he was writing his private thoughts. I asked, "Why couldn't you do that in the house?"

He responded that he wanted some fresh air and to kill two birds with one stone. He didn't look at me while he was saying it, but I was sure something was up, so I told him to let me see it. He stood up and responded saying no, these were his private thoughts and they were his and his alone.

I looked at him with intensity and I let my suspicions run wilder than ever. "Oh, I get it now, you're a psychiatrist and this was your little trick to get material for one of those books that you people write."

He responded, "What do you mean 'those books you people write?'"

I continued, "You know, those whining poor me books that blame their parents for everything wrong in their lives, somehow you people even convinced our father to let you off the hook. He was and still is a great man that you ran off on. When things were tough around here and he had a problem with drinking, you never had to deal with it. Once it got out of control, he and I had to fight about it, but I knocked some sense into him and he reclaimed who he was."

Billy was really upset and lashed back, "He was raised in a different society than we were, the fact that you think that he got over his alcoholism because you beat him up shows just how twisted you, and the things you believe are. I didn't want to say anything about it, but who the hell are you to be suspicious of me? You fought in an unjust war and killed people and I can only imagine the atrocities you committed while you were over there."

That was when it boiled over and I looked at him and said, "The law is the only thing keeping me from kicking your disrespectful ass right now."

I began to storm off when he yelled back, "I respect non-violence, why is it you only respect might?"

I flipped him off and marched home. When I came home I told my mother and father that I was leaving and that if I saw Billy again I was going to kick his ass. I saw how upset everyone was, but I didn't care because I was a war hero and convinced that I was more of a man than he ever would be. If he thought I was a heartless killer, imagine what he would have said about Mark, the guy who blew up the hut full of kids. What would he say about the Communist regime if they took over and threw him into a third world prison in Siberia? I was convinced that he knew absolutely nothing. I got in the rental car and I drove to the airport. I hadn't been this mad in so long, and the only thing I knew for sure was that I wasn't going to let Billy get his liberal claws into my kids. At that point, I almost wished that he actually was dead.

When I got home that weekend, Veronica asked me what happened, and I gave her a few simple orders: "1. Never let that disrespectful bastard Billy into this house and 2. If he calls, hang up in his ear."

I went upstairs fuming, feeling as though I had been disrespected by Billy, and betrayed by everyone else. Who was there to get our father to quit drinking and take him to his A.A. meetings? ME! Who fought for our country? Our father and ME! When our mother needed money, who gave her the money? Jason and ME! Who was it that did so many of the household chores growing up? ME! Who was the son that our father could be proud of? ME! It was like they had chosen Billy over me and were spitting in my face in the process.

I was disgusted and that night I looked in the kid's rooms after they had gone to sleep, and I thought to myself, "If any of them ran away like he did, I wouldn't let them off so easily," although it was hard to imagine your three children, who were under five years old, as adults in the first place.

That night I barely said a word to Veronica. I told her what I wanted, and how I wanted things to be going forward, and with the mood I was in, I didn't care what she had to say about it.

CHAPTER 21

★

BETTER OFF WITHOUT THEM

For the next few weeks, Billy called, my mother called, Cathy called, and even my father called and every time I refused to speak to them. I insisted that Veronica not speak to them either. My thirtieth birthday wasn't too memorable, and I just tried to push all that other stuff out of my mind and focus on my job. Jackie turned five shortly thereafter, and beyond that I wanted to focus on building my own family. I imagined a family that would respect and be loyal to me.

Unfortunately, Veronica was listening to them and began asking me why I didn't want to talk to them anymore, and because they were my family, I should work it out with them. She proceeded to say that she wanted our children to know their grandparents, their aunts and uncles.

She said with great emphasis, "All of them!"

I proceeded to tell her that they just took Billy back as if it was nothing, as if he was the one who had been there for them all of this time. She began trying to talk about the story of the Prodigal Son and I cut her off part way through and said that those people were stupid to take that jackass back so easily. The exact words I used were, "The loyal should be rewarded and the traitors should be shot."

She shook her head and walked away. I didn't want to be bothered with this stuff. I spoke to Major McLachlin who basically echoed my sentiments. I was sure when Billy's "blame everyone but me" book came out, they would realize they had picked the wrong side and they would apologize out of embarrassment and hopefully before that book came out.

The rest of the summer was spent with tension between Veronica and myself as she was taking their side in this, even though I was the one putting the roof over her head. I remember thinking that the whole world was going crazy.

President Carter was talking about conservation, saving fuel, telling us that we needed to save energy because we had run out. How could a country with so much, run out of resources? That seemed impossible. My wife wasn't listening to me, even though I was her husband, and my family cared more about a former hippie than about me. What the hell was the world coming to?

It was also around this time that I was on the verge of becoming a First Lieutenant, which was the next step and knew that I was determined to achieve this soon. The next several months involved doing everything by the book and going beyond it. I was determined to stay in the military and make things work out. In the military there was order, the loyal were rewarded and things made sense, and more and more the military felt like home. It was a place with order, everyone knew where they stood and why. Most of all, if someone didn't hold up their end of things they would pay for it, nobody got away scot-free.

Meanwhile in my actual home, Jackie was getting ready to go to Senior Kindergarten and she was so happy. She brought home drawings she did that day, she would watch Sesame Street and I remember Big Bird was her favourite. Randall was turning into a bit of a smart mouth and I spanked him a few times, with each time Veronica objecting to it more and more. The fighting began to happen more and more. We were fighting about things that seemed stupid, and she was bothered by the fact that I had put on weight since we got married.

I threw it back at her and said, "So have you."

She would yell back with, "I had three kids, what's your excuse?"

Things like that were so immature, but that was what happened and when you are in the moment, all these things seem so important, but they aren't as important as you think at the time.

I finally gave in as far as talking to my father went, and figured he would be the one most likely to see through Billy's bullshit. He was mad at me because of how I left and I had given him the silent treatment for a few months, which sparked some serious arguing between us. My father was pretty stubborn and so was I, and when you put two stubborn people on opposite sides, you have the formula for a long, long battle. The war of words was happening and I began to hear things from my father that surprised me, and he started talking about how the drinking was being used to mask his pain. He had felt guilty but didn't know how to express it – this wasn't the Barry Melvoy I had known. He was the pick yourself up by your boot straps, face life head on and hold your head high type of man. He did admit that Billy and he were still miles apart on some things such as premarital sex, and he was only somewhat bothered by it. He was glad to have his son back even if he was like that.

I told him my suspicions about him writing one of these my parents ruined my life books, and blaming him and my mother for all of his problems. My father responded that he saw that as highly unlikely and that Billy was just writing in a journal like some of his friends did back in World War II. I reluctantly backed down and he and I agreed that I would try to make peace with Billy at Thanksgiving. However, I told him that Billy owes me one hell of an apology for him accusing me of committing atrocities. Now my father was the one playing peacekeeper. What a strange, strange time it was.

The next few weeks were tense. At work I was a stone-faced authority figure who had to keep some juvenile soldiers in line by any means necessary, which occasionally included a few times when they got the back of my hand. Veronica was glad that I was trying to make peace with my family, but she also seemed very skeptical and knew that I was going to play hardball even after I got there. About a week before we left for Michigan for Thanksgiving, I received my promotion to First Lieutenant. At work I was respected and feared, while at home, I was nagged and questioned. I'm sure you can guess which one I liked better.

After dinner one night before Thanksgiving, she asked me what I was going to do when we went home for Thanksgiving. I told her, "I'll extend my hand and let bygones be bygones... after Billy gave me and the whole family one hell of an apology for abandoning us like a coward and talking to me like I was some murderer. He has a lot to answer for and I am going to make sure he does."

She put her face in her hand with dread, knowing that this wasn't going to be nice, I didn't back down from anybody and I wasn't going to start now. She asked, "Charles, why can't you forgive your brother, why can't you let it go?"

I snapped back at her saying, "That bastard abandoned us, where was he when we got married? Where was he when Cathy got pregnant and our mother was in tears? Where was he when I was fighting in wars? He was passing a bong telling someone about the colours he was seeing! It's ridiculous that you all want to let him get off so easy, well not me, he's got a lot to answer for and he's going to."

I stormed off angry, being mad about all of these people not seeing what to me seemed completely obvious.

Veronica barely said another word to me. We flew to Detroit and took a cab to Ann Arbor, and arrived promptly at 2:00 pm on the Wednesday, early enough that Veronica could help my mother and Cathy with dinner. Jason said that he bought a new car and wanted to show it to me, I said, "Sure."

We walked outside and I realized that emerald green Cadillac was his. I remember saying to him, "How can you afford this, with today's gas prices?"

He said that Game Night was going great with their sixth location starting to make money and that the other five were faring well. His expression suddenly changed as he said, "Look Charles, I have always respected you and you have been a great brother in law, but for the sake of the family, please make peace with Billy. My kids are here, and I don't want them to see their two uncles at each other's throats at Thanksgiving, or any other time, for that matter. So I'm asking you, man to man, please bury the hatchet. I have seen some ugly situations and I don't want this to turn into one of them."

I looked at him with disbelief, "You've seen some ugly situations? Where, at the bar, where a couple guys fought each other?"

I turned facing directly at him because I wanted him to fully understand the ignorance of what he had just said. "I have seen people die, I have seen people's brains get blown out of their head, I have seen perfectly healthy men return home missing arms and legs and you think you've seen some ugly situations?"

He looked at me and said, "Okay, you've been to war, but your parent's house is no place for it. Life can be really great if you let it."

I looked at him with disgust and said, "Sure, life is fun, when you are a big shot with six bars, driving a Cadillac down the road and you can brag to your rich friends about how much money you spent on Christmas."

I went from angry to sarcastically angry when I said, "Sure, why don't we all just hop down the yellow brick road into happily ever after? Where the golden gooses are running around laying golden eggs everywhere."

As he and I started to yell at each other, Cathy came outside and we both stopped. She said, "Jason, Charles, the appetizers are ready."

Without speaking a word, we both went inside and the tension was getting so thick you could cut it with a knife.

Not long after that, Billy arrived with some kind of snacks and of course the kids bought into it immediately. I didn't say a word because I was waiting for him to say something to me, like a whopper of an apology. After a little while, I went into the den and began looking through the bookshelf and that was when Billy came in. He was holding a finished wood chessboard under his arm, and he asked me, "Hey Charles, do you want to play?"

I responded, "Life isn't a game Billy, if you had grown up in the real world, you would know that."

He let out a noise of annoyance and said, "Chess games take a while, I don't know what you want me to say, but maybe during the game we can figure it out."

I looked at him and said, "I want you to suffer as much as all of us did, all of us loved you and you abandoned us."

He looked at me and said, "Charles, an eye for an eye would leave the whole world blind, why can't we find another way?"

I looked at him and said, "Okay Billy, how would you solve this?"

He looked at me and said, "You extend your arms, I extend mine and we embrace the fact that our brother is back in our lives."

I was pacing back and forth as he was saying this, and said to him, "What part of your book is this?"

He rolled his eyes telling me, "Charles, there's no book, this isn't a scam. I haven't asked Mom, Dad, Cathy, Jason or anyone for a dime, and I wouldn't have put myself through all of this if I didn't really care. I came to you first remember? I was hoping you could help prepare Mom and Dad for it because I thought that Dad would act like this instead of you. He's grown and you are still stuck in the barracks with all the rest of the soldiers – this isn't war, this is family."

I cut him off and said, "Those soldiers were my family, and Major McLachlin has been a second father to me. There was a guy who was a good friend of mine; we called him Phil "the hill." Randall's middle name is in his honour because he watched out for me and he died saving the lives of myself and many other soldiers. In that one day, he was more of a brother to me, than you ever were."

He shook his head and said, "I guess you're not ready, but if you ever want to play some chess and get to know me, the board will be ready for you."

He walked away and we had a mildly awkward dinner as I refused to speak to him and the adults didn't want to start an argument that the kids' table would hear. Before I left, my father pulled me aside and said, "Thanks for keeping the peace, it meant a lot to your mother. Did you get everything sorted out?"

I responded, "Dad, we agreed to disagree, I'm not going to pretend to like him, but it'll be fine."

He put his hand on my shoulder and said, "Just give it time, blood is thicker than water."

On the plane ride home I just kept thinking over and over about how everyone had acted, treating me like the bad guy, acting as if I'm some out of control guy who they have to calm down. I wasn't out of control, and you don't become a First Lieutenant in the United States Military by being out of control. I thought that I knew what I was doing, but they just didn't want to hear it. I began thinking about how different my life was on the military base versus away from it. On the base, I was respected, I gave a command, which others would follow, and if they didn't, everyone knew that I would lay the hammer down and no one would give me a hard time for doing what has to be done.

I began wondering what it would be like if Major McLachlin was my father, Ruth the secretary at the base was my sister, if McLachlin's wife was my mother, and if Phil "the hill" were alive and he was my brother, how much better life would be with all of that respect, order, not this chaos, second guessing and sentimental hogwash? As our cab dropped us off at the house that night, I began to wonder. As I looked at those little children and thought about how if I could just get Veronica on my side and get their respect, I would have my own family. I wouldn't need my old family in Michigan because if I was going to be disrespected the way that I had been recently, I began to think that I would be better off without them.

CHAPTER 22

★

THE NEW DECADE

1980 arrived with a party on the military base, to celebrate Christmas. I thought Veronica and I had more or less patched things up and if you don't count the recession, inflation, and oil prices, things were going really well. Many people at the time were tired of old Jimmy Carter and this was the year that we could get rid of him and what later came to be known as his "Malaise." Things on the base were pretty standard, we had moved to California almost two years ago and were nicely settled in. Major McLachlin had been promoted and he called me to inform me of his promotion and connections because he and I didn't talk that often. He had been promoted to Lieutenant Colonel some time earlier and was looking forward to becoming a Colonel. Just for perspective, after Colonel the ranks are Generals, and I couldn't have been happier for him. He also told me that he was getting the inside track on the bigger picture and that the day was coming when he would be able to speak directly to the President as an advisor. It's one thing to hear about Eisenhower working his way up, but to know someone personally who was moving up the ladder made it that much more real and fuelled my fire to pursue it further.

The other guys on the base were great and there was the odd thing but never anything serious. If a higher up was visiting, I would tell all the men that I wanted that floor so clean I could eat off it. They knew that if I was embarrassed in front of my superiors, they would suffer for it, so they always did their job well. I was thirty years old at this point, and one of the youngest Lieutenants in the military, but I was a grizzled veteran with years of experience and almost no fear. Last but certainly not least, if I ever needed someone to put in a good word for me, I had McLachlin in my corner. (Going forward I won't be listing his title anymore, I'm just going to be referring to him as McLachlin.)

Occasionally my job was difficult, but as I started the new decade, I was very optimistic. I was going to take on the un-free world, so when the next battle with the Communists happened, I was going to lead my men into battle and be victorious. I was going to take them apart, if I was face-to-face with a Russian, I would show no mercy. I was not without mercy, but at the same time I believed in that brutal version of reality.

One time during this brief period, there was this one soldier, I think his name was Percy, I began to hear rumours that he might be homosexual. So I did the only thing I thought that I could do, I called him into my office and demanded he tell me whether or not it was true. You have to remember that this was before the 1990s "Don't ask, don't tell" policy. With loads of fear in his voice he said, "Yes, yes sir."

I looked at him and said, "Well soldier we have a problem, because those men out there don't know if they can trust you, because they don't know if you are watching their back or their ass."

He spoke up and said, "Sir, please don't tell them."

I stood and looked out the window, trying to think about my options. "Here's what we're going to do, we're going to say that you have some sick family members to take care of and can no longer maintain your position on this base. Therefore, I will grant you an honourable discharge from the army and you have the perfect excuse."

He spoke up and said, "Sir, I want to be a soldier, I want to fight for my country."

I cut him off and told him that some people aren't meant to be soldiers and if he went out there, he might be the victim of not so friendly fire. He looked heartbroken but I told him that this was for his own good, as well as the good of the army.

I'm not proud of what I did back then. In retrospect it was cruel, but I thought it was the easy thing for us, and the right thing for him, I remember what had happened all those years ago in basic training. What if he ran into a guy like Mark, or what if while I wasn't around a bunch of them got together and threatened him? I didn't want any of my soldiers at each other's throats for any reason. I would hope that he would have agreed whole-heartedly that he wouldn't want to go through that. As I have mentioned before, back then people weren't so accepting of that type of thing so the easiest way to remove what I saw was the problem, was to remove him. Although in retrospect, it's a shame that I sent a perfectly good soldier away for such a superficial ignorant reason.

Despite the odd difficult situation like that, things seemed to be going okay. News began to come through about Ronald Reagan running for President and having loads of momentum. He was taking America by storm, everyone knew who he was and they were tired of Carter. I remember rooting for him and hoping that he would win, and he was confident that he could get America back on track and I believed him.

One of the things that I remember thinking at the time, was where I was going to be by the end of decade and I wrote my goals down. I still have that short list that I wrote on a piece of paper and filed away. The list read as follows: By the end of the 1980s, I hope to accomplish the following: 1. Become a General ranking at least one star. 2. Meet and shake hands with the President of the United States, hopefully Ronald Reagan. 3. Raise respectful and responsible kids; by the end of 1989, Jackie will be 15, Randall will be 13 and Matthew will be 11.

What a great list, I thought that I was ready for anything. There's a quote I heard years later from Woody Allen, "If you want to make God laugh, tell him about your plans."

CHAPTER 23

★

DECORATION, DIVORCE & DESPAIR

As they often do, things took a bad turn on Valentine's Day, and it had been a full ten years since our first date. I told Veronica that I would be working late and that we would go out tomorrow night. We did and we had dinner and basically talked almost the entire time about the kids. Something was missing from that dinner and I couldn't put my finger on what it was. After we got home I gave her a mug that said, "Best Wife," or something else like that and she just rolled her eyes. I asked her what was wrong, and she turned to me and began to tell me.

With each passing word, her voice got just a little bit louder and more upset. "Charles, some men buy their wives jewellery or something else big for Valentine's Day, other men do something that doesn't cost much but has meaning. The meaning of this thing is, I will grab the first cheap, generic and tacky thing I see and give it to her because she's too dumb to know the difference!"

That was when I started yelling back, "What do you want, to just have everything handed to you on a silver platter? I already do all the work in this family."

She started yelling back even louder, "Are you kidding me, who looks after the kids all day, who buys all the groceries, who takes Jackie to and from school and will be doing the same thing for Randy and Matthew when they go to school?"

Things took another bad turn when I told her, "You should be grateful that I look after you and the kids, you should be grateful that you don't have to face that cruel world out there."

Her exact words were, "No Charles, what's cruel is keeping me locked up in this house talking to small children all day and maybe two to three times a week I will get to see another adult and realize that their lives mean something and mine means absolutely nothing."

I wasn't done. I said, "Your life does mean something. You are Mrs. Melvoy and you have a husband you can be proud of."

That didn't help me one bit as she let me know, picking up the mug, "Well if this is what it means to be Mrs. Melvoy, being trapped in a house and only getting cheap tacky tokens instead of real affection, then I don't want this anymore!"

That was when she threw the mug and it smashed on the basement door. After that there was just a chilling quiet, she was nearly in tears when she looked at me and said, "I want a divorce. You can take the kids this weekend, I'm staying with Rhonda."

I went to the fridge, cracked open a beer and just tried to wrap my head around everything that had just happened. I must have replayed those few minutes over and over in my head at least a hundred times. I began trying to figure out what I was going to do. I didn't want a divorce; I couldn't let this happen. I called McLachlin and told him what happened and I asked him what I should do, he told me to romance her.

"Just get her some chocolate and flowers and she will melt. They all do."

So, on Sunday I gave those to her and I told her, "The last weekend was so hard without you."

Much to my surprise she didn't melt, she saw right through my gesture and said, "I guess chocolate and roses are cheaper than a lawyer."

I then made another stupid mistake. I went on the offensive, "Think of the children, they shouldn't have to say they come from a broken home because Mommy's greedy for shiny things." If I could go back in time, I would slap the taste out of my mouth for saying something so stupid.

She responded, "I don't care about shiny things. I care about respect and you get plenty of it from other people, and you have plenty of it for other people, but not me."

She told me that she wanted me to pack my stuff and get out. In my frustration I thought, "Fine if that's how she wants it, we'll see how long she lasts."

I packed my bags that night and of course the kids asked where I was going. I told them that I was being sent by the military on a trip but that I would be back soon because I couldn't think of how to tell them the truth. Children shouldn't hear about this stuff, especially when they were all under six years old. I packed my stuff, got in my car and drove back to the military base, where they had a few spare homes and I filled out all the paperwork to take one on a temporary basis.

I made sure to not just pack a few days of clothes, but a lot of them. I thought this would give her the message that I was serious and I wouldn't come crawling back. I also remember the books, which made the bag heavy. Thank God most of them were paperbacks. A few days went by, I was in a real bad mood and anyone who screwed up felt a small piece of my wrath. I remember just thinking that one day very soon, she would call begging me to come back, realizing her mistake and all would be right again.

Instead, there was silence for days, then a week, two weeks went by, and I kept wondering why she hadn't called. I had even set up an answering machine just in case, even though back then answering machines were new. Before I knew it, it was March and almost spring break when I received a letter from my wife's attorneys. They were saying that my wife was pursuing a divorce and that they highly recommended I get my own lawyer so we could negotiate how the division of property would occur. The thing that really set me off was the last paragraph that talked about how I had not been paying any child support for the last month and that I was being irresponsible as a father.

When you are in uniform, you have to be stone faced in front of the lower ranks, even if you are seething with rage on the inside. To say that this was a difficult time in my life would be an enormous understatement. I was becoming a very angry person who was also becoming very resentful of a lot of things. Some gasoline got thrown on that fire with the conversations that followed with my old friend Tony. Tony and I would talk every once in a while for the last few years and Veronica had a similar relationship with his wife. Keep in mind Tony and his wife Rebecca had introduced me to Veronica, and Tony had been my best friend since high school and the best man at my wedding. I couldn't believe that he was basically taking her side, saying that I was taking her for granted. I remember at one point asking him, "Whose side are you on?"

He responded that he was just trying to help me, and get his wife off his back as well. He tried to tell me that women are different now, that they demand more than my mother and women of her generation did. Looking back, I understand what he was trying to tell me, but at the time all I could think of was, "I am a soldier protecting my country, putting a roof over her head and I didn't beat her up like other men (I use that term loosely in that context). What more did she want? Candy, flowers, the President to give her a giant medal?"

I got defensive and before I knew it, I was getting really mad at Tony and telling him that maybe he should tell his wife that he's the man of the house, not her flying monkey. He didn't appreciate my implying that she was a witch and that he was just someone doing her bidding. Before I knew it, we were yelling at each other and I told him to go to hell and slammed the phone down. At the time, my career was the only stable thing in my life, while it seemed like everything else was unravelling.

I started trying to visit the kids and tried to pretend that they needed me to stay over at the military base and that was why I wasn't there for them the rest of the time. Matthew bought it immediately but Jackie was five and a half and was getting a little bit wiser about what was going on. I knew that she was probably going to see through this, and Randall, who was only a year and a half younger, wouldn't be far behind.

Those months were agonizing; the legal process is like peeling off a Band-Aid one painful hair at a time, except the Band-Aid is three feet long and ten inches wide. I eventually got a lawyer, who proceeded to tell me that because of the current laws, if we divorced I would have to pay significant portions of my income indefinitely. I couldn't believe this was happening to me, and I began to get depressed. I remember watching Star Wars on TV the previous year and really enjoying it. After watching The Empire Strikes Back which had come out in theatres, I knew I was supposed to be shocked by the fact that Darth Vader was Luke Skywalker's father, but all I could think about was how the good guys don't even win in movies anymore, let alone real life.

Those first few meetings with the lawyers were like stepping into a meeting where you have an adversary but the person speaking for her has a really thick accent, so you don't know what they mean half the time. This garbled language is called legalese, and all it did was make things worse and if she was mad at me before, someone was making her a woman with a vendetta. Those meetings got really tense the more I heard about her gaining the "matrimonial home," child support, alimony, and the list went on. Unfortunately, during this meeting, I told her that the house was mine, because my money bought it and she should get a job to pay her way, if she doesn't want me around anymore. This didn't help things, and once she started talking about emotional distress I just lost it.

All I could think was, "Her emotional distress? I'm having everything I built taken away from me – my wife, only seeing my kids every other weekend. This is no way to treat a war hero. I have a purple heart, did she have a heart at all?"

Things like that must have gone through my head a thousand times. I was able to stay focused and with brief moments of happiness at work, but I came home to an empty house and it reached the point that I began to wonder what my life was coming to. One day in September, I came down with a really bad cough and I stayed home that day, and as I laid there I began to feel like I was in a battle I couldn't win. I didn't even know why she was really leaving, was it over gifts, really? It didn't make sense at all. As I flipped through the channels, I began to see some of the daytime talk shows and suddenly the light bulb went on. This is the same psychobabble that I had heard Billy talk about. I came up with an idea. I could take my enemy, make him my friend and use his understanding of this to stop this divorce in its tracks, and because we were only legally separated, I was sure it could be saved.

I called Billy after I felt better, and he was surprised to hear from me, since the last six months, we had only spoken to each other like acquaintances at work, when I went back to Ann Arbor during the summer for a week to visit the family. I thought of this as a gamble but if I told him enough of the truth, he might be able to help me win Veronica back so I could stop this divorce before it went any further. He knew about the separation and that I wasn't happy about it, but I hadn't told him much else. I told him that maybe he could host a meeting where we could get to the bottom of this once and for all. He was surprised that I would suggest that, and even more surprised that I was willing to let him get right in the middle of our personal marital issues. Most of all, he was surprised I trusted him this much, and I responded that over the last year he had shown how genuine he was. Even though he and I don't see eye to eye on a lot of things, I was a desperate man.

He reluctantly agreed, and he told me that due to the tension, he would call her and get back to me as far as when we could have this meeting. He said, "She needs to feel as comfortable as possible going into this or her defenses will prevent any progress in the discussion."

I began to think of it like a strategy to let the enemy think they have more control than they actually do. So, after a few phone calls back and forth, she agreed to let him and I come over to the house on a Saturday. Billy insisted on being the impartial moderator, who would keep us from talking over each other and would listen carefully and empathetically to both of us. I remember thinking, "Whatever he has to say to get things back to the way they were, I would support it."

So the day came, and he arrived a few minutes late, then he spoke to both of us and proceeded to lay down the rules that he as the moderator would be enforcing. He asked who wanted to start, and had suggested to me during one of our previous conversations that I let her start and get what was bothering her out in the open. This seemed like a brilliant plan, where he can translate this stuff that was going on in her head into something I could understand, perfect.

She began to talk about how things had changed between us and they just weren't the same, and even Billy couldn't understand it because he asked her what she meant. She started to talk about how she had thought that we would have more time together, and she thought I would be as loyal as I can be, but then all of a sudden, it was like she woke up to nothing. A husband who would be gone most of the day, and would barely have fifteen minutes to talk to her on some days. She said that at first she didn't notice she just accepted that that was military life. However, as the kids got older, as we went from having one child to three, she just felt like she didn't have any time for anything she wanted to do. The times we went out became fewer and fewer, and she then said that to top it all off, I didn't appreciate everything she had given up to be with me, have my children, and cook my dinner when I came home every night. Billy asked if there was anything else that she wanted to say, she said that was all for now.

He turned to me to hear my side when I said, "Hold on a second Billy, for now, you see she's holding back, she can't just let it all come out, she has to keep it in and then I have to drag it out of her."

Billy stopped me before I said anything else, "Okay Charles, the rules stated that we are not here to attack or accuse the other. Now let's hear your side of things."

I looked at him and said, "I love her with every fibre of my being, all those long hours I worked were for two reasons, 1. To be the best soldier I can be to protect our country and 2. To provide an income to give her and the kids a good life. I was doing exactly that, and she didn't have to work. Plenty of women these days have to work because their husbands either don't make enough, are unemployed, or ran away from their responsibilities. I was able to provide us with everything and she thinks that I don't appreciate her, but she doesn't appreciate what I do and what I have done to build a life with her."

This was when Billy began to speak to me and said, "Charles, this isn't about money, this is about doing what's best for your partner so they feel fulfilled. Judging from what I am hearing, Veronica and you have very different ideas on what a fulfilling life is (she nodded in agreement). It sounds like she wants a career of her own, and doesn't want to be just a wife and mother."

This is where I rolled my eyes and started ranting, "Why not? That's a woman's place; it has been that way for as long as there have been men and women. Men work, women look after the kids and if the woman finds a guy who can look after her and treat her well, good for her."

Billy was trying to reel me back in, "Charles, the world is changing and we need to adapt..."

I cut him off again, "You're damn right the world is changing. It's

Melvoy's Railroad

going crazy – the world used to be so much simpler. Men had a place, women had a place and that was the way it was, and now nobody knows their place anymore."

With that rant, not only did I come off as an ass, but I basically shot my marriage in the head. She looked at me and asked, "Is that all you think I can be?"

She followed by saying, "Is that all you think our daughter can be? If Jackie tells you she wants to be an astronaut or the first woman President, are you just going to say, sorry you can't, you're a girl?"

I was stunned, I had never thought of it that way and with my stunned silence she looked at me and said, "Thanks for trying Billy, but we're done here."

Billy and I sat there in silence as I pondered if that was my last chance. Billy put his hand on my shoulder and told me that he was sorry that things didn't work out, and proceeded to say that the best advice he could give me would be for me to come to terms with the fact that we had grown apart as people.

That was a real roller coaster of a time. It was October 1980 when I finally became First Lieutenant because my outstanding work had paid off. I still had the aftertaste of that meeting that went wrong with Billy and Veronica, and I must have replayed that meeting in my head dozens of times in the months that followed. On the brighter side, it looked more and more certain that my guy Ronald Reagan would become the next President of the United States.

Then came the news that my grandmother, the one who was there when Billy ran away at Easter, had passed away. I had only exchanged a few cards with her in the last few years, as she had gone to a nursing home after she fell and broke her hip. She just had trouble keeping going after that. I had a flood of memories of the times I spent with her, the time all of us made gingerbread houses, and the times she took us to the county fair. My kids barely knew her, but I remembered her very fondly, and back then seventy-eight was considered a ripe old age.

As you can probably guess I had to fly back to Michigan for the funeral, and my wife and kids went too, but we hardly spoke a word to each other. Oddly enough, I spent more time thinking about Veronica being there than about my grandmother. When the time came, I had already agreed to be one of the pall-bearers and as we carried the casket towards the limousine, I just kept wondering what I could do, and maybe if I tried I could capitalize on her sympathy and get her back. The reception was at my parent's house, and Billy asked if I wanted to take a break from the crowd, go to the basement and play some chess. He had brought that same finished, wooden chess board and I told Billy, "No."

I told him that we had a golden opportunity to get Veronica to take me back. He looked at me with bewilderment, "Charles, I know this is hard to accept, but Veronica and you have grown apart, and this isn't right time or place."

I stopped him, "How can't you see it, she knows I have just lost my grandmother, I can leverage her sympathy."

Billy responded, "Charles, today isn't about you, it's about Grandma and those of us mourning her loss. Also, that is terribly manipulative and I won't have any part of it."

I didn't take his refusal well, "Billy, I am giving you an opportunity to prove you are my brother, why can't you help your brother with this?"

He responded, "Because you are wrong about this, I won't help you manipulate people."

I lashed back, "You came back here over a year ago because you wanted your family back. Do you want your older brother back or not?"

He threw up his hands, "I want a brother, but all you seem to want is an underling. Brothers, regardless of age, need to be equal, I hope you realize that someday."

He walked upstairs as my frustration began to boil over, and I just balled up my fist and punched a hole in the drywall. All I was thinking about was how I was going to lose a golden opportunity to get Veronica and the life I truly wanted back.

I cast my vote for Ronald Reagan, as I had high hopes that under his leadership, America would get back on track. Some of the other guys and I from the base were all rooting for him and for those few days I was able to block my divorce out of my mind and focus on the victory that had been attained. The hardest part of the remainder of the year was knowing that I would be walking into Thanksgiving and Christmas at my parent's house without my wife and kids and knowing that was going to be the elephant in the room that no one was naming.

As 1981 began, we had basically agreed that Veronica would keep the house, and we agreed that I would get custody of the kids on alternating weekends. The house was appraised and some of that money was set aside for childcare. The good news was the house on base didn't officially belong to me, so it was technically outside of the assets. As the weeks went by, Jackie, Randall, and Matthew became more and more aware that things weren't right. I remember one weekend telling Randy, (by this point he had just turned five and that was what he wanted to be called besides whatever superhero he was pretending to be that day) that none of this was their fault, "Mommy and Daddy still love you kids and that isn't going to change."

I had to make the language neutral because one time early on, I made the mistake of telling them I wasn't around because Veronica didn't want me there. Within twenty-four hours, I got a twenty-minute phone call from Veronica telling me how I was trying to turn the kids against her and how upset Jackie was by what I said.

Some people might think that being in combat is hard, well it is, but even if you are tired of it, even if you hate it, even if you are so tired of a place you never want to see it again, you can always count down to the day your deployment ends. In divorce, and anything in the legal field for that matter, no such end date exists.

My nearly ten-year marriage finally came to an end when the divorce became final on April 15, 1981. Thankfully this didn't turn into one of those never-ending ones where people fight for years over a toaster or some other silly possession. I can't imagine that and I probably would have developed a twitch, or some other serious problem. On those weekends I would pick up the kids, play board games and try to play sports with them. What made it so much worse was the kids asking if I was ever coming home, why Mommy was mad at me and so on. It was always made worse because every other weekend where I got the kids, I would have to deal with the awkwardness and contempt in Veronica's eyes as if she could barely stand the sight of me anymore. You know a situation is bad when you begin wishing you didn't have to do it anymore, even if you stop seeing your kids.

The kids weren't seeing my parents either and I took the fall for that from my mother and father, wondering what the hell I did to run her off so badly. I came home to that empty house where I knew the kids weren't and knew I was only there because I had been kicked out of my house. Although I never breathed a word about it to anyone on the base, there were a few nights where I would look at a few of the pictures I had, including the one of us in front of the Hollywood sign, and mourn my loss.

Around this awful time in my life, there was an incident where I was mad at some Private for driving his jeep a little bit recklessly and I let him have it. At some point, he blurted out, "You would suck as a Dad."

I got right up in his face and said, "If you ever talk about my personal life again, I will kick your ass so hard you will go flying through the air, got that Private?"

This was just a bad situation, and it seemed like things were going well for others but not me. I needed to get out of this, get a fresh start and as if with perfect timing that summer, my fresh start arrived.

CHAPTER 24

I GOTTA GET OUT OF THIS PLACE, IF IT'S THE LAST THING I EVER DO

One day in June, I received a phone call from McLachlin and he told me that he had kept his ear to the ground and made the right contacts because he heard about a big opportunity. The expansion of the missile defense programs that Reagan had initiated involved some additional hiring along with bonuses and would be happening in Nevada. My eyes lit up, he talked about the opportunity and that if I took a six-month training program he and I would be among the overseers of the initiative. I learned more about the program that started in September, and all I had to do was learn the system and I would be able to keep a watchful eye on Russia's most dangerous weapons. Best of all I could do it for more money, PERFECT! I never found out how he got the inside track, but it was exactly what I was looking for, the perfect way out.

As you might guess, I knew that I had to explain this to Veronica and I knew that this would be a hard thing to work around. We would have to amend our custody agreement because driving from NORAD's location to San Diego every other weekend would be time consuming, costly and just impractical.

I called her up and told her about the opportunity. She of course asked me, "What about the children?"

I told her that I would come and see them once a month or so. Needless to say she wasn't happy. She told me she was having a hard time finding work, my alimony and child support weren't quite enough and she was working as a waitress to try to make ends meet. I remember thinking, "Well you would have access to my full salary if you hadn't run off."

There was too much animosity and tension and we weren't going to be that couple that divorced but remained friends. She reluctantly accepted it though, but before the phone call ended she took one more jab and said, "You haven't changed a bit, you still care more about the military than anything else."

I didn't like that remark but she was right, I did like the military

Melvoy's Railroad

better, because it had the order and respect that I didn't get from her or anyone else. I was thrilled that this was my fresh start. I began talking a lot more frequently with McLachlin and he began telling me about how we would be able to spend a lot more time together and he would show me the wonder of golf. It never struck me as an exciting sport, but I just wanted to get away from my miserable life in California. I was so happy to get this opportunity that I would have played hopscotch.

The phone calls with the kids were the hardest, they were only seeing me two weekends a month, and after I moved they would be seeing me even less. Jackie was now seven years old and was beginning to get an attitude, saying she didn't know why I was "leaving them behind."

I could almost hear her mother's words coming out, and I don't think Veronica put her up to it, but Jackie probably overheard a lot. That's one thing they don't teach you in school, when you don't want the kids to hear it, sometimes they do, and when you want them to listen, sometimes they don't. When you are raising children, their listening does not have an on and off switch. Randy and Matthew were a little more accepting, I remember giving them the old routine that while I was away they were the men of the house. It made them feel good, even though in reality they were too young to do any of the big things a man of the house is supposed to do.

It was also around this time that Billy met a woman named Hashani. I remember talking to my father about it, and my father couldn't believe that his son was dating someone from India. We later found out that her family was from Sri Lanka, but for my father, it just "wasn't right."

Back then interracial relationships were new and strange and for once I was glad to be nowhere near this problem. I was still mad at Billy for not helping me enough with Veronica and I thought at the time, "It's about damn time our father gave him some of the crap he deserved." I just thought that it was the wrong reason.

It got closer and closer to September and I got more excited about my fresh start, or as McLachlin said it, "Melvoy, you've had a rough last couple years, so this is going to be your Mulligan."

A Mulligan in golf is a do-over, a chance to correct a mistake, and I was so excited. The thing that is so sad but funny is that I hadn't even made my biggest mistakes yet. You may be tempted to ask what could be bigger than my marriage failing, or the way I dealt with my brother. I don't just want to blurt it out. I need to tell this story properly, but keep reading and trust me, you will find out.

CHAPTER 25

★

GO AHEAD, MAKE MY DAY

I was so tired of the problems in my personal life that it was almost harder to say farewell to my subordinates on the military base, than it was to tell my now ex-wife that I was leaving. I packed up some of my things from the house and it was hard saying farewell to the kids but I promised them I would visit. As I got in my car with my suitcases with all of my belongings, I remember seeing my kids staring out the window, I knew that it would be hard but seeing their disappointed faces made it that much harder.

I hit the road for Nevada to go through the training program. I didn't realize just how hard it was to get into this program, but McLachlin knew the right people and opened the door for me. I couldn't have been more relieved to get out of California. Not only was there much more smog than in Michigan, or almost anywhere I had been before that but in California, it just seemed like there was traffic everywhere all the time, you could probably get stuck in traffic at 1:00 am.

I got to the base where they verified who I was and started a slideshow of the whole training procedure for those of us who had just arrived. The presenter, whose name I don't remember, showed us some pictures and composite paintings of past wars. His speech went like this:

"Gentlemen, you are here because of one ten letter word: escalation. Ever since the first cave man picked up a stone or a sharp stick to help him win a fight, this has been going on. Any weapon that man produced was soon either copied, imitated, or improved upon by their adversaries, whether it was knives, guns, explosives, or other machines of war. In 1944, we developed the ultimate weapon, the atomic bomb, a single weapon capable of destroying entire cities and possibly nations, which can be dropped from a plane or launched from a long distance away on land or by submarine. Hiroshima and Nagasaki were destroyed by single planes rather than armies of soldiers on the ground, preventing tens or perhaps hundreds of thousands of American casualties. When we used this our victory in World War II became an inevitability.

"There was only one problem, escalation occurred and the Russians found their own formula four years later and now they have comparable nuclear weapons with similar capabilities as ours. If they ever got the opportunity to drop those bombs on us, what happened in Hiroshima and Nagasaki would look like a picnic. If we don't stay on the cutting edge of weapons technology, they will trample us and it will take a long damn time before anyone else can challenge the Soviets. Those of you who qualify will be the most important line of defense, for us the last defense against Communism, making sure the Soviet missiles cannot sneak into our airspace without counterattack. Our ability to counterattack is the only thing that stands between us and destruction at their whim. Now that you know what you are here to do, I hope you came here ready to work."

We all applauded and the training began, and every once in a while I would hear McLachlin talking to others of a similar or higher rank about my potential, drive, and determination but most of all my passion for my country.

As the weeks went by I picked the concepts up quickly, like how to watch for missiles, where they would come from and all of that important technical stuff, procedures of notifying the President, more procedures of caution and everything in between. It seemed like they had thought of nearly everything, and if there was a scenario they weren't ready for, I wouldn't have thought of it.

The training went really well but I along with a few other people got a couple of weeks off for Christmas. I agreed to have Christmas Day with the kids but I would spend the few days before with the rest of my family. Some of the Christmases mesh together and only a couple of things made this one memorable, but the biggest thing was the conversation I had with my father on December 21st. They let me stay in my old room, and I began looking around at all those old pictures my parents had. The thing that stood out to me was seeing a picture of all of us when I was twelve, taken at Sears that said, "Christmas 1961," on the back. Those smiles, that innocence that we seemed to have as children, was now a long, long gone memory.

That evening Jason and Cathy brought the kids over and moving Christmas ahead was their idea since they were going to Montreal to see some ice sculpture festival. Billy brought his girlfriend Hashani, who seemed nice but a little nervous. About half an hour before dinner started my mother told me to ask my father if he wanted sweet potatoes with dinner or just the white ones. I went into his den only to see him opening his flask, and my eyes couldn't have been wider. I barely stopped myself from saying something that would have given away the situation.

I closed the door and began speaking quietly, "Dad what the hell are you doing? You fell off the wagon again, God damn it. When did this start?"

My father looked at me and said, "It started with Thanksgiving, when your brother brought that girl from somewhere else. It also doesn't help that I haven't seen some of my grandchildren in a long damn time because you screwed up."

His voice raised as he was saying this and I told him, "Keep it down, I don't want Mom to hear this."

He had already had a few and my mother either wasn't aware or keeping it to herself.

My father looked at me and said, "Boy, I don't get it anymore."

I asked him what he was talking about and he said, "Your sister got pregnant before she got married, thank God Jason did right by her or who knows where she'd be. Not to mention she is too easy on those kids, and one day they are going to be a big handful. Then there's your brother who I must have made miserable because he literally ran away and came back with all sorts of liberal stuff I can't believe. To top it all off, now he's dating a girl who probably rode a camel to get to the boat she came here on. Then there's you, you were my shining example then you got divorced, how the hell did this happen?"

The answer my mother was looking for was taking much longer than expected, so she knocked on the door, and asked "Barry, do you want sweet potatoes or just the white ones?"

He blurted out, "Sure what the hell, it's the holidays."

The answer made my mother pause and said, "Okay, dinner will be ready soon."

As she walked away I knew that if my mother found out my father was drinking again, it would be the end of their marriage and would ruin Christmas.

I tried to coach him to say as little as possible, and to drink some coffee, which hopefully would keep this from blowing up. As you can probably guess, things didn't go as planned. They started off okay but we just couldn't keep it together. The conversation at the table had me covering for him saying things like, "Mom he's chewing. He's trying not to set a bad example for the grandchildren."

Things were still going well for Cathy and Jason. Their chain now had seven locations and although a couple of them were struggling, they were confident that things would improve with time. We soon started talking with Hashani and her accent was almost non-existent. She apparently had moved from Sri Lanka when she was five and was a dental hygienist and met Billy because their offices were in the same building. Cathy pointed out how their jobs were opposite, when you're the hygienist you have to do the talking and when you're the psychiatrist you have to do the listening. Hashani mentioned that Billy was a great listener and that was one of the things she appreciated about him. He responded that she is a great dental hygienist because people can see what a brilliant smile looks like just by looking at her.

To be perfectly honest, I was feeling a little bit envious and my tongue got the best of me at that moment, "Well Billy, I don't have to be a psychiatrist to know when someone is showing off."

He turned to me getting a little defensive, "Charles, I'm not trying to show off. I'm just talking about our relationship because it is an important part of my life, just like Jason and Cathy's business is an important part of theirs."

Jason, trying to keep the peace said, "Besides Charles, you have things going on so tell us about your new position."

If all those years working in the bar taught him anything, it was how to spot a conflict and diffuse it.

I began talking about my new position. When my father had finished his dinner and without his food to keep him occupied, he began talking. "Hold on Charles, what the hell are you envious about? Your brother found some woman who is marrying him so she doesn't get shipped back to India or wherever the hell she's from."

My mother grabbed him by the wrist, and Billy began to get tense, when Hashani spoke up, "Mr. Melvoy I'm not being sent back anywhere. I am an American citizen who votes and pays taxes just like you."

My father then responded, "Really, you're just like me, well then, what do your parents think of you dating Billy?"

Billy cut in, "Dad, I'm begging you, stop, for the love of God."

My father kept going, "God, there's a good question. If you're like me why do you people worship elephants and cows?"

She began to get really upset and she stood up, "First of all, Hindu people do not worship elephants, they worship many Gods. Also my family converted to Christianity two generations ago before my parents were born. Finally, my family is just like you because my father doesn't like the idea of white people being in our family, which means you and he are just as ignorant."

My mother had her hand over her mouth and that was when I stood up. "Dad, that's enough if…Hashani and Billy are happy together, leave it alone."

My father and I began to argue and he blurted out, "If they get married and have kids, what will they be part brown, part white. They won't know what the hell they are."

Hashani yelled with a thunderous, "Hey!"

We turned to her when she said, "They would be children raised by loving parents, as beautiful as any other. If you would reject them because they're not all white then you are just another blind bigot!"

Jason stepped in and immediately pulled my father into his study, and then Billy turned to me and said, "Thanks Charles, I appreciate what you said."

Suddenly we heard my father yelling at Jason. I looked at him and said, "Billy, this is about to get real ugly. Tell Hashani, Cathy, and Mom to get out of here before this blows up."

Hashani looked at Billy and said, "It's your family, what do you want?"

He looked at her and said, "Go upstairs until things calm down."

Cathy, Mom, and Hashani went upstairs and Billy turned to me and said, "Okay Charles, before he comes out what's going on?"

I told him about me catching him drinking again and he let out a deep breath while rolling his eyes saying, "Yeah, that explains it."

When my father came out of the room with Jason, he was telling us to get out of his house, because we had ruined Christmas. My mother came down the stairs as we were trying to talk some sense to him and stood there at the corner with a suitcase. Like Moses coming down the mountain, she came down to where the stairs turn and she spoke in her distinctive voice when you knew you were in trouble. She stared at him with just absolute outrage, "Barry Melvoy, we only get to see our children a few times a year and you insult a perfectly nice girl and you broke a promise to me that you wouldn't drink anymore."

He responded, "I wasn't drinking."

My mother responded, "Don't lie to me, I could smell it on your breath."

He began to try to talk to her when she cut him off again and said, "I'm not listening to your excuses. I have forgiven you before, but this time it's three strikes, you're out. Get your clothes out of this house."

She threw the suitcase at him and we all stood there speechless. I told him that I would take him to a motel for the night and we drove away. Just before I left, Billy pulled me aside and told me that if I wanted to talk, I could call him in the morning before 10:00 am and in the evening after 8:00 pm. I just remember driving to the motel, thinking this was déjà vu, all over again. I thought we had fixed this problem, but it just wouldn't go away.

I had a plane scheduled for the 23rd so I couldn't stay this time to help fix things up. I guess it would be Cathy and Jason's job, although I later found out that they wouldn't have time either.

Christmas with Veronica and the kids went much, much better although that really isn't saying much. It was still awkward but that awkwardness paled in comparison to the disaster I had just been part of. One of the thoughts I remember having besides all the cute things the kids got me for Christmas and all the other things that usually come with Christmas, was the thought of, "Our divorce was agony. We weren't even married ten years, compared to my parents who were married for about thirty-five years, and I wondered how would they be able to handle it?"

The simple answer was not very well, and over the next few months I tried to focus on finishing my training and not think about it. One day my father called and he told me that even though he had gone one month without drinking, she wasn't taking him back. Apparently when she said three strikes you're out, she was very, very serious about it.

Day after day I was trying to focus on learning my new job, which was watching out for enemy missiles or other threats. McLachlin was very proud of my progress and as I finally finished my training in March, he shook my hand and told me that he and I would go out for drinks on Friday, but when I came home with this good news, there was no one. I was about to start making much more money in a more important position and in the rough economy of 1982, my job looked very secure. All that good news but no one to tell it to, which is the sound of silence when silence feels like something rather than nothing.

The first few months on the job were exciting and everything was very structured, just the way I liked it. There was no chaos, no disorganization, and I was enjoying the order, structure, and predictability. On the other hand, there was also that edge of danger knowing that if you didn't watch for any suspicious actions, a serious threat could sneak through. I knew that the odds were very unlikely of anything being launched at us but that little bit of doubt kept me on my toes.

The people I worked with were very interesting, and there was one guy named Sammy who was the big joker of our division. I remember one of his jokes, "Why are Russian missiles so big? They're overcompensating."

Of course, we all laughed, not realizing ours were just as big and that maybe we were insulting ourselves in the process.

As of the spring it was confirmed that my family back in Michigan was in a downward spiral. My parents were going through a divorce and just to make things worse, there were rumours of layoffs in Flint where my father was working. I was hoping that he would be able to keep himself together because unions are powerful, but sooner or later they can't protect you anymore. I spoke to Jason and he promised that he would make sure that no one in the family would suffer too much. He said he would find a way to make sure everyone had what they needed, even if he had to go into his pocket to do it. I think his exact words were, "Just another thing we have to do for the family, right?"

I responded, "Yeah."

If I remember correctly, Billy was still doing well with Hashani, and I don't recall them ever having any big fights, and for whatever reason their relationship just worked. I remember wondering how Billy did it, how did he find that right person, and what did they have in common? I used to fear that maybe he was just being a doormat and doing whatever she wanted, and I just couldn't imagine that he had been so lucky to find the right person. It occasionally crossed my mind, but most of the time I had a lot of other things I preferred to think about.

Most of the time I blocked out what was bothering me at home in Michigan and tried to focus on inching ever closer to the top of the military, even though for the moment I seemed to be off track a little bit. I thought that this job could still raise my stature in the eyes of my country. It was around this time was that even though Major Melvoy had a nice sound to it, what I really wanted was to be General Melvoy, because that was the dream. I realized that I originally thought at that point that being a General was the best opportunity to get what I really dreamed of. That dream was to be able to stand tall and proud one day being face to face with the President of the United States of America and having him hear my plans and strategies that would lead us to victory. I used to imagine the truly proud moment I would have when the President would say, "Melvoy, go get 'em."

Then standing toe to toe with the enemy and I could tell them, "I have the greatest army in the world, so go ahead make my day."

CHAPTER 26

★

THE FIRST SPARKS

So as the spring turned into summer, I drifted further apart from my children, because there just always seemed to be a reason why I couldn't visit. Before I knew it, it was July and Jackie, who was eight years old, was calling to wish me a happy birthday and wondering when I was coming to see her. All I could tell her was, "I don't know, they're keeping me really busy here."

Matthew was only four and he was saying, "Daddy I miss you, I lost a tooth and the tooth fairy gave me a dollar."

It was so hard to hear it, which in a way made it harder for me to schedule time. The big surprise was the phone conversation when Veronica came on and told me that she was sorry to hear about my parents breaking up. She remembered how hard it was for us to keep them together the second time. The worst part was I had completely forgotten that she had spent all that time with my mother trying to get her to give my father another chance. I thankfully remembered just in time to end the pause with, "Yes, thanks, it was a hard time."

I would say that this was the beginning of our animosity cooling off. We had gotten the yelling out of our system, we had had some time apart and maybe we could be civil for the sake of the children.

That summer in Nevada while I was working my way up, I received an entrepreneur magazine in the mail and it had Jason and the older partner's faces on it, with the headline "The Winners of Game Night."

As I read through it they were talking about how the secret behind their success was that they had found the right mix of Jason's youthful energy and ambition, tempered with his partner's extensive experience. Naturally I called to issue my congratulations to Jason and Cathy, which was a nice bright spot in a lot of the unfortunate things that had been happening recently. The older partner's name was Eric Hutchison, which got me thinking about how they had a nearly parallel relationship McLachlin and I had. He was older, more experienced and I was the younger and more ambitious one. It began to make me wonder what we could accomplish if we put our heads together and combined our knowledge, just imagine what we could do – maybe we could have America finally win. This was when I began to think outside the box and the first sparks began.

Before the end of 1982, I had seen how their system worked in the case of emergencies and I realized that it would take almost six minutes to get the confirmation to the President, who was the man who made the decisions. While this was an improvement over the seven minutes it took during the initial drills, six minutes is still a long time in the nuclear age. I began seeing where the processes were and slowly figured out where the bottlenecks were. After discussing them with McLachlin, we figured out where to cut about ninety seconds from the process. It would have been two minutes but one of the steps was more necessary than I had previously realized. However, by the time it was implemented I had been awarded for my innovation and McLachlin looked great by reflection for opening the door to my idea and to me in general.

That year went by so quickly, it seemed like when I got home I would just flip on the TV and eat dinner. At work I was proving myself, people knew me and began respecting me for what I was doing and what I had accomplished. We were turning into a united group, which had a common goal; my professional life had become the opposite of my personal life. It seemed like the family back in Michigan had split off and gone their separate ways. I didn't even want to visit with the family back in Michigan.

Billy and Hashani were staying in Sacramento and apparently Hashani had not forgiven my father for the things he said. Cathy and Jason were busy and decided to have our mother for dinner and not our father. My father arranged to spend Christmas with his older cousin Bob who had moved down to Florida for his retirement years. At least he would be warm and not alone.

I almost forgot to mention Veronica and the kids, I still got together with them for Christmas and Thanksgiving but it amazed me how much they were growing. You hear people say, "Oh kids grow up so fast," but you don't realize how fast until months go by and they've grown a few inches and she's had to buy all new clothes for them. Before Christmas, Veronica and I had a discussion about what to get each other for Christmas although it was just for the kids, it would make things look peaceful.

That was when she brought up the fact that she was dating someone new, named Todd, I told her I was fine with it. Christmas went well enough and we watched *It's a Wonderful Life,* and I remember occasionally looking over at Veronica with her arms around Todd snuggled up on the couch and thinking, "My guardian angel has a lot of explaining to do."

That jealous feeling in the pit of my stomach really was hard to see and deal with, but I held my tongue. I promised Veronica it would be fine and Charles Melvoy is a lot of things, but not a man that breaks his word.

However, that jealousy did have one positive side effect, which led me to start talking with the guys and I decided that 1983 would be the year that I found someone new. Enough time had passed and if Veronica could find someone new, so could I. After all, I was only thirty-three and a war hero and if a lady out there was looking for a real man, I was ready to be exactly that.

Of course, the dating world wasn't as fun or as easy as it was in high school. I didn't have much in common with modern women, and sometimes they would stop talking to me after they found out I had been divorced. During 1983 the dating world drove me crazy, and I remember I had started dating this girl, who shall remain nameless, and she never returned my call. I waited for a couple days and nothing happened. Finally, I was able to contact her and she said, "I just didn't feel that spark."

I remember thinking, "Why couldn't you tell me this directly?"

It was a complex game where it seemed like the rules either made no sense, were secret, or changed constantly.

Finally, it was September 1983 when I was introduced on a blind date to a new woman named Tracy, and she and I seemed to hit it off. She had been divorced too, and the big difference was she had been through some abuse. Married to a control freak guy that wouldn't let her talk to any other man. He tried to kill her and she showed me the stitches on her arm where it happened. My heart went out to her, and thankfully she didn't have any children with that maniac. Still it must have been really hard for her, and compared to that guy, I was a saint. I remember thinking that if that guy had met me, I would have taught him some respect in the old-fashioned way. She just had this vulnerable charm to her that I just fell for immediately; this was one of the highlights of that year.

I started trying harder to call my kids every week or every other week, so I would have some idea of what was going on in their lives. A few days before Thanksgiving, I got a phone call from Veronica to tell me that Randy had been acting out recently and giving Todd the old routine, "You're not my real dad."

She asked if I would speak to him about it when I came over on Thanksgiving, I said sure and as hard as it was to not spend it with Tracy, I knew that I had other obligations. Randy was seven now and he had started causing trouble in class. I pulled him aside and asked him, "What's this stuff I hear about you getting into trouble at school and talking back at home?"

I forgot to mention that Todd had moved in with them about a month earlier. Randy began to say that he was the man of the house, not Todd, and Todd can't tell him what to do. In a small way, I was relieved that he still knew who his Dad was, but I couldn't let him use this as an excuse. I admit that I laughed when he said, "Todd's a plumber, he shows people his butt."

I gave him the old, "You need to respect your mother and Todd, work hard at school and if you keep talking back to people, you're going to be in some serious trouble. Now be thankful, I'm letting you off easy this time."

Dinner went well, but unfortunately Jackie who was nine already had stopped talking to me and I didn't know why. My kids were in the next state, but I didn't want to lose touch with them altogether. Unfortunately, there was a high alert during Christmas that year and I had to stay in Nevada. Veronica wasn't happy and much to my surprise, she brought Billy into the picture and it turned into something that I really didn't like.

CHAPTER 27

★

BILLY'S WORDS

It was January 1984 when I got a phone call from Veronica saying that Billy and Hashani had come to visit her and that after a long talk, she thinks that I should have a conversation with him. I asked her what this was about and she simply said that it was about the kids and our family. I told her that if he wants to come over that is fine, but I had a busy schedule. He called later and we would meet on a Sunday, but I was undecided about whether or not I wanted Tracy to be there. On one hand, I thought that it would be good to have someone on my side, but on the other hand, things in our family were still in bad shape and I wanted to keep her a safe distance away from it, especially this early in the relationship.

Just so you know, Veronica and I were still connected but only speaking to each other on the phone once every few weeks and it seemed like those conversations had become gradually shorter and quieter. My mother was still close with Cathy and Jason, and spent time with Cathy regularly. After carefully thinking about it, I decided against having Tracy there. By this point, I knew Billy well enough to know that his "talks" were usually him criticizing me and I didn't need him making me look bad in front of Tracy.

Billy and Hashani arrived at my place and everything started out well enough, as we talked about next week being the Super Bowl, how it's become this big deal and how it was becoming more than a football game. He had brought that chessboard with him and asked if I wanted to play against him and I told him I wasn't interested. In my mind, I didn't want him playing games with me. I wanted to know the real reason why he was there. I sat there waiting for the verbal attack that I knew was coming, and seemed inevitable. He went into his fluff about how he appreciated what I've been through and the progress I had made, but that I was in danger of repeating our parent's mistakes. I asked what he was talking about, and he proceeded to tell me that I tried to uphold traditional ideas of what a man and woman were, which drove Veronica away. Now because I don't know how to be separate but still there, my children are having trouble coping with the loss of their father.

I got defensive asking him what the hell he knew about being a father. He responded by saying that he had many clients who had problems with how their parents raised them, which still caused them emotional problems to this very day. My patience was almost at its end, "So you think I'm traumatizing my children?"

He immediately tried to say that I was exaggerating and that I needed to relax and listen, but I wasn't interested. I looked at him and said, "Billy, here's the advice I would give. Tell all those people who walk into your office complaining that their Mommies didn't hug them enough, to suck it up. Maybe if you tell people how to stand up and move on, maybe they wouldn't be so damn weak."

Billy tried to tell me something about how it wasn't about weakness or strength, it was about my children missing me and it was affecting them differently. He also claimed if I didn't start reconciling with them, it could become a bigger issue. I told them that I wasn't leaving Nevada, "I am a damn good father and if you really are worried about the kids, take it up with Veronica wanting jewellery for Valentine's Day and how Todd is the sucker who will do that."

Hashani finally spoke up and said that I was being an asshole who needed to look in the mirror and look past my uniform. I told them that I was done listening and sarcastically stated, "Get out and when you replace the couch in your office, lift with your legs."

Billy left shaking his head but before he left, he turned to me and said, "Charles, you and I don't see eye to eye on a lot of things, but you are still my brother. I love you and I hope that one day you can see the world differently."

I called to him as he was going through the doorway, with the bright sun making it look like he was stepping into light itself. When he stopped I said, "Billy, you're my brother but I have to tell you, I don't think you have what it takes to see the world as I have. You are too soft to be able to walk a mile in my shoes."

He paused and said, "I know you walk in hard shoes. I just don't want you to walk into trouble with them."

As he got into his car and drove away, in a small way I respected him a little bit, no matter how wrong I thought he was, at least he said it to my face. However, I was still mad at Veronica because it seemed like she had sent them to nag me because she didn't want to do it herself.

I remember calling her up later that day and asking her what the hell she was doing sending Billy to nag me on her behalf. Needless to say, it broke down into an argument and we didn't breathe a word to each other until Easter, and in the process it meant that I wasn't speaking to my kids either. If they had their own cell phones I would have called, but when parents fight the children end up being civilian casualties in the middle of it all.

The thing that surprised me most was that a few weeks after visiting me, Billy went to visit my father. His drinking had crept back into his life and now that the divorce from my mother was almost final, the house that we grew up in would have to be sold if they couldn't find another way to split the assets. Billy tried to talk to him about giving up his drinking, but apparently it didn't work as well as Billy hoped for.

This is where Jason saved the day when he gave my parent's a simple deal. If our father were allowed to keep the house, our mother would stay with Cathy to help them with their kids. This was great for them because it was around this time that Cynthia, Cathy and Jason's oldest, was twelve, and just as my father and I had predicted, was turning into a spoiled brat. She was close to that age where she could get into serious trouble, as you will find out. So, it would be the perfect arrangement, with our father keeping his house, our mother being with her daughter and grandchildren, and Jason would have an extra set of eyes on his four children. Plus, with his money, he could easily afford having someone else live there who could help with the other household jobs.

As I heard through the grapevine, they sometimes had problems with their cleaning lady and nanny. Here came grandma Melvoy to show them how it's done. I would be lying if I said that I wasn't envious of Jason at the time. If he wasn't a millionaire by 1984, it was only because of his frivolous spending.

Billy and I had another discussion a few weeks later on the phone and I asked him if he was excited about four more years of Ronald Reagan. He started talking about how he was giving in to narrow interests that a better Republican Eisenhower warned us about the Military Industrial Complex. I translated this as "We are spending too much money on defense" which I wasn't going to hear anything about. We had to defend against the Soviets and if we let our guard down, they would wipe us off the face of the earth. As odd as that may sound to some, that was truly what I believed at the time.

If you had asked me if that was what I thought while I was taking a polygraph test, I would have passed with flying colours. Obviously, I couldn't tell Billy some things because of confidentiality, but it was still common knowledge how powerful nuclear weapons were and that Russia had plenty of them. Yet again, Billy and I didn't see eye to eye, and it was at the point where I was convinced that we never ever would.

CHAPTER 28

⭐

THE HAPPIEST PLACE ON EARTH

Some time that spring I received a phone call from Jason, who apparently wanted to take the whole family down to Walt Disney World in Florida for two weeks in July. When I say everyone, I mean everyone: my mother, my father, his kids, my kids, Billy, Hashani, Veronica, Todd, and me. To me this sounded like a disaster waiting to happen, so I told him that I wasn't sure if I could afford it. Truth was I probably could but I wasn't very interested. The last time I had done anything like that was at the state fair when I was sixteen, when I was mainly there to go on rides with Billy and keep him out of trouble. Jason then told me that it was all on him, so I asked him how he could afford this. He told me he was doing well and it would be a great time for everyone.

I truly thought that he had lost his mind, so I asked him, "What are you trying to do?"

He told me that it was the perfect place to bring everyone together and things have been difficult lately for all of us, and this would be a chance for us to reunite and truly be a family again. I shook my head in disbelief. Did he really think that this would fix my parent's now ended marriage? Did he really think that this would help Billy and I see eye to eye? Did he really think this would help my father get along with Hashani? As you may be wondering, did I go along with it? The answer is yes, and you are probably wondering, why would I do this if I thought it was such a bad idea? The answers to all of those questions might surprise you. I did it for two reasons, one I was worried that Veronica could use my absence against me. The second reason was Tracy, she and I had been dating for several months by this point and it would be a great opportunity for a romantic getaway.

I knew there might be problems, but somewhere deep inside I thought maybe Jason had a plan, and maybe everything would be great. So, for the kids and Tracy, I called Jason back and told him that I was coming, and asked if I could bring Tracy and could we have our own separate room in the resort and he said, "Sure."

During this time, my father had gotten his drinking somewhat under control, he turned sixty that year, and we were all there to throw a surprise party for him at his house. My mother refused to be there and we sent Cathy and her kids back around seven o'clock before his drinking really became obvious. His work situation was that as long as he could hold onto his job until he was sixty-five, he could retire with a GM pension. He also had several sick days coming to him if he drank too much one night and couldn't come into work. I didn't find out until later that he had stopped going to his A.A. meetings and I guess he thought he could fight this alone. He seemed like he had settled into his current mindset, which was the mindset of, "I'm going to drink when I feel like it, and it doesn't matter if I overdo it."

As July came closer and closer, my kids got more and more excited about school ending and their trip to Disney World. By this point, they had seen many of those Disney movies and were so excited to see this place. They had actually been to Disneyland in California after I left but Disney World was apparently an even bigger deal. They were talking about it like it was the second coming. Tracy and Veronica had never met and I got the sense that Tracy was nervous about this, but I assured her it would be fine and that the problems of before were behind us.

That summer the media was talking about the 1984 election and about how Ronald Reagan seemed poised to win again. The economy had improved a lot in the previous year or two and it seemed like there was plenty of good news. His phrase, "It is morning in America," was his slogan and the way he wanted to market himself to the public. That cynical decade of the 1970's seemed to be fading into a new re-embracing of patriotism and belief in how great the country was. It should be clear that he had my support, as I was a Reaganite through and through. He came across the way I thought a President should, confident, tough, aged with wisdom but able to have a little fun.

Getting back to the Happiest Place on Earth, I received a phone call from Billy telling me that he was worried about the trip and wanted to know where I stood. I told him that I was going there to spend some time with my kids, have a romantic getaway with Tracy, and I wasn't there to fight with anyone. He said he was relieved because he was worried about how I would be with everyone together for the first time ever. Todd had never met my family with the exception of speaking to Billy on the phone, and neither had Tracy. The phone call ended uneventfully, as I wondered why he called at all, "What was he looking for?"

We all met at the airport and it seemed like one of those scenes out of a movie where everyone gets along, everyone was happy to see each other, and the sun was shining bright. It was really hot but Cathy had come prepared with drinks for everyone. The first day went well enough, there were tourists everywhere so it must have taken at least half an hour to get on each ride and in some cases almost an hour. The kids were happy and while I wasn't used to all the roller coasters, I was enjoying it a lot too. The second and third day went well enough and the park was big enough that it took a lot of time to see everything.

The second night we stayed out to watch the fireworks. I remember the bangs were really loud which reminded me a little too much of my combat days so I walked away to gather my thoughts. Tracy came after me asking what was wrong and I told her that all of the explosions from the fireworks were making me think about my time in combat. I didn't go into any further detail, but she took my hand and told me it was okay. She and I kissed when the biggest firework went off with perfect timing.

The timing of that kiss was so perfect that it just felt like we had shaken the earth itself, which made our passion for each other even stronger than it already was. We went back to our room that night and that was the first night that we had been intimate. I hadn't been with anyone since Veronica a few years ago, and it was just a thrilling new experience.

In retrospect, Jason should have ended the trip around day four, because it went downhill around that time. The trouble started when Billy, Hashani, Connor (Cathy and Jason's oldest son) and my father went on the "It's a Small World" ride. As I was told, my father kept mockingly asking Hashani, "Is this where you're from?"

He supposedly asked this a couple times and she and my father began arguing, which of course began to spread to everyone else. Pretty soon he and Billy were arguing when security asked them to calm it down or they would be removed from the park. Apparently, that settled things down, but unfortunately more issues began to unfold when Cathy and my mother began arguing about how they were raising the kids and Marco talking back to her. Then as if there needed to be more issues, my father decided to visit the part of the park where they were selling beer and disappeared for hours. He did this a couple days in a row, because he was tired of dealing with everybody.

Then Connor supposedly shoved Matthew in the water park and Randy stood up for his younger brother and things got out of control leading to more problems with Veronica, Cathy, and my mother. Cathy thought that Veronica was being too hard on Connor, my mother thought that Veronica wasn't raising her kids well either, and the phrase "broken home" came up. As I'm sure you can imagine, this wasn't going well and each day that followed the tension just built and built, and all the pancakes we could eat for breakfast weren't going to keep things under control for long.

I believe it was day eight when Billy and Hashani knocked on my door while I was watching TV with Tracy, to tell us that there was an emergency and he needed my help. I asked him what happened, and he responded that our father was missing and this time they didn't know where he was, even though the last few nights he had turned up at his room and things were fine. This time he wasn't around, so he asked if I would go with him, and Hashani and Tracy could stay there in case there was a phone call or something.

Basically, we had split off into teams, with Jason and Todd, and me and Billy. As we looked around we had pictures of my father with us and we were asking security, and as we kept walking, Billy asked me what I was thinking. I told him that this whole trip was a bad idea and we should have stopped it a lot sooner. He actually agreed and said, "Charles, sometimes familiarity breeds contempt and that's definitely the case between Dad and Hashani. He just can't let go of the fact that she came here from somewhere else."

I looked at him and said, "Billy, I don't remember where she's from either. He wants his grandchildren to carry on his last name and our family traditions. Someone from who knows where is a threat to that."

He looked at me and said something that I had never thought of before, "Charles what traditions do we have that are worth anything? Our family is dysfunctional, and the last week has only hammered that point home. Now you and I are looking for our father who is who knows where, doing God knows what and won't exactly be thrilled to see us when we tell him that the park is closing for the night and he has to return to the hotel."

I didn't know what to say, is that what our family was? Dysfunctional? We had run into someone who told us they last saw him by the hot dog stand and he pointed to the area where he was a few minutes ago. He said we would have to take a left and then go over the bridge, and as we walked towards it, we saw a flashing light coming from over the bridge. We both looked at each other and knew that both of us were having the same scared thought.

As we ran over the bridge, we saw an ambulance strapping someone to a backboard, and as we ran closer, we saw that it was our father. We told the ambulance who we were and they told us to get in immediately as he was unconscious and wearing an oxygen mask. The paramedic said, "It looks like he's had a stroke."

I've seen men die, and even people I cared about like Phil "the hill", but my father, the man I've known my whole life, that was as frightening a moment as I had ever had.

Once we got to the hospital, I fell into my commanding mode and started trying to arrange things, "Billy when we get to the hospital, we each need to find a phone and get a hold of everybody and let them know what happened."

Billy agreed and we made the phone calls, and he called my room and Veronica and Todd's room. I called the other rooms, and when I told my mother she was barely able to say, "We'll be there."

The doctors worked on him as Billy and I waited. I told Billy that the family was coming and that everything would be fine. Billy looked at me with a very serious expression and told me, "Dad's tough, I'm sure he'll survive but I don't know if everything will be fine."

I asked him what he was talking about. He told me about how our father isn't going to change and whether it was a stroke or a heart attack, he would keep drinking and eating unhealthily. One of his exact sentences was, "We both know how much he loves bacon."

I didn't want to hear another word, "Billy, let's agree that he's going to pull through and shut up."

There was another awkward silence for the next few minutes, until the family got there, but not the whole family.

Cathy had asked Jason to stay with the kids at the hotel, and we could hear our mother and Cathy arguing down the hall. Cathy began talking about how children shouldn't be exposed to this type of thing, then my mother cut her off saying that this was their grandfather, and they should be here. Veronica and Todd showed up with our kids and Cathy began saying, "Why would you bring them? They don't need to see this type of thing because it would really upset them."

I began talking to Veronica, and although I was unnerved at the same time, put on my cool, calm, and collected face and tone of voice. I thanked her for being there and bringing the kids, and she stood there unimpressed and asked to speak to me in private. Once we got down the hall and into a nook, she said, "Charles, this trip was a disaster, don't ever invite me or the kids to any of your family's vacations ever again!"

I got defensive saying that I had no way of knowing that Dad would be in the hospital, but she said, "That's just the icing on this disaster of a cake."

Suddenly Todd came around and said that we could visit him now. This just felt like chaos, with one problem after another, after another after another.

We went into my father's room, and he seemed a little out of it when Billy asked him how he was doing and he said that he felt really weak. All of his words were a struggle to understand with the left side of his face paralyzed. My mother picked the worst possible time to start nagging, and she began telling him, "Barry Melvoy, if I told you once, I told you a thousand times, that your drinking and all that bacon would come back to bite you."

Billy tried to stop her saying, "Mom, this isn't the right time for this."

She continued saying, "Then when is the right time? For years I told him don't drink and don't eat so many chips, bacon and all of those other salty things, but he just wouldn't stop."

I grabbed her by the wrist and pulled her outside, "Mom, you are kicking a man that is down, look you and him are divorced so he is not your responsibility anymore, so leave him alone."

She asked me whose side I was on and I told her that I was trying to do what's best for everyone. She rolled her eyes saying, "Since when?"

I asked her what she was talking about and she continued by saying, "Well Charles, in my day, a father who left the state was called a deadbeat Dad."

I was pulsing with rage and responded, "How dare you call me a deadbeat Dad. I pay child support, I talk to them when I can and I didn't leave the state for no reason. I am in Nevada protecting our damn country!"

I stopped myself from flying off the handle and going even deeper into an angry rant. She then responded, "Well call it whatever you want, but another man is raising your children and it's because you aren't there."

I stared a hole through her for a couple seconds before I walked back into the room and told my father that I would be back tomorrow to talk to the doctor.

I stormed out of that hospital room so angry. My father nearly died and my mother accused me of being a deadbeat Dad, and it felt like my head was getting ready to explode. After I went back to my hotel room, Hashani and Tracy were still there watching TV. By this point it was probably 2:00 am, so I told them that I was tired as hell and we were going to the hospital tomorrow. Hashani spoke up and said, "You can do what you want but I want nothing to do with that old bigot."

With that insult, Hashani was about to hit my last nerve.

I responded saying, "He is a great man, a war hero, a man that deserves respect."

She obviously disagreed and I told her to get out. That night I didn't just go to bed mad, I went to bed enraged, and I don't even know how I fell asleep at all.

The next day as planned, Tracy and I went to the hospital to see my father and he was looking really frail. I spoke to the doctor about what it would take to get him better, and he told me that because of how quickly he was spotted, he should make close to a full recovery, but it would take a lot of time and a great deal of care. The doctor specifically said that he would need rehab just to get walking again. It was right then and there that I knew he had to come live with me, so I would get him back on his feet. The problem was that this would be the end of his job in Flint and no one else seemed to care enough to take on this task.

So I decided that I would take on this task. At first, he wasn't sure about getting the property ready for sale, which would be a challenge in and of itself. I figured out that his savings and the proceeds of the house would be enough to pay for his rehab and then some. Beyond that he wouldn't be alone so much and maybe this could keep his drinking under control.

However, arranging all of this from a distance was going to be quite the challenge. I didn't fully realize just how hard this was going to be for a lot of different reasons. The one thing I was sure of though was that our family had so many fractures in it that even the Happiest Place on Earth couldn't put it back together.

CHAPTER 29

RE-ELECTION, REJECTION, REFLECTION

My 35th birthday came around just after we got back to Nevada. My father wasn't too fond of having to be pushed around in a wheelchair because he was a proud man, and to him this was a deep humiliation. Although he probably took comfort in knowing that no one who knew him was seeing him like this, I did hear him grumble quite a bit about the whole situation. I made calls to Michigan to find a real estate agent who could help us sell the house and was willing to make all of the long-distance phone calls back to me. Helping my father bathe was really hard to deal with, but thankfully we found a really good home-care worker named Grace to help him.

While I was at work I began to feel torn; part of me was getting tired of looking at all of these screens which rarely had anything on them, while wondering if my father was okay. The hard part was discovering that my mother didn't want to help my father at all with any of the work cleaning up the house or anything, which was a nightmare. How do you clean up a house when you live halfway across the country from it? Jason reluctantly stepped up and agreed to hire a moving crew to help with everything. However, my father and I would still need to sort everything out together once he was a little more mobile.

He had a lot of hard work to do, but he felt like he had lost everything, his health, his job, and pretty soon all he wanted to do was drink. He was sober for the first month or so, because he couldn't go anywhere, but eventually he got well enough to move his wheelchair and went to the liquor store. When I came home that night he was watching TV and barely coherent. That August and September, I had to make weekend trips to Michigan to help organize the contents of the house. Cathy was nowhere to be found and Billy came up on the second or third weekend. We had done a lot of work cleaning up the basement, but more work needed to be done. A lot of stuff builds up when you live in a house for over forty years.

I remember Billy and I finding boxes of our old toys, including a train set that Billy and I had saved up money to buy together. He was four and I was nine and I did most of the work, but he did help and he was still a little kid so I let it slide. When he came downstairs we talked for a little while, and things were still good with Hashani and him and because my father was upstairs, she didn't come with Billy. She was so mad at our father that she didn't want to be within fifteen feet of him, even though Hashani's father had come to know Billy and accept him. This contrast didn't make my father look very good.

I remember Billy saying that I should keep the train, after all I did most of the work to earn it in the first place, and I was impressed that he remembered that. He went on to say that this house was going to be hard to say goodbye to. I didn't want to think about it so I proposed we talk about something good, like Ronald Reagan being re-elected in a couple of months. Billy didn't share my enthusiasm and suggested that we change the subject.

I shook my head, thinking to myself, "Was he really supporting Mondale – Jimmy Carter's Vice President? The country was getting better and this guy wanted to drag us back to 1979's oil shortages, to hell with that!"

Over the next several minutes, we finished boxing up what we wanted and took it upstairs. As the weeks went by, I was getting worn out, but thankfully my father was showing signs of improvement, but those were slow and gradual. I remember taking the model trains home and thinking that someday soon I would show these to Randy and Matthew, because boys love trains. It really sparked some of my happier memories; I reminisced over the memory of playing with the train and that train going around and around and only stopping when I wanted it to.

Finally, around the beginning of October the house was finally cleaned up and they began showing it to prospective buyers. I promised my father that he would get the money and then he could find a nice place in Nevada where he could live the rest of his life. He wasn't too receptive to the idea, after all he was sixty, he had lived in Michigan his whole life. He didn't know anyone in Nevada besides Grace, the guy behind the counter at the liquor store, and myself, and certainly was in no condition to live on his own.

I remember one day I came home and he told me that he had walked from his wheelchair to the bathroom by himself and didn't need to hold on to anything. I knew how proud of a man he was and how badly he didn't want to sell his house, so I asked him to show me. As he was walking, I began to notice his legs getting shaky, especially his left one. He made it there, looked in the mirror and even though he was breathing heavy, his face was red because of the extra effort. A smile came across his face, and he turned to me and said, "See, you don't need to sell the house, I'll be fine in Ann Arbor."

He took a deep breath before continuing, "Pretty soon I'll be good enough to go back to work and everything will be fine."

I knew that the exercises annoyed him, and he hadn't exercised in years. When he came home, he wanted to have dinner, read, watch TV, talk a little, and that was it, because his time was his. I asked him, "Who would be helping you with your exercises in Michigan?"

He said, "You just saw me walk fifty feet. I'm fine now, and besides I'm tired of waiting for you to come home every day so I can do things."

I looked at him in disbelief as he was in severe denial about how bad of shape he was in, so I had to lay down some tough love. "Dad, that was forty feet at most, and you were winded when you got here. I was more mobile after the surgery that got the bullet out of my leg. Besides, the doctor said your recovery would be at least six to eight months, which means we will be in the dead of winter. So how are you going to shovel the driveway, especially if there is a snowstorm and your legs were shaking walking forty feet!"

He got really upset because I was telling him the exact opposite of what he wanted to hear, because he didn't want to hear that he couldn't do all of the things that he used to, especially the things he took pride in. When I said at the beginning that he told me what being a man was in the traditional sense, here is an example: when I was a kid he would get me and eventually Billy to help with the shovelling the snow out of the driveway. He told me that shovelling snow out of the driveway was the man's job, and if the man of the house wasn't doing it, he is either a sissy or injured. There was no third category, and he told me a dozen times that hiring a snowplow was a waste of money. It seems petty, but things like that meant a lot to him and me telling him that he couldn't do it anymore was hard for him to take, and in some ways he felt like it was an insult to his manhood.

His face got even redder as he began to rant about how he had worked hard all his life and he had decided I wasn't going to take anything more from him. I was trying to calm him down, but he would have none of it and in his mind he was taking a stand and wasn't going to let his home be taken from him. I quickly lost my patience and began yelling back saying, "Shit happens in life but you get back up and you charge forward."

He then said, "Then let me do it in my own damn house. I will get a lawyer on your ass if you sell that house."

I began yelling back saying, "I don't want you to die trying to do something you can't do anymore."

He yelled back and saying, "Don't tell me what I can't do, you don't know what I can't do."

He took a deep breath and stared right into my eyes like I haven't seen since I was a teenager, "If you sell that house, you're no longer my son and when I die you won't get a dime!"

He wheeled himself into his room and slammed the door. I thought about that for the entire rest of the day, wondering, "How could he not see that he was setting himself up for serious problems? How could he say that he would disown me and get a lawyer after me? I'm simply looking out for him the way he looked out for me. When we went out fishing he would grab me by the shoulder if he thought I was leaning too far so I wouldn't fall in. When I got home Vietnam with the bullet in my leg, he was always telling me not to hurt myself. How could he not see that I was trying to do the same thing for him?"

The lawyer threat really concerned me and since I didn't speak legalese I knew that I needed help. Thankfully we had a phone book in the office and during my lunch break I called a lawyer to ask about what options I had. The lawyer told me that as long as his name was on the deed and there was no mortgage, and he didn't have any mental conditions that would cause him to not be functional, the only way to take that house from him was imminent domain. I knew right then and there that there was nothing legally I could do to stop it, and I only had one option left. I called Billy, which was a long shot, but desperate times call for desperate measures. I just had this vision in my head of my father going out one day in December to shovel the driveway and slipping on the ice, or having a heart attack or another stroke and breaking his hip on the cement and possibly freezing to death before anyone helped him. The thought was hard to bear and I just had to do something to stop that from happening. I knew what it felt like to lose people close to me and I wasn't ready to let go of my father Barry Melvoy.

My conversation with Billy was basically him telling me to try to see where he's coming from and try to show that I respect him as an adult, and validating his concerns. I resisted the urge to say, "Say it English doc." I got the rough idea, but Billy made it very clear that it still may not work and that not knowing where our father's head was at made it so he couldn't be sure of the result.

So, the first Friday evening after our earlier argument, I came home with his favourite case of beer. He looked at me puzzled, "I thought you didn't want me to drink, what are you up to?"

I told him that I wanted to talk to him man to man, and I didn't want a repeat of the other night. He said okay as he cracked open his first one, and reminded me to put the rest in the fridge so they wouldn't get warm. We had a long talk as I tried to tell him that I just wanted him to be safe and that I was just looking out for him as he did for me. He responded by saying that a father is supposed to look out for his son, but the father should look out for himself.

I tried to spin it a little bit, "It doesn't matter who is the father and who is the son, what matters is we're family, and family looks out for family."

He told me that it does matter, "I'm not going to be some invalid; I'm not one of those lifeless mumbling old farts that can't wipe his own ass anymore."

I got defensive saying that I never said he was. He told me it was great that we can agree he is not a helpless old man who can live by himself and that there was no need to sell his house. I finally conceded and said, "Could you at least wait until the spring? Then you will be all better by the time the snow comes again and mowing the lawn will be some outside practice."

This was my last-ditch effort, and he looked at me with conviction and said, "The boys from the VFW (Veterans of Foreign Wars) are expecting me this Thanksgiving and I'm going to walk in there with my head held high."

I never thought I would resort to this, but I actually got down on one knee as he finished off the beer he was drinking "Dad, please wait, the next year you can walk into the VFW with your head held high, why can't you wait?"

He began to get upset, "Because I'm doing better now and will be fine by then. I walked fifty feet on my own and in two months I will be able to walk in there good as new. I already booked my plane ticket and I'm leaving November 10th."

My heart sank when I realized that he wasn't going to stop for anything. He only had a month until November 10th and by then he wouldn't even have Grace to help him.

The next few weeks I saw him get a little bit better but he still struggled. He was becoming harder for Grace to work with and he fell on a few occasions, getting a scratch on his right forearm and a small bruise on his left knee, but otherwise the falls weren't too bad. I knew he still wasn't ready but I still couldn't legally stop him. All I could do was step back and hold my breath, which was a subtle helplessness that I couldn't stand.

The election coverage was a very helpful distraction at this time and the good news was that with all of these polls that were starting to air, we could find out that Ronald Reagan seemed to be who the majority of Americans believed should win, and I kept thinking about that and how great that would be. The only question was how would that turn out in the electoral vote? As the election date, November 6th, drew closer and closer, it was so hard to think that something so good and something so bad, were both coming in the same week.

Finally, the day arrived, and I came home around 6:00 pm which, was 8:00 pm on the east coast, and the polls had already started closing. I had taken part of the day off and made sure to cast my ballot. We turned on the TV, and my father and I had three cases of beer ready. I had talked with all the guys about it at work and there had been a little bit of concern that if Mondale won, he might scale down our defenses which could include us losing our jobs. If you think one guy will take away your job, it's so easy to want the other guy to win, no matter what.

As the polls were closing we saw victory after victory for Reagan, state after state, and I was just so relieved that the door was being shut on Mondale. My concern about Mondale winning enough of the electoral vote to win the presidency was not only unfounded, but what really happened was the exact opposite. Reagan had fifty-eight-point-eight percent of the popular vote and had won almost every state in a massive electoral vote landslide, which was one of the biggest in American history. Five hundred and twenty-five out of five hundred and thirty-eight, I don't know what the percentage is but it was an absolute takeover and my father and I could not have been more thrilled.

Suddenly, around his sixth beer he blurted out, "Nothing can stop Reagan and nothing can stop me."

I didn't say anything, but that was so hard to hear because even though I had had several beers, I still knew he was making a mistake and there was nothing I could do about it.

You might be wondering where Tracy was during all of this. Well this is what happened: She and I began spending less and less time together as I always seemed to be busy with work or looking after my father. Between going back and forth to Michigan and medical appointments and other arrangements I had to make, it left less and less time for her. I remember it happened the week before Halloween, when I called to invite her to go out for dinner. She responded that she couldn't make it and felt like I had abandoned her, and so she had just found someone else. My jaw nearly fell through the floor, as I thought with dread, "No, not again."

She told me that we had drifted apart and that pretty soon we wouldn't be anything. I got really bothered by this, and asked her what the hell she was talking about. I had to spend time helping my father, and I couldn't just abandon him.

She responded back, "But you could abandon me?"

I asked her why she thought I was going to abandon her, and she said, "You have no time for your own kids. You and I saw each other three times since we came back from Disney World. I'm just not important to you."

I let my tongue slip, "Damn it, you're sounding like Veronica."

She began getting mad back, "This isn't about gifts, it's about time; gifts mean nothing compared to time, clearly I didn't mean enough to you to get either."

I responded, "So what, I'm supposed to drop everything so you can go to the mall?"

She abruptly hung up the phone after saying, "Goodbye Charles."

I didn't know what to think, as it was all so overwhelming and I didn't know what to do. I didn't have a whole lot of time to think about it. After dropping my father off at the airport and helping him get to the plane, I went home and for the first time in a few months I really had time to think about everything that had happened the last few months. I couldn't believe that in just a few months we had gone from having kisses that set off fireworks, to it just ending with barely a whimper.

CHAPTER 30

INTOLERABLE & INEVITABLE

During the remaining few weeks, life suddenly became duller, and my father and I only talked a couple of times on the phone over the remainder of the year. I finally made the decision to pick up the phone and call Veronica, who had been mad at me since the trip to Disney World. Todd picked up the phone, apparently she wasn't home, and I could tell because he was surprisingly blunt, "Look Charles, she wasn't happy with you after the trip, she wishes we never went."

I responded, "Well that makes two of us."

She apparently had become friends with Hashani over the last few months and they were mad as hell at my father, as well as at Cathy and Jason because of the way their kids were acting and treated our kids. It was eventually agreed upon that they were going to have Christmas with Billy and Hashani, so if I wanted to come I would have to ask them.

With some degree of reluctance, I called Billy and asked if I could come, and then he asked one question, "Are you bringing anyone?"

I told him, "No, Tracy and I have broken up."

He responded, "Well, I'm sorry to hear about that, but it wasn't Tracy I was worried about, it was Dad. I don't want him bringing his prejudices into our house."

I told Billy that I wasn't interested in bringing a fight to Christmas. I had enough of that in my life already. So, that was the agreement: no fighting, Merry Christmas.

I wasn't simply abandoning my father though, I arranged to have a day or two with him a few days after my dinner with my kids, Billy and Hashani. When the day finally came, Veronica wasn't exactly happy to see me but she and I agreed to a truce for the kids. The part of this that I wasn't expecting was that Hashani's parents and her two brothers were there. I don't remember their names, but we got along fairly well. What I found surprising was the crucifix that the younger brother wore. It wasn't the basic crucifix I was used to seeing, its proportions were different and actually looked fancier.

Hashani's father asked me a few questions and was impressed that

I was an army man and had risen to the rank that I had. Christmas basically was happening without a hitch and at one point after a few drinks I had said to Hashani's brother, "So what's it like back in... uh what is your country called again?"

He rolled his eyes and said, "It's called Sri Lanka, and it is a small beautiful country right next to India. I don't remember much about it because we left when I was a child and we haven't been back there since. The two things I can tell you though are you don't see snow except on TV and people are a lot more grateful for what they have because many of them don't have much."

I just nodded my head just to move the conversation along. I was trying not to tell him that I wasn't sure how to respond.

The last thing I remember from that evening was Billy asking if wanted to play a game of chess. I told him that I was tired and wasn't interested anyway.

I told him, "Thanks, you have put on a nice Christmas."

He asked me for a favour and we went upstairs into his room, where he then looked out the door to make sure no one was around. "Charles, on January 1st I am going to propose to Hashani, and before I do I need your word as a man that you aren't going to tell her."

I immediately said, "No problem."

He then continued, "I also need you to not tell Dad about it because we are not inviting him to the wedding."

I heard this and I was instantly torn between my loyalty to my father and my loyalty to my brother, and you can guess to whom I was more loyal.

I looked at my brother with confusion and shock, and I asked him, "What? Are you serious? He's our father you cannot cut him out of our lives!"

Billy said to me, "Charles, he has been against our relationship from day one. Not to mention like many alcoholics, his stress drives him to be even more self-destructive and he will make a big scene and I don't want that to ruin our day."

I took this very seriously, "Don't you think I was a little afraid of him making a scene at my wedding to Veronica? Yes, I was worried about that but we are a family and not being invited to his son's wedding is a giant slap in the face."

Billy took a deep breath and said, "This was a very hard decision for me. I didn't want it to come to this but I know that he will cause problems, because he will get drunk, then disrupt the entire event and insult Hashani and her family. I wish it didn't have to be this way, but that is our reality."

I looked at him with disgust, as if he was betraying our family. "So, you're choosing her family over ours. You're running away again, which was just like you did when you were a kid."

He spoke up, "I'm not running from anything, I am trying to keep the peace."

I was having none of it though. "I'm not going along with this. If your wedding is too good for our father, then it's too good for me."

I began to walk away when he put his hand on my shoulder and said, "Charlie wait!"

I turned around to say, "You know damn well my name is Charles."

He paused but continued, "I'm not trying to destroy a family, I'm trying to build a new one, but I can't build a family with people that don't want to be together."

I was done listening, "Yeah, a boy who rejects his father isn't building anything."

He said to me as I was going towards the stairs, "I'm not a boy, I'm a thirty-year-old man!"

I said, "Yeah right!"

I stayed for the rest of the evening, and when I came down the stairs I was slightly tempted to ruin his surprise to Hashani, but I decided to keep my mouth shut and not ruin that part of the surprise. When Veronica asked me what was wrong, I told her that Billy was disappointed by the election results and he and I didn't see eye to eye on that. I think she bought it because even though it was a lie, she knew our politics well enough that it was not only believable but also likely.

I visited my father a few days later and he was doing okay. He had managed to get his job back at the GM plant, and his union fought for him and got him back in right where he left off. I was still worried about him standing for that long, and wondered was he really up to it? I knew I had to tell him what happened with Billy, but I was trying to figure out the right way to say it. After all, how do you tell a sixty-year-old man who is recovering from a stroke that his son is getting married and that he isn't allowed to be there? I took a deep breath and began to tell him what Billy told me. I should have picked a better time, and he was holding a glass beer mug over a wood floor. His jaw dropped and his glass fell out of his hand as he sat speechless. My father was not a quiet man, but a blunt individual who always told people what he thought, but for a good minute he just sat there in stunned silence.

I finally asked, "Dad, Dad?"

That was when he began to say something, "Well, I don't want to be at some crazy foreigner wedding anyway, they might be using trained monkeys to serve the food. I got to tell you, back in my day, not only was this not allowed, but people knew better than to mix oil and water. If they have kids, what the hell will they be? I don't know, they won't even know. They'll be confused. They won't look like the mother they won't look like the father, they'll just be lost."

I looked at him and said, "I know the world is going crazy, how did everything end up like this?"

After a pause, he said, "I don't want to talk about this anymore."

We ended up talking about other things. In a way I knew my father was wrong, but I had too much respect for him, after all he was family and you don't abandon your family, especially when that man is your father and a war hero.

When I asked, "how did everything end up like this?" I was talking more about how it got to the point of us cutting each other out of our lives.

After I went home I spoke to McLachlin about the whole situation, he basically took my father's side and said that Billy should know that his father is only looking out for him. After he asked, "Is Billy the one who's the democrat?"

I reluctantly responded, "Yes."

He responded, "No wonder, Liberals keep trying to change things that shouldn't be and don't realize how we got this far. It wasn't by smoking reefer or whatever they call it now and singing hippie songs, it was by men being men, women being women and everyone looking out for their own and protecting their own. The world is going crazy Melvoy, but at least we know that's the next battle. Melvoy, once the Soviets are gone, that's going to be the battle fought. It's going to be a culture war, a battle of ideas inside our country for its very soul."

That speech by McLachlin strengthened my resolve and I was able to go into work every day for the first several weeks of 1985, as determined as ever that I was doing the right thing. Unfortunately, people around me had to bring up Valentine's Day and I remember during the week or so before it, wishing I could just put my fingers in my ears so I wouldn't have to hear about it. When you are alone and have bad memories of the Valentine's Days of the past, being reminded about it by people who think it is just wonderful, makes your skin crawl.

Since Christmas, there had been silence between Billy and myself. My phone calls with the kids were also getting pretty short, and when your daughter isn't interested in talking to you, it's hard to deal with. I sent Randy a card with $25.00 for his ninth birthday which was a lot of money, but he seemed to be the only one who liked talking to me and still thought of me as something. Matthew turned seven not long after but he always seemed like he was trying to watch TV while talking to me. The phone calls were bittersweet but I knew that if I didn't make them, I would miss everything. I remember talking with Randy, who often talked about how much he loved Hulk Hogan and how he was a Hulk-a-maniac. It reminded me of when I was a kid and in a way, it was so great to see my son looking up to someone who was standing up for America in a big theatrical way, but still the message seemed right.

Things were going well where I was at work, despite my taking time off here and there, and they were very understanding and actually gave me very positive reviews. However the problem was that I felt like there was something more that I could be doing. I didn't go through all of that hard work in the field to simply sit behind a computer, and I felt that I needed to do something else. I had learned a lot of different things about our missile defense system and the positives and negatives of the system. The hard part was looking at that screen every day and thinking if only there was a way to have a shield that would block the missiles before they finished crossing the ocean.

Other times I used to think that it would be great if we could launch our missiles to neutralize their missiles so that we wouldn't lose anyone. I even wondered what would happen if our missiles were faster, so fast that if we got an advance warning, we could launch first and stop them before they could push their button. I began thinking about shifting into another field, and contemplated shifting my career, either going back to the military or maybe something more exciting like the secret service? Or the CIA? Or the FBI? It wasn't about money, and I was doing very well, but the issue was that I wanted something to broaden my knowledge of our battle with the Soviets. Before I could truly set my mind on a particular path, I got the phone call that I had feared, one of those calls that you hope never happens…

CHAPTER 31
★
CHURCH BELLS RING

It was Tuesday March 5, 1985 and my father had been somewhat careful during January and February, but a very bad storm with plenty of freezing rain had started that night. Since the snow didn't start until about 4 or 5:00 am, he thought that he would shovel the driveway so he could still make it to work that day. When a nearly sixty-one-year-old man who isn't in good shape goes out to shovel the driveway, and it is dark and slippery and he is alone with no witnesses, that is a dangerous game. He'd probably had some drinks earlier that night so that didn't help anything. Around 7:00 am one of our neighbours went out to shovel his driveway and he saw this large mass in the snow on our driveway. He was concerned so he went over and found our father unconscious, buried under half an inch of snow. As hard as it was coming down, he must have been out there alone like that for several minutes. If he hadn't been wearing his thick old jacket and been tough as nails as he was, he would have died right there. I couldn't believe what I was being told – just the type of situation I was afraid of.

Since his divorce, I had been listed as the next of kin so I was the first to be informed, and Jason and Cathy didn't want to be seen as disloyal to my mother. I knew that I had to fly out there, and I was worried about how this would affect work. I asked McLachlin if this was going to be okay and he told me something that really stunned me, "Melvoy, some of the other guys who are just below me aren't fond of you taking the time off that you have, but I have stood up for you over and over again because I know how good you are and you wouldn't leave if you didn't have to."

I thanked him again, and was sure that I always had McLachlin, and that he would always be there for me. That gave me a great deal of comfort in this trying time, despite everything that had happened with my family, I had one person who was always there for me.

I flew out to Michigan and walked into that hospital, and if it weren't for being a hospital with a very different layout, I would have had severe déjà vu. I asked to speak to the doctor, who told me that my father had suffered severe brain damage, and they were struggling to keep the swelling down and he was effectively in a coma. They were barely keeping him alive, and I asked her if there was anything that could be done. The doctor said that they had already done the tests and basically there appeared to be barely any brain activity at all.

When he fell it was just at the wrong angle and smacked his head on the cement, the several minutes or so lying on the driveway allowed the brain's internal bleeding to occur which only made things worse. Had the neighbour waited another fifteen minutes, he would have been dead right there. I asked if there was any surgery that could be done, basically anything they did would be guesswork at this point. The hardest part was when she told me, "I know this isn't easy to say, but realistically all you can do is say your goodbyes and decide when you're ready to let him go."

I asked to see him, and she took me to his room. I can still remember that square grey sign with white letters that said, "Room 404" and seeing him hooked up to those machines, and hearing the occasional bleep from the heart monitor. I remember wanting to cry there but hearing his voice in my head from when I was a kid, "Men need to be as tough as a rock, no matter how hard you get hit by a person or life, show no weakness, charge forward no matter what."

I knew that I would have to call everyone else to let them know what was happening. I realized that if I were pulling the plug I would have to arrange a funeral, which I had never done before. I had no idea what to do, as I had so much to think about and quite frankly I didn't have time to grieve. After careful consideration, I called our local minister first, who said that he had heard that my father had fallen but had no idea it was that bad. As I hung up the phone, he said he would be praying for me. I knew that telling Cathy, Jason, and my mother would be difficult but it would have to be done.

I remember arguing with myself about calling Billy. After all, he had banned our father from his wedding, by doing that he may as well have disowned him. When I called Cathy's house, our mother picked up and after trying to give me a guilt trip and why it had been so long since I called her, I cut her off and said, "Mom, I don't have time for this, my father, your ex-husband fell, he's in a coma and doesn't have long to live."

She was speechless, and although it wasn't really very long, it felt like an eternity, before she managed to eke out an, "Oh. I will have to tell Cathy and Jason."

That was the end of that conversation, and I finally had to decide on whether or not to tell Billy. I finally came to the conclusion that all I had to do was call during the day and leave a message on their answering machine and it would save me a hassle of a phone call. I called Veronica and Todd because I wanted our kids to know about the situation, remember that for later.

So later that day Cathy and my mother showed up, Jason had to work the late shift and couldn't make it. They said their farewells, I looked at my mother and realized that despite everything that had happened, she still cared for him and knowing that she would never see him again was too much. I asked Cathy why she didn't bring the kids, and she said that this would be too intense for them and that pissed me right off. Her oldest daughter was thirteen, so how the hell was that too young? Here she was sheltering them from reality again.

We got into an argument as I talked about how they should pay their respects, but she said she didn't want to traumatize them and this might be hard for them.

I lost it and said, "Of course it's hard, their grandfather is almost dead, but guess what life isn't always pleasant." I lifted up my pant leg showing the scar from the bullet that went into my leg, so long ago, "This was unpleasant," I pointed to my nose that my father broke during our fight on the lawn, "this was unpleasant, and dealing with life's other problems is unpleasant, but you can't protect them from the real world forever! The world is a very unpleasant place with people who would blow us up right now if they thought they could get away with it. Gangs, drug dealers, and child molesters walk the streets and no matter how many we lock up, there's still plenty more."

A nurse came in asking me to keep it down, as I was disturbing the other patients so I finished in a quieter voice, "Life is a trip through hell and no matter how many Disney movies you watch and how many smiley face stickers you put on their homework, it doesn't change that!"

I had pointed to our father lying there unconscious, as I stormed out, leaving Cathy and my mother just stunned at the fury I had unleashed on them.

I remember driving home white knuckled, blood boiling, just fixating on what was happening and how everyone was hiding from reality. I felt like I was the only one that knew how to stare reality in the face and say, "I'm still standing, take your best shot."

After the hospital, I went back to my father's house knowing what I had to do the next day, I didn't even want to think about that situation until tomorrow. So I went into the fridge, my father still had most of a case of beer left and I figured what the hell and I began chugging them back. I literally drank until I passed out, something I hadn't done since my early twenties. I woke up with a headache, and looking outside at the sun shining a bright light off the snow didn't help one bit either.

Melvoy's Railroad

I went to the hospital that day trying like hell to keep myself together, as it is hard to find an analogy that fits a situation like this. You know what you have to do, but you don't want to do it. The only thing that comes to mind was that first confirmed kill I made in Vietnam, that man was suffering and if I had left him there he would have writhed in agony for a long time. So, I took a deep breath and pulled the trigger and just like that it was over. I almost missed my turn at the corner because I was thinking so much about that moment.

I eventually reached the hospital around 11:00 in the morning, and I spoke to the doctor and asked her what was happening. She said everything was the same and told me, "If you want to pull the plug, you will have to sign the legal releases."

I agreed and she told me that she was really sorry. As I sat there waiting for these forms, every second was just a little bit harder as my impatience grew more and more.

Finally one of the orderlies brought me the forms and I began reading through them; I never dreamt that this would happen, that I would have to pull the trigger on my own father. I kept trying to just force my way through it but it wasn't working. I finally made it through the forms and signed and initialled the various spots. I handed it over and I went into my father's room and sat there next to his bed, knowing he couldn't hear me, knowing that the man I knew was gone. It was just agony looking at him so helpless like that. What do you say to someone who you care for so much but can't hear you? I just pretended that he could hear me, really it was all I could do. "Dad, you taught me what being a man was, you taught me almost everything I knew. Above all you always told me to stand up and fight for myself, my family and my country."

By this point I was in tears with a pain running through my jaw, struggling to say goodbye to this man who I loved and respected so much. "I wish...I was half the father that you were and I am so sorry that the others can't see...what a great man you were."

The nurses came in, and with a lump the size of a golf ball in my throat I told them that I had to leave and they could just do it. I didn't want them to see me crying, after all I was a grown man.

As I got into my car I was feeling overwhelmed, everything from angry, sad, frustrated and everything in between. The cold air that allowed me to see my breath didn't help anything. I ended up going back to his house and I must have replayed those moments in my head over and over again. I don't know why exactly, at this point I probably never will, all I knew was that I had to plan a funeral and I was in a mindset that didn't want to do anything.

Chapter 31 : Church Bells Ring

I didn't enjoy having to choose the casket, I remember just boiling at seeing some of these fancy caskets with all of these other pointless bells and whistles. At one point, the guy mentioned that some of the caskets that I was looking at were of lesser quality and may not do the service justice. I was not in the mood for manipulative sales tactics like this, and remember staring a hole through the guy. He immediately did a complete reversal, and he knew that if he kept taking those underhanded cheap shots, I would have kicked his ass right there. We settled on an oak casket, I had to make dozens of phone calls, and aside from the minister, no one seemed to be interested in helping. I had to twist Jason's arm just to get him to have the reception in his original Game Night location. I had to tell Veronica, and to her credit, she said that Todd, her and the kids would be there, although she could barely even eke out an, "I'm sorry for your loss."

As mad as I was at a lot of different people and things, what really set me off was my phone call with Billy and Hashani. I remember most of that conversation, when I told Billy when the funeral was and he reluctantly said that he and Hashani wouldn't be coming. I remember asking him, "What the hell are you doing that could possibly be more important than this?"

He responded that he and Hashani were planning the wedding and that they already had scheduled a meeting with a photographer. I remember telling him, "So what? Then re-schedule, when is your wedding?"

He told me June 1st, I told him, "That's plenty of time."

He then tried to tell me that it was more complicated than that. I asked him, "What the hell is so complicated? You go, you pay your respects, you talk to some people at the reception, eat a sandwich, go home, the end."

He told me that Hashani wanted nothing to do with it and that funerals are to honour the dead, and there was nothing about our father worth honouring. That was when I flew off the handle and told Billy, "Get that bitch on the phone right now!"

He immediately tried to calm me down, but I was having none of it. She knew nothing about him and she had no right telling anyone, let alone her future husband, that he couldn't go to his own father's funeral. He didn't want to put her on, until finally I said, "Damn it Billy, stop protecting her, put her on the phone right now!"

Finally, she came on and said, "Hi Charles."

I was well past having a nice conversation, "Listen up peaches, Barry Melvoy was a war hero, he was our father who loved all of his children and worked hard every day of his life to give us the best life he could.

I'm going to tell you what Billy doesn't have the nerve to: he's our father damn it, he can't say anything that offends you now, he's dead, so get over it!"

There was a pause then she said, "Are you done?"

I said, "Yes."

She responded, "Good, so am I."

She then slammed the phone down. I couldn't believe that this horrible woman was keeping Billy away from his own father's funeral. Where was her respect, where was her HONOUR? I took it upon myself to be one of the pallbearers and I remember the pain that I felt knowing that I was carrying this heavy oak casket with my father inside. Everyone I expected to be there was, but when Billy and Hashani didn't show up at the funeral, arguably the hardest day of my life up to that point, I knew that I wasn't going to their wedding. If they weren't going to be here for these church bells, I wasn't going to be there for theirs.

CHAPTER 32

IT'S TIME TO CHANGE COURSE

That spring, especially after the funeral, I began to think more and more about my childhood as a flood of memories came back, like the time my father taught me how to hit a baseball. I remember him telling me about the sweet spot on the bat, how tight or loosely you had to hold it and what happened when I was playing baseball for my team in eighth grade. I hit a great hit, which I thought was a home run and I was moving slowly so I could watch the ball, but unfortunately it wasn't a home run. As soon as I saw it land in the field I realized that I only had a few seconds. I was tagged out by the short stop, just before I could reach third.

I remember my father pulling me aside and saying, "Do you know why that happened?"

I told him that I didn't run fast enough, and he said, "Close, you weren't running fast enough because you were watching that hit. No matter how good you hit it, when you hit the ball you run, the umpires will tell you if it's a home run. Never celebrate before you get the job done. Never."

That stayed with me for a long time and I carried that with me not just in baseball but also in my football days and in a way, the rest of my life. I began to realize that my sons might have been missing out on all that. I didn't know Todd very well and he might have not known anything about sports or other stuff that is important for young men to know. Sure, he could teach them how to be handy because he was a plumber, but that is only one dimension of manhood. I needed to figure out a way to help my country but still be close to my kids. I also hadn't seen and had barely spoken to my daughter since the previous Christmas and those conversations were short and cold.

I was talking with McLachlin about a change in plans and he told me that as much as he enjoyed working with me, and as integral as I was to the team, he would try and figure something out for me. It took a while just to talk him into that because he kept trying to tell me how he needed good men like myself there, and eventually he relented.

A few days later McLachlin got back to me and he told me that he had made some calls on my behalf and found out that they were hiring at the CIA and there was an office in Bakersfield. It sounded like a good opportunity and even though my starting salary wasn't going to pay as much, it still seemed like a great opportunity to be closer to my family, while still protecting the country. If the CIA was on the lookout for spies, taking down a Russian spy would be something that I could be proud of.

What you might be surprised to find out is that the CIA hiring process isn't some big James Bond style stunt test. It starts off with interviews and background checks where they investigate your past behaviour to see if they find patterns of loyalty or disloyalty. You never know who they are talking to, but presumably they are talking to people that know you pretty well. The only person that I know for sure that they spoke to is McLachlin and I will never know how that phone call went, but presumably he spoke well of me.

They gave me a series of tests, problem solving tests and other things of that nature. By the time the tests were over, which took place over a few weeks, they called me and said they wanted to discuss the results with me. As hard as you try not to be nervous, there are times in life when you just can't help it.

I don't remember the name of the two men who interviewed me, but they told me that there were several ways that they examine potential agents. As far as ability to keep confidential information, I had scored ten out of ten, in terms of focus my grade was nine out of ten, and my ability to command was given eight and a half out of ten. My ability to think on my feet was seven and a quarter out of ten, and so they thought I needed a little more work on being more spontaneous but effective in an emergency. I was doing very well with a little extra work needed, but there were two areas of concern. One of which was my time away in the previous year. I explained that was because of my father's health and they then informed me that if I was assigned to a thirty-day mission spying in Iran or anywhere else, I wouldn't be able to leave if a family emergency occurred. I told them that my father was dead so his health was no longer an issue. They asked about my mother, and I told them she was always in great health and if anything happened to her Cathy and Jason would have to deal with it. They asked me if I would be willing to go off the grid for that long and be without contact with my children or other friends, and I told them that I could and had lived in a different state to do my job in the NORAD base.

They said that their other area of concern was my connection to a couple named Billy and Hashani Melvoy. I said that they were my brother and sister in law, and they probably sensed the disgust in my voice when I said that. The two agents looked at each other for a second, "Well Charles, are you aware of their political activities?"

I rolled my eyes, "I know he's a Democrat, he actually voted for that idiot Mondale last year. Democrats, what can you do?"

The other agent continued showing me a few pictures they had in their file, "Actually Billy and Hashani are actually part of a group of people called Peaceful Tomorrow. Which is a group that sometimes holds protests against military institutions. In fact they were videotaped having a rally for nuclear disarmament in June of last year and even did a short interview on the local news."

I could have crawled under the table in embarrassment; my brother hadn't grown up. He was still a damn hippie. I tried to explain to them that he and I haven't had a lot of interaction in the last six years and had none for eleven years before that. I haven't even spoken to him in months because of him and Hashani abandoning my father.

They went into a separate room to discuss the results. I sat there thinking to myself, "Billy, you better not have screwed me out of this."

The agents came back in to give me their decision. "Mr. Melvoy, given your service to our country, your aptitudes, but also our concerns, we have decided that you will be offered a support role and with time, we will consider giving you a field position if we find one that would meet your personality and your skills." I agreed to it, after all I needed to spend more time with my family. I accepted the job and they gave me a fake job to tell everyone I had.

As far as my family and friends knew, I was a District Manager at a local grocery store chain. It was set up perfectly that if anyone asked, I would be there and if I had to go away, it was to meet with foreign food suppliers, or head office. I was a little bit concerned but at the same time, I figured those extended periods of time would be few and far between, so that when I was home I could spend more time with the family. It seemed like a pretty good plan, and I asked them if I was allowed to disclose to McLachlin that I had gotten the job. They informed me that I was allowed to say that I had the job but anything past that was to be kept purely confidential. I was excited for this new challenge, I had made very good money for the last several years, so even with California's real estate prices I could buy a nice house. By the time I started there, it was July 1985, I had started spending more time with my kids and it seemed like things were beginning to line up.

The biggest obstacle that remained was Veronica and Todd. I hadn't been there on a consistent basis for about four years and I needed to work out an arrangement with them. Veronica basically wasn't interested in sharing the kids and started calling me an absentee Dad, and I was getting more annoyed with each little jab. Todd surprisingly took my side, when he said, "Veronica, it's not like he was passed out in a ditch somewhere. He was working for national defense and now he has found a position close to home. Let's think about what is best for the kids."

I thanked him and Veronica stood up and said, "I am thinking about the kids. You calling once every couple weeks is not the same as being here every day. I don't want the kids to get hurt again."

That was when the argument broke out, "What again, I have a great relationship with the kids, just last week Randy was telling me about the VCR you guys got and how excited he was about it."

She just shook her head saying, "You still don't get it, after all these years you still don't get it."

She walked off to her room and I just threw up my hands in disbelief. Todd turned to me, "Look Charles, I know you care about the kids. Let me talk to Veronica and we'll try and figure something out, maybe we'll try for a couple nights a week and maybe on Saturdays."

I responded with, "Thanks, Todd."

He looked at me and said, "I know there's a lot of bad blood, and you and I literally can't be best friends, but I don't want to come between the children and their father."

I thanked him again and left. I had to admit that he seemed like a decent guy who seemed to have his head on straight.

Eventually he must have said something to Veronica, because she came around and said that she would let me start spending time with the kids on Saturdays. This was helpful, but unfortunately I got the sense that she was just uncomfortable with me being there. It was as if she wanted to forget that I was their father and Todd wasn't. Veronica was the biggest obstacle but she was by no means the only obstacle. Going out for ice cream with the kids was something that seemed like the simplest thing to do, but it became more than I was bargaining for.

Jackie was eleven and it seemed like she was mad at me for every little thing, like it wasn't the right ice cream place, she had better things to do, my two-dollar limit meant she couldn't get the large twist cone, she just didn't want to be there, and nothing was right. Randy and Matthew were happy enough, but it just bothered me that this little girl that I remembered holding in my arms, and "Da-Da" being her first word all those years ago, now wanted nothing to do with me.

Back at work I began to learn about how the intelligence agencies work, like I said there weren't any big explosions or anything like that, it's basically a very covert investigation. My job became taking reports from the field and compiling them for weekly reports for the regional director. Everything was kept separate, and despite being under the same umbrella, the CIA, the FBI, the NSA or any others, were supposed to communicate as little as possible. You were even supposed to minimize communications between CIA offices; the term compartmentalization was the name of the game.

So, the first of the reports I had to compile information from was about Jamaica, a country I knew very little about but I learned quickly. We didn't just have to keep an eye on Cuba, we had to keep an eye on every country. In that era, we had to pay even more attention to the ones that were geographically close to us. They were close and the last thing we needed was another enemy that we had to potentially blockade.

We had agents with their ears on the ground, designed to watch for any growing Communist insurgency. Although it ended up being a non-threat, it's better to look and not find, than to not look and have it emerge.

After I got home I had to practice my story, so that if anyone asked how my job was going, I would have a prepared false story ready for them, and make it sound as realistic as possible. I remember talking about a fake teenager named Eddie who would show up late, but I was always being asked not to fire him because he was the son of my boss' friend. Stories like that make it sound real, and having fake allies and antagonists in a story often allows people to feel like it's more real. I had to spend a decent amount of time memorizing the story and practicing it in front of the mirror, so I would never contradict myself or talk my way into a corner. You don't want to invent a fake girlfriend or other friend, who those closer to you would be interested in meeting.

Over those months, I began to think more about family and how fractured ours was. I was still a little mad at Cathy over what had happened in the hospital with our father but she was still my sister and I needed to keep this family together. So I began talking a little bit more often with Cathy and Jason, and I discovered that not only were they over-protecting their kids, they were bragging about their kids constantly. I remember one of these brag-fests was about Connor getting a B+ in history. I went through the motions while thinking, if it was an A or A+, I would be impressed, but if she thinks that is more than good enough, she will never see any A's from those kids. She began to tell me about how bright her youngest, Melina was, and I remember thinking that every kid seems bright when they're little, so I didn't take it very seriously.

I remember her telling me about how with nine locations, Jason was barely home anymore and she wouldn't know what to do if she didn't have Mom and their housekeeper. After I got through conversations like those, I began to talk to our mother and she began to tell me what she really thought – how she wasn't happy with anybody, and she had complaints for everybody. Whether it was, Billy, Cathy, myself or anyone else, this was a side of her that I don't remember seeing before and it took me a little while to realize that this was who she was turning into.

Before 1985 came to a close, I remember getting a phone call from Jason and he told me that they were opening their tenth location and he was hoping I could come out for it. I couldn't but I wished him all the best. He had bags of money and pretty soon his kids would be able to afford any college. He actually told me that he was hoping that Game Night could become publicly traded in the next few years. He was telling me that because of the work involved he didn't see his partner as much anymore but they were getting a lot done. As much as their brag-fests became a chore to listen to, I still preferred them to talking to Billy and Hashani, especially given their political activities.

Despite these issues, I felt like I was getting back on the right track and maybe someday we would be a big happy family again. As an added bonus, I had started getting close with one of the other report collaborators in the office, whose name was Anita, and she seemed to find me intriguing. She had only ever been in an office, so my old war stories made her eyes light up with excitement, and the stories of me putting guys in line as a Drill Sergeant also showed her my strength and authority. I know this isn't politically correct, but some women love a strong man that knows what he wants and that was Anita down to a T. It was more than a little strange that I was going out with another woman, because back in the day, divorces weren't very common. Finding a new girlfriend when you are thirty-six seemed a little strange, but I got past it pretty quickly.

Our first date was sometime at the beginning of December, when we went out for dinner at a restaurant she liked and despite some of my hesitations about getting into another relationship, she had this magic about her. She made me want to throw caution to the wind and the more I talked to her, the more I wanted to risk whatever I had to be with her. I don't remember the exact moment when it happened but I decided that I didn't care that she was working. She didn't have a man in her life and somehow the fact that she was doing a job that was on the same side as mine, made me re-think the way I had thought about women in the workplace. When that date was over, I remember dropping her off at her apartment, and we had a wonderful kiss at her door.

She then whispered in my ear, "Better than any conversation at the water cooler."

I let out a laugh and I walked towards the elevator. I remember going down that elevator from the seventh floor to the ground floor asking myself, "What if she's the one?"

Christmas that year was simple, and I was invited to Michigan to spend time with Cathy, Jason and the rest of them. I was glad that my own kids weren't there, because Cathy's kids were spoiled even more, not only were the kids being given expensive clothes, but they all had their own rooms, TVs in each of their own rooms, and were being given their own VCRs with VHS tapes that they liked. You have to keep in mind in that 1985, VHS tapes and VCRs were state of the art technology and were not cheap. I kept wondering what would happen when the bubble burst and these kids had to come face to face with the real world.

In any case, this was my first Christmas without my father and another Christmas once again separated from my brother, but I was trying to make do with everyone else. As the New Year took hold I was feeling more optimistic, the economy was going well, I felt like I was making progress with my kids and my new job was working pretty well. I also saw things progressing with Anita and I couldn't help but feel like we were clicking in a very real way. I had changed course and I liked the changes, but of course even the best plans go awry.

CHAPTER 33

WHAT I WAS WAITING FOR... SORT OF

At the CIA, they began having me look into what was happening in Asia, particularly Iraq who at the time was the next-door neighbour to an enemy determined to destroy us – Iran. So keeping eyes on Iraq and maintaining their military strength was very important, because we could help Iraq fight them without putting our own boots on the ground. Some of you may not understand that putting our own boots on the ground was still politically dangerous because Vietnam was still in the back of people's minds. It became known as Vietnam Syndrome and despite all of his hard work, even Reagan couldn't cure it. By the time I began compiling reports, the conflict between Iraq and Iran was in full swing and the questions about what the long-term strategies were began to surface. One of the things that is as true today as it was back then, is that Middle Eastern Geo-politics is a science in and of itself.

While I was trying to figure out that conflict, along with my co-workers, I had another conflict to deal with, and it was the one with my kids, my ex-wife, and her husband. One of my co-workers came into work really upset one day and I asked him what his issue was. He told me he had just bought four tickets to WrestleMania 2, which was happening in Los Angeles. The bad part was he just found out that he was doing a mission during the entire month of April so he would miss it.

Before I knew it, Anita was asking, "Hey Charles, don't your sons love that stuff?"

I said, "Absolutely! Hulk Hogan is their hero."

She then said, "Why don't we go to it?"

It seemed so simple, Anita, myself, Randy and Matthew would go to this event and have a great time.

So I waited a couple days and decided to make a surprise visit to their house on Thursday evening to surprise them with the tickets, where unfortunately everything went awry when I did. First Veronica blew her stack, the kids began yelling and in the process, Jackie had stomped upstairs. I remember hearing Veronica yell, "It's a school night, they'll be dead tired the next day!"

The kids were yelling, "No we won't!"

Melvoy's Railroad

Then as I tried to explain to her that it was an opportunity to spend time with the kids, she lashed back at me. "I don't want you around my kids, and I told them they couldn't wrestle anymore after Matthew got into a fight at school."

I was in disbelief, "When was this?"

She exclaimed, "On Monday, you would know if you were here every day like I am."

I began to lash back, "Well pardon me for trying to do my best under the circumstances!"

Todd asked the boys and her to go upstairs so we could talk without the kids being in the middle and so Veronica could calm down.

I asked, "What happened?"

Todd responded, "Matthew said that some kid was picking on him so he fought back, and the teacher saw what was going on just as he was trying to drop his leg like Hulk Hogan does."

I paused and asked, "Then what happened?"

Todd went on, "They gave him a three-day suspension and when his teacher spoke to us the next day she suggested that we keep him away from violent influences."

I then asked, "What about the kid who started it?"

Todd sighed, "He was given detention for one day and that was it."

My eyes lit up and I said, "Let me get this straight. So our kid gets picked on, he stands up for himself and he gets punished, the kid who started it gets off easy and you just sat there and let it happen?"

Todd reluctantly said, "They take this stuff more seriously now than they used to and they don't want to encourage violence."

I couldn't believe what I was hearing, "Oh I see, don't fight back, just go and tell the teacher, if they are even around. I think they are encouraging victimhood. If he went too far that is one thing, but he shouldn't be punished for standing up for himself."

Todd was always more level-headed, "That is the problem you see, TV is one thing, but Veronica thinks that you are part of the problem, even more than the wrestling."

I thought that my jaw was going to hit the floor, "Me? I don't tell the kids to start fights ever, I tell them to stand up for themselves and to not let themselves be victims."

He sighed again, "How do you tell them to stand up for themselves?"

I looked at him with a cold stare, "Whatever you have to do to protect yourself. I thought we were raising those two boys to be men, not little wimps that can't do anything themselves. Sometimes you have to bring the hammer down, and sometimes you have fight fire with fire, that's life."

Todd said, "Well I disagree with your parenting philosophy."

I cut him off, "It doesn't matter what you think because you aren't a parent, you are just the handyman the mother ran off with."

Finally, Todd's cool demeanour was beginning to break, and he got up and walked to the front door, "Charles, you can leave now."

He turned the knob and opened it, I looked at him with disdain, "See you on Saturday."

He slammed the door behind me as I bristled, "Who was this guy to tell me how to raise my kids? Especially since he was clearly doing it wrong and telling our boys to back down."

During the drive home I remembered all those times I didn't back down and won, and what that did for my confidence and now I realized what they were missing out on. In that moment I truly pitied them and feared for what they might turn into, I thought to myself the last thing the world needed was more people like Billy's clients who can't handle reality and had to be coddled.

At work the next morning, I told Anita what happened and she said to me, "I hope it isn't me, did you tell them I would be there?"

I responded, "I didn't even get that far."

She put her arms around me and kissed me on the lips, when exactly at the wrong moment one of the other guys walked by and said, "Get a room you two."

I rolled my eyes but I said to Anita, "I can't wait for our date tonight."

With a lustful tone, she responded, "Neither can I."

It was an entirely different relationship because instead of keeping the woman I cared about away from my work, we were partners in it. This was the strangest thing and yet it seemed to work so well. When Valentine's Day came, it was so simple. We just went out after work and had dinner at a nice restaurant. I gave her a heart shaped box of candy, and I forget how much it cost, but I could easily afford it. The drama that I used to experience on Valentine's Day with Veronica didn't happen at all and I began to wonder if at long last, after all of these years, Anita was the one.

There was still tension with the family, especially with Veronica, Jackie, and Todd, but thankfully the boys and I were still on good terms. They kept talking about how excited they were for WrestleMania 2. Despite everything I had been through in my life, they were so excited it was like being young again and having a Birthday, Christmas, and the Fourth of July all happening the same day.

One thing that was also going on during the first two months of

Melvoy's Railroad

1986 was my preliminary spy training, most notably how to influence, what to look for, and how to get yourself out of tough situations. I learned if your cover is blown, how you have to fight your way out. This didn't involve running away from explosions, but it involved hand-to-hand combat, and what do you do if your attacker has a gun and you don't? What do you do if you are outnumbered? What do you do if you are in a place that isn't out in the open and there are walls and nooks to hide in? What if you are in a situation with all of the above? I took to it fairly easily as I was already familiar with guns and did not have the hesitation that many people did to pull the trigger. I remember at one point, they asked me, "If you are captured do you A: Escape, B: Kill the Captors, C: Stay where you are, or D: Kill yourself?"

I paused and said, "Could be any of them depending on the situation."

Their smile lit up, "You're correct, which is why we have to train you to know which situation requires which answer."

I felt more ready with each test I passed and felt stronger and more confident in my abilities. At one point, an instructor said, "Melvoy, when it comes to the combat portions of this, you are a natural."

All of that training paid off because one day in March, I was called into the boss's office and he began to lay out my first mission. My boss's name was Mr. Donovan, who was about sixty-two years old, but he was lean and had the energy of a man twenty years younger.

"Melvoy, you're dedicated, you're hard working and you work well with the team, so I think it is time that I found you a mission that will be right up your alley."

I nodded, preparing for the mission. "We have a tip that Noriega may not be doing what he was supposed to be doing down in Panama, and the reason this mission is right up your alley is that I want you to pretend to be an under the table arms dealer. Ask to speak to Noriega, so that you know you are 'secure.' Remember there is no combat here; this is about finding out where the corruption is in his government and seeing how high up it goes. No matter who makes the buy, tell us who it is and what their role is."

I seemed a little bit confused, "If you don't mind me asking, why is this right up my alley?"

Mr. Donovan continued, "One, you can handle the jungle. Any man who does three rounds in Vietnam isn't afraid of the jungle, where some of the demonstrations might take place. Two, your military background means you are already familiar with military grade assault rifles, and the time required training you to use them will be less than many of our lower level agents. We are sending you in a few weeks,

176   Chapter 33 : What I was Waiting For... Sort of

around April 18th, that way you can pay your taxes before you leave."

We both let out a good laugh, and I shook his hand telling him, "Thank you."

Before I could leave the office, he told me one more thing. "Melvoy, you can tell Anita that you are on a mission but you can't say where and why. Melvoy, just be careful how much you tell her because as secure as this agency is, you never know every time you trust someone with information, you have to hope they will handle it the right way and don't have other loyalties."

As April came closer and closer, I began to go over the basic facts of the mission and learning the minor differences in the assault rifles, the prices, the features that they would probably be looking for etc. I rehearsed those sales pitches over and over using my training of which facial ticks to watch for in their reactions. Those are the small little things that people don't even know they are doing that give away what they are really thinking.

The day of WrestleMania 2 finally came, Anita and I picked the kids up from the house, and I asked her to stay in the car to save her the grief that I was sure Veronica would give her. When I got there, Randy and Matthew were thrilled and Veronica stood there, arms crossed giving me a look that could kill. As coldly as possible she said, "Don't bring them back too late, they have to be up for school tomorrow morning."

I rolled my eyes, "Okay Veronica."

As I began to walk out the door, she slammed it behind me and I remember thinking to myself, "After I get back from Panama we are going to have this out once and for all."

That night was fun, and although I don't remember too much of it one thing that stood out was one short match where the Russian and an American were fighting in a flag match and the American won quickly. I thought to myself, "If only defeating the Russians was so easy in real life."

The match where Hulk Hogan beat King Kong Bundy in the steel cage was the main event, and he won and got his hands on the sneaky manager. The crowd loved it, but what I remember most was being arm in arm with Anita who was to my left, and then to my right were my two sons who I cared for so much, on the edge of their seats. When Hulk Hogan slammed King Kong Bundy they leapt to their feet screaming at the top of their lungs and their excitement and the rest of the crowd's excitement was infectious.

I wasn't there for my kids as much as I wish I could have been, but I will always be grateful that I gave them that night. I hadn't seen any of my children that happy in a long, long time. That night we drove them home and they fell asleep during the last half hour, and I was so glad that things had gone so well. We took the kids back, and Veronica stood there in the doorway, angry as can be, and I said, "Well here they are, I'm sure they will be fine for school tomorrow."

She told the kids to get in the house and to get ready for bed. She looked past me to look at Anita, and there was an awkward pause, "Well I will see you on Saturday."

She responded, "Yeah."

Then she slammed the door again, as I just walked on and knew I would deal with it after I came back from Panama.

I had to tell the kids that I was going to Minnesota for a convention and that I would be gone for a few weeks, and explained to them why I wouldn't be able to call. I forget what I told them, but I think Veronica knew I was lying. She knew me too well, and said, "Normally, I would ask what is really going on, but I don't care because I don't even want to see you again."

I shook my head and walked out. I was so tired of this and I had bigger things to worry about than her. I had my first national security mission and there was a possibility that I wouldn't be coming back.

I said my farewell to Anita and I knew that I would miss her so much. The strange thing was I didn't know whether it would be a few days, a week or more, but if this mission went well I knew that the sky was the limit for my country and my job in the CIA.

CHAPTER 34
★
PANAMA!

If anyone thinks that the CIA is a spontaneous institution, guess again, they plan and plan and if they strike, it is usually surgically precise. This was one of the earlier steps of what was a much bigger move. I was just a member of the team and if the report ever came out, my name would be one of dozens involved. In this instance, I wasn't a star but one of the gears of the machine, and if you asked me what the rest of the machine looked like or what its end goal was, I wouldn't have been able to tell you. The best answer I could have given was, "We are doing what we have to do to protect our national interests."

The plane ride was something else, because I had to take a plane to southern Mexico and fly in on something that looked like a half-assed charter plane that would only hold thirty people. Anything "too official" might tip them off after all. From up in the air you could see the coastline, which was a thing of beauty, something right out of a movie. As we got lower, we saw the vast stretches of jungle and the city was coming up in the distance. I knew that this might be a one-way trip, but that if I followed my instructions everything would probably be okay. I had been in a war zone in the jungle and even though it had been well over ten years, I knew that I could survive if such a scenario occurred.

I was greeted at the airport by the one of the other agents who had helped set up the meeting and I had four types of guns that I would be showing them. I would be wearing a wire the whole time to pick up on any clues or anything suspicious. Eventually the moment came when I met their defense purchaser who reported directly to their secretary of defense.

Basically, I was two degrees of separation from Noriega. This was a huge start but I had to go through the motions of telling them what they were buying and why. One of the things that almost caught me was the question, "Are these more than what they have in the U.S. coast guard?"

I proceeded to tell him, "Absolutely, these are military grade fully automatic, and a navy seal would be happy to walk into battle with this in his hand."

We went into the jungle and they said, "Just open fire, we have some cardboard people in the distance so we can see what it can do."

I began to tell them about what it could do and how many rounds per minute and I opened fire. If you ever saw the movie *Predator*, it was like that, bullets being sprayed in every direction. I did the same thing with the other guns, and they were impressed with what they saw. They then asked if they could use them, and they did and looked like they were having the time of their lives shooting bullets for close to thirty seconds straight. That was part of the plan to reach them on a personal level, not just a business level, and make the experience enjoyable.

As the demonstration came to an end, one of them began to talk to the other in Spanish, and then they both started to laugh. I naturally asked, "What's so funny?"

They responded, "He said these guns are so big they might scare the Chinese passengers, so we might have to put some flowers on them."

We all had a good laugh, but in between breaths I asked, "What do the Chinese have to do with this?"

The other one blurted out, "The refugees want to get into the U.S. and if we run into the coast guard, we want to make sure they can't catch us."

The defense purchaser told them both to be quiet. "I apologize, we can't say anything more, and I hope you will keep quiet about what you have heard today."

I responded, "Of course, I hope we can become regular business partners. I wouldn't want to jeopardize a long-term customer."

This answer satisfied the purchaser, "Okay, we will take two thousand of the model A, as you call it, a thousand of model C, and a thousand of model D."

I asked him, "What about model B?"

He responded, "It doesn't grip as well as the others, and the weight feels off. You showed us its fire power, and while it is close to the others, holding it tires your arms and if we are in any extended combat, we want our weapons to be as easy to use as possible."

I responded, "Fair enough."

I shook his hand and prepared to come back the next day with millions of dollars in fully automatic weapons.

In the back of my mind I started to struggle, because I had fired these weapons, and I knew how good they were, but the thought suddenly occurred to me that if this ever got out to the media, then I would be labelled a monster. I was selling top calibre weapons to a possible enemy that may one day be used to kill Americans who were protecting our country in border security. Before thoughts like those could take over I stopped, took a deep breath, and remembered something I had heard several times in the previous few months: "Sometimes to catch the king, you have to let them take a few pawns."

So, I just accepted that this was the first part of a much bigger plan. In the end, if we did have to fight these guys we would be ready and would know what we were up against, especially since we were the ones selling it to them in the first place.

The next day I brought the guns and they looked at them extensively, presumably to make sure they weren't rigged to explode or anything. Eventually they bought them and I was given millions in cash. I made sure that I was professional and acted like this was simply the acquisition of a new regular client, mildly enthusiastic but not too excited. Before I left, they asked me about what I had told the U.S. border patrol and I responded wittily, "As far as anyone in the States knows, I am on a beach in Acapulco, and as long as I come back with a tan and looking relaxed, no one will bat an eye."

They let out a good laugh and we shook hands and agreed to meet again in the not too distant future.

Since things had wrapped up without incident and even more quickly than I expected, I went out to get the tan that I had told them I would need. It was so strange to know that I had twenty-four hours to just relax and enjoy the scenery. It has always struck me as strange that some of the most beautiful places in the world were, for both natural and political reasons, the most dangerous places in the world.

The next day I took my return connecting flights and came back with the money and the recordings, and I sat down in my office with my boss Mr. Donovan as well as five other men. The other men were from other offices and sat around the table to converse about the report.

Mr. Donovan began, "Gentlemen, I went over everything that Melvoy gathered from them. As suspected, they are running Chinese immigrants over our borders and plan to bring conflict and major firepower to our border security. We carefully scanned the currency and all of it was unmarked, indicating that they aren't onto us, at least not onto him. They have also indicated that they may be expanding their operations, so follow up missions may become necessary. What's more, not only did they confirm this, a man two degrees from Noriega was there for the whole purchase, and if Noriega isn't directly involved, then he is at least aware because his minister of defense is."

The other men turned to me, nodding in approval, "Did you get any other indications about what they may be up to?"

I responded saying, "I don't know, but with follow up visits and future sales, whether it be weapons or anything else, I am sure I can find out more. We had a good rapport and perhaps my weapons selling connections could allow me to bring people selling other things."

One of them was taking notes and finally spoke up, "Mr. Melvoy, did you tell them anything about your background with the military?"

I responded, "No, I simply told them that I have been selling these weapons for a while, and know them and their capabilities very well."

He responded, "Good, the more you distance yourself from us the better."

Further discussions were had, but the meeting closed with Mr. Donovan saying, "In light of the information achieved, the access acquired and the trust cultivated with the potential targets, I believe this mission has been a success. I would like your permission to send Melvoy to future projects, not just involving Panama, but other parts of the world."

The other five men seemed to nod in approval, then one of them turned to me and said the following, "I would be inclined to agree that your history, relative youth, and work ethic are proving to be great assets for this agency and we look forward to your future work."

I took great pride in this approval. I was given a hell of a test and not only passed, I excelled, I walked out of that office filled with pride, filled with vigor, and the truth is I would need every bit of it during my next trip to Veronica's.

CHAPTER 35

I LEFT A DANGEROUS COUNTRY FOR THIS?

I got home and I made a phone call to sort out the problems with Veronica, but Todd picked up and he reluctantly agreed to meet so we could work out our issues. The one thing I remember him saying was, "I hope you are ready for yelling because she is not happy with you, and we may have to send the kids to my parents so they don't overhear all of this."

I agreed, and when I told Anita what I was planning to do she wanted to come with me, but I told her that I was worried about how intense it would get. She responded, "Charles, you and I are together, that means through the good and the bad, so if I have to deal with your ex-wife, I'm willing to do that."

I agreed to it, so we had an arrangement for the first Friday in May to finally have it out with Veronica.

That day approached, but as it got closer I grew more resentful, thinking to myself, "Why does she have to give me such a hard time? I am a war hero, and helping take down dictators in other parts of the world. What does she do?"

Eventually the day came, as agreed the kids weren't in the house and Anita came with me. Todd and Veronica sat on their couch as we sat on the other couch facing them. I saw the sour and bitter look on Veronica's face as Todd got started. "Well as everyone here knows, we have three kids to look after and despite the divorce, we have tried to make this work as well as possible."

Veronica immediately scoffed, letting out a sarcastic, "Ha!"

I didn't like that but I tried to keep my composure.

Todd continued, "Veronica, let's not start off on the wrong foot."

She rolled her eyes, and Todd continued, "This isn't a traditional family, but as four adults, I think together we can make this work and put the children's needs above our own desires and issues."

Up until this point, I thought that Todd was on the right track, "Thank you Todd."

Veronica looked like she was going to burst, so I decided I just wanted to face it head on. "Okay Veronica, I know you are upset so just let me have it already."

Her face began to contort as if there was so much she was trying to figure out, like what to yell about first. The tension in the air built to the point where you could almost smell it.

"Charles, when I married you I thought that I wanted to be the traditional housewife. The truth is it was awful especially because of the fact that you didn't work a nine to five job and were gone so much of the time. I was basically left alone and you never gave me the appreciation I deserved."

I thought we were getting off topic, so I interrupted to try and put things back on the topic. "Veronica I thought we were talking about the kids, not history."

She began to get an angrier tone in her voice, "It's not history, it's still happening! You come in here once a week as if that is an acceptable amount of time for children to spend with their father, and then I have to clean up the mess!"

I didn't like the accusation, "What mess?"

She got even more annoyed, "Well most recently, the fact that you ignored our daughter and you gave the WrestleMania ticket that should have gone to her, to this slut."

Anita's eyes lit up, "What did you just call me?"

Todd asked everyone to calm down and reminded us that this isn't about personally attacking each other but it's about doing what's best for the kids. That was when Veronica cut him off, "I am talking about the kids, Jackie was already hurt, she already felt abandoned by you and this just hammered that point home."

I rolled my eyes, "Gee, I wonder who was bad mouthing me behind my back to make her think like that?"

Veronica got defensive, "I don't tell her anything that isn't true. She resented you before I ever said anything."

I had heard enough. "Bullshit, you know when I have our sons out I don't say anything negative about you because I am not trying to push you out of their lives and replace you."

Her face was turning red by this point, "Well you aren't much to replace, and isn't this slut the person you are trying to replace me with?"

Anita stood up and had heard enough, "If you call me that one more time…"

I took Anita by the hand and said, "I think that is enough – we're out of here."

Todd put his hand on my shoulder, "Wait a minute, let's just calm down and get through this, remember what's important."

184   Chapter 35 : I Left a Dangerous Country for This?

Anita walked to the front door to grab her shoes, as I turned around, "I always know what's important, defending our country so our kids would have a future. You're the one who broke up our family because you wanted everything and I bet that if you hadn't spent the last few years telling Jackie what a horrible person you think I am, she and I would be great. Now I am leaving because you can call me any name in the book I have heard them all, but I will be damned if I am going to hear you talk that way about the woman I love."

I marched out and looked back out of the corner of my right eye, seeing Veronica with her arms crossed and seeing Todd shaking his head in bewilderment. As I drove home my blood began to boil, but Anita took my hand, "I heard what you said, that's why I love you too. You are a real man who stands up for the woman he loves, but too much of a gentleman to ever hit a woman."

That put a small grin on my face, realizing that no matter how wrong things went with my ex-wife, Anita would be there for me. She then added, "It's a good thing you did get us out of there. I'm no soldier, but I know enough to take her apart."

I chuckled, "I bet you do."

Once again there was a divide, at work I was respected, valued and had a lot to look forward to, but in my home life I had to deal with an ex-wife who seemed to hate the ground I walked on. I tried to call Jackie to prove Veronica wrong but she wasn't home. She was at soccer practice, which got under my skin because I didn't even know she liked soccer.

Before I could get more upset, I had a very concerned phone call from the minister at my mother's church. He told me that he had something serious to tell me, I asked him what was wrong and he said that he was worried about my mother. She seemed to be having a very hard time with Jason and Cathy's kids. I asked him what he was talking about, and he responded, "Cynthia (their oldest daughter) is fourteen and is apparently causing trouble, not doing her homework and staying out late. Your mother confided in me that she was scared that Cynthia might be hanging around with the wrong people and that if she keeps acting this way she could end up getting in some type of trouble. Your mother had tried to talk to Cathy about this and Cathy wouldn't hear any of it. Cathy can't accept that anything might be wrong with her kids. She didn't want anyone saying anything against her kids, and so she swore her to secrecy, if they knew she was telling me this, they might kick her out."

My head was ready to explode, and I remember thinking to myself, "I told them, damn it, I told them things like this would happen and now they are blaming the wrong person."

I had seen so many news stories, and stories from various people of these punk kids, these delinquents, and if they are acting that way, by the time they are thirteen they can get into real trouble. Connor was almost that age and the last time I had seen him he was a spoiled brat and I cringed at what awaited him. The hippies that we were scared of in the 1960s were now heavy metal hair dyed freaks yelling things about Iron Maiden and other bands with weird names. I remembered one of the guys at work saying, "Do you know why they are called Iron Maiden? Because their music is torture."

I laughed at the time and believed it. I liked calmer country music, and I remembered the words of McLachlin all those years ago about how the culture war on our own land was proving itself more and more. By 1986, there were a lot of people afraid of where the country was headed and I was definitely one of them.

After thinking about it, I decided I was going to try to talk to Cathy and Jason, but I would have to ask about it carefully so that they wouldn't know about my mother's concerns. Just like with Panama, if I was going to change things, I needed to lay down the groundwork and get a sense of what was going on inside. Maybe I could help them shift the power dynamics so that the rebels/kids wouldn't take over the region/house.

It started with a phone call to Jason asking him how things were going. He was doing well with ten locations and he was raking it in and talking about the future of the organization. He spoke of how the day may come when they are a national chain with hundreds of locations. They could one day expand into Canada, Mexico, and they could create a similar one in Europe but they would have to give soccer a lot more time and how they call that football.

I began to ask about the kids and as I expected, he was telling me about how Cynthia was entering grade nine and everything seemed great. He started to tell me that between the housekeepers, Cathy, and my mother, there was always someone there. I asked him if he was keeping an eye on who she was hanging around with because high school can be the time that leads kids down the wrong path. As we had shifted onto this topic, I could sense how he suddenly became a little less sure about what was really going on.

He tried to say, "Yeah, I am always telling her how I have a college fund for her and her brothers, so that the sky is the limit as long as they do their best."

I tried to ignore the fact that once again his answer involved money and once again as if that was the solution.

We ended the conversation agreeing that "being a parent isn't easy and it's a lot harder than it used to be."

I then asked where Cathy was and he told me she was having a girl's night, and it struck me as odd that she was staying out late on a Wednesday. I got a sense of what was happening; the parents weren't there and assumed someone else would do their job. Suddenly I began to understand my mother's concern, she was old school and believed that every home needed two parents, and housekeepers were not an acceptable substitute.

So then I called Cathy to hear her side of things and I was surprised by this conversation where everything seemed to be rosy, and judging by what she said, they didn't have a single problem in the world. It sounded like the sun shone every day, the birds sang every morning and that the world was perfect. She kept talking about how bright Melina was and everyone else was doing wonderfully. She didn't have to work, she was living a life of leisure and expecting her mother, the housekeepers, and the school, to look after her kids. I began to fear for my mother's well being and began to ponder what to do in terms of my mother. Do I ask her to live with me, and force Cathy and Jason to raise their own kids? Would that remove the only real parent in the house and leave the kids to completely go down the wrong path?

I had to wonder what the next step was, and I remember asking Anita what she thought I should do. She finally said, "If you want to give your mother a choice, fine, but I think your sister and brother-in-law should grow up and if their kids fail, then it is not your problem."

It seemed to make sense and I began to wonder how I could make this offer to my mother without causing more problems. After a couple days of consideration, I decided to call her. I had to hold my tongue when she started asking why I never call, and why I never bring her other grandchildren around, etc. It was very hard hearing her telling me, "I don't know what I did that was so horrible, I always loved you kids. When you were kids, I never let close to two years go by without letting you see your grandparents while they were still alive, because I don't know how many years I have left."

I grimaced, not enjoying this one bit, and I remember the thought popping into my mind, "Someone had to look after Dad, during those last few years."

In retrospect, I guess I was mad at her for getting divorced but at the time I was too close to the situation and didn't see it or didn't want to face it.

I withstood the onslaught of guilt that she levelled me with but I maintained my composure and began trying to ask her what was happening. She began to tell me that the kids were a handful and that she was worried about Connor not doing his best and getting in trouble at school. I asked her what was happening and the best she could offer me was, "Jason is so busy because when you have to run ten small businesses he is working all the time. Cathy seems to be busy all the time too, going shopping and other places. I sometimes ask why she doesn't stay home and she says that she needs time to herself and she has 'social obligations.'"

I told her I could find a place for her to live in California if she wanted to see her other grandchildren. She appreciated the offer but said that she was badly needed there. She asked me why she couldn't live with me, which is why I responded that I thought I could find her a place at a nice retirement home, so that if I went on a business trip she wouldn't be alone. I may as well have told her I was going to kill her when I said retirement home. She heard a place where she would be tied to a chair and condemned to wither in a junk pile. The avalanche of guilt ploys began all over again and her obvious fear of being labelled useless rose to the surface.

I apologized and couldn't wait to end the phone call, as there was only so much I could take. The real reason why I didn't want her staying with me was that I didn't want her to be there and in the way if I wanted to have an evening with Anita. Not to mention I didn't want her to find out anything that might tip her off that I wasn't working for a grocery chain and that I was actually working for the CIA. When you work for the CIA, they don't want you to live in a place where people might overhear your confidential phone calls.

The next day I decided that there was nothing I could do but wait and try again in a few weeks to sort out the issues with my mother. In the meantime, things with Veronica and Todd had begun to settle down, and much to my surprise they had contacted Billy and Hashani. Billy had come up with the idea of having a written agreement between the two parties and had told them that he would be willing to help us write it up. I didn't foresee this going well, so I told him that I didn't think she would keep up her end of the bargain, since she had failed so badly on "till death do us part."

Todd finally said something about this that I will never forget. "Charles, this is the last time I am saying this, she divorced you, people get divorced, get over it!"

I paused and said, "It won't be so easy when it happens to you. If you don't get her everything she wants, she will throw plates at you or worse. The day that happens, it will rip you to shreds to know your wife has thrown you out of her life."

He paused and said, "Charles, I didn't want to play this card, but you have left me with no choice. We are trying to have another baby and that is going to be hard enough on her, without all of this drama going on. I am sorry about what she said about Anita, but this madness has to stop. Billy is a psychiatrist and I think he is onto something with his written agreement idea."

After he explained what he meant, I told him I would think about it and decided I would talk to Billy about it, because something about this didn't make sense. A written agreement? Are we getting lawyers and notaries in as witnesses? The whole idea made me uncomfortable, but I was convinced that if I didn't, I might never be able to stop the parade of bad mouthing that was going about me behind my back to my own kids, especially Jackie.

I hadn't spoken to Billy in about a year and a half, since the incident about him and Hashani not wanting my father to be at their wedding, and them not going to his funeral. I was sure I was right, but I also knew that I wasn't the one making up the rules. My kids were in my ex-wife's house and I had to work around those rules. I remember thinking to myself, if I get the right information and the right techniques, maybe I can shift the agreement to my advantage going forward, so maybe let her worry about what the kids thought of her.

I was still carrying around my resentment of my brother for being a damn hippie protesting against Reagan. As I was preparing to make that call, it was just so hard to understand how he and I could be brothers. If I was like my father, Cathy was somewhat like my mother, but Billy being away for those eleven years, turned him into something else entirely. I don't remember exactly when, but I do remember it was deep into the summer because I had to keep wiping the sweat from my face throughout the phone call.

The phone was ringing when finally Hashani picked up and said, "Hello?"

I responded, "Hello Hashani, how are you doing?"

She had no time for me, "I know you don't give a damn, what do you want Charles?"

I rolled my eyes, "Okay, I wanted to talk to Billy regarding the issues with Veronica."

She paused and in an irritated voice said, "Okay Charles, I will let him know."

I waited, and after about a minute, and beginning to wonder if he was going to pick up, Billy finally came on the phone, "Hello Charles, how are you doing?"

I responded, "Well some things are going very well. As I'm sure you know, things with Veronica and the kids aren't going so well and she told me that you are trying to create some sort of agreement for us."

Billy paused, "Yes, with this much history and this many bad feelings, it's going to take a very long time to rebuild any serious level of trust."

I took a deep breath and I realized that I had to hold back my first instincts to disregard his psychobabble, although on some level, I had to tell him what I thought he wanted to hear and to mix in some partial truth.

I began to talk about how I just wanted to make things work with my kids and I didn't want every time I came over there to be tense and angry. I was planning to be with Anita for a long time and I didn't want her not to be welcome there. I also told him my concern about Veronica bad mouthing me to the kids and I wanted that to stop.

After I finished explaining that to him he said, "Okay, here is what we are going to do. I am going to fax you an agreement that I am going to draw up based on what you, Veronica and Todd have said. If everyone agrees to it and signs off we can hopefully start with a fresher slate."

We then fell into other topics, I decided to ask him what he and Hashani were up to, and he began to say, "Well, our wedding was wonderful. We still have the pictures and it was nothing less than amazing. I really wish you had been there, because it would have meant a lot to Hashani and I."

I responded, "You weren't there for my wedding either. You didn't show up because you were spending time with hippies, and the reason I didn't go to your wedding was because the last time I spoke to Hashani, she hung up in my ear. After the way she was ordering you to throw our father under the bus I couldn't stand for it and I still don't know why you did it."

There was another tense pause, "Look Charles, I know that we have a lot of bad history, but we have some good history too. You have always had an incredible loyalty, and when I was getting picked on in school, you were there."

I stopped him right there, "Why didn't you stand up to her? Who wears the pants in your house? If you are going to let her rule the house, what happens if you have a son? He will grow up thinking that men are supposed to say 'yes dear' and follow orders."

Billy responded, "Isn't that what you did for over ten years in the military?"

I let out a gasp in disbelief, "That is not the same thing, that isn't even close, that's comparing apples and watermelons."

He paused and said, "Now do you understand how your comment

sounded to me?"

I shook my head, "I will tell you this – I don't let any woman tell me what to do."

He responded, "No, you tell them what to do, right?"

I said, "Yes, if I'm their husband or father."

He let out his own groan of frustration. "Charles, that attitude cost you your marriage, please don't let it cost you your relationship with your children. The world isn't like that anymore and never should have been that way in the first place."

I wiped more sweat from my brow, "You see that is the problem with liberals. They want to change everything, take all the foundations that we built our society on and wipe them out, what sort of world will that give us?"

He responded, "Everyone's house is built on dirt, but that doesn't mean you have to keep it in every room in your house."

I thought that was the most bizarre metaphor I had ever heard and I was getting tired of listening to this. "Billy, just fax me the agreement, I will look it over and I will sign it if I agree with it. And Billy good luck, because trust me, with Hashani being such a shrew you're going to need it."

He paused and said something to me that I didn't expect to hear in that conversation. "Charles, you and I are very different people and I'm not sure if we could ever walk in each other's shoes, but I hope one day we can sit across from each other as brothers."

I was confused, "What do you mean, we are brothers. I sometimes wonder how the hell we are related, but we are brothers."

He said, "I don't mean biologically, I mean as equals. I sometimes wonder if you still see me as that kid that ran away all those years ago."

I let out a dismissive scoff, "Considering some of the people you hang around with I have to wonder if you are grown up at all, like those liberals who don't realize we are in a war."

He paused again, "Well Charles, I hope the day comes when we don't have to be in wars at all. In the meantime, look over the contract and hopefully this will be the first step towards a better time for you."

I responded, "I hope so too."

I then changed the subject, "By the way, while you are offering advice, could you please talk to Cathy and get her to discipline those kids of hers before they get into serious trouble."

I heard almost the same scoff from him, that I had made just seconds earlier. "Charles, I know exactly what you are talking about and this may surprise you, but Cathy is even more stubborn than you are."

I needed a few seconds to process what he had said and he went on,

"Between puberty, new expectations, and responsibilities, the teenage years are very tough for everyone."

I interrupted him, "What do you mean tough, they have it easier than any of us ever did, and have you seen how spoiled those kids are?"

He took a deep breath, "I think you misunderstood what I meant, because those teenage years are absolutely pivotal. Above all they need guidance to truly become responsible and I fear that Cathy is enjoying her affluence so much that she can't see the potential problems."

It had been years since he and I had agreed on anything or so I thought, "Exactly – they need to be taught to work for what they have, and if they get out of line they need to know they will get a boot in the ass."

Suddenly those few seconds of agreement fell away and he said, "Charles, harsh discipline is not the solution. They need to recognize why things need to happen and why they have to earn things, not just do as your told or else."

I responded, "That is how our father kept us in line, and I didn't disobey him because I knew I would get a boot in the ass."

He paused again, "Charles, I suggest you read some parenting books because that attitude won't help you when your children are older."

I had heard enough, "Billy, parenting books? Really? It's not that hard and it never has been. I don't know if you and Hashani are ever going to have kids, but just remember you can't convince your kid you are in charge if you are running to check a book to make sure you didn't punish them the wrong way."

I would bet money he was shaking his head, "Charles, sometimes it seems like we are from different planets. I will send you the contract, so please read it over carefully and please think about the things I have said."

Before hanging up, I said the obligatory, "Thanks Billy, have a good night."

I didn't understand him, and I didn't understand how he could see things so differently from myself, because what seemed so obvious to me was ridiculous to him, and vice versa. There were three of us raised in the same house, by the same parents, yet we were all radically different people with radically different ideas of parenting. Even though I didn't end up reading any parenting books, I do remember thinking, "Somebody needs to write a book on how to deal with family because it seemed so much more complicated than I would have ever thought."

CHAPTER 36

MAKE A DEAL, BREAK A DEAL

Today people have a tendency to take for granted how convenient e-mails are, but back in the 1980s a fax machine was considered futuristic, and tons of things were still being mailed directly and you had to wait several days before they would arrive in your mailbox. Today someone can scan whatever it is and e-mail it and the whole thing would take less than two minutes. Those few days sure felt like a long time because I knew that I was either agreeing to something I might not like, or it might be something I couldn't agree to. If I rejected it, the arguing would begin again and let's just say it wasn't something I looked forward to.

Anita and I were doing great, but for the first time things at work began to have real problems. Most notably, there was an increased tension about something and I didn't know what it was. Around the same time that I was waiting to receive the faxed agreement from Billy, I was called into my boss, Mr. Donovan's office and he asked me, "Who do you know in Sacramento, California?"

I let out a sigh and said, "My brother. I know he is a big time Liberal and was part of one of those protest groups. He and I may have had the same parents but we are almost in different worlds."

He looked unsatisfied with that answer, "What were you talking to him about?"

I was taken aback as if my loyalty was suddenly on trial. "I was talking to him about the issues with my family, the issues with my ex-wife, and what's going on with my mother, my sister and her kids."

There were a couple seconds of silence as Mr. Donovan was contemplating what I was saying. "Well we have a problem, because we have an important mission that we were considering involving you with. However we have to be careful, if peace groups like the one your brother and his wife are associated with find out about our missions, they would take them and spin them into something completely ridiculous. Secrecy is absolutely paramount."

He paused for a second and said, "This mission that we are considering making you a part of would be significant. It would raise your security clearance and would give you a good reputation among my colleagues. They were impressed by your work in Panama as well as your office work. The fact is you have what it takes to accomplish great things, so here is what might happen. We don't want you letting this problematic party get in the way of our objectives. Do you understand?"

I nodded, "Mr. Donovan, like I said, we only have family in common, in fact if I found out he had been switched at birth, I wouldn't be surprised. What's more, I want to give my all to this organization, whether I am filling out reports in this office, travelling anywhere in the world you want me to go, or taking out potential threats, I will do it all."

Mr. Donovan nodded, "Okay, I will put in a good word for you, odds are they will want to do another interview with you before they debrief you on it, but we'll know in the next few weeks."

I shook his hand and thanked him for hearing my side of things. I forget whether it was the same day or the next day, but I got the written agreement that Billy had drawn up. I don't remember all of the details, but the things that stood out the most were things like, "No underhanded jabs. Look deep inside yourself to forgive the other person, if the children bring up the divorce don't paint anyone as being 'at fault' but try to neutrally explain that sometimes people aren't compatible."

I was trying to figure out if this was at all realistic, and if either of my sons asked me why we broke up, I didn't know how I would tell them that it wasn't their mother's idea. I honestly didn't think she could keep from taking jabs at me and the part that I was baffled by was the fact that they said that we needed to forgive each other. I didn't see myself as really being at fault in this situation as I was doing my job to provide a home and secure future for the children. It took me a full day to decide whether or not I would sign it. Life is full of surprises though the clause that I barely even thought about was the one that would cause me the most trouble. I signed the agreement thinking that as long as she was held to these standards I could continue my relationship with my kids. I called Veronica and Todd and left a message telling them I had signed the agreement and would be coming over that weekend expecting them to have signed it as well.

I called Billy to tell him that I had signed the agreement and he seemed pleasantly surprised, then I followed by saying, "What do I do when she breaks it?"

He asked me what I meant, so I told him that I wasn't sure if she could go more than ten minutes without taking some shot at me about being some supposed bad husband and father. He responded with something that I found so strange he said, "Listen carefully."

I heard his hands clap. He said, "I just clapped and I can't change that."

He clapped again. "I just clapped again, and you can be mad that I clapped twice, but I can't change the fact that I clapped twice. I did clap twice, I can apologize and promise not to do it in the future but I can't change what has happened."

I was a little puzzled, "Where are you going with this?"

He responded, "We all have done things that we regret and no matter what we do, we can't change what we have done. All we can change is what we are going to do, and agreeing to do better is a big first step towards that. So instead of waiting for someone to break the agreement, try going into it with the optimism that she is one hundred percent sincere in moving forward."

I paused and shook my head, "Okay Billy I will try it your way."

I thanked him for his time and effort and hung up the phone hoping that maybe he would be right about something for once in his life.

I got to Veronica and Todd's house and Veronica came up to me and for the first time in who knows how long, she actually greeted me with a smile. She extended her hand, "Charles, Billy told me something about how we can't change what has happened, but we can change what will happen."

It was the weirdest feeling when I realized that either he had told her the same thing he told me, or that he told her to reinforce what he told me but either way it made me suspicious.

She continued, "I'm so glad we are both going to move forward for our children's sake. I know I have been a little extra edgy lately because Todd and I are planning on having another baby and that hasn't helped things, but I'm glad we are moving on."

I nodded in agreement, and as I was about to call up the stairs she asked me to speak to her in the living room for a few minutes. As I sat down I had a sudden flashback to sometime many years earlier when we were younger and happier together. It took me a second to snap out of it and that was when she told me, "Charles, part of the reason why I was so mad at you was because of the anger that Jackie feels towards you. I sat there on Jackie's bed next to her asking why you barely came around, why was it that other kid's fathers are there for them and you weren't there. So, I think that if we are truly going to move things forward, you really need to clear the air with her."

I tried to maintain my composure as I never liked any indication that I was a bad father, which this was. I had to think on my feet, so I responded, "Okay, fresh start, clear the air, I'm going up."

I tried to use a little bit of humour, "I hope I don't have to take her shopping to make up for it."

Veronica didn't laugh, and after a second of awkward silence, I repeated, "I'm going up."

It was so strange that I was almost more nervous over this than going to Panama. If my cover had been blown, I would have had a small army chasing after me or I would have been captured and held, possibly for the rest of my life. Normally a twelve-year-old girl would be nothing compared to the scenario I just described, but when it's your own daughter and your future with her hangs in the balance, that changes everything.

I knocked on the door and poked my head in. The long side of the bed was up against the wall and it looked like she was writing in her note pad. Jackie looked at me for a second and then turned away. I rolled my eyes, "Would you look at me please, I came up here to talk to you."

There was nothing but silence. "Jackie, I did three trips in Vietnam, your silent treatment isn't going to hurt me."

She said, "I know Mom sent you up to talk to me and you don't really want to."

I sat down next to her on her bed and I looked at her, but only seeing her hair, as she was refusing to look at me. "Jackie, I know I haven't been around all the time and that happens when parents get divorced. The fact is I wasn't going around drinking or gambling in Vegas. I was defending our country so that you and your brothers could live in a safer world and a free country."

The silent treatment went on and I was trying my best to keep my composure. "Jackie, I'm trying to talk to you. How can we work this out if you are giving me silence?"

She turned around and finally looked at me saying, "You think a couple minutes of silence is hard, try weeks at a time, try watching your father pack up his things and then not call. That's what you did, and then when you do come back, you're taking Randy and Matthew to WrestleMania and just leaving me here. What's so wrong with me? Why am I not good enough for you? Is it because I'm not a boy? Or is it something else?"

By this point, she had actually burst into tears and I held onto her as tight as I had held onto Anita after Panama.

It was so hard of me to see my own child burst into tears, and I followed up by saying, "Jackie, I was there the day when you were born and it was one of the happiest days of my life. When you are a parent, you will realize that sometimes when you are trying to do the right thing, sometimes people misunderstand them. One day you'll realize how hard being a parent really is, how hard it is to do the right thing all the time, and one day when you find a guy to marry, you'll realize that marriage is a lot harder than they make it look on TV. When your mother and I divorced, it was one of the hardest things to ever happen in my life. I hope you never go through anything like that, so just calm down, accept that I'm here and let's go out for ice cream."

She pulled her face up and stared at me and said, "Ice cream? You think that's the answer, because you've barely been in my life for the last few years and you think ice cream will make it all better?"

I was getting bewildered and had an impulse to tell her to shut up and remember who her father was and show some damn respect, but I had given my word to Billy and Veronica that I would try things their way. I said, "it could be a start, I mean you could fill me in on what I've missed out on and if you want help with your homework, I could help you with that right now."

She paused thinking things over and sniffled as she transitioned away from crying. "You are going to be around a lot more from now on?"

I told her that I would as much as I could, because I didn't want to miss any more of her big moments. She was very conflicted, but she said, "Okay, if this is for real, then let's start."

I wasn't much help for her homework since I hadn't been in school for over twenty years and I had completely forgotten algebra.

As I drove home, I felt good about where things were going, my ex-wife and I were on the best terms in years, my daughter and I were getting back on the same track, my sons were still very happy with me, and things were going really well with Anita. I was beginning to think about marrying Anita next year. I began to wonder if maybe I had underestimated Billy, although in the back of my mind, I had to wonder about Veronica and I being told the same thing.

The next month was great, I was with my children quite a bit and I was stunned to find out new things about Jackie since she was beginning to like boys. As we drew closer to Halloween, things seemed to be going along well, then one day Mr. Donovan told me that the interview about the mission was tomorrow. With everything that I had been told about this mission, I was nervous and tried to tell myself that his could change everything. The promise of higher security clearance was especially tempting, the thought of one day meeting with President Reagan was a wonderful thought and it would be the fulfillment of a dream that had been in my head for a long time.

I got there and they told me what their primary concern was. I told the same story, that I was talking to my brother only regarding family stuff and that I drew a hard line between my family life and my professional life. They all looked at each other, then they asked me to leave the room for a few minutes and I did, waiting and wondering what career boosting opportunity awaited me; what was the next great task that awaited me to prove myself.

They called me back in and they then raised their one new concern. "The mission in question would require you to leave October 24th and the odds are about 60/40 that you won't be back until early November or later. Is that something that you are willing to deal with?"

At that moment all I could think of was my career and the next steps up the ladder. I responded, "Absolutely, whatever my country needs, I'm ready."

Mr. Donovan's boss, Mr. Graham, came forward, "Okay, everything from this second onward is top-secret, and you can't discuss it with anyone outside this room. Are we clear?"

I nodded bracing myself to leap head first into this opportunity, "First, you are going to Israel with weapons, where you will meet up with pre-approved personnel and then all of you are going to Iran. We have top-secret negotiations going on there right now, and you will be one of the bodyguards for the primary negotiators. During your time there, you will observe everything and you will speak as little as possible. Most of all, once the deal is made, you will be expected to verify the identities of the hostages we are freeing, to retrieve the payment from the Israelis along with two other agents, and then take a quick trip to bring the money to the contra force in Nicaragua. This mission is top-secret and your role is secondary, but if you can pull this off without a hitch, it will go a long way towards us knowing that we can trust you with top level clearance."

This sounded so exciting that I thought that I couldn't say no.

Do you remember me saying that the smallest thing would haunt me bigger than anything else? Well one of the things in my agreement with Veronica, was the list of major events that I would be there for to share the responsibility, with Halloween being specifically listed. Not to mention I was going to have complete radio silence for at least the next week and a half. The worst part was I told my family the day before I left, that didn't help me. I stuck to my story of having a conference to go to for supermarket managers in Denver.

In the meantime, I had a big job to accomplish, a very big job and considering one of the places I would be going was Iran, I knew that this could end up being a one-way trip.

CHAPTER 37

IT DIDN'T HAVE TO BE THAT WAY

I got myself ready for the first trip to Israel and as I read through the whole briefing, it turned out this had been going on for a couple of years. It was unclear how many more times they intended on doing this, but I was now part of it. I was chosen, along with a few other specially selected agents, after a brief meeting in Israel and then we all got ready to leave for Iran. In the back of my mind I got a little bit of déjà vu like I was going back to Vietnam, a war zone where I would be facing an enemy. Only this time instead of fighting with them, I was there to oversee the exchange of weapons for hostages and hoping it didn't go badly, we were getting closer to some place that was an hour's drive away from Tehran. I didn't ask questions, or try to make friends because it was a mission that could make or break my career. I also didn't want to disappoint President Reagan, who I still supported whole-heartedly in 1986.

When we finally got to Tehran, one of the people we were introduced to was a short man named Naajid, who apparently had done this before and judging from how abrupt he was, he wanted to get this over with fairly quickly. One of the few things I do remember was when they brought out the hostages; my job was to look through the files to confirm that they were the people that we were promised. What struck me was the look in their eyes, they were being freed and yet their eyes looked like people who thought that they were still in a nightmare. One in particular had whispered something under his breath, I asked him what he said and he responded, "I wish I could be sure that this isn't a dream."

I responded, "This is as real as it gets."

During the exchange, my eyes continuously scanned the room for any sign of an ambush assault because when you are fighting people in guerrilla warfare, that skill is essential. I was tense during the entire time because this was like walking through the jungle in Vietnam, where if you keep your eyes open, that extra second could mean the difference between life and death.

Finally as everything was settled, we were taken to our plane, and before we took off a few others and I had to check it out to make sure no one was hiding anything explosive on board. With the safety check complete, the plane took off back to Israel and after dropping off the Israeli negotiators and the hostages, we had one last stop – Nicaragua. It felt similar to Panama in climate but the political situation was completely different. In Panama, if someone who was our guy might have stopped being our guy there was uncertainty. In Nicaragua, we knew we wanted the contras to overthrow the government. We already had Cuba so we didn't need any more Soviet allies that could launch weapons at us from our own hemisphere.

We saw the Sandinista Regime as being one step away from being the newest member of the Soviet Union, so after we got the money for the sale of weapons, we made a stop in Nicaragua to give the equivalent money to the rebels. This was a secret mission with two goals: to gradually take down a potential threat in South America, and keep a current enemy from aligning themselves with our biggest enemy. While there is more to it than that, that was the bare bones of this mission and its objectives.

I remember looking out the window and seeing the beautiful landscape, which amazed me that these places in South America looked like this all the time. I guess when you live so much of your life in suburbia that is how you perceive things. We dropped off the money and I remember them being very thankful. There was one very nice man who had a moustache and offered me a cigarette, I politely declined and he shrugged.

Before we left, one of their commanders came up to us and asked when the next drop off was. I had been told nothing and one of the other guys we came with said, "We don't have an exact date but I would probably say next winter."

We shook hands and then we were on our way back to the United States. Just like in Iran, I was on high alert, and we were meeting with the rebels, which meant that if the government had found out we were coming, that could have been a hell of an ambush. I had a short nap on the plane ride back home, finally feeling relieved that everything went well. I would be going back home to a loving woman, children who are happy to see me, and superiors who would be thrilled with how everything went.

After landing, we were met by several CIA people for a de-briefing. We went over every detail and apparently the guy who had told the contras 'next winter' upset our superiors. "You never tell them when, and we have to be careful not to promise things we can't guarantee a delivery for."

I was off the hook though and went home on November 1st for what would turn into one of the most stressful months of my life up to that point.

I came home and my answering machine had multiple messages on it, from Veronica, Billy, Anita, and I'm sure you can guess that the ones from Veronica were the hard ones to listen to. It was later that evening and I decided it was best to go to bed and face this tomorrow because I had literally travelled to two other continents armed with weapons to help my country's national interests. I didn't have the energy to deal with Veronica's complaints about me not taking the kids out to go trick-or-treating.

The next morning I made the obligatory phone call. I already had my plan figured out with the contract I had signed clearly stating that I would be there for those events "barring any circumstances that were out of my control."

Well I was sent away by work so I also made sure to downplay Halloween and already had my strategy ready. Just as I planned, I had to weather the initial storm like a boxer hanging on despite an offensive flurry from his opponent. Then as she started to tell me how upset the kids were, I explained that I would make it up to them and I would be there for Thanksgiving and Christmas. I went out of my way to point out that Halloween isn't even a holiday because no one gets the day off.

It took a couple of days of arguments but I eventually got Veronica to agree that it was regrettable, but that as long as I was there for Thanksgiving and Christmas, she would let this slide. After that, I called Billy that evening and told him that I had sorted everything out, and he responded by saying, "Charles, I'm glad you and Veronica came to an agreement but you can't play fast and loose with this. Next time might be the straw that breaks the camel's back."

I asked him what he was talking about and he responded, "One of the reasons she agreed to the contract in the first place is because she is thinking about pursuing full custody of the children."

My jaw dropped and I thought to myself, "It was bad enough that I only saw them on weekends and now she wanted to make it not at all?"

Billy continued, "This was the compromise, if you aren't careful this contract will be used against you in family court."

I was trying to contain my anger, "Does she forget who put a roof over their head, food on their table and clothes on their backs for years, and I still send her child support. She's got some nerve…"

Before I could go any further Billy interrupted. "Charles, I know this is hard for you to hear but Veronica has a very hard time forgiving people, especially when she thinks they have no remorse. As far as she is concerned, this is the last straw before she tries to obtain sole custody. This was the compromise that I convinced her to go with."

I finally asked, "Billy, why didn't you just tell her she was being selfish because the kids aren't just hers, you know."

He responded, "Sometimes the best way to get through to someone is to empathize and put yourself in their shoes as much as you can."

I wasn't impressed, "Well you enjoy putting your feet in women's shoes, bye."

I hung up, feeling like my brother was once again being more loyal to women than to his own blood. While this wasn't as bad as him taking Hashani's side over my father's side; the point was he was taking his former sister-in-law's side over his own brother's side.

I knew that Thanksgiving was going to be awkward and that I would have to win over my children's trust all over again but I knew it had to be done. The next morning, I was preparing my game plan for how to settle things with Veronica, Billy, and the kids.

It was 10:00 am when I got a phone call from the office and it was Mr. Donovan, "Melvoy, I know you weren't supposed to come back until Wednesday but we need to discuss something with you which is absolutely urgent!"

While Mr. Donovan was a very serious man and the most light-hearted thing I had ever seen from him was a mild chuckle, I had never heard him speak with this urgency, and with this seriousness. I began to fear the worst, had Soviets infiltrated the office? Did they know who I am and where I lived? My heart began to race as I drove to the office. Right after I got there, Mr. Donovan, three other men, and Mr. Graham greeted me at the door and took me into the office that was soundproofed. I feared that it was news that the Soviets had found out who we were and/or that they had spies coming for us or our loved ones. As it turned out, my guess was all wrong but potentially just as troubling.

Mr. Donovan began, "Melvoy, everything that we are about to discuss is top-secret and you are not to breathe a word of it to anyone, not your family, not your colleagues, not the news media – absolutely nobody."

I nodded, "Yes sir."

Mr. Graham then began, "Let me make something perfectly clear Melvoy, we trust you, you have proven yourself to be a great asset to this agency, but we have a huge problem. The news of the Iran weapons deals, as well as our funding of the contras in Nicaragua, has fallen into the wrong hands and was published in a Lebanese magazine. It's only a matter of days before the news hits home. While we are trying to dispose of as much evidence as we can, considering your relatively smaller role in the proceedings, you should be okay. However, we can't guarantee anything and if somehow your name comes up and you are questioned about it, I don't care what they offer you, we are all in trouble if they find out our involvement. Are we clear?"

I was stunned, "Wait a minute, we were doing our job, the President sent us on this mission, right?"

Mr. Donovan looked at the others before looking back at me, "He's aware of the mission but because of how this will look, he has to distance himself from it as much as possible. We don't know how bad this is going to get but hopefully we can destroy most of the documentation, and whoever is implicated will hopefully be able to get out of it. We don't know where all the chips are going to fall when this is done. So Melvoy, if your name comes up, you know nothing, you were shocked to hear of such news, but most of all, if you let it slip, if they get hard evidence against us, we may be looking at prison time… everyone in this room and more. Do you understand?"

I took a deep breath, "Yes sir."

They shook my hand and Mr. Graham said, "Don't worry, this leak wasn't your fault, you did a great job; some people just don't know when to keep their damn mouths shut."

I drove home and now had a new level of fear. Could I be facing prison time?

It wasn't the actual prison conditions I was scared of because I had been in the army I could handle some thugs who rob gas stations, but it was the shame that would come with it. I would never be able to live that down because back then being called a jailbird was a serious source of shame. Not to mention I didn't want to be away from my kids or Anita for years. If they found out, how would my kids take it? I would never hear the end of it from Veronica and she would get sole custody for sure. On top of that, my mother was having a hard time with Cathy's kids; it might kill her to know that one of her children was going to prison. It was hard for me to bear, how the hell did this happen, information like this was like carrying around a bomb and if it ever went off, it would be disastrous.

As they said it didn't take long for the news to hit the U.S., and not long before President Reagan himself appeared on the television to admit that it had happened. All the stuff with Veronica and the kids fell to the back-burner, and I just had to wait there wondering if I was going to get a knock on the door from the police. I remember one Sunday I was home doing some vacuuming when I heard a knock on the door, and it was with dread that I answered the door, however unlike Vietnam, if they came for me I couldn't fight back. I opened the door and it was a couple of Jehovah's witnesses who asked if I had found the lord.

I had no patience for this and responded with great agitation, "Yes I found the lord and I do his work. I have fought evil the likes of which you can't imagine, now get off my property."

I slammed the door in their faces. I admit I could have been more diplomatic but that is how tense I was about this whole thing during that time. I remember once again being at my desk when Mr. Donovan came to my desk and asked to speak with me in his office. I obliged, fearing what other horrible update awaited.

He said, "Melvoy, I have a Thanksgiving present for you. I just got the word that one of Mr. Graham's colleagues has shredded most of the documents, and the odds that our names will come up just became a hell of a lot less likely."

I let out a sigh of relief, "So I don't have to worry about them coming to my door and arresting me?"

Mr. Donovan responded, "Melvoy, with how many documents were destroyed, unless I get arrested, don't worry about yourself."

I had Thanksgiving dinner with the family and trying to get through all of this I was hoping I had just dodged one of the biggest bullets in the world. I couldn't tell you how relieved I was that I wasn't going to have to explain a possible trial and prison conviction to my kids.

That Thanksgiving, I came to Veronica's house with Anita, Billy, Hashani and the kids who were in a good mood, largely because they had a couple days off from school and a big meal awaited them. I remember going through that dinner wondering if Veronica was going to make a scene but to my surprise she didn't and everything went great. As we left that night we drove back to my place, Anita had agreed to stay over with me. That night we held each other and I felt this weird mix of emotions where on one hand I was so upset at the guy who had leaked our mission, and at Veronica for wanting sole custody. At the same time, I was so grateful for all of the things that had happened, that would keep things the way they were. I was holding the new love of my life in my arms and I was so glad to be able to, and wondered if anything felt this good.

Some of you may be wondering why I hadn't proposed to her yet, while I had seriously thought about it and would have bought the ring. However two things stopped me, the first was everything with this mission and the second was the fear in the back of my mind of this marriage turning out like the first. I knew it was going to happen but it was just a matter of time. Some people might think that a man who has done the things I have done like stepping into war zones must mean that I have no fear. I assure you marriage can scare damn near anybody, especially when you already have one that ended badly.

Anita was resting her head on my chest, and used to do that because she said she could hear my heartbeat. Before we fell asleep she asked me, "Did you know anything about that Iran-Contra deal, I mean before it came out?"

I was glad that her face was turned away when I said, "No, when I heard it I couldn't believe it."

There was a pause as if she was trying to decide whether or not I was telling the truth, she finally said, "Okay, I love you."

It took me another twenty minutes to get to sleep, and it was hard enough to lie to Veronica and the kids, but if Anita was going to be my wife, could I marry her if the relationship started with lies, even if they were for the good of the country? I didn't know but I just tried to put it out of my mind before anything could happen.

As 1986 came to an end, I was wrestling with my future. How could I reconcile the lies that I have to tell for work? How do I keep things going with my kids? What if somehow my name comes up in the investigation? Despite all the negatives going on, despite the possible investigation hanging over my head, the countdown began and 1986 ended with me thinking, "It didn't have to be this way, but somehow it's great!"

CHAPTER 38

I TOOK THE LEAP, THEY TOOK THE PLUNGE

1987 began with me having two New Year's resolutions: one to make sure I was such a good father that Veronica would have no argument for sole custody; the second was to propose to Anita. I wanted to pick the right time, though before January was over I had started looking up jewellery stores, and it seemed like engagement rings were so much more expensive than they used to be. Of course, that had been over fifteen years ago, and not to mention that California was generally more expensive than Michigan.

Speaking of Michigan, I remember getting an envelope from Jason. I have no idea how he did it, but somehow he had gotten five tickets for WrestleMania III in Pontiac, Michigan because he knew how much the kids liked it. The note said, "Tell them happy belated birthdays."

I was floored – how could he afford this? I didn't get it, but then again, I didn't get a lot of things about how they ran their home. Cynthia was about to turn fifteen and was apparently starting to hang around with the wrong crowd. How did he have time to get me wrestling tickets, yet he didn't have time to discipline his daughter?

One day that winter, I got a phone call from my mother who said she needed someone to talk to, not Cathy or Jason or their cleaning people, who were apparently indifferent to the well-being of the children. I asked her what was wrong, and she began talking a mile a minute about how she knew this was going to happen. It took several times of asking before she finally came out with it. Apparently she didn't approve of Cynthia's new boyfriend, she was fifteen and not doing well at school, her boyfriend was a seventeen-year-old with scruffy hair, tattoos and a motorcycle.

I asked if Cathy knew about this, and my mother responded, "Yes, but she just let her off with a warning and said that if she disobeys her, she'll hear about it when her father gets home. The problem is he is barely home long enough to sleep, let alone act like a father. I warned her that a boy like that only has one thing on his mind, and unlike Jason, he won't stick around if she makes the same mistake Cathy made. Cathy suddenly tells me that I am never to bring that up ever again and that as far as we are concerned that never happened."

I thought that was the craziest thing I had ever heard, that her daughter was dating a punk and she was mad at my mother for bringing up the consequences that could happen.

I finally told my mother that I would take care of this, so I called Jason and had to leave a message with his secretary. The next day I got a phone call from Jason who said he was about to go out for dinner with a supplier. Then after thanking him for the WrestleMania tickets and mentioning that my kids loved them, I told him what I had heard from my mother.

He responded, "Look, we have Cathy, your mother, and a tutor. I told Cathy that if we are going to make sure the kids go to the finest colleges we have to get everything set now. That is her jurisdiction, I'm working night and day in mine."

I tried to tell him that as their father he had a job to do, and I had never heard him get so defensive in all the years I had known him. Then he threw out stuff about "at least another man isn't raising his kids." I tried to keep my cool but it wasn't going to last much longer and I responded, "If you think getting divorced is easy, trust me, with everything you have to lose, it would be absolute hell."

He responded, "Well I'm not getting divorced because my wife is happy with her life."

I responded, "Of course she is, her head is in the clouds and she thinks someone else is going to do all of her work for her. Money can't buy your way out of this one, this takes time and if this punk kid is like Mom said he is, you are in for a world of trouble."

He had no time for my warning, "I have enough to worry about, you worry about your own kids."

He slammed the phone down and I shook my head, as it was only a matter of time now. When you plant your head in the sand, sooner or later something or someone will kick you right in the ass.

Those first few months the Iran Contra scandal would come up on the news, and I couldn't help but watch it with extra interest. In the back of my mind I was worried that the newscaster would suddenly say, "New evidence has revealed one of the people involved was named Charles Melvoy and charges are being pressed."

I was afraid of that and every time it came up on the news, I would let out a sigh of relief as soon as they would change to another topic. Over the next couple of months, it would come up and I kept waiting for the headline in the paper, on the TV or news from the office that something had been exposed. One day around mid-March, I was asked to come into the office with Mr. Donovan and Mr. Graham. I braced for the worst news and just in case, I stopped by Anita's desk, gave her a big kiss and said, "No matter what happens, I love you."

She asked, "What's going on?"

I responded, "I don't know."

I got up and walked into that office and they asked me to sit down.

Mr. Graham began, "They are starting the prosecutions and as of this moment there is no existing evidence on any of us or this office in general. So, given where we are as long as we keep our mouths shut about this we should be okay. Have either of you heard anything or had any contact from anyone about this issue?"

I shook my head, and Mr. Donovan plainly said, "No."

Mr. Graham let out a big sigh and said, "Okay, I know this has been a tough last few months and while I can't write it in stone, it should be okay."

I wanted to believe that everything was going to be okay but unfortunately it was hard to imagine because by this point, bad scenarios and worse ones had gone through my head over and over.

He then moved on to the next subject, and due to the success of my first trip to Panama, they were sending me back for another trip, to once again selling weapons. My palms began to sweat, we were looking over our shoulders because one arms sale arrangement had been exposed and now here we were about to arrange another one.

Before I could raise my objections, Mr. Donovan may have seen the anxiety and said, "Charles, before you get the wrong idea, this isn't like the deal with Iran. There are no laws against selling weapons to Panama, and on a public level, Panama does not have anywhere near the visibility and issues that Iran does. So don't worry, you did a great job last time and we want to find out more about the things they are up to. Given the information we have so far, it appears that Mr. Noriega may have gone rogue and is now looking out for other interests besides those of the United States."

I regained my composure and I tried really hard to tell myself that it would be fine, just like last time, everything would be great. They informed me that I was scheduled to leave at the beginning of April and that I would return in a few days. I let out the biggest sigh of relief on the inside. WrestleMania was March 29th and Easter was April 19th so I wouldn't have to miss either one. I walked out of there feeling better, nothing was found out, my next mission was set and it wouldn't conflict with the written agreement, so I was thrilled. Anita asked me what was happening and since I was forbidden from divulging more than absolutely necessary, I quickly took a piece of the truth and pretended it was all of it. "I was worried my next trip was going to conflict with

WrestleMania weekend and Easter but thankfully it won't."

I don't know how but when a woman knows you well enough, you can't throw a lie past her. That was what made our relationship different, and because of our jobs, we had to lie to each other, but we both knew it and we both had to accept it.

I once again came up with a story about a conference and told Veronica about it and then I said to her, "Don't worry I will be there for Easter and I will make sure to bring some things for the dinner."

She responded by asking about what was happening with the trip to Michigan, and I told her that we would be taking the flight Friday night and we would be flying back Monday morning. She was unimpressed with the fact that they were going to miss school.

I responded, "Don't worry just ask the teacher for the homework and I will make sure they get it done on Saturday."

She paused and said, "I will hold you to that."

I responded, "Just get the homework from their teachers and it will be fine."

Sure enough I picked up Anita and we had a wonderful time planned and we stopped by the house, Veronica gave me the kid's homework, Randy and Matthew brought down their small suitcases. I remember the look on their faces, they were so excited, but I was waiting for a few more minutes and Jackie still hadn't come down, so I decided to go up and see what was going on. I knocked on the door, and then opened the door and I saw her finishing packing and asked her if everything was okay.

She responded, "Yeah, I'm almost done."

I said, "Okay, we only have a few minutes."

She came downstairs and we got into the car and just before we left, Todd asked to speak to me in private and I said, "Okay."

He started telling me, "I really appreciate you guys taking the kids for the weekend because we really needed a weekend off with just us, so thank you."

We shook hands and the thought crossed my mind about Veronica asking for sole custody, "Was he in favour of it? Was he one of the people who were trying to talk her out of it? Would he go along with it just to make her happy?" I had no idea but I knew this, if this battle did ever come to a head, he could either be one of the bigger foes or my greatest ally, and only time would tell.

We took the flight and they hadn't been on a plane since the trip to Disney World and thankfully this didn't remind them of it. I decided to get a couple of hotel rooms, and this might sound strange, but I thought that despite the huge house that Cathy and Jason owned, I wouldn't want my kids to be around theirs, especially if they were the misbehaved terrors that my mother had spoken about. The next day as promised we made the kids do their homework even though Matthew put up the biggest fuss promising the old, "Oh come on, I'll do it later."

I wasn't falling for that old trick. The kids were in the next room, I was there with Anita, and had seriously thought about proposing to her on this trip, and I even thought about finding a jewellery store around Detroit and buying a ring there. I finally decided against it and had been thinking about it for several months but for some reason I just had a hard time doing it. The fact that the kids were around gave me the perfect excuse to not go anywhere away from our group.

That Sunday we went to WrestleMania, somehow in all the preparing and all of the other things going on, I hadn't realized how many people would be there. The Pontiac Silverdome was enormous and by the time it was full, there were people everywhere to the point where I thought that it would take forever for everyone to leave the building. Each match came out and you couldn't help but get caught up in all the excitement because when thousands of people are cheering for someone or something, that energy just grabs you and takes you with it.

That entire day I kept hearing about Hulk Hogan vs Andre the Giant and whether or not he could beat someone who hadn't been beaten in fifteen years. Randy and Matthew were eleven and nine respectively, so I don't remember if they knew it was all a show, but even if they did, they were so excited they didn't care. Jackie seemed to fall into the background amidst all the excitement and that night I remember looking over at my children's faces when Hulk Hogan slammed Andre the Giant, and the joy on their faces was so heart-warming. Once again, the all American good guy had triumphed against all odds and that was the type of entertainment I whole-heartedly approved of.

As sick as this sounds, I remember thinking to myself at one or two moments during the show that if someone had snuck a gun in and was a trained sniper, with this many people they would never know who fired the shot. Thankfully no such tragedy occurred and the night went about as well as we could have expected, although trying to leave took an eternity.

We came home late that Monday as promised, and I knew that they would have a lot to talk about when they went to school on Tuesday. I came home preparing for my second trip to Panama and gradually feeling better and better about how things were going.

Just like last time I went to Panama, I was met by friendly faces and for some reason the reality of this situation wasn't sinking in. It wasn't until I had been there for two days that I remembered that if things went sideways, they might kill me. As I showed them the new weapons, we even talked about body armour for some of their troops, if it was ever needed. They didn't end up having much interest in that, but the new types of guns and ammunition as well as the basic repair instructions, were very interesting to them.

It was during this trip I asked if I could meet Mr. Noriega just so I could be sure that this was being sanctioned by him and because I thought it would be interesting to meet a man of his stature. They decided against it explaining how busy he was, however they did introduce me to the Minister of Defense. He clearly voiced his interest in a continuing relationship and the one thing he said that truly surprised me the most was this, "Look, these purchases have the full unofficial support of the Government of Panama and let me tell you something else, even though you can never say it in public, we have nothing to worry about."

I couldn't help but ask why that was, and he responded, "America has bigger things to worry about than Panama, namely the Soviets, and to a lesser degree those oil countries in the Middle East. Iraq, Iran. I'm glad I don't live there."

Everyone let out a big laugh and he continued, "Noriega has close ties with America so they aren't worried about him, the American government has a phrase 'he may be a son of a bitch, but he's our son of a bitch.' That means even if he was killing people and even if he does terrible things, as long as he fights Communists, America will give us anything we want."

That was hard to hear, but keeping in character I responded, "Glad to hear."

The sale went off, I got a tan, and I got the money and even a little documentation signed by their Minister of Defense. It blew my mind what I had heard and genuinely couldn't tell whether they were really that confident or whether they were telling me that so I would keep selling them what they wanted. Either way, the remainder of the trip went off without a hitch. Just before going to where I thought we would be having drinks, I remember double checking to make sure I had a pill that could induce vomiting, if they gave me a poisoned drink.

Thankfully the poisoned drink didn't happen and we had some good laughs and told some jokes like old buddies who had known each other for years. It is so hard to have a good time while looking out the corner of your eye for movement, like someone pulling out a gun. We all parted ways and I shook hands with the purchaser who was thrilled with how things were going and said he looked forward to meeting with me again in the near future. I was thankful everything had gone well and I was going home to where it was safe. The plane ride should have been a relief, but I was still scared that maybe while I was away the investigation into the Iran deal had exposed me. I couldn't help but ask myself, "Will handcuffs be waiting for me at the airport?"

I went through the de-briefing and told them everything I had seen and heard. The moment that I had a hard time grasping was when I told them about the Panamanian official's confidence that we weren't watching them and he responded. "Well in April 1986, Noriega left the CIA and is no longer 'our son of a bitch' and if that really is what they think, a regime change will be a lot easier than usual."

What bothered me about that was the implication that if he were still working for the CIA then the idea of us looking the other way, no matter what they did, would be correct. I tried to push that out of my mind but I did wrestle with it for a little while.

After I got back, I finally realized that I had a lot more on my mind than just Panama, or Iran. I began to feel like that person who keeps putting off a diet but the longer you put it off the worse you feel. This was true about proposing to Anita, by this point we had been dating for over a year and I couldn't understand why it was so hard for me to buy that ring and get down on one knee. I loved her and if there is such a thing as a soul mate, it was becoming increasingly obvious that she was mine. With Easter just over the horizon, I knew something was scaring me away from doing it, but what?

I contacted McLachlin, hoping his age and wisdom could give me a clue as to what was holding me back. I was hoping for a simple answer, but that wasn't what I got. He started with, "Sixteen months of dating is not that long of a time, perhaps you're a little worried because of how your last marriage ended."

I asked him what he would do if he were in my shoes, and he said, "Well Melvoy, I say that since Veronica is the one who ended your first marriage, you have nothing to feel guilty over. I also think that if you really want to, and if Anita really is the wonderful woman you have described, then go for it but just get a prenuptial agreement first so you don't get put behind the eight-ball again if something goes wrong."

I thought about what he had said, but the truth was although I had thought about what if we get divorced somehow, I was more worried about the kids or Veronica. I was thinking about how our relationship would work, and would this set off Veronica? I genuinely didn't know. I remember stopping by a jewellery store the Thursday before Easter and looking at all the rings and trying to pick the right one. The truth is I don't know jewellery, I never have, I still don't and I probably never will. I just felt like I needed to get a good-sized ring but I didn't know how much I wanted to spend, and I didn't know whether I should get it engraved. They had so many types of diamonds, I didn't even know whether more carats was a good thing or a bad thing. I came to the conclusion that this was the step that was holding me back, I wanted this to be perfect, only to realize I had no idea what perfect would look like.

Finally, after what felt like an eternity I chose a ring, spent more money than I wanted to and now had to choose the right moment, would it be Good Friday, would it be Easter Sunday? Would it be the week after that? Would it be sometime in May?

Easter dinner went off without a hitch, and I left the ring in the glove compartment of my car and I remember looking around at the kids thinking how happy I was to have this time together. Once again, I kept putting off the proposal, even though I had the ring and had rehearsed what I would say, but I was still struggling with it.

We were well into May when I found out that the kids wanted me to take them to see a movie called *Ernest Goes to Camp*. It had just come out, and I thought that it was a little absurd. I thought it was ridiculous when the bad guy goes to shoot Ernest and it magically doesn't work despite the guy being so close and knowing how to use it, but once again the things you do for your kids.

I finally dropped the kids off at home and I went to drop Anita off at her apartment. I got out of the car right after she did and told her I had a surprise for her. She waited at the front door of the building, and she was thrilled when I asked her to close her eyes. I walked back to my car and reached into my glove box and finally took the big leap and I got onto one knee. I still remember getting down on one knee and feeling the weight coming down on that hard-concrete step.

I told her to open her eyes, she immediately looked across from her and saw nothing and then looked down to see me on one knee. I looked up at her with that beautiful smile that had formed on her face, with her hair that was tied behind her. I could see the sparkle in her eye possibly for the streetlights shining off the tears that were forming and I vividly remember what I said. "Anita, I have been through hell and back, my first marriage ended and it was a hard thing to get over, despite it all, you have been the best thing in my life this last year and a half. I want to spend the rest of my life with you so…"

I opened the ring box, "Will you marry me."

Her face trembled as she began to nod and through her tears said, "Yes, yes I will."

She put the ring on her finger and I stood up, we hugged and it was just a perfect moment. It was one of those moments that I wish I could re-live over and over again.

The next day we went out for dinner with one of her friends and her husband on a double date. I remember spending a good chunk of the night pretending that she worked as a secretary for a small-time fashion magazine. It was so strange to know that I was dating someone who was blatantly lying to one of her closest friends and knowing that I was doing the same thing and we were both okay with it.

We began talking about when the wedding would be, and before I knew it we were talking about it for the summer of 1988, so we could book a really nice hall and have time to properly plan the wedding. Her friends began really pushing for a much fancier wedding than my first wedding with Veronica in 1971.

I began to wonder who my best man should be; I know that tradition said it should be Billy because he was my brother. But did I really want Hashani to be involved? However, I was on great terms with McLachlin who encouraged me to propose in the first place, maybe it should be him instead. Before I could really settle into that decision, I had told the kids, and Veronica got upset saying that I should have spoken to her about it. Then I told her that when the divorce was final, she had no place to make that decision. She began to get annoyed at me and I said, "Besides, what about this stuff about you guys having more kids, are you waiting for my approval or have you already done that?"

That was when Todd told me, "She's almost two months pregnant now."

There was tension but we talked through it and I thought everything was fine. I guess that goes to show that you don't really know everything, people are as unpredictable as they get.

Like most kids Randy and Matthew had the classic older/younger brother dynamic and if Randy got a strike in bowling, Matthew had to get one too. Of course, raising a daughter, especially one like Jackie, was a challenge unlike anything I could have imagined. Somehow completely out of the blue, she began to withdraw from not just me, but from her mother and Todd, and before the end of the summer of 1987, Veronica was at her wit's end.

The conversation I had with Jackie was brutal, and after asking repeatedly she finally told me what was going on; her mother was having a new baby, I had a new wife, and she somehow thought she was being replaced. I told her that was ridiculous, and although a lot of things are replaceable, kids aren't. She didn't believe me and I couldn't understand why she was so worried about this. I had been there so much more recently and I hadn't left her out of things, I had driven her to her soccer games although that was the year she decided she didn't want to play anymore. I didn't understand that she was thirteen already and the world that she was growing up in was very different from the one I had all those years ago.

Where I really put my foot in my mouth was a conversation not long after that, when I told her that if she keeps being a drama queen, no boy would ever want her. Even Anita's eyebrows nearly left her face when I said that I had told her that. She told me, "Charles, teenage girls are very shallow, to them there are about three things in the world that matter, popularity, boys, and looks, and telling them that two of those things won't happen is scary to them."

I felt like I was trying to learn a new language, not to mention I kept telling myself that she was too young to be dating anyway. Those years go by so much quicker in your thirties, and it's very easy to forget a birthday, especially when you are so busy and have a hundred other things on your mind. This took another big leap after I came back from another trip to Panama. I learned nothing new on this one and they began to contemplate whether I had maximized my usefulness on that mission.

By this point it was October 1987, and I decided to give my mother a phone call. I knew her well enough to know her tone of voice and I could sense that something was seriously wrong. She said she would call me back, and did that about an hour later from a phone booth several blocks away because no one could know that she was telling me this. As it turned out, Cynthia's tattooed, motorcycle driving, smoking, punk boyfriend had gotten her pregnant – Cathy and everyone else had found out the day before and everyone was in a panic.

My mother was absolutely about to go through the roof, and started on this long rant about how shameful and embarrassing this was and how if she had gotten pregnant as a teenager, her bag would have been at the door. I had to calm her down and I tried to tell her that they would be okay and that they have more than enough money to look after it.

She almost lost her mind, "Are you listening to yourself? You can never have too much money to feel shame. I was afraid this would happen but they wouldn't listen to me and now they expect me to clean up this mess. Well that little brat will have to deal with this herself. She needs to marry that boy so he can make an honest woman of her."

I told her that if she needed to talk to someone, I was here and at the time it was hard for me not to agree. I remember thinking, "If you lay on your back, you better face the consequences."

You may be wondering what happened next, well I'll tell you. Apparently that kid was seventeen and showed as little care for Cynthia as he had for everything else. Before Christmas, he packed his bags, stole several hundred dollars from his parents, hopped on his motorcycle and hit the road. The story as I heard it was he told her to get an abortion and when she refused, he left, she never saw him again, and if you ask me, he probably died under a bridge.

Cathy and Jason usually had a big Christmas get together where they always seemed to enjoy showing off to their friends or the family. This year instead, they were taking a couple of weeks off going somewhere else, which I think was the Bahamas. My mother refused to go with them and must have called me every other day to talk about how mad she was about the whole situation.

At one point, I asked her if she had told Billy and she scoffed, "Yes, I told him, he was telling me all about how we have to support her, how we can create a good support structure and help ease Cynthia into adulthood. This is what's wrong with things Charles; these parents let their kids get away with everything, even when they do something terrible. I think it's a disgrace that she let that boy do that. Wasn't she thinking of her family, or herself? Charles, let me tell you something, the world is changing, you better watch that daughter of yours like a hawk because believe me it's only a matter of time before those same temptations of boys, and drinking, and sex will creep up on her."

I was pissed off at the kid who ran away and he wouldn't have been able to walk if I had gotten a hold of him. Even though I thought my mother was being overly dramatic, I listened to her. I realized that my own daughter was starting high school next year and was filled with dread and the thought of some guy trying to touch my daughter made me sick. As 1988 began, I had effectively had three big jobs: first, try to take my job at the CIA to the next level; second, get married to Anita; and third, keep my kids, especially Jackie, on the straight and narrow.

CHAPTER 39

LOVE (& HATE) ARE IN THE AIR!

So as you might expect with a wedding scheduled for August that year, a full-time job, and a fear of my children going down the wrong path, my hands were full. Valentine's Day was on the horizon and I was thinking about a romantic evening with Anita. With less than a week to go, I had a bomb drop, some boy had asked Jackie out on a date and she had said that she had to check with her parents. My mother's stern and frightening warning suddenly took over my thoughts and before I even knew what I was saying, I blurted out, "Absolutely not, she is not going, she is too young and I don't trust some boy alone with my daughter."

Todd tried to tell me that he was worried that she might not be mature enough and teenage romances usually end quickly and are really painful. I couldn't tell whether Veronica was doing this out of spite or what, but she said, "I think they should go, it might be a good first experience for them."

I was ready to lose my mind, "Do you even know this boy?"

She responded with his name, that he was in her class, and she had met him when she picked Jackie up from the mall one time. She thought he was a nice boy and that it would be a good experience for her. I absolutely forbade it and the yelling began and finally Veronica said, "Okay Charles, you don't want her to go on this date so you tell her because I'm not taking the blame for this."

I responded, "Fine, I'll go up there and do it right now."

I went up to Jackie's room determined to prove to Veronica that I was in charge and that Jackie would do as I told her. I knocked on the door and she was writing in her diary, and I told her that I had decided she wasn't going out on a date with that boy. She asked why, I said, "You're too young and teenage boys only have their mind on one thing."

She tried to tell me that she had friends whose parents let them go out on dates. I responded that they were being reckless and that there was a lot to protect her from. She didn't like that answer and sarcastically responded, "Oh yeah a movie, popcorn we might hold hands,

217

yeah hide the children."

In retrospect, everything I did next was completely wrong.

I immediately got defensive and saw this as a challenge to my authority, "Are you being a smart mouth young lady?"

She said, "Yes, you're being totally unfair."

I responded saying, "No I'm saving you from yourself so when you get married to a good man and no one is whispering about the white dress, you'll thank me."

She said, "So Sunday night while all the other kids are out on dates, I am going to be home doing the dishes?"

I said, "Yes, you need to learn responsibility and that is the end of the conversation."

She tried to appeal to me, "But Dad…"

I immediately cut her off. "One more word and you are grounded, young lady."

She crossed her arms, rolled her eyes and sat down on her bed, scribbling angrily in her journal. As I was walking down the stairs I heard Matthew say to her, "Ha ha, you got in trouble."

I turned around, "You're grounded if you don't shut it."

I walked downstairs proud that I had laid down the law. Before I left, Veronica pulled me aside and told me how Jackie was going to be mad at me for a long time and I said she would get over it. I had laid down the law and was now going to have a wonderful dinner with Anita.

The dinner went fantastic and the engagement ring sparkled off the lights in the restaurant but the sparkle in her eyes seemed even brighter. Anita had an amazing ability, I could be having the worst day and within fifteen minutes of being with her, all of my problems would disappear. I gave her the heart shaped box full of candy and a dozen roses, and we talked about the wedding she had just arranged for Saturday, August 20th. I couldn't wait to see her walk down the aisle, grinning from ear to ear. It was going to be a perfect night with the love of my life.

Back in Michigan, Cynthia's pregnancy was going well, medically at least, however interpersonally everyone was mad at everyone else. My mother was blaming Cynthia, Cathy and Jason; Cathy and Jason were blaming each other; Cynthia was blaming the guy and was mad at everyone else for getting on her case about it. Even if my mother were exaggerating, I wouldn't have wanted to be in that house for all the money in the world. It was a terrible situation where everyone was mad and no one was accepting responsibility.

Meanwhile with my own kids I was accepting a new norm, Randy was the good son, good grades, did well in school, and played football.

He was showing an interest in wrestling, although he was disappointed that high school wrestling didn't include a ring or jumping off the top rope. Matthew was turning into the second coming of Billy, getting into trouble, being a smart mouth, and I got a few flashbacks of the infamous Easter when Billy left. However, the most troubling of these developments was Jackie who was mad at me all over again. I offered her the role of flower girl for my wedding to Anita and she suddenly decided that all I saw was a little girl. She started going on about me not treating her like an adult and I wasn't taking her seriously. Being a parent is one of the hardest jobs in the world, because there are no shortcuts. I thought putting my foot down was one but I was wrong. I told her she wasn't an adult, she was a thirteen-year-old child and she was having none of it. At one point, she ran upstairs and had blocked the door with her chair and I was there banging on the door demanding that she open it.

Veronica came up and asked, "How's it going?"

Her snide demeanour wasn't appreciated, "Not now Veronica."

She had her arms crossed and was not happy about the entire situation, "Charles, stop banging on her door and let it go."

I started talking about how kids have to respect their parents, and if they don't, they don't listen to the rules and they will go out and do terrible things. She let out an irritated sigh, "Charles, she is not a little girl anymore and simply barking orders doesn't accomplish anything."

I took this badly, "You know Veronica, if she doesn't learn some respect, she could end up like Cynthia, or worse – a thirteen-year-old isn't an adult, not even close. If you are going to let her make the rules then we may as well just throw in the towel right now and wait for the cops to come and say they found her dead in a ditch."

She pointed to the stairs leading to the family room, "Get out."

I marched away annoyed because I felt like Veronica wasn't holding up her end of the bargain.

I had several conversations with McLachlin over those years but this one stood out. He told me about how everything started to go wrong in the 1960s because that was when the parents started losing control over their kids. He told me that what I needed to do was take action and tell Veronica that if she wouldn't do her job, then I would. Someone had to keep those kids on the straight and narrow and as soon as they get out of line, bring back Melvoy the Killjoy and watch how quickly they get back in line. Had they been living in my house, it would have been much easier but they didn't, so it was going to be an uphill battle. McLachlin told me what I wanted to hear and I was happy to hear it.

As we got closer and closer to the wedding day, Anita and I were trying to decide who to invite and who not to, but as we were having the discussion, I zoned out. I started remembering having flashes of my father and I got up while she was in mid-sentence and went to the bathroom.

She began knocking on the outside, "Charles, is everything okay in there."

I told her I would be out in a minute because I didn't want her to see me getting emotional. It had suddenly hit me that my father wasn't going to be at my wedding and it was so hard to imagine an empty place where he would have been. All I could think about were those good times we had, the proud moment when he shook my hand after my first promotion to Private First Class, and all of those times he was there when I was a kid. I came out of the bathroom and told Anita that I was thinking about my father and I didn't go into any more detail, because I didn't want her to see me looking weak. The man was supposed to be strong, and he had to be the pillar of strength that everyone else knew was as solid as a rock. So I pulled myself together to be exactly that, of course even stone pillars have cracks.

That spring I turned on Melvoy the Killjoy and I told my kids what I expected from them and that I was prepared to lay the hammer down if I received any disrespect. One day while I was watching the kids, Veronica and Todd were having one more night out before she would have her baby, Matthew spoke up first and I told him to drop and give me ten push-ups. Keep in mind he was ten at the time and barely pulled off seven before his arms were so shaky that he fell on his face, so I told him to do ten, not seven, and that he owed me three more push ups. He forced out two more grunting until he fell on his face again.

I stood over him, "You owe me one more."

I looked over at Jackie and Randy, and Jackie was clearly unimpressed and Randy looked scared as if he was next.

Matthew barely did one more when I said, "On your feet, so from now on, if your mother, Todd, Anita or I tell you to do something, you're going to do it, are we clear?"

They nodded and I said, "Okay, go do your homework."

They went back upstairs and I felt really good because it reminded me of the feeling of satisfaction I got years ago on a military base when I was turning maggots into soldiers. I had the power and they knew it, but of course it didn't work as well as I had hoped. The next day I got back from the CIA office and a scathing message had been left on my answering machine by Veronica telling me all about how upset Matthew was and how she thought I was losing my mind and forgetting that these are children, not soldiers.

I called back and Todd answered saying that he didn't like what I did and that if I were left in charge of his kid, he wouldn't allow it. I didn't enjoy him talking back to me and telling me how to raise my kids and if anything, I had been too soft on them for too long. I wasn't going to be one of these parents who told the news people, "I don't know what happened, they used to be such good children."

I refused to apologize and the tension between Veronica, Todd, and myself began to get worse all over again. Veronica had her baby, another daughter, and that summer I barely even saw her because between work, my own kids, and the wedding, my time was getting filled up.

The wedding day was closing in and that summer just flew by, and with some reluctance, I invited everyone, Cathy's family, Billy and Hashani, Veronica, Todd and the kids. In retrospect, it was crazy and never should have worked but somehow it did. I had originally planned to offer the role of best man to McLachlin, but with the family politics as they were, I decided not to push my luck and provoke further issues. As the tradition goes, I offered Billy the role of best man, for which he thought he would be a poor choice, given that Jason was the bar owner and would know far more about throwing a party. I thought that made enough sense but I wondered if that was the real reason, because I still didn't like Hashani and she still didn't like me. I was still mad at her because of what had happened with my father being uninvited to their wedding and not attending his funeral. Even though it had happened three years earlier, that grudge was still there and as raw as ever.

That week went as well as I could have hoped and the bachelor party was great although there are significant parts of it I don't remember. We got plenty of congratulations from people at work and to top it all off, we had a great moment during the actual wedding.

I remember looking in the mirror with the tuxedo on and had a brief flash of the previous time I had gotten married seventeen years earlier almost to the day. I was surprised at how much older I looked this time. Jason seemed stressed at every turn and even though things went well, the confident man with the world as his oyster, had been replaced by a frustrated person going through the motions. Billy came up to me and said that he wished he had been there for my first wedding but he was glad to see this one.

I responded, "Well, when you have your second marriage, I'll go to that one."

He looked at me with a very unimpressed look and there were a few seconds of awkward silence, followed by Jason changing the subject.

Chapter 39 : Love (& Hate) Are in the Air!

Outside of that, the day was going very well, and I didn't have time to really think about it because the excitement was a much bigger deal.

The minister arrived and I remember shaking his hand thanking him for being there, he asked me if everything was okay. I said, "Of course, best day of my life."

His smile went from ear to ear as he patted me on the back said, "That's the spirit."

I came out of the dressing room and the church was beautifully decorated with white lace lining the walls. The organ began to play as each of the people came down the aisle. I looked over at my kids who were sitting there, less excited than I expected them to be. I looked over at Veronica and Todd who seemed like they were doing fine. I looked and saw my mother who was emotional and sitting in the pews further back, which was something my mother had insisted on. She insisted on that because Cathy, one of the babysitters, the kids and Cynthia's baby would be there and she wanted them out of sight. Her shame of the teenage pregnancy trumped the tradition of sitting in the front row. You may be thinking that with all of these small things not being so great, why was this day so wonderful, well I can tell you.

The organ began playing Here Comes the Bride and we had held on to the tradition of not seeing the wedding dress, so I had no idea what she was going to look like. Then Anita came down the aisle and she had a smile and a brightness to her that was above anything I had seen before. With each step, my heart beat a little faster and as she got closer and closer, I felt something I had not felt in a very long time. A weightlessness, like all of the weight and concerns of my life had been completely and utterly abolished, and for those precious seconds, nothing else mattered, and it seemed like no one else was in the room. It was just her and I, and it was a truly perfect moment.

During the ceremony, the minister said something that I had never heard before. "A marriage is a life-long commitment and what it requires from both partners is not easy, but is deeply rewarding. If you move forward with integrity, honesty and love, both partners will continue to move together in whatever direction life takes them."

Then came the moment of truth when the minister stood up and asked, "If anyone has a reason why these two should not be wed, speak now or forever hold your peace."

My heart beat a mile a minute with each passing second feeling like an hour as if waiting for something to ruin my perfect day. Just like something came along and had ruined so many other things.

Finally, the minister said, "Very well."

We both said, "I do."

Melvoy's Railroad

It was the greatest feeling in the world hearing him say, "I now pronounce you husband and wife, you may now kiss the bride."

She lifted her veil and she looked beautiful, with not a single hair was out of place, and every tiny bit of her face looked perfect.

During the reception McLachlin was there and gave us a war figurine of a Civil War soldier riding a horse while holding the American flag. I thought it was fantastic, and most of the other presents were fairly standard like a blender, microwave, etc. There were a few moments from the reception that stood out. I remember Jason's speech saying, "Charles Melvoy is a remarkable man, a man who has incredible drive and integrity. When he commits to something, he is as great as they come, quite frankly Charles, I look up to you. You have to have incredible commitment to strap on a set of boots and go half way around the world to fight for our country. You have to have incredible commitment to do it repeatedly, even after getting injured. He is also a committed son, and when his late father fell ill, he bent over backwards helping him recover, and while I don't want to be a downer, he was there for him right until the end. Anita, with that type of courage and commitment, I have no doubt that he will put his all into this marriage."

The crowd applauded and I was taken aback as those were the nicest things he had ever said to me.

I remember going up to the podium with Anita and I still remember the short speech she gave, "Charles, ever since I first laid my eyes on you, I knew you were a good-looking man, but I had no idea how great a man you were until I began speaking with you. Your loyalty and the fact that you are never one to run away from any problem and are willing to carry the weight of the whole world on your shoulders for the good of those you serve, is incredible. I want to conclude by saying Charles, as long as we are together you will no longer have to carry that weight by yourself."

The crowd let out a loud, "Aw."

It was now my turn, and it had taken me hours to figure out what I was going to say. The paper I was pulling out of my pocket was either my eighth or ninth draft. "I would like to thank everyone for being here, people I worked with during my military service, friends, family, and my kids."

I waved and they unenthusiastically raised their hands in return. "Even though life is hard, it is rough, sometimes hideous, you get a handful of beautiful moments and a handful of beautiful people who make you feel like the luckiest man on earth. Anita, you do that for me every time we kiss and every time I get to hold you in my arms, it took a long time for me to find the one, but I did. Today I say," I raised my champagne glass, "thank God for second chances."

The crowd applauded as we kissed. It was a perfect night as we danced and drank and ate a feast, and I knew this had cost me a fair amount of money but it turned out to be worth every penny.

The honeymoon was great, and we went to a bed and breakfast north of us. It had a window that looked out into an open green field and although the weather was unusually cool for August, it made the perfect cool breeze. It was right out of a movie, and it was hard to describe how good that time felt and how much I wish I could go back and relive it and savour it that much more.

One of the most vivid memories I had was of the moments just after we had had sex, when we both laid there catching our breath, cooling down from the intensity. Her hair pushed up against the pillow pushing it out an inch in all directions, and she caressed the edge of her fingernails against the side of my face. The soft touch sent a chill across my face and I remember her saying, "I wish this moment could last forever."

I responded, "Me too."

After we got back from the honeymoon, I felt a special spring in my step as if I was fifteen years younger and as if I had a new lease on life. I was re-energized to carry out the mission that I had committed myself to. I wasn't going to let my sons become the new Billy, or let Jackie become a new Cynthia, who was now a sixteen-year-old teenage mother. They had made their terrible decisions and I had to stop my family from making the same ones. Of course, as you will find out, there are no shortage of mistakes we can make about people, about life, and most of all about being a parent.

CHAPTER 40

1989: A PANAMANIAN ODYSSEY

Shortly after returning from my honeymoon I realized a few people were mad at me, and Billy didn't appreciate my comment and thought that I was saying that his marriage to Hashani was doomed. I also found out that my comment about "thank God for second chances" was offensive to Veronica, which I disregarded, after all Todd was hers. However, my kids were not happy and said they found the wedding boring, and Jackie saw the entire thing as an event lying about how great I was. Needless to say, I didn't care for her comments and she hated all of the twenty push-ups I made her do in response. I was not only Melvoy the Killjoy, I was a re-energized Melvoy the Killjoy who wasn't going to back down.

I also found out about another mission I was being assigned to, but as it turned out there was someone that the U.S. was considering backing in the planned overthrow of Noriega. His name was Moises Giroldi and they wanted to know if they could trust him. So it was decided that early in the New Year, I along with someone else, would be sent to southern Costa Rica and then would meet with him in a place in Panama near the border. It was planned this way so that we could avoid their officials spotting U.S. planes. For the remainder of 1988, I was preparing for my next mission, while trying to get everything where I wanted it. I eventually came to an agreement with Billy that I wouldn't say anything else about Hashani because I had to accept their relationship regardless of how much I didn't like her.

I then had to work things out with Veronica and had to explain that it wasn't a shot at her but just a simple fact that we needed a second chance as she did. She didn't like it but after a few seconds of silence she said, "Okay I guess I understand."

There were a few other issues to sort out, and I told Jackie that she wasn't going on any dates, she wasn't going to get fast talked by some guy, but she was going to keep herself safe from that type of behaviour. She resented me for it and over those months she did plenty of push-ups. There was another very serious problem, when I came over on a Saturday afternoon to take the kids over to my house, Veronica came up to me with a great deal of focus. I was wondering what problem she had with me now, but that wasn't her problem.

"Charles, come here we need to talk about something."

I said, "Okay." Bracing myself for yet another complaint.

"Guess what Matthew did?"

I asked, "What?"

She responded, "Well yesterday after school, I sent him to his friend's (I don't remember the kids name) house and I get a phone call from Mrs. Wilkinson, his math teacher. When she came home from a staff meeting, her house had been egged and her neighbours described our son and his friend perfectly."

I was really upset and asking where he was, she responded, "You know Charles, I don't usually care for your approach, but after this be as hard on him as you need to."

I nodded, "You don't have to tell me twice."

That weekend when I brought the kids home, I sat them all down and paced back and forth in front of them. "Let me explain something to you, I expect a lot from you because I know that there is a lot of good you can do. However, there are a lot of stupid things you can do too, so for this weekend, Matthew you are going pay for what you did last night. As for the two of you, don't help him, don't make excuses for him, he alone did this and he has to pay the consequences."

Not only did he do his homework, but he did every chore, and I even made him run around the house multiple times until he was exhausted. I reminded him that it can get worse and he would know that it would be worse next time.

Before that weekend was over, I was walking past the room that the boys were sleeping in, and I heard them angrily whispering at each other, "You told them, you tattletale."

Randy responded, "I never said anything."

I kept listening as Matthew asked, "Well then how did they find out, she wasn't home."

Randy continued, "I don't know but I wouldn't rat you out."

Suddenly Matthew yelled out, "You liar!"

Then they started wrestling and I heard something fall over and I charged in. "What the hell is going on in here?"

I pulled them apart, "What's going on now?"

Matthew blurted out, "Randy told Mom on me, I didn't tell on him, he's the one who gave me the eggs and told me where she lived."

I turned to Randy, "Really?"

He looked like a deer in the headlights barely able to blurt out a word, "Well, uh, no."

I stared a hole through Randy and you don't need CIA training to know when a twelve-year-old is panicking on the inside. "Why? Tell me now."

He took a big gulp and said, "Mrs. Wilkinson was giving Matthew a hard time and she was mean to me too."

I got very angry; Melvoy the Killjoy got turned on full blast. "Line up, the two of you are in a world of trouble. Matthew what you went through today isn't even close to the end of your punishment and you have more coming for not telling the truth. As for you Randy, you are in deep trouble too, and tomorrow is going to be a day from hell. You thought your teacher was mean, you don't know what mean is, and by the time tomorrow is done, you will know what mean is. If you have any other information I should know, you better tell me right now because if I find out some other way, you will be in a world of crap! Lights out maggots!"

I walked out angry and I can only imagine how scared they were. I walked over to Jackie who was watching TV with Anita and I told Anita what I had heard. I turned to Jackie, "Did you know anything about this?"

She said, "No, if they were going to pull a prank, they wouldn't include me. Matthew is still in his 'girls are gross' phase."

I looked at my watch, "You're going to bed in half an hour and don't give me any crap. I am not in the mood for it."

The next day we came home from church, and I gave those boys a lot of grief. I started by telling Randy, who had wanted to wrestle, that he wasn't going to wrestle for a while. He tried to complain but his pleas fell on deaf ears. I told them both that they weren't going to see any movies, or go to anything fun for a long time. I also started marching them up and down the street until they were sweating buckets. I didn't let them have any of the chips or candy they liked and made sure Anita gave them the plainest meals imaginable. By the time it was over, I asked them, "Are you ever going to pull this stuff again?"

They said, "No."

I responded, "You better not, because I will come down on you even worse."

By the time I dropped them off at Veronica's house, they were tired and relieved that today was over.

I told Veronica about what had happened and why I was hard on Randy as well, she rolled her eyes, "Oh no, I thought he was the one I could trust."

I responded, "Well, after the way I ran them ragged, they will think

Melvoy's Railroad

twice about it from now on."

Before 1988 was over, I had dealt with several files, was winning over my superiors and my co-workers and I was proving my worth, especially with my continued silence on the Iran Contra affair. I remember the Tuesday of the election that year, when several of the guys at the office had an office party with the TVs tuned into the election. It was George H.W. Bush vs. Michael Dukakis, and while it wasn't as much of a crushing defeat as Reagan had dished out four years earlier, the Democrats had wrestled a handful of states from Bush but it was still nowhere near enough. As soon as the news declared that he was the projected winner, the people in the office were thrilled with the result.

In the weeks that followed, I studied my next mission and was determined to finish this mission to derail the things that Noriega was up to. I was excited to help end his regime of drugs and other smuggling. I knew that 1989 was going to begin with another risky mission and it was hard because I had a loving wife and three kids waiting for me and I had to hope that nothing would go wrong. I had been fortunate to not have any serious things go wrong in previous missions, however this time I had this gut feeling that something was going to happen.

I got my de-briefings, my alternate I.D., and due to the nature of this mission, I was also given two guns, a knife and a bulletproof vest. I remember having a sudden flashback to the day Phil "the Hill" died in Vietnam and I was surprised at how vivid it was. That bad feeling wouldn't go away and I remember climbing aboard the chopper. I had done something like this before but this time it would be harder. This time we weren't meeting with the government; we were meeting with people trying to overthrow the government. No one was going to bail us out if we got caught.

We landed in a town about twenty-five miles or so from the border and I remembered one of the people who greeted us, laying out the last-minute details. He told us about the car that was taking us into Panama and the cyanide capsules if needed. Then he said the words he told me to repeat in my head over and over again, so I don't forget them. "If things go sideways and you can get away, get across that border any way you can and get to a purple shed on the northwest part of San Vito, and call this number from that phone."

He handed me a piece of paper with a phone number that didn't have the usual number order I was used to. "We'll pick you up, and remember Noriega can't find out what we are up to."

As the car drove us, I read and repeated the number and the name of the city to myself and as we drove closer and closer to the border, I kept telling myself that everything would be fine. We got across the border with our prepared alternate I.D.s and passports and the border guard looked everything over and then let us in. We drove down a long dirt road, and we finally arrived at a nice looking home, almost the size of home you would see a rich person with today. The bright sun bounced off the windows as I scanned for any mysterious movement, nothing appeared obvious.

When we arrived, two men in sunglasses, straw hats, and Hawaiian shirts met us and that horrible feeling was still hovering in the pit of my stomach. After they introduced themselves, one of them was named Banderas, we asked where Giroldi was. They said that something came up and he couldn't make it, however he still wanted to know what we were willing to offer. We explained that if he agreed to shut down the drugs and other operations, we could make sure they were well stocked with weapons, and would be willing to send troops if anyone else tried to launch a coup against Giroldi. Additionally, he had to be completely on our side and do little to no dealings with any Communist regimes, whether they be Russia, Cuba, etc.

In response Banderas said, "Mr. Giroldi has no interest in Communism or with Cuba. You could sink it into the ocean and it wouldn't concern him."

Just as I was beginning to think this meeting was going to go well, a large window several feet from us shattered because a grenade had been thrown in. I immediately dove away, and thankfully I only felt my feet being hot as I immediately looked for the nearest exit. Soldiers began coming through the door, as I raced upstairs seeing them coming into the nearby hallway. My heart raced as I knew I didn't have long to get them off my trail.

I had no idea whether or not they had the house surrounded and even if I had opened fire, I only had enough bullets to refill each handgun once. After getting upstairs in no time, I ran into the nearby bathroom trying to figure out my next move. With only seconds to make a decision, I saw a window ahead of me, a shelf with towels, and a sink to the right, to my left was a five-foot-long claw foot bath tub, and a toilet near the window. I picked the far side of the tub up off the floor and struggled to plant the feet up against the door. It was a struggle because of how heavy the tub was but the adrenaline allowed me to move it.

As I heard them come up the stairs I kicked through the glass window, but before I could see if it was safe to jump, I heard them coming to the door and I immediately got down as they opened fire. The instant the gunfire subsided, I heard them breaking down the door, so I rolled under where the tub would fall. Sure enough they knocked it over, and the thud was deafening as it echoed within the tub. I pulled myself into the fetal position to hide myself and heard one of them yell in Spanish, "Salio por la ventana," which means, "He went out the window."

They raced away as I had to contemplate my next move and how to escape. I waited another half minute just to be safe.

Remembering how hard the tub crashed when it landed around me and realizing that another loud crash would draw the soldiers back in my direction, I laid on my back and pushed the tub up with my legs, as I moved my arms and chest under the side of the raised tub. My legs began to tire quickly. I struggled but finally wiggled all the way out from under the tub while easing it down and pulling my hands out at the last second.

I ached but I knew that I had a lot left to do so I crawled towards the window and listened intently for any sign of people or any clue of what was going to happen. While my Spanish wasn't perfect, I heard them say something that sounded like "burn it to the ground." Now what was I going to do? I drew my gun and gradually opened the hall door, looking for any sign of trouble. I quickly moved back and forth from room to room as I came closer to the stairs. I listened, and as I peered my head around the corner looking for any movement, I saw four men walk by. One of them said, "Muerto," which means, "Dead."

Immediately I knew I was alone and would not have any help. I went back up the stairs and looked out a different window, where off in the distance was a road that had cars going by. It looked like a long walk away, but it might be enough for me to hitchhike to the border. I looked near the house trying to figure out if I jumped out, if I could make it. I heard footsteps coming up the stairs and knew I was trapped in the room. I immediately ran to the corner near the door and waited repeating to myself, "This is what I have trained for."

As soon as the first soldier came in, I grabbed his wrist forcing his gun upwards in one move, firing the bullet into his own head. The second soldier shoved him out of the way leaving his head vulnerable. In one quick move, I snapped his neck and eased him to the ground. The gunshot had attracted attention, and I could hear more of them coming so I leapt out the open window, holding onto the bottom of the window and then jumping down.

I did the roll through that I had practiced over and over again months earlier and began running for the road in the distance, hoping none of them would spot me. The window I had jumped out of was on the opposite side of the road leading to the house, and every two seconds I looked over my shoulder for any sign of pursuers. I was running faster than I had in years, and I was getting winded but I couldn't stop. The road must have been over a mile away but I began to feel my energy giving way and thankfully just ahead was a small hill, where I stopped and hid hoping to catch my breath and figure out my next move.

I strained my eyes and saw soldiers coming around to the side of the house I had jumped out of, they were looking around. I had to hope that I had lost them. Then I saw the smoke and I realized what was happening. They thought I was still inside and they were standing guard to make sure I didn't make it out alive. I was caught in an odd situation. The good news was they didn't know where I was and I could catch my breath, the bad news was that if they spotted me, they would be after me and it would be easy shooting. So I had to lie there and watch the house get burned to the ground and wait for them to leave before I could move from where I was. All while the sun was beating on me and getting higher and higher in the sky. Then I had to hitch a ride to the border.

As my bad luck would have it, the road I ran towards was a mile in the wrong direction and a few men in a truck pulled over asking me what I was doing. I told them a lie about how I took a wrong turn, my car had broken down, and my family was waiting for me in Costa Rica. When acting, you can sometimes transfer real feelings you have, or had, to make your pretend feelings look more real. In this case I was trying to get back to my family, which helped make my pleas look more legitimate. They asked about my passport, and I looked through my pockets pretending I didn't have it and said, "She must still have it in her purse."

I thought they took pity on me and said in Spanish, "Okay my brother, we will take you across the border."

As it turned out the truck had bench seats that lifted up in the back. So, I had to climb into there, my heart raced, if they sold me out I would have no chance.

With great reluctance I climbed in, and waited for what seemed like forever, it was so hot in that compartment that if I was in there five minutes, it felt like an hour. As soon as the vehicle stopped, I reached into my pocket and pulled my gun, because if I was going down, I was going down with a fight. After a few minutes, we kept moving and I hoped that was the border and we were now on our way to San Vito.

The heat was really getting to me, I was beginning to fear that I would be baked alive in the back of this truck. Finally, it stopped again, my gun was drawn, and I imagined Anita walking down the aisle. I could imagine seeing her head on the pillow at home and I knew I had to get home, one way or another.

The bench seat was lifted up and they told me to get out, and I pulled myself out, tucking my gun back into my pants before any of them could see it. I fell on the ground from dehydration and exhaustion. The driver asked me if I was okay and I told him how hot it was and he said, "Well we got you over the border, we risked our necks, what are you going to do for us?"

I reached into my pocket and I gave them some money. The driver then took me by the shoulder and led me to the other side of the truck and I saw the small city. The city sign was a football field away and sure enough it said, "San Vito." I shook his hand and began the walk. I remembered the purple shed, however with the state I was in, all the people in the town probably thought I was coming from a bar.

I looked around mumbling and feeling so disoriented, I'm sure people were staring. I remember a car horn blaring and a person yelling something, trying to tell me to get out of the way. I finally came around a corner and down the road was a small almost dilapidated home with a purple shed. By this point, I was in such rough shape physically and mentally, that a tear came to my eye. I stumbled towards the shed; the sun was high overhead and had been beating on me for hours. I was really losing it when I fell face down in the dirt, and the hot sand wasn't enough to help me keep conscious.

I woke up some time later, and was laid across a few wooden chairs in a bar. I was looking around and someone said something that meant I was awake. One of the guys started asking where I came from, and I told him I had to get to the purple shed. The bar owner and two other guys helped me walk into his back room, where he spoke in broken English. "Listen, whoever you are, I saw your guns, we don't want that here, we want no trouble, why do you have to go to the purple shed? Are you here to kill someone?"

I said, "No, I can call home from there."

He looked at the other two guys, and I was in no shape to fight anyone he said, "Okay, we hold your guns, when your friend comes to pick you up, we give them back and watch you leave, deal?"

I asked, "Could you give me a ride?"

He nodded, and one of the two men who were standing there watching me left, I handed my guns over to the bar owner. I knew I didn't have much going for me, but I needed to get there by any means necessary. We got in a run-down car that looked like a car from the early 1970s and had been driven across the planet. We got in as they gave me a glass of water and I was so thirsty, I could have drunk a waterfall.

We drove to the house and one of the gentlemen came with me

and knocked on the door but no one answered, so I opened the garage door and there was the phone. I asked for some privacy. It took me a moment but I remembered what the number was, I dialed the number and left a message to come and get me at the bar in San Vito.

They drove me back as I waited. I saw the kids playing with a few adults, one of the men said to me, "Nice to see that, parents playing with kids, that's life brother. Whatever you do with your life, remember that is what life should be."

I looked at the scene but I couldn't help but wonder what life they were living and how could they be so oblivious to what was going on around them? They had a drug lord living next door and I didn't understand how they could just play there. They didn't look like wealthy people and shouldn't they be working? It struck me as so odd, as if they and I had such different priorities that it was mind-boggling.

I waited at the bar, since I had given most of my money to the guys who had smuggled me across the border. I couldn't afford much but I got myself a couple drinks of whiskey. Finally, four guys came in and asked for me by my alternate I.D. name. I stood up and the bar owner said, "Wait a second."

He went to hand me my guns and then said quietly, "Take your guns out of here and if you ever return, no guns. We don't want that here."

I nodded and thanked him as we got in the car and left. As we got to the plane that would take me home, one of the people who accompanied me on the plane, asked if there was anything he could do. I responded, "Get me a drink, after the day I've had, I need as many as I can get."

Thankfully they had bottles of water that had been kept cold, and after that experience the cold water touching my tongue was just a little piece of heaven.

They flew me back home, where I was hurriedly rushed to the CIA office to explain what had happened. As expected, Mr. Graham and my direct boss Mr. Donovan, were there with several other people. After telling them the whole story, every agonizing detail that I could recall, they were simultaneously amazed and bewildered. By the time I had finished my story, it was 1:00 am and I had been awake for twenty-one hours straight.

Finally, Mr. Graham and Mr. Donovan looked at each other. Mr. Graham responded first, "Okay we're going to get to the bottom of this, and thank you for proving to us that this guy is trouble. We will definitely be passing that information on."

Mr. Donovan shook my hand, "Amazing work, you showed ingenuity, determination and negotiation skills, you've come a long way Melvoy."

The proud smile on his face said it all, and he had been speaking on my behalf and I had proven him right.

I had to stay locked in the office until that evening, in order to maintain consistency with the story that I had when I left. That night I slept in the storage room in the basement of the office, knowing that Anita was waiting for me at home. Just eighteen more hours and she would be in my arms again.

Those hours felt so long and then finally the car came to take me home. I remember having a flashback to the moment when I was hiding under the tub and I felt that same claustrophobia for a moment and I didn't know why. Finally, we pulled up to my house and I came to the door, put my key in the lock and declared, "Honey, I'm home."

There she was, and she walked up to me, put her arms around me and I held her so tight. Right then I whispered in her ear, "I thought I would never see you again and I never want to let you go."

CHAPTER 41

NOT ALL BOMBS ARE DROPPED BY ENEMIES

The rest of 1989 was an entirely different story. I was forbidden from telling Anita what really happened and all I could tell her was that the mission went very badly and I had almost died. Even then I might have said too much, but she was comforting and supportive nonetheless. I was called into Mr. Donovan's office a few weeks later to discuss the basics of what had happened.

"Charles, I just want to say that you did an amazing job, a lot of guys would have gotten captured or not made it out alive. Thanks to your intel and a few other sources, we were able to figure out what happened; apparently someone ratted out Giroldi's meeting to Noriega. Someone in turn tipped off Giroldi that they were coming a couple hours earlier, so he sent a couple of patsies in there hoping they could wrap up the meeting in a few minutes before the troops showed up. We have heard nothing from the other agent or from our intel in Noriega's regime that he was captured, which leads me to believe you heard correctly that he was dead, either from the grenade or the cyanide pill. Yesterday we got a fax of their internal reports that mentioned the incident, but they never successfully identified you and believed you were hiding in the house when they burned it down. So if we have to arrange another meeting, you're still in the clear."

I was relieved that they didn't see me and if they knew who I was, I dreaded the thought of them coming here to get me. He then said, "After discussions with Mr. Graham and a few of our respective colleagues, we are upgrading you to senior field agent which will include a bump in pay and a little more vacation time."

I was over the moon and thrilled because once again at work I was respected and my efforts, even through the harshest of conditions, bore fruit. At home, it was a different story.

Anita was happy with my promotion, as she was always proud of me, however I couldn't tell anyone else. Maybe I could tell them the raise in pay part but that was it. It was around this time that I had a call from Veronica expressing her concern over Jackie.

She asked Jackie if there were any boys that she was interested in at school and she said, "Not a one."

I heard this and didn't know why Veronica was worried. I didn't want Jackie dating high school boys, so if she wasn't even trying to, there was no issue. Meanwhile Randy was starting to like girls but was at that stage where he was too shy to ask them out. Matthew, as far as I knew, was staying out of trouble. It seemed like things were going well enough, but unfortunately the positives couldn't keep going forever.

On the other side of the family, it was one problem after another. Cathy's two boys got caught with marijuana, and the silver lining of that situation was that they were caught by Cathy, and not the police. However, that wasn't much comfort to my mother, who actually began talking to me about them moving in with Anita and I. I told her no way that could happen because if they bring that stuff into my house and the police find out, it would be a huge problem, not to mention I didn't want that stuff around my own kids. The additional reason was that I didn't want them to know about my role in the CIA and as far as everyone besides Anita knew, I was still a regional manager of a chain of grocery stores.

As the spring of 1989 came around, things once again boiled over with Billy. One day he called me to talk about the situation with Cathy's kids and at one point he suggested that he might take them in if things get worse.

I asked him, "Why are you trying to take them in? You and Hashani are both in your thirties you should be having your own kids. Why aren't you?"

He began to talk about how they were trying to keep their careers going and decided it wasn't what they wanted for their lives. I immediately jumped to the wrong conclusion, "Let me get this straight. She's not having your kids, doesn't she know that is what women are supposed to do? You and her have been married for a few years now so what does she expect – you to get pregnant?"

I heard a groan, "Charles, this isn't the fifties and that attitude wasn't right then either."

The older brother in me came out, "Billy, having kids is part of being a man, having kids is part of being a woman. If women back in the past had taken that attitude, none of us would be here."

He was ready with his own statement, "Charles, humanity is not suffering from a lack of people. We have over five billion and counting, not everyone has to have kids and it is probably better that some people don't."

I responded, "Yeah, I guess you wouldn't want to have Hashani raise daughters to be as shrewish as she is and sons who are emasculated."

There was a long awkward pause, "You know Charles, despite our nation's political choices, the world is changing and the next generation isn't going to think like that."

I responded by saying, "You know what Billy, if the world is changing we have to stop it any way we can. Our nation was made great by men and women who knew their place."

He objected again, "Charles, did it ever occur to you that those places were arbitrary and in some cases completely wrong?"

I asked him what he was talking about. He responded, "Maybe if you hadn't been so domineering and all about you, your first marriage wouldn't have ended."

At that point, I had heard all I was going to hear, "Billy, call me when you finally reclaim your balls from Hashani."

I hung up in his ear, and was angry that he had the nerve to say that the divorce was my fault. I told myself over and over that it was her fault. She asked for the divorce, and was the one who didn't want to live up to her role as wife and mother.

I told Anita about the conversation and she was supportive, and she and I had agreed that she would keep working until we had children. I began to wonder about whether or not we should and if so, when. I enjoyed being at work with her, and all of the time I could possibly spend with her, because she wasn't just my wife, she was my best friend. We began talking about it and she was excited about the possibility of having kids, so we were trying to decide when, how many, and other details. Before that spring was over, we decided we were going to have children and she wanted to have two children, to be a wife and mother and wanted the same things I did for our country and ourselves.

That summer we tried and every month it didn't happen. While the first month wasn't a big deal, by the time that September came around and she still wasn't pregnant I began to wonder if something was wrong. I asked myself, "It didn't take anywhere near this long for me to get Veronica pregnant over a decade ago, was I too old or was something going on with Anita?"

The frustration about this situation had been building and I got a special phone call from McLachlin, who not only had been overseeing the missile defense systems, but now had a direct line to President George H.W. Bush. The reason why he called was that it was a special day. It was the fortieth anniversary of the first Soviet nuclear test, which was the shot that put the cold war in motion. We talked about how the Soviets were struggling and the internal fighting was eating away at them.

McLachlin told me something that I will remember for the rest of my life, "Melvoy, I used to wonder what it was like for the British and the French all of those centuries ago, wondering what it was like to have an enemy that they never fully vanquished. Well I have a sense of it now and it's frustrating as all hell. But if we keep at it, we may finally be able to take them down and finally be victorious. It's just a matter of when and how."

I remember asking him when it would happen and he responded, "If we keep the pressure on them – they have been stumbling recently, and they may be coming apart now. If we keep them competing with us, and given the right circumstances, they might be done during Bush's second term."

I said, "Well, you never know, the democrats could win in '92."

We both laughed because they had not just lost, but been destroyed in the last three elections and at that point, there was no star on the horizon who would be a threat.

The conversation then moved onto more personal matters. He was doing very well, his kids were doing great, he had a job for life and he was making a very comfortable living advising on nuclear policy. He asked me how I was doing and I told him some of the basics about how Anita and I were trying to have a baby and I couldn't figure out why it wasn't working. He then began to tell me about someone his brother knew who was trying to have a child, but the wife went behind his back and kept taking the pill. I asked him why she was doing that, and his response was, "She didn't want to do the work, she wanted him to try, give up, and hire a maid so she wouldn't have to do anything. Kids are work but some women try to get out of doing their job."

I asked him, "You don't think Anita is doing that, do you?"

He responded, "Well she is a lovely woman but you never know, women are the most dangerous manipulators in the world."

I thanked him for the warning; I got off the phone and began to seriously consider what he was saying.

As horrible as it was, I began to wonder if she was secretly taking the pill and wasn't serious about having a child. With this concern bouncing around my mind and for weeks not talking to anyone about it, that suspicion grew and grew. By the time October came around I was convinced that something was up, because she was getting more irritable and more easily upset. I called her doctor, I spoke to the pharmacist, I even went looking around through her purse, and that one she found out about. When I finally told her what I thought she was doing, her eyes began to water and her voice began to crack. "Charles how can you think that? I want this as bad as I've wanted anything in my life. I never accused you of putting on a condom when I'm not looking."

I then said, "Well then what's going on, we've been trying for over five months now?"

By this point she was crying, "I don't know!"

She went back to our room and I decided I was going to get to the bottom of this. I called a fertility clinic, and at first they said that I shouldn't be too worried as some women reach the height of their fertility at certain times of the year and maybe her time hadn't arrived yet. I wasn't taking that chance and I was going to get to the bottom of this once and for all. So I made an appointment for both of us to find out what was going on, and she resented me for it, as if I didn't trust her. She didn't even want to talk to me, and this was the biggest fight we ever had by a huge margin.

We went to the clinic, we did every test they had and they told us to come back in a few days for the results. We barely spoke at work, and she didn't want to speak to me in the house so it became awful, like my marriage with Veronica all over again. Finally, the day came, and she gave me the silent treatment that whole morning.

I didn't handle it well, "Would you please grow up and talk to me?" I demanded.

She turned to me in disgust, "Charles, I would never lie to you. I love you and the fact that you think I would do something so despicable as to take the pill when we are trying to have a baby is so hurtful. We are going to this appointment and the next thing you say to me better be 'I'm sorry.'"

If she was taking the pill behind my back, then she was trying to bluff me, but it was hard for me to imagine her thinking that would work.

We got to the clinic and that was when the doctor told us, "Are you familiar with uterine polyps?"

I had never heard the term before so he proceeded to show us a rough diagram, which I wasn't entirely comfortable looking at. He proceeded to explain that they occasionally can grow, and based on the ultrasound, they were growing in the walls of her uterus in such a way that were preventing pregnancy. I naturally asked what we could do, and he said there really wasn't much they could do and even if they had a surgery to remove it, the polyps could grow back, further impeding pregnancy. He gave us a very heavy, "I'm sorry, I'll give you a few minutes."

Anita was so devastated that our fight instantly ended, I threw my arms around her and I whispered in her ear, "I'm sorry."

Those weren't easy words for me to say but in that situation, even I couldn't avoid them.

As you might imagine, this issue had pre-occupied a lot of my mind in those months, which is why the next big hit got me even harder. It was Saturday, and once again I had the kids and I was getting ready to take them back to my house, and the boys were already waiting downstairs. Jackie and her friend Clarissa had a sleepover the night before and Clarissa was supposed to be on her way out. I walked upstairs to go get her when I saw it, my daughter and this blonde girl Clarissa kissing. I don't mean a peck on the cheek, I mean passionately like I would have kissed a girl when I was a teenager.

"What are you doing?" I blurted out in a loud voice, and suddenly the usually talkative Jackie was a deer caught in the headlights. I continued, "You two get downstairs now."

I came downstairs and told the boys to go outside and play. Matthew asked why and I said, "Never mind, just go."

Veronica suddenly looked confused, "Charles, what are you doing, what's going on?"

I waited until the back door closed before I said anything else. "I went upstairs and I saw these two kissing like a teenage couple."

Jackie could barely say a word and Clarissa looked like someone who was in front of a firing squad. Veronica turned to Jackie, "Is that true?"

She could barely eke out a, "Yeah."

Veronica responded, "When did this start?"

Jackie began to regain her composure, "A couple months ago, we really like each other and she helped me realize I… like…girls."

I put my face in my hand and I turned to Veronica, "How the hell did you let this happen? How did you let our daughter turn into a lily licker?" By this point I was starting to yell.

Veronica said, "Charles, it's not that big of a deal, I mean other parents have gay sons or lesbian daughters and they turn out fine. Mrs. Lockleer's nephew is an interior designer and he is charming and doing very well for himself."

I was having none of it, "Veronica, what is wrong with you? You are acting like this is no big deal!"

She hesitantly said, "Maybe it isn't."

My jaw hung open for a few seconds, "Are you kidding me? This is degenerate behaviour! If we let this slide, where will it end?"

Veronica began to get upset, "Charles, don't be ridiculous."

I responded, "No, what's ridiculous is that you let this happen. These people have AIDS and are spreading it across the country, not to mention how the hell do they have kids, they won't. We have to stop this right now before it goes any further, and make sure you call Clarissa's mother so she can fix this on her end."

Clarissa then went into a full panic, "No please don't tell my parents, they're really strict and if they find out, there's no telling what will happen. Please I'm begging you, please don't!"

I had no sympathy, "Hey, you have to face the music for what you are doing wrong here."

Veronica began to get even more upset, "Charles, you're blowing this way out of proportion!"

I didn't think so, "Oh I get it, this happened because you were letting her hang around with degenerates during the week, so now that it's emerged you're denying everything."

She said, "Charles, you are going to leave this alone and if you're not going to, then the kids are staying with me this weekend."

I wasn't giving up that easy, "Fine, I'll tell the boys that they are staying here this week and you can deal with what you've allowed to happen."

I walked out and told the boys a lie about how their mother wanted to spend more time with them. However, there was another reason why I did that. The phone and the address book were on the way outside and I had grabbed the address book on my way. I came back in and I came right up to Jackie, "This has to stop, Jackie."

I kept walking and went outside, I got home and gave Anita a big hug and kiss and she then asked where the kids were. I told her I would explain in one moment, I flipped through the book until I got to the part where the kids had written their friends' information, and I noticed by the address that Clarissa's parents were from the rich neighbourhood. I then began punching in the number for Clarissa, her mother picked up, I told her who I was and what I saw and that she had to deal with this, and she was horrified but thanked me for telling her.

Anita had overheard the conversation and she asked me what happened. After telling her what happened and that Veronica came to Jackie's defense, Anita paused. "I just can't believe that Veronica was okay with it, I mean there goes the possibility of grandchildren."

I was pacing back and forth with great anger; I tried to think about how this had happened. I never saw any real clues, I thought the reason she had stopped asking to go out with guys was because she realized we weren't going to let her. Between the revelation of Anita's infertility and this I was really pissed off at life itself.

However, the problems weren't over yet, the following Tuesday Anita and I got home from work and as we were finishing dinner I got a phone call. I picked it up, and it was Jackie. Remembering this phone call thirty-three years later still sends chills down my spine.

"Dad, how could you?"

I asked, "What?"

She responded, "You told Clarissa's parents, now they are sending her to some religious boarding school to 'straighten her out.' We begged you not to but you did it anyway, how could you do this to us?"

By this point she was on the verge of crying and I responded, "Hey I did you a favour, you'll be thanking me when you are engaged to a good man who will look after you."

She angrily responded, "Dad, I'm a lesbian, I like girls, and Clarissa and I were happy together. How could you do this to me?"

I was struggling to not give in to some sense of sympathy, "Jackie, this is tough love, like I said you will thank me one day once you get straightened out."

She then wept for a few seconds before gathering her composure, "You call this love, this isn't love, this is cruelty. Imagine if someone took Anita away from you."

I responded, "That is nowhere near the same thing, we are a married couple, not this fake lust that you fell for."

She paused "there was nothing fake about it, I cared for her so much and you just want to stomp all over it because it's not what you want. Well fuck you dad, fuck you I hope someone hurts you as much as you've hurt me."

I began to yell, "Hey I'm your father and you will not talk to me like that!"

She interrupted me and said, "Fuck you, you're not my father, parents don't do this to their children, and you don't do this people you love."

She slammed the phone down and I called back but this time Veronica picked up. She wasn't happy with me either, she had told me to let her handle it and I had gone over her head. I told her that I had to do something to stop this, and she responded, "Well you did, and you crushed our daughter in the process."

I followed by saying, "She'll get over it, and in a few years when she is grown up and more responsible, she can go find the right man and have a real relationship instead of this degenerate bullshit you let her fall into."

She paused and said, "Charles, I did fail our daughter, but not by letting her like girls but by letting you back into her life years ago. I should have known you would hurt her just to satisfy yourself, but I let it happen anyway. Well I am not letting it happen again so stay the hell off my property and I am seeking sole custody!"

She hung up on me and I was incredibly upset that she was calling me the bad parent. I thought I was trying to stop the madness and they were blaming me for taking action. Now not only could I not have new children with Anita, but I was going to have to fight for custody of the children I already had.

Over a week later I got a letter from Veronica's lawyer telling me that I had acted abusively to our daughter and that I had caused her incredible emotional distress. The letter made it sound like I had been smacking her around. I was going to go into that courtroom and fight for my rights whenever that was. A time that should have been very good for me was ruined because of these issues.

On November 9, 1989 the wall that had disturbed me in Germany was being ripped down, which was a major sign of the weakness of the Soviet Union. The following December the mission that I had risked my life for in Panama came to fruition and Noriega was removed from power by the beginning of 1990. Those few days were happy enough but it was hard to enjoy those victories that I had fought so hard for because I was losing something that meant so much to me.

That February we had the custody trial and the angle I was going in with was that I was looking out for Jackie's health and that her mother was letting her get away with anything. I thought that this would work in my favour, and in a different state it might have worked, but I underestimated where California was on this issue. Same sex intercourse had been legal in California since the second half of the 1970s, so by 1990 many people including the judge saw it as perfectly fine. I tried to frame it as being like the measures taken to stop a teenager on drugs and I thought we had to do something. I tried to bring the AIDS argument in, however Veronica's lawyer was determined to show that what I did was not just incorrect but controlling and abusive.

The judge left and came back, commenting on my blatant disregard for my daughter's well-being, my refusal to accept her sexual orientation and the excessive discipline I had used on all the kids with the push-ups, running miles, etc. The judge decided that I was an unfit parent and declared that I no longer had any custody of my children. He recommended that I make some major changes to my behaviour if I ever want any future judge to re-evaluate the decision.

In a period of six months, the Berlin Wall came down, the Panama mission was a success, I found out that I would never have any more children, and now I no longer had any custody of my current children. I went home that night, opened up a case of beer and drank until I passed out, and all I had left was Anita and my job. The 1990s didn't like me and I didn't like them either.

CHAPTER 42

FALLING THROUGH OUR FINGERS

I was given a major job, which was a big one; I had to help organize a meeting with Kuwait because they had concerns about the possibility of Iraq invading Kuwait. So, if we were ever going to take action on Kuwait's behalf, we would need them to uphold our narrative to the international community. While I wasn't the biggest player, I was given a key role to prove my worth and this would be the first report written by me that would land on the desk of the President. If this report gave them the information they needed to make decision, I could end up becoming someone the President of the United States would listen to. It was unclear whether Reagan was aware of my involvement in the Iran Contra Affair, but this would definitely put me on the map.

This mission was so important because there was an enormous amount of oil at stake and we couldn't let it fall into the wrong hands. Especially not to a regime that might give it all to the Soviets, who were on the ropes economically, and we wanted to make sure they would stay down and other countries couldn't take their place. When you're the police and an organized crime family is powerful, if you get the opportunity to take them down, you have to take it. What else was happening was a discussion about whether or not to overthrow Saddam Hussein in Iraq, and after careful consideration, we came to the conclusion that we had to keep this intervention small. The reason being was that we had to avoid creating a conflict that the Soviets might be tempted to get involved with and benefit from. Saddam was now more of a liability than an asset, as he had been years earlier, so separating ourselves from him and keeping him down was something we decided was best. The other key reason was some people still had "Vietnam syndrome" which was a great reluctance to get involved in significant conflicts unless a quick victory was guaranteed.

By late 1990, the plan was laid out and worked very well, the public support for it was high and we were able to minimize the issues, which kept the situation under control. I got a promotion having the equivalent of Mr. Donovan's job, which meant that I would be working with new people in Florida as opposed to California. After pulling a few strings, we agreed to move to Florida and I began forging new alliances there. With no access to my kids, the only thing left for me in California was Anita and as long as she came with me, I wouldn't miss too much else.

My work was going well, dare I say very, very well. My family soon had very little to say to me, Billy and I were still worlds apart, and Cathy and Jason had taken Veronica's side in the argument over the situation with Jackie. The only person willing to talk to me was my mother and even then, she wasn't that happy with me, wondering why I was moving to Florida. It was so hard not seeing my kids every week and it was so hard to think that I might not see them graduate from high school, get a job, get married, and maybe see them go to college. However, I was most concerned that without my guidance and discipline, and their mother's lax view of such degeneracy as homosexuality, I feared for their future. What else was she so permissive of? In 1990 it was so hard, my daughter's sweet sixteen was that summer, Randy would turn fourteen, Matthew was turning twelve, and knowing that I would end up missing the most pivotal years of their lives.

Anita and I bought a house in Tampa, Florida in November 1990 in order to be together. I remember looking around that house and thinking that this could be the house that we would live the rest of our lives in. This was going to be our fresh start, I was going to leave my problems in California, without kids, she and I would still have each other in a beautiful state doing well for both of us.

I was several months into the Regional Director's job, laying out missions assigning people all of those tasks and missions. I had already decided that no matter what, Anita was never going into the field, especially not in dangerous conditions. She certainly was qualified and they were nice enough to move us together, but I wasn't ever going to ask her to go somewhere dangerous because I was her husband and I would protect her no matter what. 1990 was the year when I seemed to have lost so much, now I had to focus on what I still had.

As bad as 1989 and 1990 were for me, in 1991 it got even worse. One day in June, my mother called and while she had called upset before, this was the worst I had ever seen or heard. I don't know how she didn't have a stroke, although she did get diagnosed with high blood pressure later that year. What was making her upset was that the story had spread around town that Jason was having an affair… with the twenty-two-year-old daughter of his older business partner, named Meghan. It was one of her worst fears come to life, not only was this a source of shame, but everyone knew about it. She was scared to step foot outside the house for fear of everyone's judging eyes.

I asked her, "How the hell did this happen?"

She said that the only clue that she had was the brief argument she overheard between Cathy and Jason, when he said to Cathy, "We barely see each other anymore since I do all the work, and I am sick and tired of being blamed for everything."

With that, everything going on was about to be torn asunder, and his business partner was livid. Cathy almost had a nervous breakdown and then did have a nervous breakdown when Jason officially packed up his things. She literally had to be institutionalized for a few months because this was just something she couldn't bear. I still don't know the full story, but basically she had tried to commit suicide and my mother happened to call the ambulance in time. This may sound like an extreme reaction and it is, but the truth is her status and her concern about the appearance of everything were things that she had based her life on, and within a summer it had been obliterated.

I couldn't understand how Jason could do this, and sure we all have problems, but I couldn't believe he had taken it that far. I repeatedly had to talk my mother down from going over the edge herself and every few days it was the same damn thing that summer. A part of me actually contemplated hiring a hitman just to take Jason out and end this, because he was a cheater and I didn't give a damn about him anymore. Jason decided that he had had enough of married life and left with the twenty-two-year-old Meghan. That summer was so painful, and it also didn't help that my mother repeatedly brought up the situation with my own kids, constantly asking, "What is happening to this family?"

Despite all of this I still had Anita and my job, and then yet another bomb was dropped in late September 1991. She went to a doctor's appointment and then she told me that she had to go for more tests. I just assumed everything would be okay, and reminded her that she was still young and that doctors are always being extra careful because it's their job to be. Well, once again I was wrong. She had gone to the doctor's office to get the results, and when she came home, I could see the smudges around her eyes that showed that her eyeliner had been running from tears. "Charles, they did more tests, and... I have breast cancer."

I was part way into my second beer and I dropped it in shock. I was so stunned that I didn't even hear it hit the ground. I held her as she cried herself to sleep and I was overwhelmed wondering how it was that almost everything I loved was slipping away. Before I fell asleep, I held her extra tight and told myself, "I am not letting her go, they will have to pry her from my cold, dead hands."

CHAPTER 43

★

TWO BATTLES

After everything that had happened, I was livid, I was angry at Veronica and the courts for taking away my kids, I was angry at Jason for running away on Cathy, and also at Cathy too for letting their kids fall down the wrong path. I was mad at Billy for letting Hashani run his life, I was mad at the Soviets for threatening America for so long, causing us as a nation to spend so much time fighting them that we couldn't fix our local problems that seemed to be mounting. I made a promise to myself that I was going to do everything I could to make sure that everything would be okay. Anita and I were going to have our happily ever after and America was going to be triumphant. One way or another, I was going to make this happen if I had to move heaven and earth to do it.

The first thing I did was take Anita back to the doctor's office to figure out what the next step would be. As it turned out the tumor was in her left breast and that if we did a mastectomy quickly enough we could probably stop it right there. The doctor said that they could arrange one for mid-November and I asked if there was another way.

He said, "Chemotherapy has many negative side effects and is better for treating cancer that is spread throughout the body. However, if it is in an isolated area, surgery is the preferable option."

Anita took a deep breath and said, "Okay, surgery it is."

I wasn't entirely comfortable with it because I liked her body the way it was, but given the alternative, this seemed like the least difficult option. I asked that we delay it a few months until the New Year, so she wouldn't have to go to family events with one breast. The doctor told us that sooner was better, however Anita took my side and said, "Book it for January."

The next few months I tried to make her feel sexy and appreciated and bought her flowers and took her out for a few dinners. We had our special dinners with her family for Thanksgiving and Christmas, and of course we didn't talk about the cancer with them because we didn't want them to worry. The original plan was that we would tell them after the fact when the issue was solved.

One of the biggest highlights was the very end of 1991, when we in the intelligence community celebrated something I had waited for my whole life. On December 26, 1991 after three years of systematic collapse, the Soviet Union officially disbanded. It was glorious, while Boris Yeltsin didn't see America as a friend, by all accounts he had no interest in pursuing the United States in a military race. He was more interested in rebuilding Russia as a country, so our government didn't simply defeat them as we had defeated Germany and Japan in 1945. Despite this fact, it was still a tremendous victory for our country. The world was changing and it was the first time in the previous year that I had become optimistic about anything. As 1991 came to an end, I convinced myself the surgery would go perfectly and everything would be great.

It was January 21, 1992, the day of Anita's surgery, I remember being there in the waiting room and giving her a big hug. I could feel how nervous she was. I told her, "Everything will be fine because we have the best doctors in the world."

She went in and those hours went by so slowly and I read through magazine after magazine trying to keep my mind off of worrying. By the end, I was reading a golf magazine even though I thought golf was a boring sport. As boring as it was, it was still better than worrying.

The surgeon came out and called my name. I asked him if she was okay, and he responded, "The surgery went fine, and we will be keeping her for a couple of nights for observation."

I asked if I could visit with her and he said, "In a few minutes. Just remember she will still be groggy and may not be fully coherent."

I walked into the room and sure enough she was groggy and seemed confused. I kissed her on the forehead, hoping that this cancer nightmare was finally over. Those next few days at work I struggled to focus on anything but Anita's condition. The day she came home we agreed that I would keep going to work but she would get lots of bed rest and that she didn't want to keep me from work.

It was so strange seeing the way she looked with one breast missing. She had to talk to a specialist about getting a prosthesis to hide this fact in public. I tried to be as supportive as I could and told her she was still beautiful to me. She really appreciated that and seemed extra eager in sex, and it was as if she had to prove to herself that I was telling her the truth about her attractiveness.

After a time she went back to work and I thought things were going well. I was enjoying my new job but I began to wonder about what was left to do. I mean, the Soviet Union was officially gone and the remaining threats paled in comparison. So, was my battle which I had committed myself to, officially done? It was very difficult to determine and it was strange that we weren't celebrating as a nation. In 1992, the end of the Soviet Union was significantly down the list of headlines and the issues on the minds of the average person. It seemed like people were more shocked that Canadians, the Toronto Blue Jays, had won the World Series.

While all of this was going on, Cathy was back at home and on medication, Jason was participating less and less in the business, and as I heard from my mother, the business was beginning to face major problems. The older business partner hated Jason for committing adultery with his daughter. By contrast Jason seemed to be annoyed at him for being less ambitious than himself. By the spring of 1992, the business partners were beginning to fight among themselves. People were beginning to be a part of "Team Eric" or "Team Jason" and the question was how long could this go on until the business' internal struggles became external. How long until one partner would have to step aside for the sake of the company?

Cathy, my mother, and even the kids who were now in their teens, and Cynthia, who was now twenty, began to worry about the financial future of their family. After being told about this every week, it was hard for my mother's concern not to rub off on me, not to mention the divorce was getting messy, and the lawyers were apparently licking their lips at the money they could make getting a millionaire family to tear itself apart.

Before I could begin to think about what I could do, Anita had begun to feel a new lump on her right breast. We went for tests and yet again it was cancer and the doctors feared that it was going to spread even more quickly if she didn't get surgery immediately. This drove her into a complete panic, the cancer had spread from one breast to the other and where next? What else would they have to do? Would she even survive? This time we wasted as little time as possible and went for the other mastectomy. The doctors insisted that we go for even more tests to see where else it may be in her body. Those days felt like an eternity, and the burden of knowing that something was trying to kill my wife and there was so little I could do about it, was absolutely infuriating.

We had the second mastectomy scheduled for a Monday and the additional tests scheduled for the following Thursday. She was absolutely exhausted from the ordeal and I wasn't far behind her. When we went in for the additional tests, we found out that while the surgeon had removed most of the cancer, some of the cells were still there in her chest and may have begun to spread to her vital organs.

It was enough to send me into a flying rage; I wanted to scream at the heavens demanding that God explain why this was happening. Of course, a doctor's office isn't the time or the place for that type of thing.

    We went home that day, and I decided to leave for a few minutes to buy her favourite flavour of ice cream and I knew that she loved strawberry. By the time I came home with it, she was in tears watching the wedding video, and I could see what that day meant to her. It was priceless, just like it was to me. I told her that she wasn't going anywhere and we were going to fight this and win. My attempted pep talk wasn't enough to convince her, because I could tell just by looking into her eyes that I would need to do a lot more to put her mind at ease. This nightmare had been going on for months and just wouldn't end, but I was determined to find a way to beat it. I told myself that no matter what it took, I would do it.

CHAPTER 44

⭐

THE RAILROAD BEGINS

Around June of 1992, in the midst of all the turmoil, all the anguish, the fear, and the frustration, a report that had been co-authored by McLachlin came out. To be perfectly honest, I had called him McLachlin so much that I had totally forgotten that his first name was Theodore. The report was an examination of the current state of Russia and quite frankly they were in a state of remarkable disorganization that Boris Yeltsin was trying to clean up. There was infighting, there had even been some left over Soviet militias who tried to retain control for a little bit into 1992, despite the official disbanding on Boxing Day, 1991.

The report's closing paragraph is something that I still remember because it sent chills down my spine. It read: "In conclusion, despite their current state of disorganization and major shift in priorities, they could pose a major problem in the future. They still have a large population and significant resources including nuclear capability; with time and a major shift, they could once again challenge the United States as a world power. This appears unlikely in the near future, however the twenty-first century could potentially see Russia take a new imperial form under a different flag and different political ideology."

This was terrible news, and it was as if our victory barely meant anything, and was like reading in 1946 that the Nazis might return by the 1950s. There was so much going on in my life and this conclusion, however accurate, was intolerable. The thoughts raced through my head, "I haven't devoted my entire life to fight the Russian Bear only for it to hibernate and return. I wasn't going to let that happen, I wasn't going to let them get back up and I was going to make our victory permanent, but how?"

I don't remember what made me think of it, but when I was a kid, I used to be jealous of a friend of mine who had a model railroad, and this was what made me decide to start saving for my own with Billy. I remember asking my friend why he set it up that way. It just went around and around and around it a big loop (that's what train sets did). I remember asking him why he didn't buy more tracks for it so the train could go anywhere. He told me his parents told him that was all he was getting and at one point his younger brother got jealous that we were playing with it and he wasn't. As the train was going around the far side, his brother kicked it over. That was similar to our situation, going around and around for over forty years, to finally win this we had to kick their train over.

I picked up the phone and spoke with McLachlin, and told him that I had read his report and while I complimented him on how well researched it was, the conclusion was genuinely concerning. So I asked him a question, "If I can come up with a way to stop the Russians from ever challenging us again, could you arrange a meeting for me with the President?"

He responded, "Charles, if you can find a way to do it that allows us to keep them out of our way without starting any major fiascos, I would be happy to."

So I began working on my own plan, I researched, I read, I drew upon my own experiences and by the time August came around, my plan was ready to be pitched.

Operation Railroad was ready and McLachlin was as good as his word, and it was hard not to be so proud but also so nervous, while not initially envisioning how this would come about. This was the dream, I, Charles Melvoy, a small kid from Ann Arbor, Michigan, who worked hard all of his life serving his country was finally going to fulfill his dream. I was going to meet with the most important man in the world, the President of the United States, to discuss the future of the country.

As an added bonus, it was even more than that. McLachlin would be there, along with the President of the United States, George H.W. Bush, Secretary of Defense, Dick Cheney and a few other military and intelligence specialists.

Anita wasn't feeling very well but I made sure she came as this was the opportunity of a lifetime to meet the President of the United States, and although she seemed reluctant, she came anyway. I personally introduced her to them and despite being very tired, she put together the biggest smile she could muster. After they waved at everyone in the office, they came in and one of the military advisors began speaking.

"Mr. President, just a little background information about Mr. Melvoy, who has a stellar record of service for our country. Over thirteen years in the military, reaching the status of First Lieutenant, and known for an exceptional record, he earned a purple heart in Vietnam. Worked four years for our missile defense base in NORAD with an excellent record, and even helped us shear many valuable seconds off of our missile response time. Since 1985, he has been working in the intelligence community and not only helped keep a lid on the Iran Contra affair, he risked his life repeatedly gaining us valuable information that assisted us with the Panama regime change."

I couldn't help but look at the President who smiled and Dick Cheney who nodded his head in approval. As exciting and validating as this was, I had a presentation to make, the biggest of my life.

"Thank you I appreciate that. Mr. President, like myself, you are a veteran who fought in a war against a dangerous regime. However, Mr. President, you shouldn't have had to because we beat the Germans in World War I, but we took our victory for granted and left them to their own devices and they returned in an even worse way. As the director alluded to, I have been serving my country for almost twenty-five years and put my life on the line repeatedly. I don't want the Russians to be left to their own devices, and given the opportunity to return in a worse way. While I know you still have spies there to keep an eye on them, we need to take a grander step than that. We need a solution that will allow us to make sure that if the Russian Bear comes out of hibernation, we'll have it where we want it before it is five feet out of its cave."

I looked over at McLachlin who had a subdued smile on his face, like a proud father seeing his son graduate college. With that tiny bit of encouragement, I continued, "Imagine if mutually assured destruction was no longer mutual? How can that be? Let me tell you, as you know they have the same nuclear triad as we do, so we need to render them unable to counterattack should we decide to finally strike. Due to the disorganization mentioned in the report that came out in June, co-authored by Mr. McLachlin, now would be the best time to begin infiltrating, and within a few years a collection of several hundred well placed spies and double agents could get into the positions where we need them.

"If we assign spies to get into their subs, their bomber fleet and their land based launches, they will be defenseless. Any attempt to strike at us would result in futility and our strike on them would be absolutely obliterating. One of the key details I have to stress is that this plan can't just be in place for a few years, so we need to keep a consistent flow of spies going throughout their system. As they get higher in the system, they open the doors for others to take those places. Piece by piece their defense establishment becomes our ticking time bomb. It will only be a matter of time to put everything in motion. Once fully implemented, it will only take roughly twenty minutes for us to go from telling them to shutdown, to pressing the codes. Not long after, our missiles will be in the air and their system will be shut down from the inside.

Before they can find out where the problems are, they will be history and the Russian Bear will be completely vanquished. Do we have any questions?"

The slides had shown more detail and I sensed that there was a hesitant interest in the operation.

They all looked around the room as Mr. Cheney spoke first. "Mr. Melvoy, while I can certainly see your concerns and intentions, what would stop one of the spies from revealing the entire plan?"

I responded, "We do what the CIA does best, compartmentalize. The spies in their bomber brigade wouldn't even know about our efforts on the other two corners of the triad. The only time a spy would know about any other spy, is if he is hiring and elevating him or her, and even then, they are never allowed to discuss the mission with any outside contacts."

One of the military directors spoke up, "Mr. Melvoy, your plan is contingent on two things. First, that we will be the ones making the first strike, what if the Russians try to make a first strike, it gets stopped and they figure out something is wrong?"

I had thought of that, "Like with the bombers, we would have at least a couple of dummy missiles that have no real capability and the instant they launch, we launch our counterattack. What few of their missiles reach us will do almost no damage whereas ours will cause mass devastation."

The military advisor continued, "The second contingency is that future Presidents will keep this going. We have an election in November but even if Mr. Bush keeps this plan going, he will have to step down after 1996. How do we keep it going despite the possible objections of future Presidents?"

This was the one that I hadn't thought of because quite frankly, it seemed so obvious that we needed to do everything in our power to stop Russia… ANYTHING! So, after a pause I said, "Well there are a couple ways to keep it going. First, once it gets started, stopping it suddenly risks exposing the operation in the first place and I think anyone, even a democrat, can figure that out."

This line gained a few chuckles in the room. "What even they should be able to figure out is that this is an option of last resort, it's not the first option but it is the ultimate contingency plan. This operation is the guarantee of America being the leader of the world going into the twenty-first century and beyond."

They seemed to nod in agreement as President Bush finally spoke, "I need to know three things. First, McLachlin, how big is the window that we have to make this plan work before the Russians get their act together and then we can't do this?"

McLachlin responded, "Well the window would never completely close, but if we waited five years to start, it might take decades to see it fully implemented. The sooner we start, the quicker it should come together."

The President turned to me, "Mr. Melvoy, my second question is this, how much of this can you organize and how much of this would fall to us?"

I responded, "You would barely have to touch any of it, all of it can be implemented by myself with some advisement from Mr. McLachlin and some help from current spies."

I could see the wheels turning and while Bush was never the beacon that Reagan was, he was always Presidential and never showed too much of his hand through his facial expressions.

Finally, he took off his glasses to rub something in his eye before he spoke again. "My third question is if this is discovered, it's going to look really bad on the world stage and to John Q. Public who doesn't know what we do, so who takes the fall?"

Everyone immediately looked at me and just before I could speak, McLachlin chimed in, "Mr. President, I think the best thing would be for you to put the blame on me. I will be helping him with this project. In the end if something goes sideways, either you or one of your associates can guarantee us a pardon, like you did for other people in previous operations."

President Bush took a moment and said, "Could everyone except Cheney please give us a few minutes to discuss this?"

Everyone went outside as my heart raced, I thought I might be part of an operation to save America, which was a mission from the President of the United States himself. McLachlin pulled me around a corner and said to me, "Melvoy, no matter what they say, don't complain, just say 'thank you sir' and accept the decision whatever it is."

I nodded and waited, hoping that they would understand the mission and see it as worthwhile.

After several tense minutes, we were called back in, I tried to put on my poker face and I remembered what McLachlin had just told me. We all took a seat as the President, with his hands clasped, looked at everyone around the table, "Any operation, especially one of this size and scope, brings with it a great deal of risk. However, given the detail and research, given the potential threat outlined by the report authored by Thompson, Gall, and McLachlin, I have decided that this operation would be a worthwhile contingency plan to ensure that the Russians are never again a major threat to the United States."

On the inside, I was ready to burst because I was so happy to hear those words, so happy to hear the President of the United States validate my work. He then said, "On a more personal note, Mr. Melvoy your service to our country is admirable and I can't stress enough how proud I am to see a man so dedicated to our national interests. So, while this operation will require assistance from various departments, Mr. Melvoy and Mr. McLachlin, will be the leaders on this and every two to three weeks I will expect a report on the progress of this operation."

I said, "Thank you sir."

I shook his hand and was so proud of this moment. The President and the others all left and I swelled with pride as I felt such joy that my dream had for all intents and purposes come true.

I remember McLachlin pulling me aside and saying, "You know Melvoy, when I saw you all those years ago, I saw someone who reminded me of myself, gritty, determined, someone who doesn't run away when things get a little rough. You not only impressed me then, over these last twenty years you have exceeded my expectations and now we are going to finish this once and for all."

We shook hands, and with that Operation Railroad was born.

That night Anita and I went home and I was absolutely thrilled. I spared Anita any of the details but she knew that my plan had been approved and I was on a mission from the President of the United States. I was so excited I couldn't understand why she was in no mood to celebrate. It was as if I had forgotten all about her problems and all I could see at that moment was my success. I had done it; I had convinced the President of the United States to adopt my Operation, an Operation that would change the course of my life and our country forever.

CHAPTER 45

★

THE STRUGGLE

The initial stages of Operation Railroad were looking for the right foreign operatives who either were working for us already or had a history that may allow them to be swayed to our side. For example, if they had family that had been killed under the Soviet's rule. Every few weeks we sent the reports and things seemed to be going along well enough. I had my mind on so many things that I wasn't paying attention to the polls. The day the election came, I was watching it at home with Anita hoping that the American people would give the great George H.W. Bush a second term. As the night went on, the Democrats started racking up electoral votes until finally Bill Clinton was declared the next President of the United States. Just like that, twelve years of Presidents I admired was gone, I didn't hate Bill Clinton but I didn't put him on the same level as Reagan or Bush.

I called McLachlin that night asking him what we were going to do, "The plan is still in its earliest stages, we could potentially lose the whole thing."

McLachlin responded, "Melvoy, I can't guarantee anything but if necessary I will call in as many favours as I have to. If we have to arrange your pitch all over again we will, but I am not letting this die without a fight."

That made me feel better that I had a big player in my corner and someone who would give me a fighting chance. Unfortunately, I didn't have that when it came to Anita's condition.

The summer of 1992 Anita and I discussed whether or not to go ahead with chemotherapy, and although we had her mastectomies paid for, the deductibles had taken a huge toll on our savings. I hated buying things on credit and we had signed up for a short-term ten-year mortgage, because I figured we wouldn't spend a whole lot of money and our house would be paid for. We were less than two years into it and the savings had been depleted because of my court battles for the kids, the car we bought in 1990 and now these surgeries. On top of it all, her sick leave was going to run out which would mean that we wouldn't even have her income. If I hadn't gotten that promotion, I would have been very worried. The point is we didn't have a whole lot of money lying around, which meant that we needed the insurance company to pay the large majority of the bill and suddenly they were saying they wouldn't.

I was already pissed off and already hated what this cancer was doing, but now this? I couldn't stand it and demanded to know why not, and then they started by feeding me the excuse that the mastectomies should have cured her so this was an unnecessary expense. I thought I had cornered them when I got the x-rays and other stuff that clearly showed what was happening, but they still wouldn't pay for it. Keep in mind if we mailed them the documents it would take weeks for them to get back to us. I don't even know how many phone calls I made that fall trying to get a straight answer out of these people. Her sick leave was going to run out in March and then she would basically be getting time off without pay. I got angrier with the insurance company with each passing week.

By the time January 1993 came around, they were telling us that they wouldn't be insuring her because of something she had misstated. I asked what they were talking about, and suddenly they started telling me about how when you first apply for health insurance you have to state your accurate medical history. They then claimed she didn't tell them about two yeast infections she had had in 1973 and 1978 respectively. I didn't even know what they were, let alone why they were relevant. They told me they wouldn't be insuring her, so I told them that if they didn't I would be taking my business elsewhere. It didn't take long for me to find out how hard that was, because as February and March came around, I contacted every insurance company I could find to cover the insurance. Every single one of those companies declined to take on our situation and told us some version of "we hereby deny Anita Melvoy coverage due to her pre-existing condition."

If I had been sent to assassinate those people who made these decisions they wouldn't have had to ask me twice because this wasn't some frivolous claim and she was going to die without these treatments. I then started calling around to different hospitals asking what we could do to see about some sort of pay-as-you-go plan. They proceeded to tell me that the whole round of chemotherapy would cost over $50,000 and we would need a bare minimum of sixty percent down. Well there went all of our savings and we still had roughly $7,000 to account for. All of this happened at the very same time her income had dried up entirely. I tried to talk the hospital into lowering it and one of them said they would do it with fifty percent down.

I scraped together the remaining $2,000 between having a yard sale and getting people at the office to chip in so that she could go through her first round in late April 1993. At that point, we were basically out of options and had to find $25,000 from somewhere to cover the other half of the treatment. I began asking myself where else could I find the money and they told me they wanted the other half by June 10th or they wouldn't continue with future treatment. I talked to a few people at work about where else I could get the money and they suggested I ask my family and one suggested that I ask McLachlin. Over the course of April and May, I had put together a couple of thousand dollars but it wasn't enough. The only thing that could save Anita's life was too expensive and if we didn't find a way to pay for it, I knew I might lose her.

President Clinton finally got around to meeting with McLachlin and I about Operation Railroad in later May, and if I was going to ask McLachlin for money I had to do it in person. The day before I had met with McLachlin, he mentioned to me that I needed to be a little bit slower in my implementation of Operation Railroad. He asked me what was going on and I then told him about the money situation, that I needed over $20,000 and I feared that without it Anita would die.

He suddenly said something that shocked me, "Melvoy, you are a great soldier but it's not my fault that you didn't manage your money better for an emergency like this."

My eyes nearly came out of my head and I couldn't believe what I was hearing. This was a serious situation, I was fighting for my country and my wife and he almost didn't care that I was fighting for the latter. I didn't say anything at first because I was so stunned, and he finally said, "Don't say anything about this to President Clinton because the last thing we need is for him to think that we are playing the sympathy card."

I had to shut all of that out of my mind to talk to President Clinton. I don't remember that meeting very well because I was going through the motions and astonished that Theodore McLachlin, a man who I considered a second father that I would have taken a bullet for, didn't care.

The meeting ended with Bill Clinton saying that he was willing to keep the Operation going on the condition that his secretary of defense and himself receive monthly updates. Another constraint he put on it was that we would not be putting any U.S. operatives, who were not Russian nationals, on the ground without his express permission. Thankfully the plan required virtually none of that but it was still annoying that he thought he had to keep Operation Railroad on some sort of leash. I was relieved that he was allowing the Operation to continue so that we could finally finish the job. As upset and disappointed as I was with McLachlin, I kept my mouth shut because I knew that if he left the Operation it might fall apart.

So, with June 10th quickly approaching and Anita looking frail, worn out and exhausted, I knew I had to do something. I began calling my family, as I was out of options and was becoming a desperate man. I called Veronica and Todd, and while Veronica was still mad at me, she did say that she felt sorry for Anita. The truth was she said they were having a hard time paying for the kid's college as it was, so she couldn't. I don't know if she really did not have the money but if it was an excuse, it was a good one. Next, I turned to some of my distant relatives but all of them had said they couldn't afford to help us.

That meant there were two phone numbers left, the first was Cathy's and the other was Billy's. I hadn't been on good terms with either of them as of late and even though my mother and I would still talk, even that had begun to subside because she was asking that I move back to Michigan to help them manage the bar. I decided to get what I thought would be the painful one over with and called Billy. I told him how I wasn't able to pay for the second half of her treatments and I couldn't afford a second mortgage, but once she got healthy and working again we would pay back every penny.

He said, "Let me talk to Hashani and I'll call you back tomorrow."

He couldn't see it, but I rolled my eyes because I was sure what her answer would be, I knew she wouldn't lift a finger to help me. That left only one option, my sister Cathy and the hope that she and my mother would loan me the money. If anyone had it, I knew that they did and if anyone was kind enough to part with it, I knew it would be Cathy because that was always her issue, she was too kind for her own good but this time it would save Anita. I took a deep breath and hoped that this phone call would save Anita's life.

The phone call began with the usual pleasantries, "How are you doing? How's the weather?"

It didn't take long for me to bring up the situation with Anita and how desperate we were becoming but unfortunately Cathy wasn't in her most charitable mood and began talking about how scared she was for the company. Her youngest daughter Melina was planning to be a surgeon and that would require a lot of money. Medical school would be expensive and if things continued to go poorly for the bar, then she might not get her chance. I steered the conversation back towards the subject of Anita. "I am really scared that we will lose our place on the queue for chemotherapy."

I explained what might happen, and that I was gradually becoming more and more scared of losing her. She said that she felt sorry for my situation but they couldn't be giving away tons of money until they were safe.

That was when she tried to trap me, "Charles, look, we have been asking for your help and the business is in chaos. You have been the manager of a chain of grocery stores so you can take those skills into the bar. If you sign an employment contract and help us manage the bar, I'll make sure Anita's treatment gets paid for. I will wire that money to you and you will have it in forty-eight hours."

June 10th was in a week and the money that could save Anita's life was one career change away, however to do it I would have to walk away from the battle I had been fighting since I turned eighteen. Not to mention I was on a mission from the President of the United States that I believed I would have to fight to keep alive. With just a few seconds to think about it, I told her that I couldn't.

Cathy was just astonished, "Charles, I know that you are loyal but you have a sick wife and a sister who needs you, so what does that other job have that is so important?"

I came up with some excuse to get off the phone and told myself that there had to be another way.

I didn't tell Anita about the offer, and how could I? I just told her they couldn't because of the situation they were in. She went to sleep that night in my arms, and I noticed her skin was pale, her hair was thinning out, it was as if she had aged twenty years in the last year and a half. I told her that somehow, some way everything was going to be all right.

The next day I came home from work miserable because there had been a problem. One of our operatives had been in a car accident and now we had to find a new one in one of Russia's least populated regions. Anita greeted me with the brightest smile she had had in months. "Charles, Billy called today to get our address and he is mailing the money to us tonight."

I asked her how much it was, and she said, "He said it was $18,000 and something."

With my latest paycheque, we were going to be less than $700 short.

I remember thinking to myself, "I can't believe it, he finally grew a pair and came through for his big brother."

I regret not calling him that night but instead I sat down with Anita trying to figure out where we could get $700 by Thursday. I started calling around to see who wanted the leftover furniture we had in the basement that belonged to Anita's uncle. I spent that Saturday calling around and that Sunday I managed to drop it off in exchange for

Chapter 45 : The Struggle

around $300. The church was having a bake sale that Sunday and Anita had convinced them to give some of the proceeds to go towards her chemotherapy. I was against it initially because I didn't want us taking charity so I made her promise the church that we would eventually pay it back. Even with that, we were still about $100 short. Thursday was fast approaching and I was waiting to get Billy's cheque and I tried to talk to the guys at work about chipping in again. The remaining $100 came together as I got down on my knees that night and prayed that Billy's cheque would arrive in time.

It was Wednesday June 9, I was at work when Anita called saying that his cheque had come in and was over the $18,000. It came with a note, and the end of the note read, "P.S. please deposit or cash ASAP."

She offered to go to the bank that day and I told her absolutely not, that I would do it tomorrow before we stopped by the clinic.

That morning we went to the bank and when we went to deposit the amount, they told us the news, "Due to the size of the amount we will have to hold it for a couple of days for it to clear."

I asked what they were talking about. They told me that they always hold any cheques over $10,000 for more than two days and given that they weren't open Saturday or Sunday, the funds wouldn't be available until Monday. I thought I was going to snap and I began to get angrier as I told them my situation the teller began telling me to calm down. In the process the teller suggested that I write the clinic a post-dated cheque that would be good on Tuesday. I remember asking the teller, "Do you think that will work?"

She responded, "Every company has different policies."

Such an ambiguous answer for something I was so desperate to find certainty in was infuriating but nevertheless I calmed down.

So, I wrote out the post-dated cheque as suggested for Tuesday, June 15th. We got to the clinic and I gave them the post-dated cheque, then the woman behind the counter gave it a bad look. "Oh, post-dated."

I asked her if there was a problem and she proceeded to tell me that due to the size of the cheque it would take a few days for them to get it, and now I was adding a few more days on top of that. I responded, "Look you are getting your money, that's what matters isn't it?"

She then gave me this forced answer about how they had people with cash who were ready to take Anita's reservation, so I immediately asked how long the waiting list was. She told me three months and I felt like I was ready to lose my mind. "Are you kidding me? This is how you treat a war hero's wife? I fought for my country, I saw people die, where were you in 1968 when I got a bullet in my knee? Where the hell were you?"

She then told me that if I was going to act that way I should just leave and I said, "Fine."

I ripped the cheque up in front of her. "Kiss the money goodbye."

I took Anita by the arm and stormed out and told her that we would call around and find another clinic to pick up where the first one started. I wasn't giving up that easy, Charles Melvoy fears nobody, absolutely nobody.

For the next couple of weeks, I called around looking for any place that we could get treatment sooner than September. We finally found one two hours away in Northern Florida with an opening for late July, as well as a preliminary evaluation in mid-July. I didn't give up and now I had found another way so I didn't have to give up on Operation Railroad. She still wasn't well but now it was going to work. I was sure of it, but when we went in to speak to the doctor regarding the tests, that was when it hit me.

I remember holding Anita's hand when the doctor let out the disappointed sigh, when you know the news can't be good. "Mrs. Melvoy, the chemotherapy did help significantly however, it has still spread which means that if we start treatment as scheduled, we would need a more intense treatment regimen. The payment you put down will allow us to start but it won't be enough to finish all of the treatments you may need. Additionally, I would say that even if we complete the treatments, your odds of survival are between forty to fifty percent."

I was floored; after all of the hoops I had jumped through, the best we had was fifty percent? Those may be great odds at the racetrack but when someone's life is at stake, it is an entirely different story.

The less control I felt at home, the more I demanded it at work and people began to like me less and less. If I got bad news, I wanted to know where it went wrong and I was potentially ruthless on whoever it was that made the mistake. Operation Railroad began to turn into an obsession and when I was at work I had to block out what was happening with Anita. I was focusing with relentless intention making sure that Operation Railroad went off without a hitch. Every time I got word about one of our operatives being hired or being given new information, I was thrilled. I was hoping that before too long this Operation would come to fruition.

At one point during the summer of 1993, two operatives were being investigated for possible espionage. This could have exposed at least part of Operation Railroad but by the end of it, the charges were dismissed due to them not finding anything substantial, although this meant that their place in the submarine division would be compromised for the foreseeable future. I was also arranging other spy missions in other countries. It was almost strange being the person handing out the missions, as opposed to going on them, but my office needed me and I wasn't leaving until the job was done.

As the summer of 1993 became the fall, Anita was once again going through chemotherapy and I was once again in the situation of needing another $12,000 or so in order for them to do the next rounds in November. I had managed to scrape together about $3,000, which obviously wasn't enough, and while I was worried about that something else was on Anita's mind. She didn't feel attractive anymore and she hadn't felt good in over a year and a half and she also was getting more convinced that she was going to die. She and I had a discussion about going on a cruise in January, and I told her we couldn't afford it and we had too much to do here. She burst into tears, and started trying to tell me that every day was either treatment or staying in the house feeling like an invalid. One of the things I specifically remember her asking was, "What do I have to look forward to?"

I responded, "Getting better, that is the only thing you need to worry about, okay, that is your only job. I'm the one who is still going to work and carrying the weight of a nation on my shoulders. So stop worrying about something else and just focus on getting better!"

That answer wasn't good enough for her, perhaps because she was convinced that it wasn't going to happen.

I made another round of calls and this time Billy told me that he had sent me a lot of money last time and the best he could do was another $2,000. I managed to get another $1,000 from other people but by the time October came around, it wasn't enough. They told me they would continue the treatments the moment I put $12,000 down on the table. Billy sent me another $500 the following month, and I saved every penny I could. Finally on December 12th, we almost had the $12,000 when my car had to go to the shop and before I knew it we were down another $500. It took another few weeks to scrape it together and at the end of December we finally had the money with the treatments ready to resume that January. She and I had drifted apart in those months and I began to wonder if she even wanted to live. We went in for the next evaluation at the beginning of January and this time the doctor was even more sombre. "It appears to have spread even further and it is now surrounding this artery coming out of the left ventricle. I would say that your survival odds now are less than ten percent."

I asked him if there was anything else they could do, and he responded, "Charles, very aggressive forms of cancer are difficult to fight and we are using the best tools at our disposal."

After we went home I began preparing dinner and when I brought it to her on the couch, I saw her eyes getting watery and her jaw trembling. I asked her what was wrong, she said, "Charles, I'm going to die, the treatments aren't working and they are tearing me apart, use that money to pay down what you owe Billy and let me go."

I couldn't believe what I was hearing, "No! Less than ten percent is better than zero and I didn't go through all of this effort just to give up now."

She barely pulled herself up, her head now with no hair left, pale and exhausted, "What you went through? I'm the one who has been getting torn to shreds with cancer and radiation. I have had to give up on everything I love, my job at the CIA, going out on my own, our marriage is dead."

I immediately shot back, "No it's not, I'm right here."

She said, "We haven't had sex in a year. You haven't kissed me with any passion in months, I'm just this thing you have to take care of. Well don't bother, just let me go."

In retrospect I responded poorly. "Anita, snap out of it, you are going to get better if you set your mind to it and go through with the rest of the treatments. You will get better and you will see that this is just a hurdle."

She lay back down on the couch and turned away from me, "What is this, the silent treatment?"

She then said, "Leave me alone Charles."

I paused waiting for her to say something else. There was just silence. I was so tired of this, so I went to the fridge and pulled out a beer and sat down on the living room chair and turned on the TV. That beer went down so quickly that I went to get another within five minutes. That one went quickly as well, and that night I probably had seven beers before I stumbled to bed. She opted to stay on the couch, and if cancer were a person I would have unleashed violence on it that most people couldn't imagine. But it wasn't a person I could attack, it was this thing I couldn't even do anything about, and such is the heartbreaking nature of diseases.

We tried to go through with the treatments and Anita hated every moment of it, but I wasn't giving up, ever. That round of treatments was devastating as it made her so tired that she didn't even want to get up out of bed during the day so we had to buy a walker. She was in worse shape than my father was when he had stayed with me all those years ago.

Every day I would go to work, I would come home and she would have barely eaten anything. She began to get bedsores because she would only get up to use the bathroom, which was only a few times a day. It went on like this for weeks and it was hard for me, but in retrospect it was agony for her.

CHAPTER 46
★
THE LOSS

That Valentine's Day I bought Anita chocolates and we watched *Ernest goes to Camp*, the movie we watched the night that I had proposed to her. It was the first time I had seen her even crack a smile in the last month. I held her frail body as I felt the few weak laughs she could muster and I kissed her. Unfortunately, her laugh was interrupted within seconds by a cough she let out. The next few weeks were more of the same and she fell back into her depression, finally the end came on Monday March 7, 1994 when I came home. Operation Railroad had really picked up the last few months and I was being given a raise for my efforts, I came home at least somewhat happy and excited to tell her the news.

I came home and I heard nothing, I called to her but I heard nothing, I called her name louder, my heart raced as I looked over the top of the couch and saw that she wasn't there. I immediately ran into our bedroom as I called to her again, but I heard nothing and she wasn't moving. I checked her pulse, begging to feel something but there was no heartbeat. Not only had she died, but I wasn't there for her during her final moments on earth. I barely willed myself to the telephone where I called for the ambulance. I sat in a chair in our room staring at her, looking for some movement or something and whatever movement I saw was only my eyes tricking me.

The coroner appeared almost an hour later and determined that she had died around 3:30 that day. If I had somehow gotten home just two and a half hours earlier I could have said goodbye. The entire thing was like a bad dream and the next few days I woke up hoping that I would see her lying next to me, even if she were sick. However, there was nothing, those repeated disappointments hit me harder and harder every single day. The funeral was heartbreaking, her family was there, some of our co-workers were there, but none of my family was. I had a few people telling me they were sorry for my loss but that was it.

I remember calling Billy to tell him what had happened and he told me, "Listen don't worry about paying the money back, you have more than enough to deal with right now."

Melvoy's Railroad

With the mood I was in, I took that exactly the wrong way and began to get mad at him for treating me like a charity case. The phone call didn't end well, I had so much grief, so much rage and I had no real place to put it. The closest thing I had to an outlet was my vision of President Clinton or some other President actually pulling the trigger and sending those damn Russians on a one-way trip to hell. I funnelled my rage into my work and doubled my determination to finish Operation Railroad. Everyone was astonished that I didn't take any time off with the exception of the day of the funeral; I was working late, coming in early and was undeterred. I was going to finish Operation Railroad if it killed me. I had to stay busy because I would come home to nothing, a place that may as well be a graveyard.

When I came home on Saturday nights, after working an extra day, I would just start drinking until I passed out. I just didn't want to accept that Anita was gone; I was prepared to do anything to keep from thinking about it. That was hard to do, especially after getting the funeral bill for $7,200. Her life insurance paid for it but that reminder was painful. My mother called again asking if I could please help them with the bar, and by this point the divorce had been finalized, and Jason had left leaving Cathy with a fifty percent share of a business that was struggling. They had lost three of their locations and two others were losing money. She couldn't understand how I put my job ahead of my family. I told her to stop right there, but she kept going and I hung up in her ear. It was the spring of 1994 and I was miserable, all I had was Operation Railroad and had no more friends. My acquaintances at work had been keeping their distance and I got an obligatory phone call from Veronica when Anita died but that was it. All I had was the mission; all I had was Operation Railroad.

At one point McLachlin called me, asking where my head was at. I told him it was on the mission as always, but he told me he was worried. I responded by asking, "When did you start giving a damn?"

He knew exactly what I was talking about, he responded, "Look Charles you aren't in your right state of mind, and how could you be, your wife is dead and you had to deal with these damn Russians. Could you imagine if those Russians hadn't started causing us all of these problems for all of those years? How many of our top scientists would have found the cure to cancer by now? Who knows, Melvoy I just wanted to make sure that your resolve wasn't wavering."

I was lacking in restraint and I said to him, "Do you want to know what I think? You're right, if I didn't have to keep these Russians down I could have been there for her when she died. I could have taken the deal that my sister offered me last year. I could have done a lot of things differently, but they were threatening all of us. I don't give a damn what you think of me, but McLachlin, let me make this clear, I am finishing this Operation once and for all, and I better not hear any bullshit from you trying to cut me down behind closed doors."

He immediately went on the defensive and began to tell me that he wouldn't do that, he and I were partners and if we started fighting amongst ourselves the entire Operation could unravel. I told him then that as long as he doesn't try anything with me, then he had nothing to worry about. He said okay then, and that was the end of a tense phone call that required all of my remaining restraint not to simply lash out at him.

My 45th birthday was the hardest one of my life up to that point; grey hairs had begun to form on the sides of my head just above my ears. In some ways, I had accomplished so much but in other ways I couldn't shake the haunting feeling that I had accomplished nothing. It was the afternoon and I was flipping through the channels on TV and I found that there was a wrestling pay-per-view that night. On the guide, it said Hulk Hogan vs Ric Flair and I ordered it saying to myself, "What the hell, it's my birthday."

It was fun enough initially seeing some wrestlers I had never seen before and a couple that I had, it was a different company, with a different show. Finally, I was on either my fifth or sixth beer, and the main event began, during which I began having flashbacks to those previous WrestleManias I had gone to with Anita and my kids. The emotion finally began to pour out as all the pain began to overwhelm me and I suddenly heard my father's voice telling me not to cry, like he had told me so many times before. Just so you don't get the wrong idea, it was a memory, not psychosis, although that death then came back and by the time the match was over I was a wreck who went to sleep a shattered man.

The alarm went off the next morning just as it had for the previous four months, I looked to my left and there was just nothing. For almost six years the woman I loved would wake up next to me and now every morning the first thing that went through my head was that she was gone. That painful reminder every morning forced me to get out of bed and it worked again. I poured myself some cereal, shaved, showered and prepared to go to the office, which was the only place where my life still meant anything. I got there and to my surprise there was a concerned voice-mail that had been left on my machine from the secretary of defense, William Perry.

I called back and I waited for him to come on the line, he then asked how I was, and I lied and told him, "I'm fine, I had a nice relaxed birthday yesterday."

He seemed surprised by my answer, "Well happy belated birthday, Mr. Melvoy. The reason why I am calling and asking is because over the weekend Theodore McLachlin suffered a severe heart attack and is in critical condition. The cause has yet to be determined so we wanted to make sure that we haven't been compromised."

He then followed up by saying, "Please be careful and make sure that nothing regarding the mission is anywhere near your home or anywhere civilian eyes can see it."

I thanked him for his concern and then called a meeting with the staff in the office that day. "One of our top military advisors has just had a heart attack. As all of you know sometimes things happen by accident and sometimes they don't, so please be extra careful of any suspicious behaviour. If he is compromised, then I am potentially compromised, if I am compromised, it's possible all of you could be as well."

They all nodded, accepting what they had heard and one of them went out of his way to thank me for the warning. After what had happened between McLachlin and myself, I was only concerned about some operatives coming after me and the mission, rather than his health. I got another private phone call two days later from William Perry's assistant informing me that the cause of the heart attack was McLachlin's tradition of going out for Sunday Brunch every week. This tradition included eating bacon, sausage and other things that doctors tell their patients not to eat too much of. His physician verified that he had a history of high blood pressure and cholesterol. So I was relieved that we were off the hook, however there was still a problem, who was going to pick up McLachlin's share of the work?

One conference call with President Clinton later and it fell primarily onto me for the foreseeable future. By this point I was already used to working seventy hours a week, so I was already on top of everything on my end. For McLachlin this was only a part time job anyway, so I was willing to take it on although it added some more stress, however now my name was the primary name on this Operation. Some things wouldn't move as fast as I had wanted so I came up with a few steps to move this process along, including giving a few of our operatives instructions on how to kill one of the authority figures and frame one of the other top candidates. As 1994 progressed I was becoming a little bit desperate and was prepared to do anything to make sure everything was in place.

By this point I hated the Russians, I hated anyone who sounded like them, and was basically at a point of effectively blaming them for Anita's death. Operation Railroad was not just a national security measure anymore, it was the ultimate revenge, everything I had gone through in my life was going to come raining down on them sooner or later. Each day was exhausting and I gradually drank more and more, just trying to numb the pain. I was miserable and I was willing to do anything to get over it. I also did this to stop the nightmares, some nights I would try not drinking and I would have one. I remember one night having a dream that I was in the jungles of Vietnam looking for Anita and calling out to her but I couldn't find her. My heart raced, fearing that the VC's had her, but there was no sign of them or her. Finally, I walked out of the jungle and I saw her in the distance as she was years ago before she came down with cancer when everything was so good. I dropped my rifle and ran to her, I ran and ran, then, just as I was one stride away from having her in my arms again, my alarm clock went off and in that blink of an eye it was gone. That moment was so cruel that I almost couldn't stand it and I am surprised I was able to pull myself together and walk into work that day.

You might be wondering how I could have lived like this with a heavy workload, hardly anyone to talk to, and dreams that almost give me back what I wanted with every fibre of my being only for it to be ripped away all over again. The answer is it couldn't go on and if you keep reading you will find out exactly how.

CHAPTER 47

★

POINT OF NO RETURN

Just like my birthday and Thanksgiving I spent Christmas alone, I had stopped going to church because of the hangovers I sometimes had on Sunday mornings that came after several drinks on Saturday nights. I convinced myself that watching the TV sermons in my bathrobe was just as good. So for Christmas I cooked myself a steak and a bunch of other stuff and watched the 1950s version of *A Christmas Carol*. For some people it would have been so lonely, but for me I was so angry at the world that it suited me just fine and was happy not to be bothered. Of course, 1995 came around and we celebrated New Year's at the office, although celebrating was certainly not on my mind.

The only part of 1995 that I was looking forward to was making sure everything was in place for Operation Railroad. I remember in March finding out that we had secured the air division and we had enough people in key positions, so that if the Russians tried to launch an air strike they would be carrying defective bombs. When I say defective, I mean they contained no nuclear material and/or were designed to go off when they reach a certain height, so that they would effectively go off while still in Russian or other foreign airspace. That was one of the nuclear triad down and two to go.

I think it was around that time that I found out that McLachlin wasn't coming back and was retiring after the triple bypass he had the previous fall. So I was left to work all the hours and finally the day came when I was asked to meet with President Clinton. I wasn't sure what he wanted to meet about, so I sat down there with Bill Clinton, Al Gore, William Perry, and half a dozen other members of the intelligence community.

President Clinton began, "Mr. Melvoy, I appreciate the work you have put into Operation Railroad but we are beginning to see it as more of a liability than a safety net."

I blurted out, "What?"

He went on, "Our working relationship with Russia has changed dramatically under the leadership of Boris Yeltsin because he has re-introduced more free markets and has been supportive of our efforts in dealing with the Middle East. It appears that we are in a new situation and the revelation of something like this could jeopardize this new positive relationship."

I couldn't believe what I was hearing and everything I had worked on for the last few years was about to go up in smoke. I responded, "Mr. President, with all due respect, that would be an extremely short-sighted move. I admit that Mr. Yeltsin has been co-operative but this is so much bigger than him. A kid born in Moscow or Saint Petersburg in 1970 was raised as a communist and then was suddenly told when he was twenty-two years old 'guess what we're not communist anymore.' Do you think that kid who is now an adult will suddenly start smiling and say, 'yay capitalism'? Do you really think it will be that easy?"

That was when one of the other military advisors chimed in, "There is a growing backlash against Yeltsin, it's smaller now but there is the risk of it growing and becoming violent. To Mr. Melvoy's point, they were raised with communist ideals and now seeing a free market and the wealth disparity may not be acceptable to them. There is already outrage over what they see as 'oligarchs.'"

I could see the wheels turning in President Clinton's mind when Al Gore chimed in, "Mr. President, the last several years of the Soviet Union were awful for large segments of their population and they are in no rush to return to those policies and those conditions."

I decided to continue, "Mr. President, I'm not asking you to pull the trigger but I am asking you not to throw away the gun. Even if there is zero risk of Mr. Yeltsin turning against us, what about the next President? Or the one after that? What if there is another communist revolution that comes to power? We are close to getting them exactly where we want them. Dare I say that before your first term is over, all of the players could be in place."

Bill Clinton paused, "Mr. Melvoy, I understand your point, but at the same time if this leaks, and somehow gets out, we are in big, big trouble and I don't know how we would keep that from escalating."

I once again had to speak up, "See right there, do you notice we aren't afraid of Cuba escalating? It's because on their own, they are a small threat and our army would make quick work of theirs. Russia is a different story and I don't want us to have to worry about things with Russia escalating. We shouldn't have to worry about whether or not Russia might change regimes. Mr. President, this is the ultimate safety net and this will be the guarantee that we won't have another cold war. As far as the discovery goes, I thought of that, and they only know little bits here and there, at most no one knows more than three other agents and there are hundreds that we have arranged infiltration for.

Even if they catch one, the plan will still be in place and we will be able to stop them before any war ever gets started."

Again, Al Gore spoke up, "Mr. President, this is not about self-defense or holding onto a gun for self preservation. This is about taking the first shot whenever you feel like it, which isn't right and would cause enormous problems on the global level if it ever occurred."

I responded as follows, "Mr. Gore, with all due respect, if you see that someone is about to shoot at you, you shoot first, and if someone is coming at you with a knife and you can strike first, you should."

From what I could gather Mr. Gore didn't like me, and showed a surprising amount of passion for someone who was known for being so wooden at the time. "Mr. Melvoy, this isn't just about shutting down a potential attack. You have expressly stated in the original plan that this could be used to render Russia defenseless so we can attack them without counterattack at a moment of our choosing. That is not a plan of self-defense, it is a plan of outright aggression, pure and simple. How would we explain such actions to the United Nations and more importantly to our own people?"

I happened to look over at Bill Clinton and right away I sensed that he was finding Al Gore's point of view convincing. Before I could muster the next argument, another person from a different branch of the CIA chimed in. "Mr. Gore, the answer to that is so simple, tell the American people that they were going to attack us, but we attacked first." He then went on in a condescending tone, "Operation Railroad is one of those things we call confidential."

Suddenly Gore turned to the other guy, "Look Mr. (I forgot his name), don't you understand that if we launch nuclear weapons and kill tens of millions of people, you can't just slap a classified stamp on it and make it go away. We would face outrage, the likes of which we haven't seen since Vietnam. In fact, the global outrage would make Vietnam look like nothing."

At that point, I had heard all I was going to hear. "Mr. Gore, what exactly is your problem with Vietnam, I served in that war, three (I held up my fingers) tours of duty. From where I sit the only problem was that we didn't finish the job and win it."

Al Gore rolled his eyes, "Mr. Melvoy, I appreciate your service as I do every veteran but the fact is, that war was a disaster and we lost tens of thousands of soldiers for no good reason."

My eyes almost popped out of my head, "We could have won, but we didn't go all the way with it, we have to finish the job otherwise it will hang over our heads until the end of time."

I turned back to Bill Clinton, now I was upset and my passionate anger came through. "Mr. President, this whole thing started after World War II, we didn't want the world to fall into chaos again, Russia decided it was going to run things and started trying to catch up to us. We have a golden opportunity to make sure that we never let that happen and this will guarantee that World War III never happens. If we throw this plan away, those casualties that Mr. Gore was so worried about will be nothing by comparison."

I had said that on purpose because I wanted to take Gore's words and throw them back at him.

Before he could collect himself, Bill Clinton said, "Okay everyone calm down, now Mr. Melvoy raised some excellent points, and before I make my decision I need to know one thing, Mr. Melvoy, do you believe in this? I mean really believe that maintaining this Operation is in our national interests?"

I responded, "Of course."

He paused, "Very well, if there are any issues you will be disavowed and you will be prosecuted, and if this ever comes out in order to maintain our relationship with Russia, I am prepared to jail you."

I told him, "Well that won't happen so we have nothing to worry about."

He said, "Very well, Mr. Melvoy, as the President I reserve the right to return to this issue should circumstances change, but for the time being we will keep this going. And Melvoy, keep up the great work."

Al Gore tried to speak up, "Mr. President, I think you should reconsider."

That was when one of the other intelligence officials condescendingly chimed in, "You heard the man, Gore."

Then Bill stood up and said, "That's it, this meeting is over, everyone shake hands and we will keep Operation Railroad as a contingency plan and that is final."

We all shook hands although I went out of my way to shake Gore's extra hard to show him what I thought of him. I knew that I had to take an extra step to guarantee no one could ever pull the plug on this operation. God forbid something happens to Bill Clinton and President Gore decides to pull the plug. I believed that I had to stand guard against any attempted dismantling of this Operation.

Meanwhile back in Michigan things had taken a turn for the worse, the other partner of Game Night was finished and had effectively sold the bar to Cathy. She had no idea how to run a bar, much less six of them, and they feared that if things didn't improve that they would be shutting them all down in a few years. They were still asking for my help but since I continued to refuse, they had hired a business manager who was supposed to turn things around for them. However, after several months they discovered that he was a con man and by June of 1995 he had stolen over $12,000. Unfortunately he too had fled town before they could find him but they eventually caught up to him pulling the same scam in Wisconsin. They were now down to five locations and were scared for their future, so they hired another manager who was honest but was also disorganized.

I continued working sixty hours a week if not more, drinking at night, occasionally throwing up as a result before trying to get back to sleep. I knew that if I drank enough I wouldn't dream the awful dreams, and nightmares were more than I wanted to deal with. I would occasionally ask myself if I was drinking too much and sometimes try and stop for a few days. Pretty soon, I would have a brutal nightmare or a rough day I would be cracking open a beer again thirty seconds after walking through the door.

That fall saw me secure the second corner of Russia's nuclear triad, their submarine force. Those who couldn't suppress it entirely had replaced the missiles similar to the air force that could be altered to make them ineffective. Those ones were also designed to go off when faced with a change in pressure, which in this case was while they were still underwater. If they tried to fire it, within seconds it would blow up in their faces. This left us with the final and most difficult one which was the land based launches, and like my own job at NORAD, were the hardest to break into and they were watched the most closely. The good news was that once the operatives were in place and they reached the status of secure, they would only have to send updates weekly as opposed to every other day.

Thanksgiving and Christmas 1995 I spent alone and my mother asked me to come out, but I told her I was busy. I knew that if she saw me having multiple beers, she would just give me a hard time and in truth I knew that once I got there they would just go on and on about how hard they had it, even though they were living in a mansion. Before Christmas, my mother told me that unless they got a major influx of customers, they would be shutting down another location and then they would be down to four. As 1995 came to an end, we had a breakthrough on the land missile defense system. One of our people was given a job of hiring future candidates and another became one of the top four officials. All we had to do now was get a few people out of the way and everything would be in place.

It was sometime in 1996 when I began having a drink in the morning as a way of reducing my stress for the day ahead. I began to wonder if I was letting it get out of control but I would usually tell myself, "It's just one drink in the morning, it's not like I am driving drunk."

I got a terrible phone call from my mother just a few days after the Super Bowl, they didn't get enough business and they were shutting down the location and the other four were struggling. She began to tell me about how depressed and scared Cathy was, and how the doctors had to increase the dosage of her medication. By this point I was tired of hearing about it and tired of hearing the same routine about how bad things were for them.

We were able to further solidify the other two corners of the triad so that many of our operatives had back-ups who could potentially take their place. I found out that we were one top replacement away from securing the last corner of the nuclear triad. The problem was this person reported directly to Boris Yeltsin and was a trusted friend. This was the last major step and we had to find a way to execute it because the 1996 Russian election was months away. After careful consideration, I was left with only a few options.

The first option was assassination overt, which was one of the least desirable options since we were trying to avoid an investigation and we needed to do this as quietly as possible. The second option was assassination covert, where we make it look like an accident or a natural death. While this one is less risky, it could still cause people to snoop around. On the positives of both, our guy would most likely move into that key administrative position in short order. The third option was frame him for scandal, and while this option could work it was the least likely to succeed based on his friendship with Yeltsin. With this we were in a bind and one key promotion away from completely locking in Operation Railroad. We had to take the guy out, but the question was, how?

I typically avoided such tactics but I knew that desperate times called for desperate measures; we had to kill him in the most careful way imaginable. We found that way, as it turned out the guy's marriage was hanging on by a thread and one of the problems was the wife having to do housework. The plan wrote itself and our operative casually suggested that he hire a housekeeper so we sent in an operative from Ukraine who went by the name Nadia. She was very attractive and knew that she had one job, which was to seduce, kill, and frame. The plan worked like a charm, and week by week she slowly used her allure and charisma, making it look like an organic attraction was growing. When the time was right she had to kill him, and make it look like his wife did it, and Nadia was a master. She set everything up to look like the wife did it and made the gun shot go off when it was in the wife's

Melvoy's Railroad

hand, so that even the wife thought she had done it. That summer it all unfolded and on August 12th the last piece of the puzzle was laid bare. The wife plea bargained herself down to the equivalent of a manslaughter charge and Nadia left town because of her "embarrassment of being discovered as a scandalous woman who had committed adultery."

The story added up so well that no one thought it couldn't have been anything other than one of the oldest stories. The guy falls out of love with his wife, falls in love with a younger woman, the younger woman falls for a powerful man, the wife finds out, and hell hath no fury o'er a woman scorned. Some people might think that intentionally arranging something like this was cruel but when you are in the middle of a war everything seems legal, the only thing that matters are the results and I was very happy with those results.

On September 3, 1996, I wrote my report on the success of the implementation of Operation Railroad and now all that was required was maintenance and occasional replacement of personnel. Just like McLachlin's report four years earlier, this went to the top of the different intelligence agencies as well as other top people in the CIA. I received many compliments from those in the community on the stellar job that I had done on this. However, one question remained, what if something happened to me? Who would run things? I knew that Gore still wasn't happy about it and I needed to find a few people who would help me prevent any repeal. Even though Clinton was going for a second term, there were rumours about who would run for President in 2000 and Al Gore's name began being passed around.

While I was figuring out these details and setting up the last part of the plan, things were taking a bad turn with my family back in Michigan with the disorganized business manager quitting, and during the Labour Day weekend some guy had drank too much and drove and was suing them for letting it happen. By this point, Cathy and my mother were at their wits end and while the kids had started working in the bar to help out, they didn't know the ins and outs of it. I was so focused on my mission that I repeatedly ignored my mother's cries for help. At one point even Billy called and asked me to go and help, and he told me that he had been talking to Cathy and was very concerned that she was falling into a state of hopelessness. I still didn't take it seriously and was still a little mad about him offering me charity two years earlier.

Then on October 22, 1996, I got home after figuring out my successors to run Operation Railroad and I was on my second or third beer when I got the phone call from my mother. I saw her name on the call display and almost didn't pick up but I thought to myself, "I may as well get it over with."

Suddenly I heard it, "Charles, she's dead."

I was stunned. "What? Who?"

My mother was heartbroken. "Cathy, she wrote a suicide note and took too many pills and by the time I found her it was too late."

I heard my mother bawl her eyes out for over almost half an hour and my heart broke with her. How could she do this? What was going to happen to their business? What was going to happen to their kids? I fell asleep that night hoping this was a bad dream, then I remembered that with how much I drank now there were no dreams, no nightmares, only a reality that felt like one.

CHAPTER 48
★
TOO LATE?

    I decided to take a week off to go to the funeral and talk to them about the next step. I packed up everything and I hadn't gone a week without drinking in a long time but I had no idea how hard it was going to be. I got there on the Thursday and the funeral was scheduled for Saturday. My mother was so glad to see me that she held onto me so tight I couldn't believe she had that much strength. I found out Billy was flying in from California the next day and I cringed wondering how that would go.

    For the first time in a very long time I had seen all of Cathy's kids who were so much older than I remembered them and they were devastated. Cynthia's son was now an eight-year-old named Caleb. It wasn't until I arrived that I found out exactly what had happened, the lawsuit verdict had come down saying that the person who was suing them was being awarded $45,000 and that was apparently the last straw. Cathy had started taking placidyls, which is a very powerful sleep aid, and one is plenty, but she took what was left of her entire month's prescription and taken them all, which was over twenty. That was all it took because she thought they were going to lose everything. Reading the photocopy of her suicide note was the hardest thing I had read in my life. I couldn't help but remember how happy she used to be in her younger days, how she used to walk out from the kitchen being proud of the latest dish she had cooked with my mother when she was a child. I remembered how thrilled she was to have this big house and how happy she was on her wedding day. I remembered some of the other times in her earlier life when she was so bright and so optimistic. By contrast, the note reeked of self-pity, hopelessness, and the belief that she had failed as a wife and as a mother, which in turn made her a failure as a woman and a person.

    The one sentence that stood out the most read, "My older brother won't lift a finger to help me and my younger brother thinks I'm crazy."

    That was so hard to read and it was hard not to wonder if there was something I could have done to help her not give up. I began to wonder if that question was going to haunt me for the rest of my life.

The next day Billy and Hashani arrived and I was already in a really bad mood and wasn't looking forward to meeting Hashani again. It had been over ten years and I disliked her so much that I didn't want to deal with her. Billy and I started talking about the situation, I remember asking him if he had read her suicide note and he said, "Yes, if only she had held on a little bit longer."

I asked him what he was talking about, and Billy responded, "I was in the process of shutting down my practice in Sacramento, my last appointment was October 30th and I was going to come over here to help her through this crisis. I knew she was in a very bad place, but it took time to wrap everything up."

I paused, wondering if that would have saved the day, but once again, it was too little too late, I asked him what he would do now. He responded by saying that he would be staying in town for a while and he was glad to see me there as well as he knew it meant so much to our mother. I responded that she was really upset and I didn't know what would happen to their kids. Billy responded, "I am very concerned about this family and what they might do to deal with this tragedy."

I asked him what he was talking about and he responded in his doctor voice. "Our family didn't do a good job teaching us how to deal with bad situations and they are more afraid of how the situations would look to everyone else than whether they dealt with things properly. Those talks I had with Cathy made it clear that she was scared to talk to a counsellor directly because she didn't want people to think she was crazy or that their family was anything less than perfect. I tried to tell her that she needed help and that if she tried to just internalize it and medicate it, that would not be good."

Suddenly her suicide note made a lot more sense and I had an easy way out of my own guilt because Billy had convinced her she was crazy and now it was his fault. "So, that's how it happened, you used all of your psychiatrist terms to try to tell her she was crazy and you pushed her over the edge, and you were on your way here to have a full-time patient."

He responded defensively, "Excuse me, I was talking to her the last couple of months trying to help her, trying to help her cope since she didn't know how to cope on her own."

I responded, "Oh yeah, forget the placidyls, you wanted to be her crutch!"

He got very upset, "Charles, I was prepared to leave behind my life and my wife in Sacramento to come here and help her, what the hell were you doing other than saying sorry I can't. What were you doing? Anita died over two years ago, what were you still doing there?"

Without realizing it he had struck one of my most sensitive nerves, "You keep Anita out of this, unlike your wife she was actually a good woman."

I hadn't seen him this angry since we were children and our voices raised. "You don't know a damn thing about Hashani, she has been looking after her diabetic father for the last three years. Despite you and her despising each other, she was willing to send you that money to help you because she knew what Anita meant to you."

I wasn't in my right state of mind, "Whole lot of good that did, we didn't get it in time and her treatment got delayed and she died anyway. I guess that's always your excuse, you mean well but you're too late."

That was when my mother came in deeply upset, "Both of you stop it, this isn't what Cathy would have wanted, now shake hands and apologize."

I turned to her, "Not what she wanted, she didn't want him getting in her head and convincing her she had a problem that she didn't have. That's what these psychiatrists do, they're like crooked mechanics, they make more problems than they solve so the suckers keep going back to them."

Billy responded, "Speaking of not solving problems, her note said that you wouldn't lift a finger to help her and you're the one with the business experience. You are the one she asked to help her save her company over and over and you were more loyal to a chain of grocery stores than your own sister. She wanted you to be there but you were too busy feeling sorry for yourself."

My mother seeing this situation getting out of control stepped between us, "Boys, boys, calm down, just because there has been a death in the family, there is no reason to act like this."

I responded, "Mom, we aren't boys, we're men, and Billy if you want to step outside so we can settle this like men, let me know."

He responded, "There it is right there, caveman mentality. That is why you always vote republican because that is their mentality. Here's something for you to think about, maybe if they cared about people we would have universal health care and Anita wouldn't have died."

There was a long, stunned silence and by this point Cathy's sons were standing in the doorway. I was so enraged I could have broken him in half right there, but my mother was standing between us and I had heard enough so I walked away. I hoped that he would fight me outside but I knew he wouldn't because I would have torn him to pieces.

The funeral went on and it was so hard hearing them talk about her life and how much she loved her children and that her kindness was an example to all. It was hard for me to listen to that, but I put up with it. I stood there and listened to all of the people issuing me their condolences for her passing. It was so hard picking up that casket knowing that my younger sister was inside, knowing that she was only in her forties and it was over for her. It was hard to accept that this was really happening, this person who I always thought I would get together with later was no longer going to be there.

I sat down with my mother the next day and asked what was going to happen, she said that she didn't know because there was no leadership and the three remaining locations could fall apart. The good news, if we could even call it that, was that Cathy's life insurance would be enough to pay for the lawsuit, her funeral, and leave about $15,000. I was left with a tremendous conundrum in that if the business went down they might lose their large home that they wanted to keep so badly. However, I was still in a situation where I had to protect Operation Railroad, and my mother with tears in her eyes begged me to please save the business. With her right in front of me I couldn't say no, but I bought myself some time by saying that I would need a few months to sort things out so I could move and be there for the business.

We had a meeting with the four kids, my mother, Billy, Hashani and myself. My mother wanted us to clear the air once and for all before I went home so we could sort everything out. Cynthia spoke first, "Uncle Charles, our family has had some bad times, but I don't want to lose everything for my son, because if we come together we can save this business."

This was when Hashani chimed in, "A lot of things have happened but Charles, if you're willing to let bygones be bygones, we will too."

I looked at her in disbelief, "So once again, you're speaking for him now?"

Her jaw clenched together, "No, he is more than capable of speaking for himself but I'm trying to speak for me because we have not liked each other for over ten years."

I then stood up, "Oh yes because you didn't want your family to be offended without giving a damn about ours, but what really drives me crazy is that you didn't let him go to his father's funeral. That was the most low-class thing I have ever heard of!"

She sat down and Billy stood up, "Charles, the other reason why I didn't go to his funeral was because I was trying to avoid the inevitable conflict with you. Ever since we were teenagers, we have been worlds apart and at each other's throats. I have visited his grave and paid my respects, I wish things had gone better between us, I wish I hadn't run away all those years ago and damn it, I wish you could learn to let things go when it matters most, like right now!"

We were on different sides of the table, with my mother around the corner to my left. There was another awkward pause, when Cathy's son Connor spoke up, "What the hell happened between you two, Grandma, Mom and Dad were never clear about it."

I responded, "Okay Connor I'll tell you. When we were growing up, I did everything to help him, I helped teach him sports, I stood up for him any time he needed it, and then he turned into a brat listening to hippies and ran away from this family and ruined the Easter of 1968."

Billy responded, "Charles, I have long since apologized and taken responsibility for that, I am amazed that you are still mad about something that happened almost thirty years ago. We were teenagers then, we are now men in our forties, Cathy's kids and your kids are older than we were at that time. I came back and have since made many efforts to make up for it and be a real brother."

I did not take what he said seriously, "Some brother, you spent all your life in an office telling people that everything is their parent's fault and why they need to pay you to listen to them for the rest of their lives."

His own anger began to emerge, "It's called listening Charles, maybe if you did that once in a while I wouldn't have had to save you."

I asked him what he was talking about, and he responded, "When Veronica wanted to pursue sole custody, I listened to her complain about you for hours and hours and hours, and I repeatedly stood up for you and defended you. Did you forget the contract I drew up so that she wouldn't pursue sole custody?"

I responded, "Some plan Billy, it happened anyway."

He responded, "That is your fault, if you had asked me how to respond to your daughter's lesbianism and you had listened to me, you would still have a relationship with her."

I responded by saying, "Oh yes, you would have told me to pretend it was just fine, who cares that my ex-wife let her become a deviant? Who cares if she never has children or comes down with AIDS because of it?"

My mother spoke up, "Honey, I know you are upset, but please calm down."

I responded, "No Mom, I'm tired of this guy pretending to be looking out for us and then telling us how to run our lives. You call yourself a brother, you have some nerve."

Hashani started to say something when he put his hand on her shoulder. "Gee Charles, I was enough of a brother to send you over $18,000 for Anita's chemo, but now that you need someone to blame, suddenly I'm the bad guy. You expect me to keep apologizing for things that happened three decades ago and you won't take responsibility for your actions three months ago."

My fist was balled up and I was ready to punch him in the face, when Cathy's third child and second son Marco stood up, "Okay, this is getting too real here."

My mother exclaimed, "Marco, don't interrupt!"

If I had wanted it badly enough, my CIA training would have allowed me to kill everyone in this room, but I knew I had to keep it together. This man was my brother, a brother that I didn't understand, a brother who I was blaming Cathy's death on, and a brother who seemed to be my opposite in almost every way imaginable.

After a very awkward fifteen seconds, Hashani spoke up, "Charles, your mother told me that you are going to be helping up here full time?"

I responded, "Yes, it will take a few months to sort everything out back in Tampa, but yes."

She suddenly had the answer, "Well how about this, Billy can stay here to help out until you can come here and take over."

I looked around at these young people, who were now effectively orphans, and I looked at my mother who just wanted us to get along. I walked away from the table to the nearby window and realized that they needed me, even though I had trouble admitting it.

I turned back towards everyone and said, "It will probably be January or February before I can move up here full time. Billy do you think you can handle that?"

He paused and said, "Yes I think I can."

I responded, "Good because when I come back I want you gone and you better not try turning anyone else here into your next customer."

I walked away, packed my things and stayed in a nearby hotel until the day of my return flight home. Not only did I not want to be around Billy, by going to a hotel, I could finally drink again, which after the days I'd had, was all I wanted.

Shortly after returning to Florida, the 1996 election was held and to my personal dismay Clinton had won a second term. "What the hell is happening to this country?" I pondered to myself.

With that I had to create some type of exit strategy. I requested a meeting with Clinton and other members of the intelligence community and they granted it to me at the end of November. During the meeting I laid out my situation that I couldn't continue in my current capacity. So I proposed the following: first, I laid out three top candidates who would each manage our initiative within each corner of Russia's nuclear triad. Second, I continued by saying that I would still be accepting the occasional request for consultation and finally a monthly report to keep me on top of what was happening. I would be separate but still enough in the loop to keep my eye on things, especially because I was concerned about Mr. Gore potentially stopping the Operation after four long years of hard work.

While I always preferred Reagan I have to admit that Bill Clinton had grown on me a little bit as commander in chief, and I certainly liked him better than Jimmy Carter. He issued his condolences and said that my request was perfectly reasonable and would be very helpful going forward.

One of the other intelligence advisors spoke up, "I'm afraid I have one concern, are you planning to move into the house with your mother, your nieces and nephews as well as your great nephew?"

I said, "I'm not sure, I know that was my mother's idea."

He paused, "We cannot send you confidential documents, especially with so many civilians around who could see it, so I'm afraid that we won't be sending you any monthly reports until you are in your own place and can keep these as secure as possible."

I accepted that caveat and began the process of wrapping up the last of the operations I was overseeing as well as selling my house. The good news was my house was in a good neighbourhood and there were several people willing to buy. The other good news was that the house was largely paid off because Anita and I had originally had a ten-year mortgage, which we were five and a half years through. The sale happened far more quickly than I expected and now I had to arrange to find a small bungalow that I could buy outright in Michigan. Thankfully the numbers worked out and by the closing date on March 1st, I was starting over in Michigan to save my dead sister's business. I had almost $30,000 in my bank account, a small home to myself, and I would still be able to keep my eye on the Operation I had put so much time and effort into.

You may be wondering if it was hard to sell the home that Anita and I bought together, and in some ways yes it was, because when we originally bought it, it meant so much. In other ways, it wasn't because it was just a cruel place that reminded me of my greatest loss. It wasn't quite the way I wanted but I was going to make the best of it, as hard and as painful as that would be.

I didn't know how long I would be doing this for, three years, five years, ten years? All I knew was I had a mission to do but I hoped that I could eventually return to the one I really wanted.

The day before I left, I paid one final visit to the cemetery in Tampa and looked at the burgundy tombstone with the name "Anita Melvoy" carved into it. I put a hand on top of it and I said, "Anita, I miss you so much, I wish you were here and… if I could go back in time and do more to save you, I would. Maybe in the next life we will have each other, maybe in the next life I can run into your arms and you won't disappear when an alarm clock goes off. Maybe in the next life, we can stand in the middle of the street and have the celebratory kiss that we should have had here when we would have completed the mission."

I walked away knowing that I had to leave Tampa and be a family man who was going to keep one foot in the CIA.

CHAPTER 49

★

SAVING THE DAY

They teach you a lot of things in the CIA, and one of them is what to watch for, most notably where your lies, alibis etc. could become exposed and how to keep them covered. While I had learned some managerial techniques as a regional manager of the CIA, there were other things I would or should have known as a manager of a grocery chain. So I spent a good few weeks with one of President Clinton's friends who had been running his own business for years and who gave me the basics. Simple things that could easily be forgotten about, like filing Sales Taxes quarterly, how to negotiate better deals on your inventory, easy ways to cut costs and motivate employees, etc. It was so strange being the student but I was going to need this crash course, so that I could help the bar and keep my family from finding out that I had been lying to them all of this time. I took notes and memorized as much as I could so by the time I went back to Michigan, I had to be able to walk in there and lead the team to victory.

I was driving a moving truck to Michigan, to say that I was nervous about how all of this would go and how long it would take, was deeply concerning. I remember pulling off the road at a local restaurant in Kentucky for dinner, the meal was fairly average and I ordered four beers with dinner. Over the course of it, I had asked the waitress where I could find a decent hotel to stay. She said the best place around here would be up the highway in Lexington.

I took that highway up and somewhere around an hour later on the very exit I was taking, there was a trap set up by the local police trying to catch people who had been drinking and driving. By the time I saw the trap it was it was too late, the only good news was there were at least fifteen cars ahead of me. I didn't have any other food or drink packed so basically I just had to wait, each minute felt like an eternity. I got closer and closer, trying to think of what I could do and finally I got there and I knew that I had to stall for every second I could get. My heart began to race, they asked me how I was doing and if I had been drinking, I told them I had a couple beers with dinner but that was it. I knew that if they gave me the breathalyzer, it wouldn't be zero. I tried to stall by asking questions about where a good hotel was, that only lasted a minute and a half, and finally they brought it out and I blew into it fearing the worst.

The machine beeped and he looked at it, "0.078," he then put his arms on my window and said, "Sir, it doesn't take very many beers to put you over the legal limit. You got real lucky we didn't catch you half an hour ago, because you are under 0.08 you can move along and be more careful next time."

I didn't enjoy the condescension this local cop was giving me, but I tolerated it and moved along, relieved that I had gotten through that ordeal unscathed.

I checked into that hotel and began wondering if that local cop was at least partially right. If I had been caught drinking and driving it would have endangered everything I had worked for from Operation Railroad to Cathy's family's failing business. I realized that my drinking had gotten out of control and I had to put a stop to it now. I woke up the next morning and I promised myself while I was shaving and looking at myself in the mirror, that I wouldn't let that happen again.

I finally arrived in Lansing, at least this way I would be in the same city as my mother and Cathy's kids without having to share the same place. One of the three remaining Game Night locations was there, the other two remaining locations were in Grand Rapids and Saginaw, respectively. To tell you how desperate the situation was getting, the Saginaw location was $3,000 away from not being able to function. I had to start telling myself that with Operation Railroad fully implemented and competent people maintaining it, that the war was effectively over and my new primary focus had to be saving Game Night.

Some of the changes required were more obvious, for example under the stupid directions of that bargain basement business planner, the bar was opening at 7:00 am every day. Some of the employees liked working that early shift because it meant a good three hours of not having to do anything. I changed those rules in a hurry so that we would be opening no earlier than 11:00 am to potentially catch the lunch crowd. On Sundays, we wouldn't open until noon, when I say it was dead in the mornings, I mean you could have heard a pin drop.

Suddenly our electricity and labour costs dropped. I picked a Wednesday to have a company meeting at our Lansing location to talk about the changes that were going to be made. Some of the people were not living up to their responsibilities and I told them that if they weren't doing their jobs, I would fire them and replace them with someone who would. Apparently, that ruffled a few feathers, but I was certain the backlash would be short lived. With fewer hours, I was able to let a few people go and get the other employees working at the two busier locations to come to Saginaw to pick up a few extra hours and shore up most, if not all of the difference.

Here I applied not only the lessons I learned from Clinton's friend, like looking for the most obvious places to cut wasteful spending, but I also applied lessons I had learned in my previous careers.

In the military, they teach you teamwork and respect and I told everyone, "We are all part of the Game Night team. If you wear that uniform you are one of my soldiers, you will respect this team, you will respect me, and you will give your best every single day."

This resulted in a couple of people quitting, and others stepping up, one of the supervisors began to tell me how they were getting more done and that the mood of the place had picked up.

I learned from the CIA that if you find out everything you could about your competition then you can find a way to exploit their weaknesses. As it turned out, one of the biggest reasons why the Saginaw location was barely scraping by was because just a block down the road was another sports bar. That sports bar had gone out of their way to hire attractive women as waitresses to lure in more of our target customers. How we would retaliate will come up later.

cost?

There was something else they teach you in the CIA, which was to make connections. I spoke to our suppliers and began ordering bulk amounts of non-perishable items, so we would be well stocked at a cheaper price. The other thing I did was begin talking to the local sports teams, including the stars of the local major league teams. As luck would have it, if you tell people that the players from the Detroit Red Wings would be coming to sign autographs, people would come in droves. We also got a member of the Detroit Pistons to come out and sign autographs and answer questions before the start of the 1997-1998 NBA Season.

By the end of the summer the Saginaw location was making money again. Grand Rapids was doing better, and Lansing, which had always been our best location, was getting some positive press over a charity event we had done that summer with the Governor of Michigan. After all, if there is one thing a politician always needs, it's good press and in the process, we raised over $11,000 for the local homeless shelter. With each passing week, as the sales returned and the good press began to grow, my mother became more and more convinced that things were going to be okay.

There was one area that didn't turn out the way I had expected, since our competition in Saginaw was using sex and women with low cut shirts. We responded by having Monday evenings be "cheerleader nights," and some of our waitresses liked the idea, others thought it was pandering. One guy actually grabbed one of them one night and even though I wasn't there, she later told her supervisor that she was never doing that shift again and if we tried to make her do it she would quit. You may be wondering why on earth I would do that in the first place. Well it was actually a careful plan, men like what they see, the way to top a low cut top was to create a fantasy. Sure enough, the competitor's business would plummet on Mondays, which was one of their key nights as it was ours.

I knew exactly what their retaliation would be and they fell right into my trap. Our cheerleader outfits only showed bare arms and legs beneath the knee. I knew that they would put their own previous strategy on steroids and next thing you know their girls were showing full cleavage and a good chunk of their bellies. Then all it took was one of my mother's friends writing an article in the local paper, about how low class they had become. Suddenly wives were keeping their husbands away from there and making sure they went to our place. Of course, the backlash I suffered for my cheerleader idea paled in comparison to the other place's new dress code, which also included short shorts. While our business did fall off, I knew that they were a ticking time bomb and I just needed to take this one step further.

I started a campaign with the slogan, "On Game Night We Are Your Friends," which involved our cheerleader waitresses taking pictures with our clients.

They tried to top it by pushing their girls to take more provocative pictures with their male patrons, and now I was just one move away from getting them right where I wanted them. Connor and one of his friends went to a strip club that was in another town and we convinced the owner that he should pursue some of the other place's employees as potential new talent.

I didn't tell Connor my actual plan and I sure as hell didn't tell my mother about this. I told Connor that the plan was to get the strip club owner to pursue them as a prank because of a nasty phone call I had received which never actually happened.

I knew that there were only two ways this could go. Scenario A, the club owner offers the women way more money and they leave, disrupting our competitor's business for an extended period. Or Scenario B, the offer is so insulting to them that they get mad at their boss for making people think they were strippers and so they quit or revolt.

My last trick was having a lawyer, who was a colleague of my mother's lawyer, come in that same week and pull one of the waitresses aside asking her about her working conditions. By Thanksgiving, the other place was attacked from all sides for being demeaning to its employees, whereas ours was so tasteful by comparison that no one noticed. The sexual harassment lawsuit that followed became local news and ripped them to pieces. I set the trap and they fell right in.

By the end of 1997 it seemed like things were going reasonably well, and all three bars were making money again, wherein the debts that had piled up were getting paid down. For the first time in a long time my mother actually felt good about what the future held. I remember a conversation she had with me, telling me about how they were running out of money and they had been taking money out of Melina's college fund. She and Marco were the ones who didn't want to work in the family business even though Marco was doing barely anything at the laundromat. However Melina's dream was being a cardiac surgeon and thanks to all of the hard work I had been putting in, that dream wouldn't die.

CHAPTER 50

THE ENEMIES WITHIN MY WALLS

While all of these positive changes occurred, I was still keeping on top of Operation Railroad and I couldn't wait for the fifth of every month to get my reports. The reports would be about eight to ten pages and would lay out the status of everyone in the nuclear triad. All the basics were covered and it was almost funny how some members of the team were concerned about someone knowing their part in the plan, even though that person also knew about it. This anonymity was perfect because it meant that if one got discovered, they wouldn't know if anyone else was, no matter what happened.

As the 1990s progressed, Boris Yeltsin was becoming less popular and it was becoming clear that someone would be taking his place after he finished out his term. I had accepted that Clinton was more or less correct that Yeltsin wasn't a threat to the United States, but I also believed that this plan was essential for stopping them while we could. The next President of the Russian Federation may not be anywhere near as interested in working with us as allies. I had bought a locked file cabinet and even when I wasn't reading those reports, they were safe in that file cabinet. I would set aside time to deal with any issues raised and on a couple of occasions I had been asked to consult about the next step for the Operation by my successors.

I never breathed a word of this to my family and as far as any of them knew, I was there to help the family and that was it. I spent the early months of 1998 battling the temptation to start drinking when I was at home. It's one thing to have a couple beers on New Year's or a beer at Christmas but I was having a hard time keeping myself from drinking at home. I knew that if I got started again, I might have a hard time stopping and I was having a lot fewer dreams about Anita or other bad things than I used to. Having one of these nightmares once every three or four weeks was nowhere near as bad as having them every night or every other night. However, I didn't have time to think about my nightmares as I was thinking about my drinking, Operation Railroad, and running the business. Just when I thought things were going well, I was in the Grand Rapids location when I happened to overhear two of the waitresses saying, "Craig said we could be getting $8 or $9 an hour with benefits if we vote for the union."

They saw me and immediately split up and went back to work. I knew we had a problem now and just as we were getting our costs under control and our revenue going up, I believed that this would ruin everything. Just with those few seconds, I knew what they were being tempted with and I knew one of the people pushing it. I also knew that they were still trying to build support among their people and the movement was still weak which is why they were actively hiding it.

I told Cynthia and Connor to keep their eyes and ears open to see how quickly this was spreading. I called up Clinton's friend and asked him about how I could shut this down before it got out of hand. He told me that there were a few ways; the first was to watch for the laws in our state, as each state has different rules. Some would let me get away with more than others, but he said a good general rule was this, first, remind the staff that unions aren't free, they charge dues and you can't opt out once they're in. The second part is to remind them that they stop the best from getting promoted and getting the hours they wanted.

I also had to do things to squash the movement before the vote, whenever that was. The first would be to intentionally hire new people to dilute the percentage of employees who are in favour of the union. I then asked about the fact that I would now have additional employees and he said that after the vote I could slowly let them go. Maybe I could even hire the ones who are clearly incompetent, so my reason for letting them go becomes a self-fulfilling prophecy. I asked him what else I could do and he said that the big companies like Wal-Mart sometimes will shut down a store once it becomes unionized, but our organization was too small and too close together to do that without taking some major hits.

He then told me that there was another approach that might work and he suggested that I tell the staff that if we hit a certain goal, they would all get a raise. This way they could feel like what they want would come anyway without the unions. The truth was most of the staff were earning minimum wage plus tips, which back then was just over $5.00 an hour. Over the next month, I started listening to what the staff wanted and the biggest thing was that the girls were tired of doing was cheerleader nights and since the enemy was falling apart, I reluctantly agreed.

I used another trick from the CIA, only lie when you have to and to keep consistency. The most effective lies are half-truths, therefore the truth was the company had struggled for several years and while things had improved, the company was still digging itself out of the hole. Therefore, we couldn't afford a raise at this time but I told them that if they gave it a year that would change. The truth was we were still clearing profit in early 1998 and we were much busier than we used to be, however I pretended that we were in worse shape than we really were.

The vote finally came to a head and I had used almost all of those tricks suggested, except threatening to shut down. The vote was defeated and now it was only a matter of time to see how long it would take to slowly find out who the troublemakers were and slowly phase them out so no one would really notice. This consisted of giving them fewer and fewer hours until they quit, which I knew would only take a few months.

While that was going on, I was keeping a close eye on Operation Railroad. I was getting concerned about Al Gore becoming President because if anyone was going to derail it, it would be him. Then the Monica Lewinsky scandal hit, which turned into comic fodder for months and years. To give you the most basic summation, a young woman named Monica Lewinsky started working at the White House and President Bill Clinton had an affair with her. I took a bit of a sadistic joy in this because the Democrat President was being roasted from all sides, and if this kept up, a future Republican President would be inevitable. The Republicans were still my party, my team after all.

One of the other things that came to light during that time was Marco started dating a girl named Alison. Normally I wouldn't have taken too much notice of this, but it came up on my radar because Alison had gotten in his ear about how he should be running the business and how it was rightfully his. Without saying too much, she was a gold digger who saw a guy in his early twenties with a big house and absent parents, who could one day have a fortune.

After the divorce, my sister Cathy had adjusted her will to say she was leaving everything to my mother, on the condition that the children were allowed to stay in the house, which of course they did. Alison proved to be a real pain because she would start asking my mother what was in her will and why she would leave her money to her kids, when her grandchildren needed it badly. Nobody liked Alison because she was bossy, demanding, and genuinely thought that she deserved our family's barely recovered finances. After only three months, she started pressuring Marco into marrying her and that was when I had heard enough and I wasn't letting this piece of work into the family. So one day I told Marco to come over alone and I started telling him what she was doing. Then he started telling me about how she loved him and wanted the best for him and that he was seriously thinking about marrying her.

This was when I knew what I had to do and I told him that I could prove she didn't love him. He told me I couldn't and he began to walk away when I said, "I will call her, you listen and when she thinks you can't hear it, she'll brag about it."

He didn't want to believe me and he kept walking and that was when I said to him, "What are you afraid of?"

He came back and said to me, "I'm not afraid of anything, she and I are getting married and there is nothing you can say that will talk me out of it."

The one thing that I did do was talk to my mother, who made him promise that he would wait and not rush into it. Everyone could see what Alison was doing but Marco didn't want to admit it.

By the summer of 1998, he had proposed and the wedding was set for October 24th. She was trying to push for it for the end of August but that was the compromise. She wanted every damn frill and literally wanted a horse drawn carriage to take them from the church to the reception. This girl was so entitled I wanted to vomit. She must have had twelve credit cards, a $250 purse, and was saying that after they got married, she deserved to be driven around in a Lamborghini.

Since he wasn't listening to reason, I did the one thing that I thought would turn the whole thing around. I convinced my mother to tell the kids that she changed her will so that everything would go to me and to make sure she told the kids that. She didn't like this one bit but she decided that if it broke up Marco and Alison's relationship, then it might be worth it. The one condition she put on it was that I had to tell Billy what was really going on so that it wouldn't complicate things. I wasn't looking forward to this call but it had to be done, so this was a small price to pay to fix this enormous problem.

Hashani picked up the phone and wasn't happy to hear from me, but asked what I wanted. I responded that I needed to talk to Billy about something important. She said, "Charles, if you want money we're not giving you any and if you expect us to help you with something, you can forget it after the way you have treated Billy."

I told her that this wasn't about money and it was about helping Cathy's son and not me. She reluctantly passed the phone along to Billy who already knew about the wedding and agreed that it wasn't a good idea. So it started out well enough but then it took a bad turn. I told him that I needed him and Hashani to pretend that if our mother passed away, that neither Cathy's kids or Hashani and himself were getting anything.

He asked why, and I laid out my plan, "They know I don't like Alison and I am against it, so if we tell her that I'm getting all of the money and they aren't getting any she will run for the hills."

There was a long pause, then Billy began talking, "Charles, not only is that manipulative, it is dangerous."

I asked him what he was talking about, "We need to keep this wedding from happening and this seems like the best way."

He responded, "Charles, did it ever occur to you that the problem isn't with Alison, but with Marco?"

I responded, "Yes and I tried to tell him that she was just after money but he wouldn't listen, so when he sees her run off, he'll know I was right and that will be the end of it."

I sensed Billy was getting annoyed with me as I was getting annoyed at him for not seeing what seemed so obvious.

He went on, "Charles try to understand, the fact is this relationship is built on his lack of confidence in himself which she is capitalizing on, and simply ripping them apart could be hard for him to deal with."

I was baffled, "He's a man, what are you so worried about?"

Billy responded, "Charles, you're right he is a man, but you need to remember that he is a man and not a robot. He doesn't have the best emotional maturity in the first place and both of his parents left him in the last five years, traumatizing actions like that get internalized and can make someone feel like they need validation. This in turn causes them to sometimes pursue it in destructive ways."

Once again Billy and I were on different planets, "Hey Billy, get out of your office and back to the real world. She's using him and I am going to expose it, so just keep quiet about the will being changed and I don't need you to start quoting Sigmund Freud."

Just before I hung up he said, "Charles, I'm asking you to find another way, if he really believes this and you just rip it away like this, his internal emotional problems could get much worse."

I rolled my eyes and sarcastically said, "Thank you for your concern but I don't think everyone is as fragile as the little flowers you have to talk to every day."

So I put the plan in place and sure enough that week I called a family meeting and conveniently invited Marco to bring Alison. I played this deadpan serious, "Hello everyone, as you know your grandmother is getting... older."

Melina being very quick witted said, "Careful Uncle Charles."

I responded, "I am being careful, which is why she and I went to a lawyer earlier today and we modified her will so that everything including the bar and this house would be left to me."

They all looked at each other in disbelief and I paused for a few seconds before continuing, "So after discussing with her about what we were doing, she and I decided that if anyone of you gets married, you are out the door."

They were all stunned but I saw Alison being devastated and it was as if someone had told her that credit cards had been abolished. This was when Marco stood up, "Oh I get it, kick me out so that I have to dump her. Uncle Charles you never knew what love was and that is why you and Uncle Billy hate each other. We don't need your money and we don't need you."

He took Alison by the hand and said, "Come on baby, as long as we have each other we don't need this."

They were part way to the door when she said, "Hold on a minute, how are we going to afford our own place? You only make $6.50 an hour."

He began to say that she could help him find another job and she could get a part time job so she could contribute, but she suddenly began to back out and started saying that this wasn't what she wanted.

I listened carefully around the corner waiting for it, and when they began to go outside, I went closer to the door and opened it a crack. That was when I heard it from her, "I'm not going to live in some dumpy apartment with some loser who can't take care of me."

He then said, "What about us, we were going to get married?"

She responded, "The wedding is off, and I am not doing some cheap wedding with some cheap guy."

I raised my head to the side window, and when she walked away, he stood there, stoically and as the summer wind went by, he barely moved. He began to walk back into the house as I called over to Melina, "Melina, get your brother a beer, he'll need it."

He came in with a look on his face that said one thing, "Devastated."

My mother asked what happened, he responded, "She broke up with me. I wasn't good enough to care for her and she just left me." Melina handed him a beer and his steps were slow as if he were losing the strength to walk.

Everyone surrounded him as he could barely utter another word, my mother began to tell him, "Don't worry honey there are plenty of fish in the sea and you will find a better one soon."

I was beginning to lose my patience as I was waiting for it to sink in, the fact that she was using him and he was better off without her. I finally said to him, "Look, take a day, have a few drinks and everything will be fine. You're better off without her."

He looked up at me with complete despair in his face, "We could have been happy together, we were going to get married, we were going to have a family…"

He turned away putting his hands on the wall, "We were going to have a wonderful life and you killed it, you son of a bitch."

I responded by saying, "Hey it's better you find out now than later, you'll thank me tomorrow when you come to your senses."

He stormed angrily upstairs as everyone looked at me with almost a degree of disgust. I looked back at them, "What?"

Cynthia spoke up first, "I knew she was trouble and he needed to find out, but not like this, look at him he's devastated."

I responded, "Sometimes the truth hurts and this is a good lesson for him."

Connor spoke up next, "I know this is off topic but why did Grandma sign all of her money and our house, over to you? You don't even live here!"

Connor then turned to my mother, "Grandma did he threaten you or something?"

She reluctantly responded, "No, nothing like that."

Connor went on, "Grandma, if he threatened you, I will kick his ass right now."

I cut him off, "Connor, I went to war, I have killed many men and I would break you into pieces."

That was when my mother finally broke, "Oh for Pete's sakes Charles just tell them and get this over with!"

She put her face in her hands and Melina ran to her side to comfort her, Cynthia turned to me, "What is she talking about Uncle Charles?"

Connor, trying to act tough, stood next to her asking, "What did you do?"

I responded, "We didn't change the will, the entire thing was a white lie so that Marco could see Alison's true colours. If my mother dies, her estate is still being split with you getting the house, and other assets being split between you, Billy and I."

Connor got really angry, "You played this whole thing just to end Marco's relationship?"

I responded, "Yes, we were eight weeks away from their wedding and now it isn't going to happen. I just saved all of you from being screwed over by that gold digger. You're welcome!"

I walked away leaving them stunned at what they had just heard.

During the brief few months that Billy was helping run Game Night, someone had suggested that they start showing wrestling pay-per-views so that they could bring in a bunch of extra business on certain Sunday nights. Apparently, the WWF and WCW were doing so many that it seemed like every time you turned around, there was another one coming up. The previous managers had dismissed the idea because it "wasn't a real sport." Billy and I may have been worlds apart but he saw it as a positive opportunity and pursued it. So with Sunday being a big night, I went to our Grand Rapids location to supervise for the big crowd expected for SummerSlam.

I had called that family meeting on the Thursday night and I hadn't heard anything from any of them in those few days that followed. Part way into the night, we were watching a blonde guy get his hair cut because he lost the match, when Marco came in, "Uncle Charles, my shift ended a few hours ago and I came here to tell you to come outside so we can settle this."

I rolled my eyes, "I saved you and this family from a gold digger and the will wasn't changed, so what the hell are you so upset about?"

He responded, "You walked into our house, played with us, and Connor told me about how you did it all to ruin my life."

I responded, "Maybe you should take all that energy you have and get over it."

He responded, "When I knock your ass out, you can just get over it."

I responded, "If you go through with this, I will embarrass you in front of all of these people. I went to war and I don't mean some fight with some random guy, I mean I was in Vietnam fighting and killing."

His bravado was getting the best of him, "Fine, I'm ready to go to war, see you outside bitch."

By this point, the crowd had stopped paying attention to what was on TV and was watching us because they were sure a real fight was about to break out. They gave the big reactionary, "Ooooh."

I responded, "Don't egg him on, he's just being stupid."

He finally pulled back his left sleeve and said, "If you aren't outside in two minutes, I will wreck that piece of crap you call a car."

He walked out, I shook my head and I began to wonder how far I should let this go. Of course the crowd followed us, with part of me wanting to just knock him out, part of me just wanting to trip him and embarrass him but I was still deciding.

People had begun to surround us and it was a hot humid night so we were both lightly sweating before we even went outside. I had to remember that he was much younger than me and was angry, which meant that he wasn't going to quit easily and probably didn't have a strategy and was running on pure fury. He charged at me, clearly with the intention of throwing the first punch. I hit a strike aimed right at his stomach that would not only hurt, but would make him nauseous.

He fell to his hands and knees, and I had hoped that would be enough, but he pulled himself back up and took another swing but I grabbed his arm, tripped him up and threw him back to the pavement.

I told him, "Just stop, you're only going to get hurt."

He pulled himself back up, and I was surprised how determined he was to fight me, he charged at me yet again but I spun him, kicked his legs out from under him and he hit the ground again. The crowd was probably not helping the situation with all of their oohs and ahs and the odd person yelling, "Fight harder, you're getting your ass kicked."

I told him that if he didn't stop, I would have to knock him out. He wouldn't listen and he charged one more time when I grabbed his arm into an arm bar. I did three hard knee strikes to his jaw and by the third one, he was out. I picked him up, lifted him onto my shoulder and asked one of the waitresses to get him a pack of ice for his jaw.

He came to about five minutes later, and apparently stumbled out telling people to get out of his way. I didn't think anything of it, although he was angry I had stopped him, so I figured he would just go home. I called the next morning and my mother was scared to death wondering where Marco was, as he hadn't come home that night. I told her what happened and she was angry with me, so I told her that he wouldn't stop so I laid him out. She immediately called the police and they gave her the old line, "He has to be missing for twenty-four hours."

That day felt like an eternity and as luck would have it, we received a phone call from the police around 8:00 pm that night saying that he was in downtown Detroit, looking like he had been really beaten up. I went with her and Connor, and as it turned out, he had left my bar with his pride hurting and drove all the way to Detroit. He walked into another bar, threw a little bit of money around and picked a fight with three guys who did a serious number on him and left him in an alley. He was there all night and was found by the police when he woke up almost an entire day later. My mother was mortified that he had gone to a seedy bar in Detroit and had been picking fights with people. I heard an echo of Billy's warning go through my head and I began to wonder if this was what he meant.

He told everyone that he was sorry for acting so crazy and that everything was going to be okay going forward. I hoped he meant it but I couldn't be sure. As that fall began, I was faced with a difficult decision because the employees were becoming impatient about getting the raise that I had promised the previous spring. After hearing some grumbling, I finally told them that it was coming February 1, 1999.

With all of this going on, the problems with Marco, and the employees, I had begun having drinks when I came home at night again.

Melvoy's Railroad

By the end of 1998, I was back up to four or five beers a night and although some things were going really well, other things continued to weigh on me.

I had a dream at one point in October that year, where I was walking through what looked like the street I lived on back in Tampa and I was walking into that house but everything seemed to be coloured an apple green. I walked over to the stairs and they stood out because they were the only thing that was a different colour, they were navy blue. I walked up there looking for Anita but then as I got up to the top of the stairs, everything was still green. Then to my left, next to my bedroom door, I saw McLachlin sitting there in a chair. I asked him what he was doing there and he told me, "I was wondering how long it would take."

I asked him, "What are you talking about?"

He then told me, "It's too late, they're gone."

I asked him, "What are you talking about?"

He just repeated himself, "It's too late, they're gone."

I shoved open the bedroom door and saw that it was empty, no people, just nothing, the floor of the room was scorched black. I then looked at him, "What did you do to them?"

He repeated himself one more time, "It's too late, they're gone... all gone."

He began to laugh as I threw a punch, and just as the punch would have made contact, I woke up. Due to how vivid the dream was it took me a moment to re-orient myself to reality.

I was left lying there absolutely confused and wondering what he was talking about, and what did it mean? Did it mean anything at all? I began to wonder as I was lying there what my future held, would I return to the CIA full time? Was I going to run this chain of sports bars until I turned sixty-five, which wouldn't be for sixteen more years?

Around October or November 1998, some business magazine had heard about our newfound success and wanted to do an article, where they talked to the kids, the employees, and took some pictures. It was so strange taking bright smiling pictures in front of the bar and in the bar and so on. We tried to gloss over the tragedy that caused the partners to disagree and eventually split. We tried to claim that Jason had "retired because he was under tremendous stress and he felt that the bar needed new people behind the scenes and gave us the bar to run."

We struggled trying not to let the beans spill but we managed to keep the entire thing sounding rosy, so people would read it and want to come and have a great time. As luck would have it, we were featured in their January issue, which was released on newsstands in mid-December. Connor, above all, was so proud of that magazine story and went out of his way to frame the magazines and put a copy up in all three bars and in the house.

1998 ended with everyone seemingly in a good place, Cynthia was doing fine and looking after Caleb who was now ten-years-old. Connor was excelling as the supervisor of the Lansing location of Game Night, our cash reserves were building and the employees had accepted my promise of the across the board raise on February 1st. Marco seemed to have gotten over Alison, but the star of the family seemed to be Melina who was getting great grades at Michigan University. She was determined to be a cardiac surgeon and how she ended up being so smart was a mystery to most of us. Connor and Marco would occasionally refer to her as Lisa in reference to Lisa Simpson. My mother was seventy-four years old and was doing well for her age, and it seemed like things were finally stabilizing and they might be okay for a while. If there is one thing I should have figured out by this point, it was that things don't stay that way, not for me and not for the Melvoys.

CHAPTER 51
★
LIGHTNING CRASHES

I did quite a bit of driving for those four kids and during those trips I got caught up on what the young people were listening to in the 90s. I didn't understand why their music seemed so sombre and gloomy and even when it sounded upbeat, the gloominess seemed to sneak in.

I remember one of those conversations with Melina, who tried to explain to me about how a song that sounded like a song about having the greatest day, was about suicide and I was just baffled. She always read so much into everything it was sometimes hard to know how she knew so much. I had always remembered her as being so young and now she was twenty and in her third year of university. She was so bright and it was hard for me not to be so proud of her and what she was accomplishing. Perhaps what made talking to her so refreshing was that she had this innocence about her. Despite everything that had happened, she had this natural upbeat viewpoint and it was impossible not to like her. It was slow at first, but she and I seemed to share this bond as if I had taken the place of her father.

The year of 1999 was going reasonably well, and it appeared to be clear sailing ahead with Game Night and our three locations were back on track, so now we could begin to think about once again expanding and reclaiming the bar's former glory from the 1980s.

The biggest problem on the horizon came when I received the February fifth report that said that Yeltsin was intending to step down at some point within the next year. The question of who would take his place haunted me, what would they stand for? I had also since discovered the dark side of the Monica Lewinsky scandal and there was talk of impeaching Bill Clinton as President. This of course would have led to Gore becoming President, whom I feared would undo what I was working for. For everyone else, Clinton's statement, "I did not have sexual relations with that woman," was a source of laughter, but for me it had stopped being funny. My successors were doing well enough keeping everything going but I didn't know what the future held in the long term. If I ever forgot about Operation Railroad, my reminder came every time I saw the President on TV.

Around the time of Valentine's Day, I received some very unpleasant news. Marco was back together with Alison and had bought her a diamond necklace that cost over $400. When I heard that I almost fell off my chair and I came up to him asking, "What the hell are you thinking getting back together with that gold digger?"

He responded that she had called him a few weeks ago and told him how much she missed him and the truth was he missed her too. I wanted to smack him upside the head, I had gone to all of that trouble and he hadn't learned a damn thing.

One day it was my turn to pick up Melina from her biology lab and I asked her how her day was and she began to tell me about some of her lessons. "We were learning about the dangers of blood clots, how they form and how to spot them in potential patients. The more you study the human body, the more fragile you see that it is. Like with cholesterol, it is a small substance, you could crush it with your fingers easily. But when it is inside your veins or arteries, all it takes is a blockage that is so small to bring a person down and cause them to have a stroke."

I was amazed; she wasn't even twenty-one yet and she was so smart. I finally said, "Maybe you can explain this to me, why are you so smart, yet Marco is such an idiot?"

She paused, "Do you mean him getting back together with Alison?"

I responded, "Yeah, what is wrong with him? My father would have given me such a hard kick in the ass if I did something that stupid."

She let out a small laugh before responding, "Well I don't think that would solve anything, you kicked his ass six months ago and it didn't work."

I then asked almost rhetorically, "What is it going to take to get through to that idiot?"

She then began to say, "Well, Uncle Billy thinks that he may be feeling a type of desperation and we need to help him feel better about himself."

I turned to her, "Melina, look I know that you are young and idealistic, but your Uncle Billy doesn't know what he's talking about. I am going to have it out with Marco when we get home."

Then she said something that surprised me, "Uncle Charles, one of the other things I learned at school was that when people are under a lot of stress, it is hard for people to think clearly so if you and him are arguing, it may not help."

I paused and said, "Okay, how would you do it?"

She responded, "I would ask him why he forgave her for dumping him the way she did?"

I reluctantly said, "Okay Melina, we'll try it your way."

We were almost home when I asked, "What else have you learned in school lately?"

She responded, "I am taking a philosophy class as one of my electives and last week they talked about the story of the *Ring of Gyges*."

I asked her to elaborate and she went on, "The ring of Gyges was a ring that if you turned it inward, would make you invisible and the Professor used it as a thought experiment to explain how power corrupts."

She then followed by saying, "I was asked first, 'If you found that ring in the parking lot and found out that it would turn you invisible, what is the first thing you would do?'"

I spoke up, "So what did you say?"

She said, "I responded, 'Get out of the parking lot before someone runs me over.'"

We both laughed and as we pulled up to her house, it was so hard to realize that I had missed out on so much with my own children, but I now had a new chance to be a father for Melina.

We got home and sure enough she asked Marco the question that she said she would and he said something to the effect of, "Well I missed her and wanted her back."

She asked, "Why? Don't you realize you deserve better than a gold digger?"

He suddenly got defensive about the term and although she tried to calm him down, he started backing away from the conversation. I was only listening, but I wondered what was wrong with him that he needed this annoying materialistic woman so badly?

We went through March, and I was concerned about whether or not Marco would bring Alison to Easter Dinner. Finally, we approached that day and he brought her, everyone was pissed off about it and at one key point, she started pushing him saying, "When are you going to do it?"

He said, "In a minute."

I had a terrible feeling in the pit of my stomach about what she was referring to.

After a moment, he got down on one knee and I immediately stood up and walked around to that side of the table. As he reached into his pocket, I grabbed the box out of his hand and I threw it through the open door into the kitchen.

She blurted out, "What's wrong with you?"

He picked up the dull knife that was next to his plate and pointed it at me, "Don't do this to me again Uncle Charles. She loves me and I'm not letting you break us up again."

I knew he wasn't thinking straight because not only had I kicked his ass before, the weapon he picked up was probably one of the least effective knives possible.

Cynthia immediately took Caleb out of the room, and he yelled on his way out, "My money's on Uncle Charles."

There was more tension in the air with each passing second and then it was broken by Melina, "Stop this both of you."

She stood up and was standing next to Alison, "Marco, she doesn't love you, but we do and that's why we don't want you to make a big mistake. Uncle Charles, I've heard of tough love but you've really gone too far. Marco, don't rush into marriage, one of my Professors waited more than five years before they got married, don't rush into this."

That was when Alison said, "Keep out of this bitch."

Alison shoved Melina to the ground. I charged over to pull Melina away and then I pointed at the door, "Get out of my house!"

She said, "Marco, come."

I then said, "Marco, she just attacked your sister. Are you going to let her do that?"

He looked at Alison, he looked at Melina and I could see the conflict in his eyes. He finally said, "I have to go."

Alison said, "Good, let's get out of this place."

Marco spoke up and said, "No, not us, just me."

We heard his car pull away, as she took out her cell phone and called her parents. Melina asked what was happening and I said, "Hopefully he's going to think about everything and come to his senses and dump her."

My mother spoke up, "Charles, I am exhausted and I am going to bed, this is just too much."

She had started doing that more and more in the last year. She had brought this up to me a few times about how she was feeling so much more tired lately and she didn't know why. I brushed it off and told her to just get more bed rest, and she went to bed that night as the rest of us stayed and waited for Marco to come home. This blow up had happened around 7:00 pm and finally around 3:00 am, we received a phone call from the police saying they had talked him off of the edge of a bridge.

Cynthia stayed home with my mother and Caleb, while Melina and Connor went with me to the police station. It was late at night and I was ready to tear his head off for being such a drama queen.

A local psychologist pulled us aside when we arrived, "Marco is in a very vulnerable place right now, he is breaking up with Alison and he now realizes she was using him but he feels worthless. I think he needs some counselling and possibly some medication. I recommend booking an appointment for him with your physician as soon as possible and looking for a counsellor as soon as you reasonably can."

He then looked at me skeptically, "Are you his Uncle Charles?"

I said, "Yes."

He responded, "Stop being confrontational because he needs support above all else."

After he got home I told him to stop losing his temper and to be a man. I thought that maybe he had got the message but I had to watch him carefully. April went by with everyone basically taking turns trying to keep an eye on Marco because he was prescribed anti-depressants by his doctor. Marco quit his job at the laundromat and just started lying around watching TV all day. What I had forgotten was that because there were so many new channels, boredom didn't set in anywhere near as easily as it did for me thirty years earlier. My first thought was that if he didn't get his act together by the end of April, I would insist that he start working at the bar and stop feeling sorry for himself.

The day after her last exam, Melina was going to be staying at her friend's dorm and then she was going to need a ride home around noon. I picked her up, and she felt pretty good about how she did, I knew that she had studied a lot and was hopeful of the results. She was in such a good mood that she wanted to listen to some music, some of it wasn't that bad and some of it I didn't understand. However, the last song that started playing before we pulled up to the house was called *Lightning Crashes*, I forget the name of the band. She was enjoying herself and it was hard for me not to feel such pride, because over the previous two years, I had become her father figure seeing her succeed on an incredible level.

We finally pulled up to the house and she wanted to stay in the car to finish listening to the song, and when we finally went into the house, it was disturbingly quiet. I kept calling and didn't hear anything, and I suddenly got a bad feeling in the pit of my stomach, just like the quiet reception I had received the day Anita died. I told Melina to stay in the living room as I went upstairs. I walked up the stairs with dread hitting me right in the stomach.

I kept calling and finally I heard Marco call back, "I'll be up in a moment."

I walked into his room asking him where my mother was, he said, "She was tired and took a nap."

That was when I knew something was wrong; my mother could hear a pin drop in the house next door and so repeatedly calling up the stairs would have woken her up. I immediately went into her room and she laid there on her side, her eyes closed and her mouth hanging open. I called again with no response, I put my hand on her shoulder and lightly shook her with no response, and my heart raced as I feared the worst of possibilities. I immediately grabbed her wrist and took her pulse, just like I did with Anita five years ago and I waited for something, anything, but there was just nothing. I sat down on the floor but facing away from her and saw Marco standing there asking, "What happened?"

I began to get upset, "Go downstairs, I'll handle this."

I began to walk downstairs, trying with every fibre of my being to keep my composure and when I picked up the phone and called the ambulance, there was a lump in my throat so I barely eked out the words. "We need an ambulance at 345 Unique Avenue, my mother is dead."

I thought that the air was going to leave my lungs, and I put the phone down and then I sat down at the kitchen table, only to see Melina standing in the hallway saying, "I'm so sorry."

We hugged each other, and Marco even came in and we embraced, and it was one of the hardest moments of my life, but the silver lining was that I had them there for me in that moment. We had to make three calls, Melina agreed to call her sister, I agreed to call Billy the next day, but Marco just wanted to go back to bed.

I finally snapped on him, "Hey, she was my mother and your grandmother if you can't make one damn phone call then you aren't worth a damn."

Melina immediately volunteered to make the other call to Connor, and I told them that I would make the funeral arrangements the next day. Despite Melina's requests, I knew I had to get out of there, because I didn't want them to see me cry and I could still hear my father giving his old advice that he had told me one hundred times about never showing your vulnerability.

I finally got home and walked into the den and I just became so overwhelmed that I put my fist through the wall until I broke through the drywall. I was tired of things being torn away from me, and I walked over to the fridge and drank every bit of beer I could. This wasn't gradual as I was determined to knock myself out, to take this day that had punched me in the stomach and sever my connection to it.

The next morning I woke up on the floor, exhausted, with my head pounding when the reality of what I was trying to get away from hit me once more. Just when it seemed like things were getting on track, just when it seemed like I had my hands on a happy life, once again lightning crashed and someone I loved was ripped away, gone forever.

CHAPTER 52

⭐

I HATE THE 1990S

I called Billy the next day and knew it was going to be unpleasant but I knew that I had to, and when I called and he picked up, he happened to be taking his lunch break at his office. I told him that our mother had died in her sleep and they were still determining the cause of death.

He suddenly changed gears and said, "Charles, I'm sure that this has been very hard on you, so I want you to be able to tell me what you're feeling."

I responded with great irritation, "Good God, do you never stop looking for new suckers?"

He then started trying to tell me something about Freud figuring out that if you bury feelings, they come up in other ways and I was getting less and less interested by the second. I finally cut him off, "Billy the funeral is next week so I'll fax you the details and please stop trying to convince me of a problem that I don't really have."

That was when I hung up shaking my head; once again he was on another planet.

I got another phone call from the coroner and as it turned out, it was heart failure and based on what had happened, she had effectively died in her sleep and he assured me that she didn't suffer. That was only a very mild comfort, but the pain was still very difficult because I had spent the last two years here helping her deal with Cathy's kids and now she was gone. What were we going to do now? I finally got the funeral arranged for a week Saturday from when she had died. It was so hard visiting Cathy's house without seeing her there holding everything together. I didn't have a whole lot of confidence in the four kids, despite them all being in their twenties.

My temper began to get shorter, especially with Marco who came home one day from some local convenience store with candy, soda, and two videotapes. I asked him what he was doing and he responded that he was hanging out.

I asked him, "When are you going to get another job?"

He responded, "When I run out of money."

I couldn't help but ask where his money was, and then he responded that when he had returned the ring he had bought for Alison, he had over $1,200 and since it had only been a couple weeks, he still had over $1,000 left. I made him go to the bank to pay off his credit cards, and by the time he had paid them off, all he had to his name was $113 and change. I asked him if he was going to get a job now and he responded, "I still have some money, so when that runs out I will."

I asked him why the hell he didn't just go get one now, "$113 is hardly anything."

He started telling me about how he wasn't ready and something about how he wanted to have a little fun before his life turned into crap.

That was when I lost what little restraint I had left, "Look around you, life isn't about fun, life is about getting through it and doing your damn job. Sometimes you are going to have to do things that you don't want to, do you think I enjoy planning a funeral for my mother, I don't. I had to do the same damn thing for my father fourteen years ago and for my wife Anita five years ago. I didn't enjoy having to carry your mother's coffin three years ago, but I did it all while you just sat there. You are a man now, so put down the damn gummy worms and start acting like one."

I slapped him in the face as he stared at me in disbelief and he slowly walked away. Over the days leading up to the funeral, I just felt this weight on my shoulders as if I was waiting for the other shoe to drop.

It was the Wednesday before the funeral when I got a phone call from Veronica, who I hadn't heard from since 1996 when Cathy died. At first, I thought that she was just calling to give her mandatory condolences, but then she dropped the bomb – they were all flying from California for the funeral, bringing the kids that I hadn't seen in nine years. Suddenly the memories of missing them came flooding back and I told Veronica, "Okay, I have to go."

I hung up quickly because this day was going to be hard enough, without them being there to kick me while I was down.

Billy and Hashani arrived the Thursday before the funeral and I told Billy that he was going to be one of the pallbearers along with myself, and a few other men from the church. He accepted that and it seemed like he was being relatively cordial, although I didn't trust him and kept waiting for some other bad thing to happen. Hashani was being nicer than I had seen in a very long time and I was hoping we could get through this tough time without any more problems.

The day of the funeral was so hard, with thick grey clouds hanging overhead as if there was a colossal rainstorm in the works. I got to the church and I said "hi" to a few people.

I waited for everyone to come in, and occasionally looking over at that casket and seeing her lying there was painful, like I was in another bad dream, except this one I couldn't wake up from. Billy stood there next to me as various people walked over to give their condolences. I was talking to my cousin who told me about a few of his happier memories, and as he was about to move on, Billy whispered in my ear, "Stay calm."

Suddenly there she was, Veronica, now with her hair cut but it was dyed darker than it was when I had last seen her nine years earlier. She shook my hand and said, "I'm sorry for your loss."

I managed to block out my personal feelings and responded with a, "Thank you for coming."

Todd came by and looked like he hadn't shaved in four days and said the same thing. I had to make myself numb as if I barely knew these people and barely recognized Matthew who was twenty years old, and now he was a man. Randy was now twenty-three, they were both nicely dressed and I was struggling to reconcile what I saw with what I remembered. Then I saw Jackie, who was a full-grown woman, almost twenty-five who said the same, "Sorry for your loss."

There was so much I wanted to say at that moment, everything ranging from anger to regret. A part of me wanted to throw my arms around her and tell her how sorry I was that I missed her so much. However, I stopped that and after a deep gulp just said, "Thank you for coming, it must have been a long flight."

She moved on and I felt exhausted as if the shock of seeing each one of them again was like its own mile run.

The actual funeral was so hard to sit through because when someone has always been there in one form or another for almost fifty years of your life, it's hard to imagine them just not being there anymore. I don't remember too much of the funeral service, but one line that stood out to me was the moment when the minister said, "In an age when families are separating, she did everything in her power to keep them together; in an age of selfishness, she was unfailingly generous and in an age of loose morals, she held onto hers tightly."

It was hard to listen to because it reminded me of the things that I wanted to say to her, but I clearly couldn't and there were so many questions left unanswered. Questions about what I should do about Cathy's kids, my own kids, Billy, I was now the oldest member of the family and I had to be a source of wisdom but I had this sinking feeling like there was so much I still had to learn. Later on when we were having the reception, I started talking to one of my distant cousins that I hadn't seen in years, when I overheard Melina talking about her school and then I heard Jackie telling her how great it was to hear what she was doing.

I didn't want to interfere with them getting along, but then I heard. "Don't let my Dad come too close, if you love something that he doesn't, he will do anything to destroy it."

I turned and focused on that conversation so much that it seemed everyone else was silent. Jackie continued, "I was in high school with my first girlfriend, we were young and maybe it wouldn't have worked out anyway, but he called her parents and told them about us even after we begged him not to. She was taken away and basically brainwashed for two years until she was convinced that she was straight and the next time I saw her, she told me that what we had wasn't real and was just 'lustful thoughts of fornication.' It broke my heart, and he did that on purpose because he couldn't accept that I was a lesbian."

Melina was silent for a few seconds, but then responded, "I know what you mean. When he was trying to get Marco away from his ex who was using him, he wasn't nice about it but I think underneath that is his desire to do the right thing."

Jackie paused, "Melina, you're a smart girl and everyone knows it, but trust me a tiger doesn't change its stripes, and my dad will betray you because all that matters is what he wants."

She moved on and I was stunned at how she said that with such seriousness, as if I was some ticking time bomb. I was amazed that she was still that angry with me after all of these years. I also couldn't help but feel like I had received a back handed compliment from Melina saying that I had a rough way of going about things but I meant well. Over the last two years, Melina had become something of a new daughter to me and seeing my actual daughter telling her that I would betray her was hard to listen to.

Before leaving the funeral that day, I ran into Billy who told me that he was glad that I maintained my composure when seeing my family. I asked what he was talking about and he said, "It's very easy to get into a defensive mindset when you are dealing with people who you ended up on bad terms with."

I paused, "Thanks Billy."

I went home that night depressed, actually very, very depressed, because so many of the people who were closest to me were dead and the ones who remained saw me in a poor light. I went back home and I started looking around in my old stuff even though I didn't even know what I was looking for.

I saw a picture of my high school football team, which was the one that almost made it to the championship game and then I saw a picture of our graduating class from the military, before I got shipped off to Vietnam the first time. I saw that list I had made at the beginning of the 1980s and I scoffed at how optimistic I was back then.

Then I saw the present my father had given me all of those years ago when I received my first promotion in the military to Private First Class. It was a framed picture of me in my uniform and at the bottom of the frame was a bible quote from 2nd Timothy 1:7, "For God did not give us a spirit of timidity, but a spirit of power, of love and of self-discipline." I just stared at it, as if I was looking back in time almost thirty years and it was almost an out of body experience. I remembered something that my father had told me even before I had shipped out.

He had said how proud he was of me and suddenly I remembered this one piece of advice: "Charles no matter what happens, don't cave. You have to stand by your convictions and it doesn't matter if the whole world is against you, if you are right, then fight for it. Fight for it like your life depends on it."

I then had to ask myself a very difficult question, "What did I believe in? What were my convictions and did I believe them enough to stand against the world to uphold them?"

Over the next few weeks, I decided that what I stood for was protecting America from enemies foreign and domestic. Whether it be the Russians, laziness, or degenerative culture. By this time I had reached a point where I was almost fifty years old and I didn't like the way society was changing. I looked around and didn't like what I saw, these disrespectful kids, with a lack of respect for authority and tradition and kids never being told that they were wrong. Well I wasn't going to back down, I was going to stand against them. Right on schedule, the May fifth report arrived and I came up with my new plan. I was going to turn Cathy's three oldest kids into people who would manage the three locations, so that I could return to the place where the world made sense, in one way or another: Our defense establishment.

The biggest impediment to this plan was Marco who was still slacking off. According to the will, my mother had about $4,300 in the bank, but when you split that by her three principal children, that's about $1,400 each and when you divide that by four kids, that was about $350 each. So, Marco had just gotten a fresh bit of cash to do nothing with. I remember coming up to him lying on the couch at the beginning of May. "When are you getting a job?"

He responded, "I have $337, I will get a job when I need the money."

I was losing my patience, "Look, I cut you some slack because your grandmother died, but if you don't get a job in one week, I will drag you down to the bar and make sure you scrub toilets, mop floors, clean dog crap from the parking lot and every other dirty job, until you get some damn ambition."

He looked up at me in disbelief, "Ambition to do what?"

I responded, "Something! It's called pulling your weight and doing your part, just like everyone else is doing. Cynthia is working full time, and so is Connor, and Melina is starting another summer working at the movie theatre to save some more money to help pay for her textbooks and other stuff. What are you doing?"

He shifted from his side to his back to say, "I don't know what I want to do. Everything I thought I was going to be fell apart when I broke up with Alison."

I finally said, "The countdown is on, and you have T-minus one week, and if you don't have a full-time job by 8:00 am next Monday, I will drag you down to the bar and you will work for me and I will ride your ass all damn day."

I walked out hoping he would get it together and start working at the bar trying to do something that would be less demeaning than the tasks I listed. I thought that he wouldn't be able to get a job and in his panic would take the easy way out and come to work at the bar and put my plan into motion. Sometimes however life is a cruel joke. I came over the following Monday and he said to me, "Uncle Charles, I figured out what I am going to do."

I paused and said, "Okay, this better be good."

He responded, "It is, I am going to get a job as a taxi driver and I will use that to help pay for my schooling as a psychiatrist."

I rolled my eyes, "What the hell are you thinking, we don't need another one of those people in the family. Billy is one and that is more than enough."

He responded, "That's where the idea came from."

I then paused, "How the hell are you going to drive a taxi when you don't even have your licence."

He said, "Look, I spoke to one of my friends and we are going to work on it until I do."

I stared in disbelief, "First of all, you are getting a job that you can start working at today. You are not going to school for four years to go around telling people that their problem is that they weren't hugged enough."

He then said, "You told me I needed a plan, this is a plan and it's something I can feel good about."

I paused and said, "Why do you want to do this?"

He responded, "I wanted to feel like I was doing some good and if I can learn to listen to people and help them get where they want to go, both figuratively and literally, I can feel like a more fulfilled person."

I wanted him to work at the bar and to get him into a position to manage it so I could return to serving my country full time, not to mention the whole idea of another psychiatrist in the family was enough to make my head spin. I told him he was working at the bar and that was his top priority but he didn't want to go along with it so I finally said to him, "Before your grandmother passed away, she used to tell me how worried she was about you and worried that you would turn into a slacker, so don't let her down."

He then rolled his eyes, "Okay fine, let's go to work."

We went in my car and I was going to put him to work, hoping that I could cut this terrible idea off at the knees.

Over the next few weeks, I began to see him get to work and I felt good about what was happening, and as the summer took hold, I discovered that Melina had a boyfriend. What surprised me was that she never seemed to bring him around and I began to get concerned that he had something seriously wrong with him. I also began to talk to Cynthia and Connor about learning to take over some of the responsibilities, so that the business could one day be theirs in its entirety. Technically all four kids owned a twenty-five percent share but they were paying me to manage it and if they could take my place, they could all be business partners who could do it themselves. The last few years had been very good and I wanted them to step up and I knew that getting Marco into that role would take the longest, but I didn't want to waste any time. I had to protect Operation Railroad from the possibility of President Gore and the clock was now working against that goal.

I was hoping to have a great fiftieth birthday at the bar, and although the employees were there, it was hard not to notice that many of them were avoiding talking to me. It was as if they saw a birthday party as nothing more than an obligation or a chance for a free piece of cake. We were also spending more money on a babysitter for Caleb because Cynthia was working and an 11-year-old wasn't old enough to stay home on his own. The summer went by and I thought that my plan was progressing, with Cynthia now a supervisor taking on more managerial roles and Connor beginning to do likewise and beginning to get a grip on inventory management, which sounds boring but is essential to any business.

Of course, the plan as I previously imagined it, didn't end up happening that way, because life is full of surprises and the last few months of 1999 brought a big one.

CHAPTER 53

THE MAN COMES AROUND

One night in September, I was working at the Grand Rapids location and suddenly to my absolute shock, Jason walked in with Meghan, the girl he had left town with all those years ago. I suddenly saw him there, and had the visceral feeling of kicking his ass. He had cheated on my sister, he had run out on his kids, so what the hell was he doing here? I swallowed my rage and walked up to him, "Hello, how are you doing today?"

He responded, "Charles, it's me Jason."

I responded, "I know who you are, just answer the question."

He took a step back realizing my anger. "Actually I am doing pretty well and I came here to take a look at the return on my investment."

I asked him what he was talking about and he proceeded to tell me that he had already looked at the Saginaw location yesterday and the Lansing location that morning. He had a legal contract indicating that he was prepared to become a partner in the business. I was ready to stare a hole through him, "What the hell makes you think you can walk out on their mother, ditch them for years and then just walk back in here?"

He responded, "First of all Charles, you are way down the list of guys who should be lecturing me on my fatherhood skills. Second of all, you know who contacted me, Marco, he wants to sell his share and use the money to pay for school so he can become a psychiatrist. Based on what he told me, Melina doesn't want to be part of the bar either, so maybe if I buy out her part of the ownership I can be full partners with Cynthia and Connor and everyone will be better off."

I was now in quite the conundrum as this would immediately solve my problem and would quickly allow me to go back to the CIA full time. On the other hand, I knew that he wasn't here to be with his kids but only here for the money and it was only a matter of time before something bad would happen. After staying quiet for a moment, he asked me what I wanted to say, I responded, "Well if the kids want to sell you their shares, there is nothing I can do about it. But what I can say is this, I never cheated on my wife and when I took the wedding

Melvoy's Railroad

vows I meant every word… clearly you didn't."

He rolled his eyes, "You know it's so easy to criticize when you are looking at a situation from halfway across the country. I was working my ass off in this business and I came home to kids who were acting up and everything was always my fault. After hearing that, week in and week out for years, I found someone who understood and who was actually there for me."

He took Meghan's hand and she smiled and I was trying not to wretch in disgust.

I paused again trying to keep my composure, "Jason, if you want to look around that's fine, but I will be the one following to make sure you don't screw anything up."

He responded, "Why would I screw it up?"

I responded, "To bring down the purchase price."

This was when Meghan finally spoke up, "What's your problem?"

I responded, "Well, the person he cheated on was my sister who is now dead and this coward didn't even go to the funeral and then he ran off and left this business to die until I rescued it."

He then said, "Tell you what Charles, if I get a majority ownership I will write you a cheque for $10,000 as part of your severance package and you will never have to see me again."

I responded, "Let's just get this tour over with."

We did the tour and after closing time I went home very conflicted, wondering what was I going to do? It might take two years to get Marco into the right state of mind to help manage the family business. Also he wanted to sell his shares and unfortunately he could sign any contract he wanted to and there wasn't a damn thing I could do.

There was only one thing I could think of to do, and so I asked to meet with all of the kids at their house to figure out what they wanted to do in the face of this new development. The reason why I did this was because I didn't know who knew what and where they would stand. I was conflicted but if I knew where everyone stood, I could figure it out from there. Another thing that you learn from the CIA is to get as much information as you can and if there is a potentially volatile situation, try and find out as many of the variables as you can without revealing your own hand.

We had a meeting with everyone sitting around the table and Caleb was at the babysitter's. I started by scanning the room and noticing that everyone was on the edge of their seats as if they knew I was calling this meeting because it was very serious. "As all of you know, for the last two and a half years we have turned Game Night into a successful sports bar chain and we have enough cash flow to begin opening up new locations. A few years from now, we could have five or more locations since Dearborn and Kalamazoo look promising. Now with that being said, last night while I was working in Grand Rapids, your father, Jason, came back... with Meghan, saying that he wanted to buy back the shares of the company. Apparently, he has real contracts drawn up and intends to buy most, if not all, of your shares, and that he would be terminating my employment once he acquired the majority. I am currently the manager but as per the will, you four are still the official owners and you are all adults, so I want to know where all of you stand on this."

Melina looked confused, "What are they doing back?"

I noticed a nervous look on Marco's face as I looked over to Connor and Cynthia. Connor began, "Well, he does have the experience and if we are going to expand, it could help."

Cynthia looked back, "I don't want him anywhere near us, besides he walked out on all of us including my son. He and his slut can go to hell."

Marco braced himself and then he spoke, "Look, I called him, and I don't want to be part of the bar scene for the rest of my life. He can buy my share so I can pay for my school. Melina, he can do the same for you, getting your doctorate won't be cheap."

Cynthia looked back at him in anger, "How could you, he hasn't been there for us in years. He just ran off and picked a blonde over his kids, his grandchild, and he's only here because he sees this as a chance to cash in."

I now knew where two people stood as I saw the conflict in Connor and Melina. Connor turned to me and asked, "How much money is he offering us?"

I paused and said, "The contract that he showed me claimed that he valued the business at $1.2 million, so at twenty-five percent each, he would be paying $300,000 to each of you."

Connor's eyes lit up and he began to wonder if it would be worth it. Melina then said, "I don't care, I don't want to give him anything."

Marco said, "You know the divorce wasn't all his fault you know. Mom wasn't always easy to deal with either you know. She blamed him for everything and when your wife does that, it's no wonder he started looking elsewhere."

Cynthia cut him off, "I don't care, he could have gotten a divorce and still been here. Instead he ran off, hell we didn't even know where he was."

Marco chimed in, "He moved to New Jersey and has been there for the last few years. He called me one day when I was home and he and I started talking."

There was so much that I wanted to say, but I had to keep my mouth shut.

Finally, Connor turned to me and said, "Charles, what do you think we should do?"

Suddenly I was on the hot seat and I was still split on my decision because I wanted to go back to the CIA but I knew that this wouldn't end well. So after a few seconds, I said, "First of all I think we should get a proper assessment to see what the business is actually worth. On a personal level, I despise him for cheating on my sister, and I think he's a piece of shit, however he is a businessman who could help with the expansion. So personally I hate the idea but business wise it might work."

I then suggested that they all take a day to think about how they wanted to move forward with this because at the end of the day it was their decision instead of mine. In a sick kind of way, I was trying to get out of the way of this, because I didn't want it to look like I was leaving, but I also didn't want to make it look like I was pushing them in any one direction. I just knew that I had to get out of there within the next year one way or another and do so without leaving them high and dry. A couple of days later, Cynthia had basically said some version of, "All or nothing, either he isn't involved or we are all gone."

I had called an accounting firm to do a professional evaluation of the business. They came back and determined that the business' professional evaluation was roughly $2.2 million. I faxed Jason the new evaluation and told him that he had undervalued the business and would have to change his evaluation and the base number would be $2.2 million, which would be $550,000 each.

I was tempted to offer to buy Marco's portion but I didn't have anywhere near that much money to work with. Even if I had re-mortgaged my small house, it would not have been anywhere near enough. As it turned out, after I sent the fax Jason had apparently found the money and was ready to buy all one hundred percent if necessary. By the beginning of October, Marco was ready to sign on the dotted line so he could start his schooling in January. Melina was now starting her fourth year of school and still was dead set against the deal. Cynthia was against it, Connor was still undecided, and Jason was apparently invited over to their house by Marco and Jason came with a notary.

I was there and waiting to see how this would unfold and at one point I asked Marco, "Are you sure that you want to do this? Why do you want to be a psychiatrist so bad? Is this another one of Uncle Billy's bright ideas?"

His response caught me by surprise. "Uncle Charles, when I was going through my stuff with Alison, you and other people wouldn't listen. I want to be the person who will listen to other people. By the way, selling the business to my father wasn't Billy's idea, in fact he told me that he was concerned about it. I'm not worried, because my father is back and he's here to make things right. He's here to take Game Night to new heights and he is here to free me from this burden."

Connor said to Jason, "This is a huge amount of money but I don't want to be shoved out the door. I want this to be my business as well, so here's the deal. If you can get fifty percent from the others, I will sell you five percent of my twenty-five percent on the condition that you make me the supervisor of the location closest to whatever house I am going to buy. I want to hold onto the remaining twenty percent and be a part of this."

Melina looked at her two brothers and then looked at Jason, "There isn't enough money in this world for me to give you back this business that you almost ran into the ground." She said, "I would rather sell those shares to Uncle Charles for a dollar than sell it to you. When I graduated high school you weren't there, when Mom died, you weren't there, when Grandma died, you weren't there."

She walked out as I then turned to Cynthia, who began to think about it, and then Jason spoke up, "You know Cynthia, I know I haven't been there for the last few years but Meghan and I want to make this right, just like your Uncle Charles did. He wasn't there for a long time either but he came back and made it right and now we want to do the same."

Cynthia got a stern look on her face, "I'm not calling her Mom."

He responded, "Of course not, look it was a bad situation all of the way around but now is the chance, think about it, you can stay on if you want. Imagine how far $550,000 would go towards your own house, Caleb's education, a new car, perhaps all three. You would still have your job, I would happily listen to your advice and we could put this family back together."

I could see her conflict, I could see the struggle inside of her as she looked back at him and finally said, "I want to believe you but I don't because you talked about making it right like Uncle Charles, but there is a big difference, we weren't his kids, we were yours."

She turned to her brothers, "I think we should go on our own and tell Mr. Mid Life Crisis and his slut to hit the road and go back to New Jersey or wherever the hell he came from."

She then walked out, he then turned to me, and quietly said, "Charles, look you only came up here because they needed help and they don't need it anymore, I'm back. You don't want to be doing this for the rest of your life; you have other things you would rather be doing, whatever they are. You don't want to be stuck in Michigan, you fought in a war to get out of here."

I responded, "I don't have any shares to sell you."

He stopped me right there, "I know you don't so I need you to talk to Melina and Cynthia, there has to be something you can do, and they still respect you. If you can get them to sign over their shares, that severance package will be upgraded to $20,000."

I told him that I had to go home, because I had some important phone calls to make, and although it was a lie I had to get out of there and think about what I had to do.

CHAPTER 54

★

A DEAL WITH THE DEVIL

I received the October fifth report that told me how things were progressing. As previously noted Boris Yeltsin was stepping down at the end of the year and a new Russian President would be named after the March 2000 election. The particularly terrifying detail was that of the three candidates who appeared to be leading, none of them were particularly appealing. First you had Vladimir Putin a former KGB operative, Gennady Zyuganov the leader of the communist party, and Grigory Yavlinksy who was the leader of the social democratic party, which was another party on the far left. That leader would take power in late April or early May and I had tremendous fear that everything would fall apart shortly after.

I decided to do something, something that I knew was going to cause problems but at the time I absolutely felt had to be done. I calculated that $550,000 would be more than enough to cover the rest of Melina's medical school and surgery residency. I put together a pitch and if I could sell two Presidents of the United States on Operation Railroad I could sell a university student on selling her shares. I found a different lawyer and notary, because using the same one as Jason would have been suspicious. I drew up a contract, stating that she would be paid $50,000 on November 1, 1999 and the remaining $500,000 would be paid in five $100,000 annual installments.

I then called Jason and made a deal, "Jason, it's obvious that this is going to be a deadlock, and you want to run this company. If things stay as they are, there is going to be a huge amount of infighting and the company will fall apart with two equal parties each with fifty percent ownership. I don't want to go right back to where we were when you and your previous business partner were at each other's throats. So here's the deal, if you trust me, I can get Melina's shares to you, if you can get me the $550,000 by November 1st."

He paused and said, "What are you planning to do?"

I responded, "Look, this money will guarantee that she can become a cardiac surgeon, which she wants to be and I want her to be able to do it without the infighting ruining everything. The problem is she is

323

having trouble separating business from personal. I don't like you one damn bit, but it will be good for business."

He agreed he would buy the shares from me, after I bought them from her.

This was like a covert mission; I had to sell this deal to Melina as I had sold those weapons to the guards of Panama. I took her for a drive and we were going to get ice cream and then to the legal office. I began by reminding her how hard she had worked to get the degree that she would be receiving in the spring. I expressed concern that there was going to be a lot of infighting among the others and that I needed a way to make sure they couldn't just get rid of me, so I could keep things flowing smoothly so that her future could be secure. She asked me what I meant and I told her that I would buy her shares and the funds could be responsibly invested while she went to school. While that was going on, I could keep the business going so that if she ever needed more money it would be there.

She looked at me a little bit concerned wondering what I had in mind, then she asked, "Why can't you just talk the others out of it? Better yet, why can't you just use that money to buy Marco's shares?"

I proceeded to explain that I didn't have $550,000 right away and that the best I could do was $50,000 now and five annual payments of $100,000 each. I then said, "Not to mention the fact that he doesn't like me and is convinced that your father is the second coming. Why would he take an installment deal if he can get the same amount all at once?"

She reluctantly agreed, "What about Connor, can't you talk him out of his?"

I then responded, "I'm working on it, but there are no guarantees. I know this may be hard but I'm asking you to trust me, because after this you won't have to worry about money, and all you will have to worry about is your school. Based on what you have told me already you have enough to worry about as it is."

She let out a mild chuckle, and I said, "Besides we can stop and get some ice cream on the way home."

She then stopped to ask one more question as we arrived at the lawyer's office. She said, "With everything that has happened there aren't very many people I can trust, but I know I can trust you and I'm glad to know that you are looking out for me."

She gave me a big hug as a wave of guilt washed over me but I had to stop it in its tracks so I immediately changed the subject. "Hey what happened to that guy you were dating during the summer? How come you never brought him around?"

Our hug ended as she said, "I don't think you want to hear this."

I responded, "Why not?"

She said, "Okay, as it turned out he thought I wasn't getting into bed quick enough and he started cheating on me."

I paused as the guilt of what I was about to do hit me that much harder, but I forced myself out of the car and we walked in, and the lawyer greeted us. The office was immaculate, with not a single paper out of place, his suit was perfect and he was confident and friendly. He then laid out the basics of the contract, which she agreed to as I had already told her most of the basics.

The lawyer finally said, "Do you have any further questions?"

She asked, "What about the other shares?"

The lawyer looked confused, "What do you mean?"

She responded, "Do you have anything drawn up for any of the other purchases?"

The lawyer responded, "Charles can only afford to do this, and he assured me that under the circumstances this was the best option for all involved."

She looked at me and I could sense her trust. The lawyer pointed to the various places she had to sign and initial and with each one I felt a weight off my shoulders immediately being replaced by a heavier one. We spent the rest of the afternoon together, talking about her school, what I had planned for the bar, even though all of that was a well-crafted lie and that was a nice day that I wished didn't have to end.

The next day I went back to the same lawyer's office with Jason and Meghan. The lawyer showed him the form declaring that as of November 1st, she would turn her shares and all legal rights including the right to sell, over to me on the condition of the completed payment. From here I had him where I wanted him, he had to pay me before then in order to acquire the shares that would legally be mine.

He said to me, "Charles, you did it, I don't know how but you did it. I'm ready to give you the money so that we can move forward with this. I will have Marco's shares in a week and this will give me fifty percent. Unless Connor changes his mind, he will sign over some of his and I will once again be the majority shareholder."

I responded, "Make sure it's after November 8th before you tell Connor, Marco or anyone outside of this room about your fifty percent. We have to make sure the deal with Melina happens first."

He paused, "You mean, she doesn't know that you are selling them to me?"

I responded, "No she doesn't and we have to keep it that way until everything is set in stone." I concluded saying, "When she finds out she

Melvoy's Railroad

is going to be mad, but this is going to be the best thing for her."

He agreed, Cynthia wasn't budging and she and Marco were giving each other the silent treatment over this fiasco. While I counted down the days until November 8th, when the full transfer of shares to Jason would be complete, I had to pretend that I wasn't going anywhere. In reality, I had already called the CIA to discuss coming back full time to be a Regional Director. They informed me that as luck would have it the Director for the office based in Minnesota would be retiring in March and he would be happy to have me come there in January to begin the transition. Somehow, I barely thought about the nine to ten-hour drive and was focused on my opportunity to get back to doing what I loved which was protecting my country. My mission in Michigan was almost finished and I began cleaning up in preparation for selling the small house I had bought in Michigan. I dreaded one part of this, which was when it was discovered that I was leaving, and I knew it would be hard but my mission came first, Operation Railroad was my top priority and I couldn't let it go.

November finally arrived and the transfer from my account to Melina's was completed. I had also set up a fund with a mutual fund advisor with the clear instructions of sending the other payments to her every November 1st for the next five years. It was good to know that I would have a little extra money to work with after November 1, 2004 and that I could come back and get it if necessary.

November 8th seemed so close yet so far, and I could almost count the minutes, but on November 8, 1999 at noon, my formal obligations to the bar were finished. Jason called me the day before and asked me how long I wanted to stick around after the sale. I told him that I was fine to leave after a week so I could begin working on selling my house and buying a new one in Minnesota. Finally, the day came, I woke up that morning feeling far worse than I expected to, and I felt like someone who had woken up on death row. Jason had called a meeting with all of the staff and announced that he had acquired a majority share in the company and was now the new President of Game Night. That night I was at the location in Saginaw when everyone found out, everyone turned to me and wondered what was going to happen. I simply told everyone I was moving on after this week and I was sure that everything would go wonderfully.

Late that night when I got home, I heard the voice-mail messages from all of the kids. Apparently, Marco had been told first, "Hey Uncle Charles, it's Marco, look you and I didn't see eye to eye, but thanks for keeping the business going and I hope that you are happy with whatever you are moving onto... bye."

Connor called next, "Hey Uncle Charles, I know this has been a rough situation but you did what you had to do and I appreciate it. Let me know when you are free and I'll buy you a beer."

The next message was from Cynthia who had clearly called in a rage. "Uncle Charles, you son of a bitch, how could you do that? How could you lie to us like that, you are just picking up and leaving, I thought you hated Jason but now you just gave him exactly what he wanted. You know what, I don't care what your excuse is. Just Fuck You!"

The last message was the hardest to listen to and it was Melina, "Hey Uncle Charles, I, I don't understand, I thought that you were trying to be there for me. I had to find out from Cynthia, who found out from Jason, that you are leaving and I don't just mean leaving Game Night, you're leaving the state to take some higher paying job in Minnesota?"

There was a noticeable whimper, "How could you do that? You have been a more of a father to me in the last three years than my own father has been, but just because he's back doesn't mean I don't need you anymore. If he really cared, he wouldn't have waited this long to come back or he wouldn't have left in the first place."

At this point her crying had made the rest of what she was trying to say barely comprehensible and then she just hung up.

It was as if a knife had been plunged in my heart. I was so proud of her, she had been like my daughter for the last three years, but I believed that I couldn't stay, because I had an opportunity to get back to saving this country. I finally told myself that she would thank me later, and those funds I had arranged for her would guarantee her future.

That last week at Game Night barely anyone wanted to talk to me, and they were either glad to see me go or hated that I had left under the terms that I did. I remember standing there on the Sunday, the last night I would be working there. There was an extra big crowd for the wrestling pay-per-view that night in Grand Rapids and watching the big crowd and the money flow and all of the happy people, I couldn't stop thinking about all of the good I had done here.

I was able to sell the house surprisingly quickly, and as it turned out, my lawyer had a friend's brother who was looking for a place like that and we were able to agree on a price. I was all set to leave by January 15th but before that was Christmas. I had bought all of them gifts, even Jason and Meghan purely for appearances sake. I arrived at the house and I was met with an unwelcome presence, because the family was torn in half. I had spent a fair amount of money on Melina's gift but she didn't want it. The especially heartbreaking part was even after she opened it, tears came to her eyes, "Just, just get out."

I told her that I knew that she was mad but in the long run it was the best thing, but Melina walked out of the room towards the basement and I followed. Cynthia was not far behind us, and Melina who was on the couch in the basement shaking her head.

"Melina, look this is the best thing, for everyone."

She turned back to me, the pain in her face was obvious, "You think some fancy leather notebooks, paper, and pencils are going to make up for you tricking me into handing my father majority control of the business? You think that makes up for you leaving for Minnesota where you'll visit what, once or twice a year? I trusted you and you threw me under the bus anyway."

She wiped the tears from her face as she continued, "The last time I saw Jackie she warned me that you didn't care about anyone else but yourself and damn it I stood up for you."

I responded, "Look, this was a difficult situation and what I did guaranteed your future. You want to be a cardiac surgeon and now the only thing you have to worry about is finishing school."

She responded, "Like hell, I am going to be looking over my shoulder for when Jason and Meghan are going to run off again, or what other tricks they are going to pull to regain this house or whatever else they think they are entitled to."

I finally began to lose my temper, "Would you get over it, I did something important for you, why can't you see that?"

She responded, "Then why are you going to Minnesota? More money. Money matters more to you than me, or any of us. I have had it with this, get out of here."

I then said, "Would you come to your senses. People make hard decisions regarding their careers all the time."

That was when Cynthia came in, "Yeah and based on what I heard from Aunt Veronica, that was your problem then too, because your career mattered more than anything else. I wouldn't put anything over my son but clearly you don't see it that way, which is why you lost custody of yours."

I turned around in disgust, "Who the hell do you think you are, I was being responsible. If you were more responsible you wouldn't have gotten pregnant and you could have had a real child in wedlock with a real father."

She then pointed up the stairs, "Get out!"

I looked at both of them, "What is it with women, your brothers understand this, why don't you?"

I marched up the stairs, said goodbye and went home. I spent the rest of Christmas Day sitting at home watching various Christmas movies and drinking beer. I was ready to leave this place, I made visits to the tombstones of my father, my mother, and my sister and I said to the same thing to all three of them. "What the hell happened?"

CHAPTER 55

YOU CAN'T SPELL MINNESOTA WITHOUT MINE

I drove to Minnesota in another moving truck and even though I was so glad to be moving on, I was still haunted by what had happened back in Michigan. I knew it was hard but I kept trying to tell myself that it was best for everyone. By that point, I had already read the January 2000 report and I knew that what awaited me was a fully implemented plan that risked being unravelled by the incoming President of the United States.

The day I was moving into my new bungalow was difficult because the moving truck was too big to fit into the garage and it was snowing heavily. It just kept coming down with no end in sight, but thankfully I had a cart to help wheel the bigger items in. That night was Sunday January 16, 2000, I had the TV plugged in but I had to call the cable company to get the cable plugged in and turned on. This was hampered by the power going off and coming back on. I knew that the following Monday I had two months to observe the landscape and get ready to return to the job I had excelled at years earlier, when I was still living in Tampa.

While I was frustrated by the weather challenges, what really threw me for a curveball was a nightmare I had one night. In it, I was standing in front of an instrument panel and amidst all of the other switches and buttons there was one big red one. I remember staring at it, suddenly I reached out to something and someone else's hand pushed my hand into the button. I suddenly felt an explosion hit me and I woke up in shock. I didn't know what to think, whose hand was that? What button was I pressing, what did it mean? Once again, there were more questions than answers and I tried to just go back to sleep knowing I was starting the next chapter of my life tomorrow.

I got to the office where I was introduced to Mr. Blackwell, the man who was retiring in March. He told me that he was thrilled to meet me and had been briefed on my file. I had been notified that he didn't know about Operation Railroad, but knew the rest of my record. He was particularly impressed with my work in Panama and found my story of escaping the ambush to be very impressive. I was introduced to everyone in the office and they seemed to welcome me with open arms, although I still had to keep my guard up. I was also told that he hoped that this transition would go as smoothly as possible. Mr. Blackwell's balding head and greying hair showed his age and I looked much younger than he did.

He finally told me one last thing, "Mr. Melvoy, one of the reasons why I am thrilled to have you here is that your management history shows success, thorough research and best of all, a clear sense of objectives. You only left the agency because of something absolutely essential and even then, you kept your eye on things, that is admirable and it shows how committed you are."

I felt a great swell of pride in the face of all of these compliments and I dove in head first, but what surprised me was how much the priorities had changed in the last ten years. After events like the Oklahoma City bombing in 1995, the Columbine shooting of 1999, the fear of attacks had gone from standing on the border looking outward and were now turned more inward. While I had seen the earlier stages of this shift in 1996, by 2000 it had fully turned around.

At a key point, I happened to ask Mr. Blackwell how closely we were watching other countries, his response was, "Well we are keeping our eyes on the India/Pakistan situation, we have to watch the Israel/Palestine issue, and we are also keeping an eye on North Korea."

I was taken aback, because now our top concerns were domestic instead of foreign and among our foreign concerns, there was one Communist regime listed and Russia was not on that list. I began to wonder if Mr. Blackwell had a short memory or whether he had bought into the Clinton mentality of "The Russians are our friends now and Boris Yeltsin is interested in working with us and not against us."

I was going to change that as soon as I could, I was sure that the Soviets were lying beneath the surface waiting to re-emerge and take over in one form or another. Those people who had lived the first thirty years of their lives as Communists hadn't changed, and if we let them get back up, it would be a disaster. I remember thinking to myself, "They are a nuclear power and they are our biggest threat."

In 2000, I watched the Russian and U.S. elections very closely. In the case of the Russian election I didn't see any good options, I was slightly relieved that the Russians didn't vote for the Communist party and appeared to be in no rush to return to the way it used to be. They elected Vladimir Putin, while an ex-KGB he had since disavowed Communism. I didn't believe him but at least that meant that he couldn't just put the red flag back up. If he was going to do anything it would have to be subtle and I was surprised how unconcerned other members of the intelligence community seemed to be. The way some of them talked about it, it was as if the Russian election was as inconsequential to our national security as Canada's, which was later that year.

With the 2000 U.S. election there wasn't really any brutal grudge matches on either side, and it became obvious by the spring that it was going to be Gore vs Bush. In a way it was going to be a battle of Legacies, Al Gore continuing the Clinton policies and Bush Jr taking America back towards more conservative policies of his father. I was obviously rooting for George Bush Jr. because I knew there wasn't going to be a second coming of Reagan, but I had always liked Bush Sr. and I expected something similar. Not to mention the threat of Al Gore cancelling Operation Railroad was still on my mind and wasn't going anywhere.

The year 2000 was going by in a flash and before I could turn around, I had spent the entire summer in the office. Before I could realize what was happening, it was October and the polls were showing Al Gore ahead and I remember being petrified of that scenario. I had heard all sorts of accusations of Bush Jr. not being smart but I didn't think very much of it. He grew up and was going to surround himself with the right people with Dick Cheney being named as his running mate. The one thing I had to begrudgingly admit was that Bill Clinton wasn't the incompetent tax and spending fool that I had expected him to be.

Finally Election Day came and it turned into a very long night, because for those of you that don't know, the state of Florida was extremely close. When you have a state with tens of millions of people and it is decided by a margin of just a few hundred votes, it is hard for people to accept the outcome. There were also accusations of machine malfunctions and some people even claimed outright vote rigging. So it was a fiasco that went on for weeks and finally ended with the Supreme Court declaring that George W. Bush was the winner and the President of the United States.

The operation I had spent so many years putting together was riding on this, so during almost the entire month of November, I was on edge and when I found out that it had finally been decided that Bush Jr was the winner, I was thrilled and relieved. I also knew that once the new administration took over I was going to be meeting with the new President to discuss the Operation.

Unfortunately the meeting with me fell down on the list of priorities so I began to fear that he was going to cut the Operation and when I went home that night I began drinking beer and lots of it. The truth was some of the people in the office thought that I was too focused on former enemies and didn't put enough focus on the Muslim extremist groups in the Middle East. Despite various delays, I was finally scheduled to get my opportunity with President Bush on Wednesday May 9, 2001.

They came into my office, President George W. Bush, Vice President Dick Cheney, and Secretary of Defense Donald Rumsfeld, as well as a couple of other key intelligence officials. So it began with Bush Jr asking, "So Mr. Melvoy, tell us about where we are with Operation Railroad and what we need to do going forward?"

I took a deep breath and prepared to sell yet another President on this plan.

"Mr. President, you have enough to worry about, the economy, social issues and not to mention foreign countries with nuclear weapons. The truth is however, our position as the country that keeps a steady hand on the world, requires us to keep other challengers to that role from emerging. A decade ago, the biggest threat to our country fell and this plan allows us to keep a close eye on them from re-emerging. During the 1990s, I worked tirelessly with our agents to infiltrate and take over all three corners of Russia's nuclear triad, and we have succeeded not only to infiltrate them, but so that our top infiltrators have back-ups within their organizations. These came about as a mix of recruiting their current employees and sending new agents in.

"As planned, should the Russians attempt any sort of attack, we will be able to shut down that attack before it begins, because we will be notified immediately and will be able to wipe them out without any counterattack. Additionally, in the event of a first strike of our choosing, their attempts at a counterattack would be undermined before they began. All we need to do is monitor and maintain what we currently have in place, we don't need any other major expenditures and we have the Russians right where we want them. We can now be exactly what we have wanted to be since the end of World War II, the hand that steadies the world and the hand that does not let another world war happen. The world won't police itself, which is all the more reason why someone needs to, and I can't think of a better country than us."

A few chuckles rose up as Donald Rumsfeld spoke up, "Mr. Melvoy, you have said to previous administrations that if this Operation ever leaks to the public, you would take responsibility for it even if it included jail time. Do you still stand by that statement?"

I responded, "Yes and I still would."

Dick Cheney spoke up next, "Mr. Melvoy met with myself and President Bush, the elder, back in 1992 and since then he has done an excellent job co-ordinating this Operation and keeping it under wraps. Given that, Mr. Melvoy we live in the age of the Internet, all it would take is one rogue agent sending an e-mail to the New York Times and the Operation would be exposed. Does that concern you?"

I responded, "I understand that, but this is where I have been most careful, because no one besides myself and the President's office has the whole picture. Everyone else only has one piece of the puzzle, so even if the information leaks here or in Russia, they will never have any idea of the whole story. This is also why I have looked for possible successors who could carry out the Operation so that others can carry this forward. This Operation does not end until Russia is no longer a threat, either we wipe them out or we fully take control of them politically. We fought them for forty years, I don't want to go through that again and neither should anyone else."

Everyone seemed to nod in approval, when Dick Cheney spoke up again, "Mr. Melvoy, while you have made an excellent case for the continuation of this Operation and you have certainly gone to great lengths to ensure its success, my concern is perhaps we are too focused on Russia. Perhaps we now need to consider expanding this Operation to keep other countries that are emerging threats from perhaps attempting to challenge our place in the world."

I asked, "What countries were you thinking of?"

He responded, "Well Mr. Melvoy that is where it gets interesting. We are still deciding, and this summer we want you to investigate it and choose the countries that appear to be the biggest threats to our future that we would not go after on a military level. Given your background, I have no doubt that you will have some names for us by the summer and a way of expanding Operation Railroad."

The meeting wrapped up shortly thereafter and I went home stunned because not only was Operation Railroad not in trouble, they wanted to expand it and to see if they could do something similar to keep other countries from challenging us. That summer was either going to make or break my career at the CIA, and I began to think to myself about how I was going to be an American hero once the smoke cleared.

I couldn't just pick countries out of a hat, and the first thing I needed were criteria, so I came up with four primary categories called W.I.S.P. which stood for Wealth, Ideology, Stability and Population. The basic ideas were as follows, if a country is dirt poor, they wouldn't be able to fight us on our level or even close. The second was Ideology, they may be wealthy, but if they have no real interest in pursuing a military presence in the world then we have little to worry about. For example, I doubted that Iceland or Norway were interested in trying to establish any sort of empire. Now the reason why Stability was the next one, was the simple fact that regimes could change, especially in less secure areas, so stability was the next risk factor. The last one was Population, and in order to be a big threat, you need a good-sized army. A country with a population of 300,000 people and a land mass that is smaller than Vermont, would also be fairly easy to overpower.

I spent that summer sending spies here and there for covert missions to the top suspects. I specifically would ask them to observe various areas and would be looking into the way things were on the civilian level. Determining the population is easy, and the wealth factor isn't much more difficult, but it was the middle two that required greater research. What was interesting about this research was that it seemed like there was an inverse relationship between Population and Stability. I systematically compiled the various reports and what came through were the following conclusions:

First, Saudi Arabia was a country full of extremism and a royal family that had a tremendous amount of wealth to their name. Despite being one of our biggest trading partners, many of their citizens looked at the United States as the enemy. One of the key things to remember was that depending on the degree of provocation, we could go after Saudi Arabia militarily and that over the next few years, that should be our goal. We would need a catalyzing event, a straw that breaks the camel's back, if you will. I concluded the statement with the very real human rights abuses the Saudi Arabian people have suffered, and they may greet us as liberators, rather than conquerors and offer very little unofficial resistance. It would also be easier for us to gather support from other countries that could be made to sympathize with their people.

Secondly, Europe, where in theory most of the Eurozone was full of stable first world democracies but there were two risks that I foresaw. First, if the notion of the Euro and the idea of uniting Europe under one umbrella, could potentially combine with an underlying nationalist movement, that could once again grow and morph into a "continentalist" movement. Europe had no shortage of wealth, and England and France both already had and were maintaining nuclear weapons. Such a power would be on the United States level in almost every way. The hardest part would be to infiltrate every single government, although the top priority would be the ones that possess nuclear power or other weapons of mass destruction. However given the ideology of Europe, such a notion would come across as unpalatable to the vast majority of Europeans, especially given that many were easily and frequently reminded of the effects of World War II.

Chapter 55 : You Can't Spell Minnesota Without Mine

Melvoy's Railroad

Third China, whose communist history could not be ignored, and although they had a population of over one billion people, due to the trade relations that we had opened to them three decades earlier, their economy was growing significantly. With that wealth combined with their underlying Communist ideology, it could potentially lead them to begin their own attempt to create an empire.

Fourth, Iraq and Iran, where I pointed out that they were two very predominantly Muslim countries with strong anti U.S. sentiments. They both had pursued nuclear weapons in the past and both regimes could have been looking for a way to defeat the United States. The reality however, was that in order for that to happen, they may have to join forces. The reality was that the sanctions were keeping Iraq in their place and the regimes of Iraq and Iran had hated each other for over twenty years and Saddam Hussein was far more worried about keeping Iran's Islamist movement out of his country than in joining it to attack the United States. My recommendation was that they be militarily overthrown in carefully planned and completely separate regime changes, and only if either escalated these desires on their own. I felt that we needed to focus on other countries for the foreseeable future.

I looked forward to sending this report to President Bush by Thursday September 13, 2001 and giving him all the information needed to begin to maintain Operation Railroad in Russia, expand Operation Railroad into China and to prepare a military regime change of Saudi Arabia. That was what I expected to happen, but all of those plans were about to change.

CHAPTER 56

IT ALL COMES CRASHING DOWN

If you will pardon the cliché, I will always remember where I was when 9/11 happened. It started out as just another morning, I had left home to get to the office by 8:00 a.m. and by that point the first plane had already crashed into the first tower. My phone rang from people trying to tell me or ask me what was going on. There was a big forty-five-inch TV in the office and we were watching the footage, which was haunting and it was like watching a movie, except this was real, very, very real. Everyone in the office was left wondering what was happening, we were also stunned to hear about the Pentagon attack and we had to wonder what was going to come of this.

This was the worst attack ever to happen on our own soil, making it worse than Pearl Harbor. That night I went home and finished off several bottles of beer and I feared what was going to happen. I was sure that some people were going to get fired for this, I was sure there would be a mass investigation and a few people might even get thrown under the bus to make the administration look good. Our organization's existence was supposed to help prevent attacks like this and there it was in our biggest city in front of the entire world, the single biggest attack in our nation's history had slipped through the cracks.

As I am sure you can guess, my September 13th meeting with the President was postponed until further notice. He had speeches to make and had to talk with other intelligence officials who had been more focused on the Middle East region. Eventually in late October, I got the chance to meet with them and I laid out my findings about the future of Operation Railroad.

I chose to lead with Saudi Arabia who, by this point, had revealed that fifteen of the nineteen hijackers were Saudis which I thought would be the catalyzing event. Right away they started shutting that idea down, and I was barely three sentences in when Dick Cheney interrupted, "They are one of our biggest friends in the region."

I responded, "I would disagree, they are taking our money with one hand and raising terrorists with the other. If they were truly trying to prevent things like 9/11, their Internet censorship, which blocks pornography with no problem, wouldn't let Islamic extremist recruiting websites operate with no restrictions. I had also mentioned that many Imams, which are the Muslim equivalent of ministers, were often directly voicing anti-Americanism, in a country where the church and state are so close, that is deeply concerning to say the least."

That was when Donald Rumsfeld said, "Mr. Melvoy, Saudi Arabia isn't among our concerns."

I paused, "Well with all due respect Mr. Rumsfeld, considering what happened on 9/11, once we deal with Bin Laden in Afghanistan, I think they should be the next target."

That was when the President spoke up in annoyance, "Move on to the next subject, it isn't going to happen!"

I was baffled, so I explained my opinion on Europe. They seemed to be in agreement that they could be a threat one day and that we had to watch for any further nuclear pursuits or any sort of European Continentalism that could potentially lead to greater actions.

We then got on the subject of China and this was where I really began to win them back. Dick Cheney pointed out that the battle in Afghanistan and future battles would require greater military expenditure, which would in turn require more debt. The Chinese seemed to be turning into a country that had a great deal of interest in U.S. bonds.

Bush turned to Cheney, "So you think they might have some leverage over us through these bonds?"

Cheney responded, "Exactly, so a plan like this might help us level the playing field. China's wealth is growing as Mr. Melvoy noted and this could result in them making greater military investments, which in turn could lead to them wanting to play on our level."

Rumsfeld spoke up, "Mr. Melvoy, how long do you think it would take for you to secure China with a similar plan?"

I responded, "I estimate about six to eight years, because there are a lot of variables to consider."

George Bush responded, "Alright well as far as I'm concerned, you have the green light, go for it."

I then moved on to the last subject, which was Iraq and Iran, and suddenly they went from listening to hanging on my every word. I began talking about how if they escalated, we may have to topple their regimes and we would have to do so carefully and separately, so that we avoid the possibility of them joining forces.

That was when Cheney spoke up, "Do you have any evidence of Iraq or Iran escalating?"

I responded, "At this point in time no, the sanctions are working well enough and Iran, if they are pursuing a nuclear presence, they are doing so at such a snail's pace, they are anywhere between ten to fifteen years from a nuclear bomb. This means at this point, they would be several decades away from our level, barring anything unusual, sanctions seem to be the best option at this point in time."

All three of them looked genuinely disappointed by the answer, and while I didn't say anything, the entire meeting struck me as odd. I understood sometimes looking the other way and the old "he may be a son of a bitch, but he's our son of a bitch." However, this leniency towards Saudi Arabia and the eagerness to go after Iran and Iraq didn't make sense to me.

2001 ended with me putting the first steps of Operation Railroad in China in place and I had begun to identify people who were part of their defense establishment that could help us. It was just the beginning but what was so strange was the difference. Nine years earlier I was excited about starting Operation Railroad but for some reason this just felt different and dare I say a little bit empty. I was working on this during the day as well as sending people to investigate possible terrorism leads. Many of the leads went nowhere and often consisted of someone seeing a brown person and assuming the worst.

As 2002 went on, I began to get various notifications that the U.S. government was shifting the focus to Iraq. I noticed fairly quickly that the news organizations were suddenly talking about how big of a threat Iraq was and how if they didn't do something soon, it was going to be awful. While there was certainly a possibility of Hussein getting nuclear weapons and although that possibility was horrible, there was little if any evidence of that being the case. I began to hear about people in other offices leaving in protest and I was baffled, because this wasn't why I signed up, and something about this didn't add up. I was still keeping an eye on Russia, who already had nuclear weapons, North Korea had nuclear weapons, China had nuclear weapons, Iraq didn't have nuclear weapons and it seemed unlikely that they would be able to acquire or create them.

What I began to tell myself was that just like I used compartmentalization to keep my missions from getting leaked, they were doing the same thing. I began telling myself that other people must have the information and once it came out they would be proven right. After all, these men knew what they were doing, this was the President of the United States who was the son of George H.W. Bush, this was former defense secretary and now Vice President Dick Cheney, Donald Rumsfeld, Colin Powell, Condoleezza Rice, so these weren't stupid people.

Melvoy's Railroad

I remember looking in the mirror one day asking myself, "What are you going to do?"

I then said to myself, "You know they're right, just because they didn't like your idea it doesn't mean they don't have America's best interests in mind."

Every quarter, I submitted updates to Donald Rumsfeld and within a couple of weeks I would get responses, and there were gradually growing amounts of criticism with most of it consisting of questions about the next steps. They were beginning to get impatient about the lack of progress we had made in China. As it turned out, China had its act far more together than Russia did in the 1990s and breaking through it was like trying to break through a cement wall with a hammer. This was very important to them because as it turned out, Dick Cheney's prediction was beginning to come to pass as the U.S. ran up hundreds of billions in debt and the Chinese purchased a lot of U.S. bonds.

During my time at the office I was very closed off and reserved at first, but I had gradually opened up to one of the people who I slowly became friends with, a man named Max. He was a twenty-eight-year-old man with curly light brown hair who had started working in the office six months before I did. Max was a die-hard football fan and even went out of his way to get season tickets to the Minnesota Vikings for the 2002-2003 Season. He began inviting me to come with him to the games and he even paid for my ticket the weekend after my fifty-third birthday. It was so strange feeling like I once again had a friend, once again I had someone who was actually on my side, but at the same time I could never be sure what I could tell him and what I couldn't. I remember one game the Vikings had won and we left the arena quite happy and we saw a father buying a football for his son, and it almost brought a tear to my eye hearing his son say, "Thanks Dad, you're the best."

My own children were long gone and they were only a few years younger than Max, it was a painful reminder of what I had missed over the last many years and in many ways even the years I was there for them. I suddenly stopped myself before I could show any emotion and changed the subject, asking him what his favourite moment of the game was. What I didn't realize until the fall was that he was planning to marry a young woman, but he had been lying to her about what he did for a living. He had been telling her he was working in an office that managed distribution of different types of beds, he was trying to figure out how he could balance this work and his marriage. There was a split second where I wanted to say, "run," but I began to wonder what

Chapter 56 : It All Comes Crashing Down

I wanted to tell him to run from, marriage or this job, all I knew was they didn't work together.

By the fall of 2002, we had only set up five operatives in areas that would barely make any difference at all and none of them were with the land-based missiles where most of China's missiles were. China had very few nuclear submarines and we only had one operative in the air force and he still didn't have access to the payloads yet.

Around November 2002 we received the big break we needed, not only did we find out who one of the key administrators in China's missile defense system was but we had dirt on him. As it turned out, Mr. Hubei had been going to a certain part of town where you not only could find sex, you could find sex with children. This last year of trying to crack into the management of the Chinese defense infrastructure had been very frustrating, so frustrating that when I heard this news all I could think of was, "Finally, we have our way in."

Our operative threatened him and told him what we knew and that if he wanted to keep this from surfacing, he would have to hire the people we wanted and find ways to fire the people who were currently holding those places. According to the field report, as soon as Mr. Hubei saw the pictures, he turned absolutely pale. By December, two of his underlings were conveniently fired for incompetence and disrespect, and he had pulled the strings that were needed to ensure that our operatives were hired. The door was now open to China's ground-based missile system and now we could begin really locking everything in place. When I sent that report in December, I received a rave review for finally breaking the administrative wall. The exact words were, "We had successfully identified a key player and successfully exploited his weakness for the success of the Operation."

2002 ended in a very strange way, with all signs were pointing to a war with Iraq. I had a gut feeling something was wrong but I had convinced myself that these people knew what they were doing and they had a clear plan that would make it all go smoothly. I was convinced that they were going to be just as careful as I was, if not more.

The early months of 2003 saw a lot of pro-war sentiment and some anti-war sentiment as well. I came into the office and Max and a couple of other people were talking about the Oscars and how Michael Moore had said something against the war.

My first response was, "Who's Michael Moore?"

They proceeded to tell me that he was a left-wing filmmaker who had made a documentary that claimed that America was a violent nation. I then said, "What's his next movie going to be about, how jumping in a pool makes you wet? This is a violent nation because this is a violent world, so does he think we beat the Nazis by dropping presents on them?"

They all laughed and then Max said to me, "I hope someone makes a documentary that actually knows what they're talking about."

I responded as I was lifting my coffee, "Yeah that would be nice."

On a random Friday night in April of 2003, three guys in Boise, Idaho came out of a bar and saw a brown guy with a briefcase walking down the street. They jumped to the conclusion that he was a terrorist from Iraq and there was a bomb in his briefcase and proceeded to beat him to death. However, this person was not a terrorist, or from Iraq and as it turned out, he was a lawyer who had lived almost his whole life in the United States but had been born in Sri Lanka and who had a late-night meeting with a client. This man was not only the victim of a hate crime, he was Hashani's younger brother. When Billy left a message on my voice-mail to tell me about this and to let me know about the funeral, it was genuinely hard to think about.

In their defense, the guys tried to say, "We thought we were doing our job and stopping a terrorist attack."

Apparently someone had asked them where they thought he was going to plant a bomb in Boise. They then said, "The mall, the Wal-Mart, you never know where they're going to hit."

Keep in mind the mall was on the other side of town, the Wal-Mart was also several blocks away and he was literally walking the opposite way from both of them. I fought with myself about whether or not to take three days to go to the funeral. On one hand, Hashani's brother and I had barely spoken, but on the other hand, I wanted to know where Billy stood and my curiosity won in this case and I reluctantly decided to go for it.

I remember flying out to where the brother had lived in Oregon and when I got there, I was surprised at the change in the security measures because I hadn't flown since 1996 when I had to fly to my sister's funeral. I got there and Billy and her family were greeting people but quite frankly he stood out like a sore thumb. Billy thanked me for being there and gave me a huge hug and quite frankly I felt uncomfortable, because I literally hadn't hugged anyone in four years since my mother died, and I had honestly forgotten what it felt like.

As it turned out, Veronica, Todd, Jackie, Randy, and Matthew issued their condolences over the phone and couldn't make it. I found out that Jackie's kids were there. Jason and Meghan weren't and when I asked Connor, he told me, "He is staying back because he wanted to keep an eye on things."

I asked him how the business was doing, he responded, "It was doing well for a while and now I don't know. It's like the business is starting to taper off and those plans for the new locations are on hold."

I asked him what everyone else thought and he responded, "Melina was really hurt when you left and she hasn't been the same since."

There was so much I wanted to say to all of them but I kept my composure and forced myself through the event, and afterwards a bunch of us went back to Billy and Hashani's house. As you'd expect, her parents were devastated and her other brother was angry as all hell. He and I began to argue when I heard him blurt out, "God damn Republicans."

As a Republican voter for over twenty-five years, I was pissed off and I asked him what he was talking about. His response was passionate and you could feel the fury behind his words.

"Ever since 9/11, Fox News and the rest of the news media are doing nothing but drumming up fear and convincing people that brown people are something to be afraid of."

I responded, "How do you know that has anything to do with this?"

His response was quick, "According to the witnesses in the bar, that's what they were watching, Fox News. Then they went out with hate in their heads and their hearts, they saw my brother and killed him in cold blood. My brother is dead because Republicans love to pander to fear and they got their wish and the morons who watch it acted on it."

I tried to say something in return, "Look this is a terrible situation and what happened was wrong but you can't blame the President or that party because of what a couple of drunk guys in Boise did."

He responded, "Are you blind? Fox News is an arm of the Republican Party. They tell Fox News what to say, they tell people that brown people are the enemy and now my brother is dead!"

I was about to lay into this guy for attacking the President and the news network that I had enjoyed watching over the last few years, when Billy grabbed me by the shoulder and said, "Charles please come with me, I need your help with something."

He took me downstairs to his basement and I asked him what he was doing. He responded, "Look Charles, I know you're still a Republican and that is the way you are, but please try and keep a lid on it. The man's brother was murdered and he isn't in his right state of mind, how could he be? Hell, how could anyone? So I'm asking you to please hold the politics today, alright?"

I reluctantly nodded and then he changed the subject. "You know there is a chess board down here that I don't get to use as often as I would like, and I was thinking it might be nice to finally play a game with you."

As he went to get the board I asked him, "Do you agree with him?"

He asked, "About what?"

I responded, "That stuff about it being the Republicans' fault that this happened?"

He let out a deep breath as he picked up the board, then he looked up at me. "Charles, it's a complex issue."

I then said, "Cut the crap, what do you think?"

He paused and looked at the ceiling as if he were hoping there was a reminder of what to say up there. "Charles, you and I are very different people and we always have been and I don't know if that is going to change anytime soon. This isn't a time for us to argue over our differences, there has been a tragedy in the family, so this is the time when we should be able to come together."

I could tell what he was doing. He was trying to get off the subject to avoid a confrontation, and I was in no mood to play these games.

I started to go into a rant, "Billy I am amazed that after all these years you haven't learned anything about how the world works. You are still buying into this hippie stuff about 'the man' working against the people. I'm glad that you are at least working, even if it is a job that doesn't do any good and you aren't on drugs. But you haven't figured out that sometimes you have to face a brutal truth, which is that there are people in this world who aren't like us. They want to kill us and on 9/11 a few of them succeeded, so don't be mad at the Bush Administration and Fox News for telling Americans to be vigilant. Maybe you should be supporting our war on terror and our mission in Iraq. Sometimes you have to do things that aren't so good, when you are dealing with people who are very bad."

He looked off to the side as if he was contemplating what I said and then he came back with something I didn't expect, "Charles you never stop reminding me that you are the older brother, who always thinks of me as this person who you have to tell what's what to. Well maybe instead of telling the world according to Charles, maybe you should be asking yourself this, when does it stop, Charles? Where do we draw the line, or is there no line that we shouldn't cross to ensure victory?"

I responded back a second later, "We aren't just talking about victory, we are talking about survival, there are people who want to wipe us off the face of the earth and if they get the chance they will."

Billy shook his head, "Charles, Iraq isn't a threat to us. Their leader, as horrible as he is, isn't trying to take over the world and drop bombs on civilians. For us to get him is almost like knocking down a building because of a cockroach."

He took one more deep breath, "Charles, violence only leads to more violence and this quick, easy victory is nothing more than a fantasy. Hell we might be in Iraq for as long as we were in Vietnam, which was another bad war."

I had heard enough, "Billy, you naïve fool, those leaders are making the tough choices to do what we have to do to protect our country and your attempts to make it sound like anything else, are just proof that you don't know what you are talking about."

I began to walk away and was at the bottom of the staircase, thinking I had told him off but I underestimated how transparent I was at that moment, when he said, "Who are you trying to convince Charles, me or you?"

I walked out of there trying to block out what he was saying and trying not to let those liberal mind games take hold. I remember the whole drive home, trying to convince myself of how wrong he was, but it was that suspicion that was needling at me and driving me insane.

Unfortunately Billy began to be proven right, despite a very hopeful moment when George Bush stood on that ship with the "Mission Accomplished" banner it all began to fall apart as the guerilla street fighting began to flare up. The comparisons to Vietnam began to be thrown left and right. Every reminder of that comparison began to drive me mad and I didn't even want to hear about it. I had to send agents on missions to the surrounding countries to make sure that new weapons weren't being funnelled to the insurgents from Iran and Syria, but apparently Saudi Arabia was off limits even though they were right next door. That annoyance also fuelled my frustration with how things were going, and I felt like I was being handicapped in my job.

Speaking of being handicapped in my job, I kept getting orders to move things forward in China but the initial progress made with Mr. Hubei wasn't moving things along as quickly as expected. Mr. Hubei was also putting up more resistance than we expected, as if he was doing everything in his power to make sure the government of China wouldn't suspect anything. The problem was to do that, he kept delaying our implementation which added to my continued frustration.

Despite these issues, I had something to celebrate because near the end of 2003, Saddam Hussein had been captured and on that day in the office, everyone was in a great mood. The reason why was we had just taken a big threat off the table and after months of mixed news, we had a big victory in this street battle that had no end in sight. It was either that day or the next day, Max had told me about a movie he wanted to see and invited me to come with him.

He asked, "Do you remember when I said that instead of Michael

Moore, we should see a documentary by people who know what they are talking about?"

I responded, "Yeah."

He then said, "Well now there is one in Minneapolis. They are playing *The Fog of War* and it's Robert McNamara talking about his life."

That peaked my interest, because he wasn't just some fat guy from my home state. He was the Secretary of Defense under Kennedy and Johnson and he understood war because he was there in the first half of Vietnam. It was the first time that I had been excited to see a movie in a very long time.

Those years went by so quickly, it was hard to believe we were at the dawn of another election year, but here we were and I was about to go see a film about someone who would tell these hippies what reality was. He was smart and was always prepared. Some of you may be wondering why I had such admiration for a Democrat and the answer is, he was not a career politician, because he had worked hard in industry and did very well for himself. He was a brilliant thinker and manager through and through, which was what I admired about him. He could have been chosen by a Republican just as easily and he still would have brought his expertise to that important role. I remember watching him on TV and he seemed to be the picture of professionalism and intellect, and when he spoke people listened and so did I.

That was the 1960s and this was now the end of 2003, I was sitting in a movie theatre in Minneapolis as the film began and I was repeatedly stunned to my core. The regret, the loss, him admitting that America was wrong to go into Vietnam, floored me. Him talking about his meeting with the foreign minister from the North Vietnamese side and him saying that he had no idea what sort of people they were facing. I heard the audio recordings of him and Kennedy talking about pulling out by the end of 1965, so that they could get out of this bad situation. The two things that stunned me the most were first, the look on that octogenarian's face filled with such remorse and regret that it was hard to handle. The other thing was the line where he seemed to be asking rhetorically, "How much evil do we have to do, in order to do good?"

Walking out of that theatre I was stunned; I was having a hard time finding words to say and that question began to go around over and over in my mind. That question was like one of those annoying songs on the radio that get stuck in your head and won't go away. By the beginning of 2004, Iraq was getting uglier, the Democrats had a former veteran quickly gaining support and I was having a hard time returning to my mission, as my fear of being that same old man with all of that regret haunted me. I had nightmares every now and then, one where

I looked in the mirror and McNamara's old face was staring back at me, and another where I looked out the window of my house and saw a graveyard where there had originally been a view of the some of the houses in the neighbourhood. My grip on what I wanted and what I believed was slipping and I couldn't get rid of the gut feeling that something was going horribly wrong, but I couldn't tell whether it was me or whether it was something real.

Unfortunately I began to drink more than I already was and I went from having rum at night to having an eye opener in the morning. I drank a lot on my days off because Operation Railroad in China wasn't going as well as it should and it seemed like a great weight on my shoulders.

Operation Railroad in China had barely made any progress and one of the people we had installed tried to sell us out. Thankfully because of the money that he was supposed to be getting, we were able to pretend that he was lying for monetary gain. The Chinese seemed to believe it, but they were going to be watching their people even closer now, which would only make things slower. Despite my previous determination and sense of purpose it gave me initially, it was feeling more and more like a burden, and my feelings towards the President were changing also. The benefit of the doubt I had given him before was being shaken by his poor decisions and frequent gaffes. I was still a Republican but I didn't have that same patriotism that I had two decades earlier and going into the 2004 election, I didn't feel the same excitement for a second Republican term. It was hard for me not to be a little bit bothered that the guy who I was supposed to support was only ever in the National Guard, whereas the other guy had served in Vietnam as I had.

Eventually it reached the point where I was beginning to feel less and less interested in what I was doing. That year I became more and more depressed and that same pride I had taken twelve years earlier, in fully implementing Operation Railroad was long gone. It went on like this for a long time, and a lot of those days just meshed together. The election was over and we found out that George W. Bush was getting another term, and I barely let out a golf clap, let alone any real excitement. I spent yet another Christmas by myself and I had barely any presents to open and didn't even bother to decorate my house. The neighbours were probably confused and were wondering when I had become Jewish.

It was January 18, 2005 and I had a really bad day at work. I heard that our North Korean Operative had been captured and killed and we had China asking if the guy was ours, but we had to deny and very

Melvoy's Railroad

carefully explain our way out of it. We barely did, but quite frankly, it was exhausting. When I wasn't communicating with them, I was getting yelled at by a CIA Director for letting such a slip occur. By the time the day was over, I had taken several sips of the rum that I had in my desk. I went to drive home and felt a little bit drowsy, but I assumed that I was just tired and I was fine. Then before I knew it, I had slid off the road and hit a power line so hard that it fell over onto my car, but thankfully it was on the passenger side and I wasn't directly hit.

As bad as the crash was, what was so much worse was walking out of there with scratches on my head from the broken glass, tripping over myself onto the pavement. I had taken out the electricity for the whole block but I wasn't even thinking about how much trouble I was in. There was no excuse, because it was cold but the roads were dry and there was barely any snow falling. I came over to where the post had broken and I looked down at it yelling, "God damn cheap posts! One bump and they fall over."

After kicking the base of the post in anger, I noticed that the blood that had come out of my head had started to drip onto the snow. Before I could think of anything else, I remember the last time I had seen blood on snow so clearly which was when I fought my father. Before I could process the parallel, the police showed up and put me in the back of their police car.

The only good news was I had taken a wrong turn and I was driving through a neighbourhood nowhere close to where I lived and the entire process was humiliating. It was horrible getting a mugshot, being fingerprinted was distressing, and I was a fifty-five-year-old man who had acted like a stupid teenager. I knew that as soon as the office found out about this, I was going to be in some major trouble and I was going to have to go to court. This was painful, dare I say agonizing and I realized that no one was going to help me, no one.

I expected to be fired, but instead I was suspended for ninety days without pay. The next two months between the day of the offense and the trial, were beyond miserable. Unfortunately I had screwed up on a very serious level, and if it had been a different type of offence, they might have been able to make the evidence disappear with phone calls. But this offence was a public one and sweeping it under the rug in a small town wasn't so easy. My licence was suspended, so I had to walk to the grocery store and the liquor store, which were always long walks, especially on those cold nights in January, February, and March in Minnesota.

I spent my days staying home watching TV, feeling old, alone, useless, and I began to have days where I wished I hadn't woken up and simply died in my sleep. One of the few things I remember from that time was a James Bond movie playing on TV. I forget which one but I remember thinking about how different my situation was from his. How glamorous and exciting it was, and how my reality was hardly like that at all, and began to think back to that mission in Panama that went wrong that I barely survived. How badly I wanted to live back then and how now I was beginning to prefer death; I began to think that perhaps in death I would have Anita back, perhaps in death I could see my mother, and perhaps in death I could see my father. Perhaps in death I could go somewhere I belonged, perhaps in death I could finally have the peace I now craved.

CHAPTER 57

★

WHY AM I STILL HERE?

My court date came about on March 22nd and to get it over with, I pled guilty to the charges of DUI and destruction of property, if they waived the reckless driving charge. They accepted it but the judge wasn't letting me off that easy. I ended up with a fine of $5,000 and was ordered to attend mandatory Alcoholics Anonymous meetings for three months. I woke up the morning of March 23rd feeling like I had hit rock bottom. I couldn't stop replaying what I had seen with my father in my mind and the only difference was I didn't have a son to help me and I was all by myself. Max decided that he wanted nothing to do with me after finding out what I had done. As it turned out, one of his friends in high school had been paralyzed after an accident with a drunk driver and he was disgusted with me for that reason.

My remaining days of my suspension were the first days of Alcoholics Anonymous and I took a hard look at what they wanted and began to hate it. The twelve steps didn't make any sense to me: "Admit I was powerless over alcohol," so then my first thought would be, "If I was powerless, then I was as good as dead."

I began to hear the sob stories and I couldn't stand it. Also I couldn't tell them my stories, or at least much of it, because most of them hadn't seen people die, watching cancer and chemotherapy slowly kill the person they loved most in this world. I didn't even do a good job listening, and maybe one or two of them had a story like that but I just didn't care.

I was trying to decide how much I should tell the truth and how much I should lie to get this over with. I decided that the most effective lie would be a half-truth, and I would stop drinking for those ninety days. I would do as many of the steps as necessary to make it look like I was doing what they asked, and then the instant that paper was signed, I would do something else. Of course, the question was what would I do?

I finally was allowed back into the office where one of the top people in the CIA met with me. They began to tell me about how they had been impressed with my work ethic but that my work had fallen off track over the last few years. They also said they felt like I was performing under my potential and cited where we fell short in the Chinese version of Operation Railroad. I didn't appreciate the dig at my work ethic and they decided that going forward I would report regularly to someone else, basically it was a hidden demotion. I hated it and thankfully this other person had done an okay job keeping Operation Railroad on track in both Russia and maintained what we had in China. I began to view this as less of an exciting challenge and more as a chore, just like my meetings.

I woke up with headaches when I was dealing with withdrawal. I had taken all of my liquor and put it in a box in the basement and had closed it with duct tape. I would go to the meetings and try to talk for an obligatory couple of minutes: "My name is Charles, I drank and drove, hit a power line and I have been sober for x number of days." They tried to get me to open up more but I resisted each time to give any additional details and any added in were kept to the barest of bare minimums. I didn't want these people in my head and judging me for what I did for a living or what happened with my family. I was literally counting down the days and it took every bit of willpower I had to not stop by the liquor store or not just go to the basement and open up the box.

One of the things that baffled me was that the people in this meeting started asking me about which step I was on and while most of them were fairly easy to lie about, the fourth, eighth, and ninth ones required some careful planning. How do you convince people that you have done "a searching and fearless moral inventory"? Not to mention how do you lie about "the people you have hurt and making amends to them"? I came up with the simplest one, which was the people at work, most notably Max. I did in fact call everyone to attention in the office because they knew I was in the program and I apologized to them all and especially Max. He amazingly forgave me and he promised to listen anytime I needed him. They seemed touched and were very encouraged by my "sudden progress."

In reality, I was miserable and putting up a front. The thing you have to remember is that when you are a spy for the CIA, you are basically a trained actor prepared to call yourself Mr. John Smith from Everytown, U.S.A. You have a backstory with an entirely fake life with fake facts ready to go. So I put those acting skills to use and the people at the meeting were thrilled at the progress I was making and I even made up a story about another co-worker. I fabricated a story that he was always going out to the bar after work and I had convinced him he was on a slippery slope and now he was cutting back dramatically on his drinking. That qualified as step twelve and by the end of June I was free of the meetings, but free to do what?

My work was still a chore, I still came home to no one, and the person who had to oversee my work was a micro-managing pest named Ray Crocker. Everything was always wrong, this was taking too long, this was rushed, this was too risky, this was playing it too safe, I swear he was doing everything he could to make my life hell. Amazingly I didn't go back to drinking right away after I completed my meetings but there was a period of about a week where it seemed like I was still able to keep away from it.

Finally, the day came, it was Monday July 4th, I had the day off and Max was having a barbeque at his house. We were having a good day and that was when Ray Crocker came over and spent the entire day giving me backhanded comments. I wanted to punch him in the face and then there was one comment that finally stepped over the line. "Hey Crystal, don't let Melvoy have a beer or you won't be able to watch TV for a week."

I turned around, "What the hell does that mean?"

He suddenly tried to pretend he didn't mean anything by it, but I knew better and I couldn't take it anymore. "That does it Crocker, I have had it with your bullshit, you have been making my life hell for months and I'm sick of it. I screwed up okay, you know it, I know it, but you know what, I have done more good for this place than you ever have, so shut the hell up!"

He said, "Mr. Melvoy, that's insubordination and if you don't apologize, I may have to write you up."

At this point I didn't care, "Go ahead, I came here to serve my country, not to be an underling to some bureaucrat who's never even picked up a gun in his life."

I went home so pissed off that I finally went downstairs, ripped off that duct tape, picked up a half full thirteen-ounce bottle of rum and drank it as quickly as I could. I was getting so tired of everything in my life, everything from the Operation, the lack of respect, and I had had enough.

As you might guess, this led to a meeting with the CIA National Director who asked me about my insubordination and I told him exactly what happened, but obviously not the going home and drinking part. I told him what had been going on at work over the last few months. He then asked Crocker if he had said that in front of people and he denied it. My pulse was racing as I got angrier and angrier, "He's lying through his teeth and I have ten witnesses who were all there and heard it. Do I have to go get them? Because I will!"

The CIA Director saw my intensity and my sincerity, "Mr. Crocker, when we assigned you to this job we asked you to observe and keep an eye on things, but based on what we have seen, including the reports you have been re-writing, you have been overstepping your boundaries. Additionally we spoke to the other people who were part of the incident and they corroborate Mr. Melvoy's counter-accusations. I think it is in the best interest of this department for you to be reassigned and we will find another person to oversee what Mr. Melvoy is doing."

My eyes rolled, "Why? I screwed up, I corrected it, I took the twelve steps, and I have been working to remove the major obstacles that would impede China's Operation Railroad from being fully implemented."

The CIA Director explained, "Mr. Melvoy, I was told to keep an overseer on you for a year so that we could be sure that we wouldn't have another incident. Up until the last few years you did some tremendous work, but the Chinese version isn't going anywhere near as well as you suggested it would four years ago. We need to make sure that you will continue to stay on track so we will start seeing real progress on that front."

I paused and took a deep breath, "So you're saying that as long as I behave myself and keep doing my work, I will just have to cope with this for nine more months."

He responded, "Yes, we believe that is the responsible course of action, given what is at stake, because we have a lot riding on these operations."

He then proceeded to say, "Mr. Melvoy, we are starting to shift our focus from Iraq to Iran, which will result in us borrowing even more money from the Chinese. That will give them a huge amount of leverage over us and we will need this plan even more to guarantee that we will have the final say. Your country needs you Mr. Melvoy, and we need you to finish what you started."

With that I tried to swallow my pride and continue the Operation, and even though that little pep talk helped a little bit, it didn't take long to wear off. Over the course of July and August, I began to drink more and more here and there, and by September I was back to drinking until I was ready to pass out. As October and November progressed, I hit a wall and became depressed because our plan to overthrow the Chinese advisor had failed. We were going to make it look like an accident with food poisoning involving his favourite seafood restaurant. There were two things we didn't count on, one was that he had a small appetite and two, the foods we were expecting him to eat were gobbled up by his fat cousin. Now the restaurant was under investigation and the advisor was fine, but we had to come up with something else and fast. By this point, Mr. Hubei was either changing sides or was being given a better offer. He suddenly demanded $5,000,000 to continue his side of the plan, which was now a liability that we had to eliminate.

We thought to ourselves that we had to do something else, but what? Finally, we had the plan, "a neighbour" came forward and the story came out about Mr. Hubei's sexual appetites. We had one problem left, "What if he talks?"

That one ended up being fairly easy to solve, we gave him a note promising him an escape out of the country and $10,000,000 if he kept quiet. We broke him out of custody exactly as planned, except we killed him in an alley across town and wrote the Chinese characters for "filthy pedophile" on the wall of the alley. That way it looked like some angry people who wanted street justice, and so it worked. If the Chinese suspected anything we never heard about it, probably because they wanted to minimize the bad press of one of their officials being a pedophile in the first place and the corruption.

By the end of 2005, my depression was barely being held off by the success of preventing a major leak, but we were still left with very little leverage. What really did it was the month between Thanksgiving and Christmas. I saw it and heard it everywhere, sounds of family, Christmas, joy, getting together with people etc. I heard this every day on the radio and it seemed like I had to change the station every minute to avoid having to listen to these nauseating ads. I overheard it from the other people in the office about going home and how much they were or weren't looking forward to it. Whatever boost I had gotten from the progress of the Chinese level of Operation Railroad had been obliterated.

I woke up the morning of Christmas Eve beyond depressed remembering all of those Christmases with my parent's, Cathy and Billy as a kid, those Christmases with Veronica and my kids, and even the ones with Anita. Before I knew it tears had formed in my eyes, my jaw was trembling and I genuinely didn't know if I was even going to get up. Those next four days, I barely even left my house and the closest thing I did to leaving was shovelling the snow out of my driveway just in case I had to get called into work. I drank those entire days just trying to numb the overwhelming feeling of emptiness, the feeling like I had nothing, and even worse had become exactly that – nothing. With Christmas over, all the news people seemed to talk about was either the Boxing Day sales or the fact that 2006 was just around the corner.

My first thought was that I had barely pulled myself through 2004 and 2005 and I couldn't stand the thought of doing this for the rest of my life. I saw *It's a Wonderful Life* and I couldn't understand it, because

I was a war hero, I had fought the good fight my whole life, so how did this happen? There was no angel telling me about the good I had done, and no one was rushing to help me. At one point, I looked outside and saw a couple of kids in front of their house across the street having a snowball fight, laughing, enjoying their lives and I couldn't stop thinking about everything I had done and it didn't seem to matter.

I woke up the morning of New Year's and I was feeling overcome with dread because I didn't want to celebrate a new year, I had no reason to think that 2006 was going to be any better than the previous two years and not to mention I wouldn't even be allowed to have champagne. If anyone from the office saw me having a single drink, I would be in trouble and I was having a harder and harder time keeping up the act that everything was fine.

What was especially frightening was that I had begun to imagine myself parking my car on the train tracks that I drove over on my way to work and how it might be a relief to know that would be the end. I had been doing this for so long at this point that it was a habit. The full securing of Operation Railroad in Russia had been the case for some time, China was looking less and less likely to happen at all, and Europe appeared to be doing fine with few if any troubling signs. Iraq was just the same mess and I could almost hear Billy talking about how it was just like Vietnam. I could almost hear him thinking from Sacramento "I told you so." I couldn't stop wondering if the people I had trusted and had voted for twice were about to double or triple their problems with Iran. On top of it all, it drove me crazy every time I thought about it, why was Saudi Arabia still getting a free pass?

I remember walking towards the front door of the office and I could just imagine seeing myself jumping off the third-floor roof headfirst and crashing into the cement of the sidewalk down below. The proud, almost exuberant steps that I took to walk into that building six years earlier were now slow and exhausted. I even began to hesitate in merely opening the front door and as soon as that door opened I tried to put on that façade, but by January 2006 it was cracked and people began to see through it. I just remember closing the door to my office, lifting open my bag, and picking up the vodka that I hoped would help me get through the day. Vodka was less obvious than rum or beer hence I brought that to the office instead since the DUI. That January I felt more and more removed and more and more empty.

You always try to tell yourself that no one notices and that you are doing a good job keeping it under control, even when you're not. Obviously I wasn't, because one day either at the end of January or the beginning of February, Max asked to speak to me in our boardroom and closed the door. I asked him what he wanted to talk about and that was when his big intervention speech started.

"Charles, myself and a few other people have been noticing that you aren't the same and you look miserable. I mean yesterday when you were pouring coffee it was like you were going to cry, what's going on?"

I was trying to make up a lie as quickly as I could, "Everything's fine, my eyes were watery because there were onions in my sandwich and you know when you cut onions it irritates your eyes, and well that's what happened."

Of course, by this point he was well trained enough to see through that, who am I kidding? Even without training, he would have seen through it.

"Charles, I hate having to ask this, but are you drinking again?"

I sarcastically responded, "If I was, I would be in a much better mood saying, 'I love you guys.'"

He didn't think my joke was very funny, "Charles, I'm serious, are you drinking again?"

I was finally reaching my breaking point and everything I had been holding inside began to rush out like water through a collapsing dam. "What if I am? Everyone needs a little help every now and then and I have a brutal job, I carry the weight of the free world on my shoulders. I am arranging missions that involve millions of dollars and trying to protect this country from terrorist attacks, and if I am not careful the next 9/11 could happen. Every time I send someone on a mission, I know that if they don't come back I have to live with knowing that I sent them to their death. Which, by the way, happened three times in the 1990s and twice since I came here. I have to come to work with people that don't like me and talk crap about me behind my back, without thinking for one second that I have done more for our national interests than most of the people out there put together. I live in a cold, boring state in a neighbourhood with cold, boring people, doing a cold, boring job waiting for the next person I know to die. Who's it going to be next? My brother? One of Cathy's kids? Maybe it will be Veronica or one of my own kids and I will have to carry another damn casket on my shoulder into another early grave. I guess it never occurs to you or anyone else out there, that maybe I'm tired of working for an administration that expects me to go into a boxing match with one arm tied behind my back. Maybe I'm sick to death of being watched every damn day by Lewis, who isn't as bad as Crocker, but is still a pain in the ass."

After all of that I was standing, my face was red, I could barely keep my jaw from trembling, and I was struggling to talk past the lump in my throat when the tears had started again.

"You want to judge me for what I do, you came here from college, I came here from the missile defense system and before that from Vietnam. I nearly died repeatedly, Phil "the Hill" and thousands of others died for a war that we didn't win and everyone, even McNamara, says shouldn't have happened! I have tried to do everything to protect our country and secure our future for almost forty years in one way or another, and yet the decisions made at the top are stupid and poorly planned. People, including my own brother, have been calling Iraq the new Vietnam and all that bad press has given them everything they need to say, 'I told you so!' Rather than getting Iraq under control, they are trying to start an action on Iran, which I even told them not to do unless they had to, and to make sure Iraq and Iran are never given the opportunity to join forces. Fighting them both at once risks exactly that!"

I screamed and slammed my fist twice onto the wooden table so hard that I cracked it and then I began to kick over the chairs in the meeting room as Max tried to grab me to get me under control. I shoved him off and looked at him as if I was about to fight, he then asked, "Charles, what are you doing?"

I paused gasping while trying not to break into a full-blown crying fit, "I don't know anymore."

I walked out of the room, grabbed my bag and walked out of the office. My sudden leaving and the shocked look on Max's face caused people to wonder what happened, but I was at a point where I didn't care anymore.

CHAPTER 58

★

GOODBYE CIA

That night I got as drunk as I ever had been in my life because I was so tired of everything that I didn't care if I even woke up the next day. Sure enough the next day I did wake up, my alarm clock was pre-programmed and that was enough to barely get me out of bed. I went into the office and I had had enough so I called the National Director and told them I couldn't do this anymore and I was quitting. They were stunned, and they asked me, "Who's going to finish things?"

I sarcastically responded, "Operation Railroad in China isn't going well anyway, let Lewis or someone else do it to your satisfaction."

Much to my surprise I did get a video-conference call from Donald Rumsfeld who told me that he thought I had "an outstanding record" and I still had "a tremendous future with the intelligence community."

I could see that he was simply saying a rehearsed speech. I responded, "I can't do this anymore. You have what you need, just straighten out Iraq, keep out of Iran, and start putting some pressure on Saudi Arabia, but since you aren't going to do that, there's no point in me being here."

I passed off my duties and was finally going to be finished on Friday February 10th. I was going home, I had no idea what I was going to do and I didn't care anymore.

When you are in a downward spiral, the last thing you need is something else to make you feel worse, but I had exactly that with Valentine's Day just a few days later. I was alone and on a day when you are supposed to celebrate love it is a horrible time for people who are alone, which only made things feel even worse.

I was in a terrible place, I had no idea what to do, I had spent so much of my life in the military and other defense institutions and I used to find such comfort and order in it, but now it no longer made any sense to me. The world didn't make sense to me anymore, the music didn't make sense and the movies seemed weird. I missed the life so much that I had decades earlier. By this point, I had a fair amount of savings and could live off of them for a while but I didn't know what I was going to do. The TV wasn't helping as I began to hear on the news how they were starting to push for war on Iran and increasing the presence in Iraq. It was increasingly depressing, because people began to point out how it was like the ramp up of troops in the 1960s and 1970s in Vietnam. I never heard anything against Saudi Arabia and people were getting angrier and angrier about the entire middle-east situation. I didn't know what I was going to do, so as February and March went by with nothing going on, I didn't know if I had any place in this world anymore. Suicidal thoughts began to circle around my head and I was beginning to seriously consider how I would do it.

Those months were bit of a haze, and I didn't care about the world anymore. My alcoholism had gotten completely out of control, and the only reason I wasn't being called the town drunk was because I barely left my house more than once a week.

After being cooped up for so long, I decided I needed to get some air. The particular day I'm referring to was some point in April when I walked outside and began to wonder what reason I had to live. I didn't even know what I could do, if anything, to make things better. I reached a very strange point where I walked over to a bridge and looked down and began to think about it, and then I realized that the stream might not be deep and might not finish the job. Before I could think about the next step, I heard a siren and it was a fire truck driving by which briefly interrupted that perilous line of thought. I didn't want to live anymore and no one even wanted to talk to me anymore. Billy and I were worlds apart, my parents were dead, my sister was dead, my wife was dead, Cathy's kids didn't want me anymore, and my own kids didn't either. I walked and walked, having no idea where I was or where I was going. I finally arrived at a place called "Delicious Dancers" which was a strip club on the outskirts of town. I had some money in my wallet and I went in saying to myself, "What the hell."

You have to remember it was 3:30 pm on a Wednesday, so there were only two other guys in there and I just sat down figuring that I had hit rock bottom and might not be alive tomorrow, so why not? One dancer came out wearing a nurse's costume, with her cleavage protruding out of the obviously fake uniform. She swayed back and forth and I would be lying if I said that she didn't have my attention. The owner came up to me and asked me who I was and I said, "I don't want any trouble, if you want I'll leave."

His shaggy hair and scruffy face said, "No, no nothing like that. I actually want to talk to you for a few minutes."

I paused and began to worry that maybe the Russians or one of the other countries I had arranged to be infiltrated, had somehow caught up to me. We went into his office and he started flipping through an

Melvoy's Railroad

old magazine, said, "Ah, there it is, is your name Charles Melvoy?"

I paused, "Yeah, how did you know?"

He said, "My name is Gill, and I never forget a face, never. I have a bunch of old magazines out there in the waiting room, some of them are so old, they're asking how MC Hammer is going to follow Hammer Time."

He let out a big laugh and I barely eked out a chuckle. He then said, "In this magazine here is a story from 1999 about Game Night. When I'm bored, I read through some of those old articles and I always thought it would be great to have a good manager in here, but most people don't want to touch our business because they think it's smutty. I was wondering what you were doing in town and if you were looking for a job?"

I paused and said, "I have been living here for the last six years, I kept mostly to myself and I left my other job a couple of months ago, and I don't even know why I'm here."

He let out another big laugh, "Hey maybe it's destiny, I've been looking to drum up new business and you know how to do that."

I responded, "I managed a sports bar."

He responded, "Well it's not that different, I mean there they have a spotlight, here we have the headlights."

He let out another big laugh and I could barely force a grin. He then said, "Look Mr. Melvoy, you probably haven't been in one of these places in a long time and maybe you're a little nervous, but let me put your mind at ease."

He stood up and said, "Come with me." I got up and followed him, then he sat me down in a small curtained off room by myself and said, "Wait here, this one is on me."

I paused looking at him, "This what is on you?"

I waited there very tensely, almost scared that any second I was going to get gunned down by spies who had finally caught up with me. In a sick way, a little part of me would have been fine with that as long as it was quick.

Suddenly a woman walked in wearing a strange green corset, grey-green leggings, a red wig, some strange green cuffs around her wrist, and some metallic green things around her eyes. She approached me seductively and said, "I know all about plants and let's see what else grows in here?"

I blurted out confused, "So, you're plant lady?"

She then said with disappointment, "Poison Ivy, Batman & Robin."

I was confused since I barely went to the movies and had not watched anything *Batman* related since the Adam West show of the

360   Chapter 58 : Goodbye CIA

1960s. She saw my complete ignorance and rolled her eyes at how out of date I was, and she then said, "Okay, just talk to me."

She began to move around and I let out a sarcastic chuckle, "I really have hit rock bottom."

She says, "I've heard that before."

I sarcastically responded, "You don't say."

As she began to take off a grey green stocking, "You know everyone has a different idea of rock bottom."

I said, "Really?"

As she was removing the other stocking she said, "Yes, if you were Bono rock bottom would be a small house and playing in a bar in front of a hundred people."

By this point she was gyrating over my lap and she asked me to unzip the back of her costume. I begrudgingly agreed as she continued, "If you were Will Smith, having to do small time local plays in front of three hundred people would be rock bottom."

She then turned to me as the green corset began to slide off revealing a thin bra and panties, "For me, my rock bottom was two years ago as a prostitute in Detroit. I was thrown out of the house at seventeen and started turning tricks when I was eighteen. I went into motel rooms with guys with a gun in my purse and I didn't know for sure whether I would come out alive. I eventually got out of that and found this job, which is much better."

I asked, "It is?"

She said, "Of course, I'm protected. I work with my best friends and I can work good hours, for decent money, and I don't have to worry about being arrested or raped."

As she got on top of my lap and moved her hair around she said, "It's not where your rock bottom is, or how hard it hits you, it's if you are willing to climb up from it."

By this point her breasts were exposed and I was too confused by the green metallic things on her face and the experience in general, to be aroused, "I'm pretty good at reading people, because in this business you have to be, and I bet you have been through a lot."

She then got up and turned around slowly dropping her panties, and she stood there naked, as she stretched her leg over mine she said, "I bet that you have what it takes to find that better place, whatever it is, wherever it is."

She then grabbed my head, "It could even be right here."

She pulled my face into her ample breasts and shook them back and forth as the song ended and she grabbed her clothes. She waved farewell and I sat there confused about everything that had just happened.

About a minute later Gill came in and said, "So, how super do you feel?"

I responded, "I uh, don't know what just happened."

He said, "It's her Poison Ivy routine, she hasn't done it in while. That's one of the older costumes that isn't in demand much anymore. When we only have a couple customers, I let them do whatever they want, you know, keeps them happy."

I came up with some excuse to tell Gill and I left wondering what had just happened, Anita died twelve years ago and I still felt guilty over what had just happened. I went home and washed my face and took a hard look in the mirror. I was now in a place I had never dreamed of, getting a lap dance from some weird woman who I had always thought of as the bottom rung of society; the type of person that I used to be afraid of my daughter turning into and now she was giving me life advice. I tried to separate the act from the advice and it seemed like she had a point, I mean somewhere in all the gyrating, red hair and other strangeness, was the advice of getting up and doing something better.

Maybe beneath all of that other stuff was a good point. I needed to climb back up and even if I never again was meeting with the President of the United States or having my full family, I could value any improvement no matter how meagre it is. The only question was, where was I going to try to climb to?

CHAPTER 59

★

WHERE IS HOME?

I knew that I wanted to leave Minnesota, the question was where I wanted to go next. Do I go back to Michigan? Do I go back to Florida? Do I go back to California? Do I go to Canada? I honestly had no clue where I wanted to go or what I wanted to do. The thought crossed my mind about running for office but then I realized what kind of patience I would need, basically if those idiots pushed me far enough, it might end like that movie *Scarface*.

While I had thought about re-joining the military as a Drill Instructor, I realized two things: first, I would be training people to fight in a war that I no longer believed in or another one that I knew was a bad idea; second, was that I didn't have the energy that I had twenty-five years ago, because I had allowed myself to get somewhat fat during those years in the office at the CIA and my drinking didn't help with that. I struggled with this idea for some time and knew that I didn't want to work in a strip club, even if I would be the manager.

I thought about it and I realized that I could start calling myself a business advisor and could apply for jobs anywhere in the country. I started trying to send out resumes looking for some new opportunity. I knew that my age of fifty-six would work against me but what truly surprised me was how many places didn't even bother to contact me for an interview. It was depressing and while I wasn't doing as badly with my drinking I was still drinking quite a bit at night. Those continuous rejections didn't help one single bit and as the spring turned into summer, I was struggling to keep my drinking under control. I did phone interviews and more than a few of them didn't go very well. I was very confused, "I thought we had a booming economy, what is going on here?"

Before it could truly get me down and depress me anymore than it already had, I got a phone call that I thought would never happen. Connor called stating that Jason had convinced them to invest their money with his guy and they were going to make money in the market. As it turned out, their money guy was in fact an illegal tax shelter and Jason had run off with it. He took money from the business, he

363

took money from his kids, and the only person who hadn't given him their money was Melina. The problem was by the time she took what was left of her school fund to cover paying off the problems, she was $7,300 away from having the money she needed to finish her surgery residency.

I called up the person who had been managing the payments to Melina's college fund, which had technically remained in my name, and as it turned out there was about $21,000 that had been sitting in there slowly growing over the last several years. After immediately agreeing to come back and help, I was filled with several emotions and on one hand I was relieved that I once again had a purpose. I felt worried that I was going to come face to face with the rage of Melina and I felt my own rage towards Jason, because how could he do this to his own children, scamming them out of millions of dollars and nearly bankrupting them. I didn't have a whole lot to live for but I thought maybe I could help them like I did last time and help get them back on track.

I began the process of moving and it turned out to be far easier than I expected, because there was a real estate developer buying up land and agreed to pay me almost double what I paid for that home in late 1999 and I thought great, no objections here. I drove back to Michigan once that was settled. It was September 2006, and I was on my way back to Michigan when I stopped by the graveyards, the one where my father was in Ann Arbor, and the one where my mother and sister were buried in Lansing.

I remember standing over my mother's grave looking at the date of death of April 22, 1999 and it was so hard to believe that it had been seven years already. I stood there saying, "I've done a lot of things wrong and I will probably do more things wrong, but I'm going to try to make things right, somehow, some way."

I finally drove up to their house and I was greeted at the door by Connor who shook my hand and reminded me how happy he was to see me. He explained all of the details, basically Jason had run off with so much cash and had talked them into putting the house into a lot of debt, supposedly to reinvest in the business. He and Meghan were supposed to be going on vacation and by the time the week was up, all the accounts had been raided. Basically, they were doing even worse than they were last time and I asked him to call a family meeting, and what I didn't count on was that Billy had agreed to be there.

I walked into the dining room that night hoping to finally start doing things right and I was stunned at the cold-blooded glares I received from Cynthia, Melina, and even Marco, to a lesser extent. I saw Billy and asked, "What's he doing here?"

Melina said, "That was my idea as soon as I heard you were coming back, I wanted to bring someone here we could trust."

I took that personally, "Of course you can trust me, why do you think I'm here?"

Billy stopped me right there, "Charles this isn't about who is right, or who is wrong, these people have been through a lot so let's focus on listening."

I rolled my eyes, "Okay Dr. Phil whatever you say."

Billy glared at me, "Charles this isn't a TV show, this isn't going to be fixed in forty-five minutes plus commercials, and there is no studio audience for you to alienate."

I paused and said, "What do you mean alienate?"

This was when Melina came in, "I trusted you, you knew that I didn't want Jason to get back into our lives but you tricked me and gave him my twenty-five percent. Then you ran off to Minnesota and then he scammed all of us out of our money."

Billy then spoke up, "Charles, I think what Melina is trying to say is that when you have people betray your trust which directly paved the way for another betrayal, that is a very hard thing to forgive."

Then Marco chimed in, "I think that Melina needs you to accept her very real hurt feelings and not invalidate her perspective."

I paused and put my face in my hand, "Good god, now there's two of you."

Cynthia responded, "Look, why don't we just cut to the chase, we are in deep trouble here, and Charles we need to know that you aren't going to run off or sell us down the river like last time."

I raised my head up, "Look, I regret what happened but I didn't make a penny off of any of this, I was trying to secure Melina's education and I thought that Jason was back to make things right. However I was worried about things going wrong, which was why I set up that fund so that Melina's education would never be in jeopardy. You don't have to worry about me running off with money because I will never ask for any money and I will never promise you any riches. I have been to hell and back and I am here to help this family. I wouldn't have sold my bungalow in Minnesota and come here if I wasn't serious."

Melina stared a hole through me, "I don't believe you, I don't know what your game is but I don't care." She got up and walked away.

Marco looked at me, "It will take time."

I looked at Connor who said, "Charles, I do think you mean well but just be very careful."

I turned to Marco and he said, "I get the feeling there is something you aren't telling us."

I responded defensively, "Like what?"

He said, "I can't tell, but there's something."

I turned to Cynthia, and Caleb, who was now eighteen. Caleb looked at me and said, "You were in the military right?"

I said, "Yes, everything and a purple heart."

He said, "If you ever run into Jason, beat the fuck out of him."

Billy spoke up, "Caleb, violence is not the answer."

He responded, "It is to the question of what Jason deserves and what he will get if I get a hold of him."

Billy rolled his eyes and turned to me, "So Charles, tell us where you are right now."

I looked at him confused, "I'm right here sitting across the table from you trying to keep this family together which is what I have always done, even when you didn't."

He loudly scoffed at my remark, "Charles, why don't you just let it go, that was 1968. Since I came back in 1979, I have tried to do what I can to make things right and fully become a member of the family."

I was really irritated, "Oh is that what you call banning our father from your wedding?"

His voice continued to be raised, "Charles, he was against the wedding from day one and would have only caused problems."

I then responded, "Well I took that risk when I married Veronica because I wanted to do things right."

He then responded, "You mean up until the wedding day."

I asked him what he meant and he said, "You neglected her and you made your marriage all about you and your career. I came to your defense over and over but the fact is you didn't communicate and your marriage fell apart. Maybe if you had communicated more and judged less, you would still have a relationship with your own kids."

My fist was balled up and the tension was so thick you could have cut it with a knife, "You have some nerve telling me how to raise my kids, you never even had any."

He responded, "No, but every week I talk to people whose parents messed up and have learned some things that you haven't."

I responded, "See, there you are pretending you know so much, you never gave anything for your country, you never gave anything to anyone and it was always you talking down to everyone else."

He came back with, "I sent you five figures to help save Anita and you think I'm condescending and didn't give anything? You have talked down to me ever since we were kids, when I can help you, it's great I'm your brother, but as soon as we disagree I'm your dumb little brother. You still think I'm that kid who ran away thirty-eight years ago, well I'm not Charles, look right here."

He pointed right to his face, "This is the face of a fifty-two-year old man who is tired of fighting with his fifty-seven-year old brother. Mom is gone, Dad is gone, Cathy is gone, we are all that we have left of our household so are you ever going to let it go?"

Suddenly Marco chimed in, "It seems that you are holding onto some things as well, that you haven't fully confronted either Uncle Billy."

We both looked at each other across the table and in reality we were five feet away from each other, but inside we were miles apart. Cynthia looked at both of us and then Connor chimed in, "Charles, Billy, I can't settle what happened back in 1968 because I wasn't born yet, but what I can say is this, we need all the help we can get now, so just shake hands and be done with it."

Billy extended his hand and I looked at it confused, this was his hand and it was so old, he really was a fifty-two-year old man, how did that happen? We shook hands and I said, "Okay, from now on, we let bygones be bygones."

I said to myself, "Okay, let's see what happens."

That was around September of 2006, but by the end of 2006, the bars were beginning to recover and the cash flow was beginning to recover as well. Everyone was living in the house again because Cynthia and Connor's homes were foreclosed on in the wake of Jason's fraud. Basically, we were back where we were in 1997, the only difference was Marco was getting experience as a counsellor and Melina was in the last year of her surgery residence before she could be a licensed cardiac surgeon.

Melina didn't have much time for me and I was trying to get her to forgive me but she still didn't trust me, and I didn't know how to get her to. I had begun 2006 at my breaking point and now I was back in my home state and I had a purpose but no end goal in sight. The one thing I did know was that if I was going to help get these kid's business back on track, it was going to be an uphill battle. However, as you might suspect, every plan has problems and every year brings with it some unexpected issues.

CHAPTER 60
★
UNFINISHED BUSINESS

At the beginning of 2007, the business was making a little bit of money, the problem was the company had taken on so much debt that it was hard to determine how long it would take to save things. After a very difficult decision, we decided that the only way we could even begin getting out of all of this debt was to either sell two of the locations or try to sell the shares, which we wouldn't get a whole lot of money for because of all of the debt. The other thing that happened was we had to set up all new bank accounts for everyone that Jason wouldn't have access to, so he couldn't make any digital withdrawals from wherever he was hiding out. I tried to talk with all of them about this and they unanimously agreed that they should try to hold on and keep their locations. Since I didn't own any shares and it was their family's business, it was Connor's decision since he was still a twenty percent owner.

What proved to be a complete nightmare was trying to legally make the business theirs again, since Jason was still officially the eighty percent owner and so trying to figure out how to officially change the ownership was nearly impossible. The last thing we wanted was him potentially coming back and selling the business out from under them and the employees. As it turned out, we only had a few options and the only thing that would secure the business for them was if he was legally dead which would take years.

At that moment, I had a choice, which wasn't easy but I had to think about it. What if I contacted someone in the CIA to hunt him down, kill him and Meghan and make it look like a drug deal gone bad? Depending on where he was in the world, a simple cash payment to authorities would fix that right up. On the other hand, he was their father and maybe he could work things out with them. I still had a handful of memories, which were hard to ignore where he had helped me with a few things. My anger towards him was enormous and the vengeful thought stuck in my head for quite a while, and I even thought about killing him myself after the terrible things he had done. I would have loved to have seen the look on his face looking down the barrel of my gun and knowing he had screwed with the wrong family.

As those early months went on, I got more and more worried about the state of the business because it was hard for them to make any major business dealings when people found out that the majority owner of the company had run off. The location in Grand Rapids was doing poorly and despite doing okay business for the Super Bowl, it was becoming a losing entity. How do you sell something when the controlling interest is MIA? I finally did something, something I'm not proud of but something that I believed had to be done. I called Max at the CIA office and asked him for a final favour which was to track down Jason. He made me promise that I would never breathe a word about this favour to the CIA or any other government official.

While I waited for the response of the investigation, a bomb dropped and as it turned out Randy had gotten married back in 2004, to a woman named Dorothy, and now Jackie was getting married on August 18, 2007… to a Japanese woman named Chantel. Suddenly a flood of memories from that painful time in 1989 and 1990 came flooding back and I felt beyond torn. It was my daughter's wedding but it was something I thought was wrong. Everyone in the family thought it was no big deal, somehow, I was the one of the very few who didn't like two women marrying each other. At that time, California was one of only a few states that had legalized it. Even Billy told me to stop worrying about it and try to get invited so I could make up with her. I was still stuck wondering how she would ever have kids and even if she somehow adopted, how would those kids turn out without a strong father figure in their lives?

My problem with it was just too great and I decided against having anything to do with it and because I hadn't received an invitation anyway, why beg to go to something I didn't want to support in the first place. I was more grieved at missing Randy's wedding from 2004 and wishing that I had been able to go to that instead.

Around late April, I finally found out where Jason had been hiding out. He had driven down to Georgia where he took a plane from Atlanta, bounced off a few other places and was now spending his days on a beach in Jamaica. From there I knew what I had to do, somehow and someway I had to get down there. I made an excuse that I needed a vacation and I was going to visit one of my old war buddies from many years ago and I told them he was running a bait shop in Florida (this way I could cover my tracks in case they noticed me coming back with a tan).

I flew out to Jamaica and knew where to buy a gun and I knew who to pay just in case Jason tried to call my bluff. I got there and was

Melvoy's Railroad

stunned at how beautiful it was, perhaps even more I was stunned at how warm it was for that time of year. I called a cab and as it turned out Jason wasn't home so I let myself into the back door and got everything out of my suitcase and set up. Just to be as careful as possible, I put on my gloves to prevent fingerprints. They came home and as they walked in Meghan screamed seeing me sitting at their kitchen table with a gun in one hand and a small bottle of rum in the other. I did this partially because I wanted to have some drinks and also to make them that much more scared that I was unstable.

I had had a few but I still knew what I was doing. Meghan hid behind Jason with only her big brown hair and blonde streaks and a little bit of her eyes remaining visible. Jason, in a panic, said, "How did you find us?"

I let out a mocking laugh, "That's not what you should be worried about, because you see seven years ago I made a huge mistake and I flew all the way here to correct it. The only question is how that's going to happen."

Meghan ran for the phone when pointed my gun and said, "Stop right there. I unplugged it, and even if you plug it in now it will take 60 seconds to reset itself, which is thirty times the time I need."

She walked back to Jason as they leaned up against their kitchen counter scared to death.

He was struggling a lot to find his words, "Charles if you kill us, you will spend the rest of your life in prison."

I responded with another chuckle, "I have ten bullets in this gun and if I kill you, I just have to pull the trigger a third time and my problems are over."

I aimed it at my own head to further add to the perception of instability. Meghan was genuinely in fear for her life. I believed that I had them right where I wanted them, "Now if you want to live to see another sunset and drink another margarita, here's what's going to happen."

I opened up a folder I had brought with me. "These are contracts which stipulate you sign over control of Game Night back to the kids, with no money, no questions asked. I brought a scanner with me that will hook up to your laptop in the den, then you will sign them, scan them and e-mail them to Connor and their lawyer, whose e-mail is still the same. You will also write an apology, and if you do all of that and keep your mouth shut about what happened here today, you can keep the money you stole and live on. If you breathe one word about this to anyone, if I don't get you, someone will. I was away for over seven years and I have met some really bad people who have no problem gunning down two yuppies on a beach."

As I moved the gun to indicate which way I wanted them to go, Meghan turned around and said, "You're a psycho."

I responded as I took another sip of rum, "Well if I am, then you better do what the psycho with the gun tells you to do."

I watched both of them very closely as Jason signed and scanned the documents, and I dictated the e-mail and he typed it. Finally, he hit the send button and as soon as we confirmed that, I took out the cord that led to the phone jack and cut it in no time. They stared at me as I threw the cord back on the floor and I said, "Well do we have a deal?"

Jason reluctantly spoke, "You saw I just sent the documents."

I said, "Exactly, now here's what's going to happen, you will never tell anyone about today and you will never have to worry about me ever again. If I come back here, you're both dead, I have killed people for a lot less than what you've done. Do you understand?"

He said, "Yes, I understand."

I then added, "One more thing, don't you ever come back to Lansing, because you have done enough damage to everyone and I am not cleaning up any more of your messes."

I walked out that door and hoped that they were smart enough to keep their mouths shut. I flew back into town, and invented a fake story about seeing my old war buddies with a few fake moments to tell them about.

Sure enough, Connor couldn't wait to tell me the good news that Jason felt so bad about what he did, that he was giving them their shares of the company, as they were no good to him now. I pretended to act surprised but I was relieved that I could save their future.

One day, I think it was a week or two after I came back from Jamaica, I was at the house dealing with the flu and the only other person in the house was Melina. I felt absolutely horrible and on some level she felt obligated to help me since her next day at the hospital was tomorrow, and somehow on that day our bond began to regrow. After watching some DVDs with her, we began talking and we finally approached the awkward subject that had been hanging over us for months.

I told her how sorry I was for what had happened and I regretted ever helping Jason get his claws into the business again. She looked at me after pausing the TV, "I still don't get why you left. Why did you have to move two states over? Even if Jason twisted your arm and said you had to leave Game Night, how come you had to leave the state? What was so great about Minnesota?"

I blurted out under my breath, "It wasn't."

She said, "So then what was it?"

I didn't know what to say, I couldn't help asking myself, "Do I tell her the truth? Do I come up with a lie? If I tell her the truth, how much do I tell? If I tell her a lie, will she believe it? If I tell her the truth, will she believe it?"

As I struggled to find the words she asked, "Well, what was it?"

I decided to tell her a half-truth that I left because I despised Jason. I didn't want to be around the man who had cheated on my sister and I thought she would do great without me but I was wrong. I didn't tell her that the first time around because I was trying to keep the business in a stable place, even though Jason had other plans. I worked up a real apology and told her how much I regretted what had happened and how it happened. I wanted to be there when she graduated university and when she finished medical school and I regretted it every day since. She seemed conflicted, and I think she believed some of it but not quite all of it.

She stood there and turned the TV back on, while telling me, "I guess we all make mistakes, and you did make sure that I would have enough money for my schooling. I guess you had good intentions, just poor execution."

I took her hand and told her once again I was sorry and it was such a relief that after all this time she had finally forgiven me. I told her how proud I was of her and if I had anything to do with her turning out so well, then I was happy with it.

During that spring, I had to drink a lot less than before because I was still living at Cathy's family home and if I did have drinks, I had to make sure they couldn't tell. It was a lot harder for me to just drink until I passed out like before and I still wasn't healthy but it was still a step towards getting away from those problems.

Caleb and I stayed back that summer while the other kids flew out to California for Jackie's wedding, and apparently in my absence, Jackie and Melina had become closer friends despite the distance. The night when I knew it was happening, I drank more than I should have and the guilt of missing it was driving me insane. I was home that night and whatever progress I had made in getting my drinking under control was quickly going out the window, until the rest of them returned.

CHAPTER 61

★

LIKE ME?

By this point my skin was starting to dry out and the years of drinking were starting to catch up with me, hell I hadn't even had an annual check-up since 2002. By October 2007 I was seeing some progress in our company's attempts to get out of debt and I was starting to feel better about the family. Melina had finished her surgery residency and despite telling her how proud I was, those words were still hard to say because I longed for those days eight and nine years earlier when I would pick her up from school and she would tell me how well it was going. Our relationship took a big step back and she thought that my lack of interest in my daughter's wedding was a sign of me being a bigot. That had caused new problems to the relationship but we seemed to have partially rebuilt it in the spring.

Cynthia had warmed up to me since, and Marco was constantly trying to figure me out as if he was a detective trying to solve his first major case. The ones who I seemed to get along the best with were Connor and Caleb. What I didn't count on was how much Caleb liked me, as it turned out he thought I was cool, not because I was fifty-eight but because I had been to war. I would occasionally hear him refer to me as a "real man," and he liked hearing my war stories, but I didn't tell him how Phil "the Hill" died or the story about Mark killing kids, I just wanted to tell him the good ones. What I didn't realize was how this was affecting him, and he was losing interest in becoming an electrician.

One day around March of 2008, Cynthia came up to me and told me what he had been thinking about and asked me why I was trying to derail his career. I took that personally, I wasn't trying to derail anything or anyone, I was just trying to bond with my great nephew and she said, "I don't care how you do it, but I want you to tell him that war isn't glamorous and that people die."

I paused and I said, "I guess I told him too much of the good stuff and not enough of the hard times."

She said, "Uh, yeah."

I didn't appreciate that tone, but I pulled him aside and spoke to him, "Caleb can I talk to you for a moment?"

He said, "Sure."

I began to tell him about basic training and about some of the things I went through and how it isn't so easy and some guys don't come back. He then started to say, "Yeah, but you made it through and it made you a stronger man, right?"

Part of me wanted to say "of course" and wanted to embrace the message of being a man's man that my father would have instilled in me at that age, but I instead chose to say, "Don't do it, it's not worth it."

"Uncle Charles, I'm not signing up for the service."

I suddenly became confused asking, "Caleb, well then what is all this stuff about quitting trade school and going to war?"

He looked at me defiantly, "It is time to fight for freedom and for our people."

I looked at him and said, "Who is 'we,' fighting how? Caleb what are you talking about?"

He got even more defiant, "I'm fighting for my white brothers, the war isn't just overseas it is right here, on our streets, for our society."

I told him that I thought he sounded ridiculous and that he was talking like some nut.

He responded, "Don't tell me you're one of these guys who thinks we can all sit around a campfire and sing kumbayah. You can't talk to savages, the Muslims want to wipe us off the face of the earth and I'm not going to let that happen. If it takes my whole life, I will put a stop to it."

He got up and walked away, but he wasn't getting that from me. I had barely said anything about the Middle East since I came back, but it turned out he was getting it from somewhere else. Replace "Muslims" with "Communists" and he sounded like me, but he was a year older than I was when I was in that mindset.

I had to go and tell Cynthia that there was more going on than listening to me, he was listening to someone else or something else that was convincing him that he should go to war with non-white people. She told me to find out since he wouldn't tell her, and as it turned out he had stumbled onto some websites that were quite frankly propaganda. The type of stuff that even Fox News would say took it too far. Racist and homophobic, even Anti-Semitic terms abounded and I looked at him astonished, this little kid that I had known all those years ago, was following this trash. What nearly brought me to white hot rage was the Nazi symbol on the website and calls to find more "Aryan brothers and sisters." The Nazi symbol was the last straw and I lost my mind on this kid.

I slammed the top half of the laptop down and I went off on one of the angriest rants I had ever been on. "What the hell are you doing reading this garbage?! That Nazi symbol is a symbol of America's enemies that your great grandfather risked his life to fight against. That is not what I stand for, that is not what this family stands for, and I will be damned if you're going to bring any of that crap or people like that in here. If you ever try and bring people like that over here, they are leaving in a series of ambulances. I don't roll open the welcome mats for fascists or communists, end of story!"

He stood there, "I thought you of all people would understand. We have to look out for our people, our way of life, and we are fighting people from outside this country and inside this country that are trying to replace us."

I responded, "What the hell are you talking about?"

He said, "The white man built every great society and invented the civilizations that made the world what it is, and now all these other people are trying to mooch off of our hard work. Not to mention feminists and other people are trying to get men to stop being men and women to stop being women, and make them gay to weaken us. I thought you understood because they got to Jackie and screwed her mind up. You always saw through Uncle Billy's 'let's talk everything out' bullshit, and you laced up your boots to fight those gooks in Vietnam. Well now the society trying to destroy us are a bunch of brown savages and if I can't fight them there, I'm willing to fight them here."

Once again I was conflicted, part of me wanted to punch him in the face and part of me wanted to find the right thing to say to make him stop. I decided to call his bluff, "You're ready to fight?"

He said, "Damn right I am."

I responded, "I don't believe you. I think you're a punk who talks big over the Internet but doesn't have the guts to do anything."

He said, "Yes I do."

I then said, "You don't even have the guts to tell the family what you're thinking about. I dare you to tell them tomorrow night at dinner what you believe in."

He then said, "Yeah, I will."

So the next day we were having dinner with everyone there and everything was going along fine and I waited, but he didn't speak up. I waited and waited, I looked at him a few times and he kept looking away and the big announcement never came.

I walked up to him while he was watching TV in the basement, and said, "I knew it, you aren't a warrior, you are a coward. You are another guy who can talk all the trash in the world about Mr. Smith but as soon as he walks in you lose your balls."

He stood up and looked at me right in the face, I said, "You want to shut me up, go upstairs and tell your family what you've been doing."

He went upstairs and I followed about ten seconds later, only to see that he had taken his jacket and left. Cynthia said, "Do you know why he left?"

I then had a bad feeling in the pit of my stomach, but I tried not to let on, "I'm not sure."

Later that night we got a phone call, the police proceeded to tell Cynthia that Caleb and a few other guys that were his age, had got into a truck and assaulted a middle-eastern couple who were leaving the mall. As soon as she hung up the phone, she turned to me and said, "Charles what did you do?"

I asked her what happened and she told me, and then I told her what I knew and she was livid that I had not told her. I tried to move things along by driving her to the police station but she kept yelling at me the entire way. By the time we got to the station, I was ready to give him a beating that would make the one I gave Marco nine years ago look like a five-year-old who fell off his bike and scraped his knee. As soon as we came in and he saw us, he said, "How about it now, how's that for guts Uncle Charles? I got a set now, don't I?"

I responded, "If you really have guts, you'll come home and meet me in the back yard where I will send you crying for your mother. I told you to tell the family, not assault a family."

The police told us what the bail was and I said, "No, don't pay it, this guy isn't worth it."

I grabbed Cynthia by the arm as we walked out and she asked me what the hell I was doing and I said, "He needs a night in the slammer."

She then said, "We need to get him a lawyer because he could go to jail for years."

I said, "Good, maybe he'll get the hell beat out of him and he'll learn something."

She became livid, "That's my son in there."

I responded, "Yeah and you should be glad because he's safer in there than he would be if I could get my hands on him."

As we got back into my car she said, "Is violence your answer to everything?"

I responded, "Well you can't talk to… savages."

I was stunned silent the entire drive home when I realized that he did get this, at least in part from me, and Cynthia and I went home that night. I didn't sleep a bit, I was his great uncle, I thought, "Did I send him down this wrong path?"

That question haunted me in the days to come, and the media attention wasn't helpful either, especially when it was discovered that we ran Game Night. There were protests and boycotts and it became a nightmare. We finally bailed him out after a week, and there were charges on the table of assault causing bodily harm and hate crimes. I was so disgusted but I began to wonder if it was my fault, what could I have said or done to cause this? Business would end up suffering for months or maybe even years. We had to do a press conference saying that we didn't stand by things like this and we were absolutely disgusted by what had happened.

The question of "was it my fault?" wouldn't leave me alone and it haunted me like the McNamara question: "How much evil do we have to do in order to do good?"

It was just like the song on the radio that won't leave your head. I had to do something; this had been going on for months and the court dates had happened. Finally I swallowed my pride and called Billy and I told him what I heard from Caleb, what I had done and dared to ask, "Was this my fault? Should I have seen it coming?"

The answer wasn't going to be an easy one. "Charles, I would have to do a more personal examination, but typically when people join groups like this, it is a mix of factors. It comes from a feeling of inadequacy and the need to belong. A group that tells you that you're special and you are part of something close and special can be very appealing. In the case of this particular action, I think what happened was, groups like this tend to value aggression and domination and the goal of being 'alpha males.' Given your war record, he may have seen some of what he wanted in you, unfortunately when aggression is what they value and you question their manhood, they think that aggression and violence are how they validate it."

My heart sank, "So it is my fault."

He could tell how much this affected me and said, "It's more like you accidentally spread the fire that was already there."

I couldn't help but think back to the day that I married Anita and saw Caleb for the first time, he was a baby so tiny and so innocent. This was another painful reminder of how badly I wanted to go back and live in a different time. A time before all of this when Caleb looked up to me and saw my service as glorious, if they had seen what I was like on the inside, I wouldn't have had anyone looking up to me.

That summer Caleb and the other three were found guilty and were sentenced to five years in prison with no possibility of parole for at least three. With Barack Obama running for office, the issue of race was once again at the forefront and just when I thought that I couldn't regret my beliefs any more, the stock market plummeted which had been caused by market de-regulation that dated back to Reagan. Reagan's famous "turn the bull loose" speech was really a speech letting bad rules into the game. That year 2008 ripped me apart from the inside and I decided that if this nightmare of an economy, which was run recklessly, family dysfunction and hatred, was where my conservative, traditional beliefs led, then I was finished with them.

CORPORATE STRUCTURE

COMPANY

LEAST BUILT IES

VIP B

UGLY

UNUSUAL

TO OWN

BUILDINGS

CHAPTER 62

THE LONG ROAD TO RECOVERY

When Barack Obama was elected on Tuesday, November 4, 2008, it almost seemed like a fresh start for the country, because he was the first Democrat that I had ever voted for and I did so partially out of guilt over what had happened with Caleb. The family backed off on blaming me when they saw the Internet history and the blame seemed to shift towards racist websites. Unfortunately, the business had been hit hard by the scandal and by the time the heat from it began to let up, the recession had hit and a lot of people weren't going out as much. This brutal year took such a toll that we finally had to close down the Grand Rapids location on April 30th. At this point the Lansing location and the Saginaw location weren't far behind them, because the incident had also gotten us blackballed by the sports stars that used to help us bring in the crowds.

I was still drinking as a coping mechanism to deal with all this, the family wasn't happy and I just needed to see something get better. Week in and week out we were trying to hold on, trying to maintain some level of stability.

The summer of 2009, we had to close the Saginaw location due to cash flow issues and it appeared that the Lansing location wasn't far behind. This recession was brutal and had done a lot of damage, and that combined with the money paying all of those debts, became more than we could bear. As an added problem, the recession had driven down real estate so we couldn't sell the buildings for what they were really worth and even if we had, it was only a temporary solution.

I began to wonder what we could do to save the last Game Night before it went under. The bad press from last year hadn't fully gone away and we were struggling to keep up our level of service, even though we had to keep costs down. I finally came up with one last idea to try to save the business; what if we adjusted our business model and offered an all-you-can-eat buffet? Let's maximize the bang for their buck, imagine a great buffet while you celebrate the big games such as the ones at Thanksgiving and most of all the Super Bowl?

I had a gut feeling that if we could make it through 2009, we could make it in general.

By the time the summer of 2009 had come around, I began to hear the rumblings of the tea party movement. While some of it sounded good enough in theory, with no socialism, free markets and so on, what surprised me was the accusation that Obama was the one who wasn't responsible with fiscal policy, even though they had eight years of Bush Jr and he had run up trillions. I genuinely couldn't tell whether they were liars with a hidden agenda or whether they were just very misinformed. I didn't agree with all of his policies but I looked at Obama and I got the sense that he was an intelligent man who was at least trying to do good. At one point, I was reminded about Operation Railroad and I remember thinking, wouldn't it be great if he stopped it? Wouldn't it be great if all the stuff that the previous administration did wrong, Mr. Obama could turn it around and find a better way to ensure peace?

As you can probably guess, my views had begun to change and as it turned out, as I got closer to Melina she began to reveal that she was very liberal and began to show me a different way of seeing things. A way that was different from anything I had previously thought of, and at one point when she and I started debating health care, I tried to tell her about how dangerous socialized medicine was. She came back with arguments of her own that were very well thought out, and I knew that she was special but it was hard to think of just how much smarter she was than me. She showed me a few different documentaries, including one that had been made recently called *Sicko*. I had my doubts beforehand, and I had heard all sorts of stuff about Michael Moore being a liberal propagandist, but even if he was cherry picking his footage, it didn't change the truth within it.

It stunned me because the people he was talking to were telling a story, not that different from what I had experienced fifteen years earlier with Anita. Story after story of people being denied the health care they paid for with their insurance and people dying. They even had people who used to intentionally find any reason to deny people coverage and were rewarded for doing so. I had a sudden flash of our honeymoon with Anita's head lying on the pillow with her beautiful hair spread out on it. I began to remember those delays in her care, one after another and suddenly it was like March 7, 1994 all over again and her death was as fresh and raw as it ever had been. I couldn't stop thinking to myself, "She could have lived."

I walked out of the room and went into the bathroom to pull myself together, because I didn't want Melina to see me getting all emotional because of a movie. However, I don't think I did a good enough job of hiding it because when I came back out, she gave me a big hug and said, "I know you miss Anita."

You might wonder why this stands out so much, but the truth is, it stood out because of how different my life was becoming during 2009. It was as if I was experiencing a brand-new way of living, a way that I hadn't experienced in years, and even then, never fully to this degree. The civilian way, the way where I think about home issues rather than trying to fight the world.

Before the end of 2009, Melina had a surprise for me and told me that she was flying in everybody for Christmas: Billy, Hashani, Veronica, Todd, Randy, his wife Christina, Matthew, Jackie and her wife Chantel. I was stunned, and wondered how could she afford this, but of course as a cardiac surgeon, she was making a lot more money than she used to. I had to take a deep breath and ask myself if I was ready for this. I missed my kids so much and what I now had with Melina, I would have loved to have once again with my own children. By this point, I was a sixty-year-old man who was now beginning to think about his own mortality, my father died at this age after all, and unlike four years earlier, I wanted to live again.

I made a resolution and I decided that I was going to give up drinking now cold turkey, I didn't wait for New Year's and I quit on December 7th, and what a random choice that was. They were all coming in on Tuesday the 22nd and I couldn't help but feel nervous, as if I was coming face to face with my judgment, as if I was coming face to face with either my redemption or my damnation. As simple as a hug is, when you go years without having them, especially from people that you care about, they end up meaning so, so much.

I remember talking to Melina and Cynthia about it the weekend before they came in and Cynthia said, "I'm sorry that we can't all be here, but Caleb's sentence is going to go on for a while longer."

I couldn't tell whether or not that was a jab at me, but Melina changed the subject, "Yes but this is our chance to bring as many of us as we can together, to reunite Uncle Charles with his family."

I told her how nervous I was and the truth was I was not only nervous, I was petrified. Melina said to me, "Charles, I spoke with them on the phone. I've told them about how you have changed over the last few years and how much regret you have. I think that they do want you back in their life on some level, otherwise they wouldn't be coming."

All I could do was hope that she was right that they were willing to give me one more chance, one that I honestly didn't deserve.

CHAPTER 63
★
MIRACLE OR MASSACRE?

Billy and Hashani flew in first, as it turned out their flight came in three or four hours before Veronica and the kids' plane arrived. I couldn't stop thinking about that plane coming in. This was the first Christmas I had spent with him in years and I hadn't seen Hashani since her brother's funeral six years earlier. I was stunned by how young she looked with barely a grey hair or a wrinkle on her face and although she was in her mid-fifties she looked forty. Billy looked a little more like his age and I was surprised by how well I was greeted by her and Billy. This may sound crazy but I had a sudden paranoid thought, "Is this really a heart-warming family get together or is something more insidious afoot? Because I had put together spy missions that were subtler than this."

I was sure that something wasn't right, but I couldn't tell what it was.

Eventually they came in and I saw them all, and it was hard to realize the moment was coming. My heart was beating a mile a minute. Jackie, that little girl who I still remembered holding in my arms, was now a full-grown woman and was holding hands with her wife, which I was still trying to accept. Randy was there with his wife and Matthew was there too. I don't know why but Matthew looked the most like me, although it wasn't quite like looking in a mirror, but it was still surreal. Veronica and Todd were there and had brought the daughter they had together. I had almost forgotten this girl existed, her name was Martha and I had barely seen her in the last twenty years. I had forgotten what the rules were, so was she my stepdaughter, or was she just a person I didn't know, and trying to figure it out was more effort than I felt like putting into it.

I didn't know what to think about Chantel, even though she was a beautiful woman, but it was hard not to feel weird about the entire relationship. I shook everyone's hand as they came in and we had rented a couple of vans to take us all back to the house. Cynthia was there making some snacks and at one point Melina pulled me aside and told me something that really floored me. She said, "I believe in you, this is your chance to start making up for lost time."

I nodded hoping that she was right and that everything would go well.

I was genuinely scared of saying the wrong thing and I was genuinely scared of destroying what I was sure was my last chance to make up with my kids. I had missed so much over the years that I was scared that if I chased them away now, that would be the end. I tried with the basic questions, "How was your flight? What's the weather like in California?"

Of course those conversations don't last long, so I took a deep breath and began asking the more personal questions, and I asked Jackie how she and Chantel had met. She seemed surprised by the question, but she started to tell me. "Well, um it is hard to find someone. I had tried online dating which was disappointing, the bar scene just wasn't for me, but thankfully we had a mutual friend who set us up. We met at a Starbucks and we just clicked."

They looked at each other and a little smile came across Jackie's face. Chantel suddenly spoke up and said, "Sometimes you're just lucky, and I am so glad I found her."

They shared a quick kiss and I did my best not to feel some general discomfort. I responded by saying, "That's really nice, and I'm glad that you found someone who makes you happy, that's important in life."

I then shifted the conversation to Randy asking about him and his wife Dorothy and then I asked Matthew about his girlfriend who had stayed in California with her family.

As that conversation ended, Billy changed the subject and started talking about something else, which came out of nowhere and I didn't understand it. I was so worried that I was trying not to go grab a beer, or rum, or something. At one point, I went to the bathroom and as I was washing my hands, I looked in the mirror. I began to wonder what I was going to do, because it was so much more awkward than I had imagined. I was trying so hard to pretend everything was fine, but there was just so much animosity even relatively recently, that I didn't know how long it would be before the judgment began. I had to ask myself what I would do, how much I would tell, if asked. I thought, "If they knew everything, would they even look at me?"

Before I could panic, I took a deep breath and tried to tell myself that everything was fine, all those years of training at the CIA would help me keep my cool.

I walked back into the room and they began talking about politics, and now I was really worried, was this the beginning of an ambush? They knew I had been a Republican for over thirty years and my previous views on things had further exemplified that point. I began trying to think of what I was going to say. At one point, Connor turned and said, "Well Charles, you're the biggest Republican here, what do you think?"

I paused and scanned the room knowing this could be the moment of judgment. Once again, I knew I had to tell a half-truth and that would be it.

I responded by saying, "Actually, I revoked my membership in 2006 so I'm just an independent now. I voted for Obama and decided that we needed a change."

A few people in the room seemed surprised as I continued to make sure an awkward silence didn't begin. "I thought that George W was going to be a competent man who was guided by wiser people, and as we all found out, they weren't wise at all. I used to think they knew what they were doing but I learned that my faith in them was unfounded, so I hope Obama does a lot better."

I took a drink of juice and people were almost staring at me in disbelief, as if they had never expected to hear me say those words.

Billy once again took over the conversation and I let out a big breath just thankful that I had saved myself from another moment of judgment. Before the night was over, I had gone downstairs to relax and watch TV with Connor and that was when Veronica came down and asked if she could speak to me in private. Connor obliged and walked upstairs and I said stood up to say, "Okay, I knew this was coming, just let me have it."

She then said, "Something really has changed you, you saw Jackie kiss her lesbian wife and you told her you were happy for her. You left the Republican Party, I'm not sure whether you had some life changing experience or whether you were taken over by an alien."

I responded with what must have been my millionth half-truth, "Well I lost sight of what mattered and I'd like to think I'm seeing things more clearly now."

She began to walk around the couch shaking her head in confusion, "You know Charles I almost didn't come, and neither did the kids, they haven't forgotten what happened. I don't think Jackie will ever forget it, but between Melina and Billy saying that you had made some major changes, we took the chance. Charles, I really hope this isn't an act."

I responded by saying, "No it isn't, I have lots of regrets and I want to try to make things right, if possible."

She looked at me and said, "Well I hope you really do mean it because I don't want to see it again, I don't want to see you hurt them again. I have to go back upstairs, but I'll talk to you tomorrow."

Sure enough the next day, I knew that I had to try to make things right but I had to tell them only little bits of the truth because if they knew about my CIA actions, would they understand? I had no idea and it was a risk I wasn't willing to take. As Christmas progressed things seemed to be going well, the awkwardness slowly began to subside and I began to feel like we were really bonding.

The morning of Christmas Eve, I woke up scared because they were going to be in town until the 26th, and I began to think that I was in over my head. How long could I go without saying the wrong thing, even accidentally? How long could I go until the past would be brought up and thrown in my face? My talk with Veronica showed me that it wasn't a completely clean slate, because they remembered and may have still been holding it against me.

Christmas Eve went very well, we watched some various Christmas movies, and everything just felt wonderful. Slowly but surely my defenses began to lower, that paranoid idea in my head of something happening, slowly began to subside and all I could think to myself was how well it was all going. We all went to sleep and that night I had a very strange dream, like nothing I had ever had before. Somehow, I was in Santa's sleigh throwing down presents to people and it all seemed so fun, when suddenly I felt the sleigh shake and I looked down and the presents had turned into bombs and had left homes destroyed. Then I looked forward as the sleigh suddenly began to nosedive and before the reindeer hit the ground I woke up wondering what was going on, "What was that?"

I looked at the clock and it said 3:47 am so I knew I had to try to get another few hours of sleep and even though I struggled to get back to sleep, I eventually did.

Melina knocked on my door and woke me up and I felt a little bit groggy but I continued on through the morning anyway. Everyone unwrapped their presents and was happy with them, even though we didn't spend very much money because of our financial situation, but having this one spending spree wasn't going to kill us. As we all talked about things, the weather, how busy the malls still are, I went to the kitchen to get a glass of water and much to my surprise Chantel followed me. I think she was trying to surprise me but I had sensed her coming and saw her warped reflection in our silver refrigerator. I started to worry about what was coming, "Can I help you?"

She began to walk around me as if she was preparing for a conversation and she said, "You know… Charles, I don't feel comfortable calling you Dad. I made a promise to myself before we left California, that one way or another I was going to make you give Jackie the apology that she deserves."

I paused and said, "Well, I think that I should do it when the time is right and I haven't found the right moment yet."

By this point, she had completely come around to my other side and said, "What are you waiting for? Are you afraid that you will look bad in front of Melina, your replacement daughter?"

I responded, "First of all, she's my niece, not a replacement daughter."

She then interrupted, "Of course she is, she's the one thing Jackie isn't... straight."

I then responded, "Look I have grown past that, okay. Secondly, this is a sensitive topic for everyone involved and I don't want to ruin everyone's fun conversation with 'oh by the way, do you remember that horrible thing I did in 1989.'"

She looked at me with disgust, "You think I want you to apologize for one thing? No, it's not just one thing. She had to go to counselling for years to get over everything you did and she's told me about every bit of it. I have despised you ever since for hurting someone I love so much, who was also your daughter."

I then said to her, "Look Chantel, if you want this to happen so badly, fine. Let's find a place where the three of us can talk without bringing everyone else down, alright?"

She looked over at the kitchen counter for a moment and said, "Okay, but I will be watching you very closely and you had better mean every single bit of that apology."

I responded, "I will because it's been on my mind for years."

So I came back with my glass of water and everything seemed to go just fine for another hour or so, then as people began to go into different rooms, I got tapped on the shoulder by Chantel, who gestured upstairs. I went upstairs bracing for the impact, waiting for what I feared would be a tornado of fury and perhaps this would be the moment of judgment, the moment of damnation that I had feared after all this time.

We were in my room, which was formerly Cathy's, and Jackie sat there on the edge of the bed with Chantel standing to my right leaning on the dresser. I grabbed a chair out of the corner and I shouldn't have been intimidated, but I was because I had to weigh my words carefully, and to tell the truth but not too much. I let out a deep sigh and hoped I had a good plan. "Jackie, where do I start?"

She said, "From the beginning."

I said, "Okay, you were born only eleven days after my birthday and it was like the world's greatest belated birthday present. That day at the hospital when I held you in my arms meant more to me than you'll ever know."

I looked at her, still seeing some skepticism in her face.

"When you were growing up, I thought that I had to work overtime to protect you from the threat of Communists, twenty-four hours, seven days a week, three hundred and sixty-five days a year I was living and fighting the Cold War. In the process of fighting that war, the truth was I didn't spend enough time with you, or your brothers, or your mother for that matter. I have regretted that so much, I regretted every time I missed one of your school plays, every time I missed something, I was so focused on that mission that I missed what was right in front of me."

I reached out and took her hand, but she pulled her hand away, "Dad, do you know why children love Santa Claus?"

I looked around confused by the question and then she said, "It's not because he's always there, it's because when he is there, it's great, and with you it rarely, if ever, was. I had to hear you and Mom fighting for years, and I still remember the day you left for Nevada and I looked out the window and saw you driving away. I barely saw you over those years and I was a child and so were Randy and Matthew, and some job in Nevada was more important than us."

I had put my face in my hand, I then looked up, "Jackie, it wasn't just a job, I was working in NORAD, our nation's missile defense system. The other thing was the divorce with your mother was so hard and I just couldn't stand to be there so I found a more lucrative job in Nevada."

She said, "So your awkwardness and money were more important than us?"

I said, "No, they weren't. I have had to spend a long time trying not to think about those mistakes and a whole bunch more that I've made, but the fact is I was wrong. I've learned a lot since then and I want to be there for you and your brothers."

She continued, "What about being Sergeant Melvoy, the Killjoy? Do you remember all those push-ups, and those laps that you made us do, as if that was somehow a good way to deal with children? Do you remember or care that you did that to us?"

I was so worried about the other details, and I hadn't thought of those. "Jackie, I was raised in an era where kids were punished very hard and I thought that was what I needed to do. I took no joy in that and as I found out with Caleb, showing someone harshness doesn't bring out their best. Since then I have also seen some of the studies Melina showed me about how parenting works better using other methods; I have learned a lot since then."

I reached for her hand again, and again she pulled it away.

"What about Clarissa?"

I asked, "Who?"

She rolled her eyes, "My first girlfriend, the one you sent away because you couldn't handle the fact that I was a lesbian."

I thought she had stepped a little over the line. "I didn't send her anywhere, her parents did that."

She said, "Because you told them, even after we begged you not to."

By this point she was beginning to get upset, "Do you care so little that you forgot about that?"

I responded, "I forgot her name but I never forgot the pain that I caused you, I never forgot how badly I hurt you and I have regretted that for years."

She said, "Oh so you're okay with me being a lesbian now?"

I responded, "Yes, I have accepted that is who you are."

She responded, "Really? If you accepted it and if you really changed, why didn't you come to our wedding? It was only two years ago."

I said, "I know I wasn't invited but I could have asked. When I saw what Caleb turned into and I realized that he got there by looking up to me, I had to take a long hard look at who I was and what I stood for and I realized how completely wrong I was about a lot of things. I have been trying to make up for some of those mistakes ever since."

I got up off my chair and sat down next to her, "Jackie, the fact is I can't change what happened, but I can be a better man now and try to make things right."

She turned to me and she said, "I don't know if I can trust you, and I need some time to think about this."

She got up but before she went out the door, I stood up as she looked back towards me and I said, "Jackie, from the bottom of my heart, I'm sorry."

She turned away and kept going and Chantel then said, "Well, you've got a long way to go."

She walked out of the room and I sat there on the bed contemplating, "Maybe it was too late, maybe too much damage had been done. If that wasn't enough, what would it take?"

I had similar conversations privately with Randy and Matthew and I apologized about how things had happened, how I had spent so much time away and how I was too hard on them and drove them away. They seemed to accept the apologies, although I think Matthew was a little bit less convinced.

When Christmas was over, it wasn't that it ended horribly or great, it was a big question mark and with the decade ending, I began to ask myself where were we going to be ten years from now at the end of the 2010s? I had no idea, and all I knew was that I had to somehow save

Game Night and save my relationship with my kids. How long would it take? What would it take? I had no idea but I thought that there had to be a way, there had to be some way, how I would do it, the only answer I could give was, somehow.

CHAPTER 64

GETTING THROUGH THE STORM

2010 began with everyone being angry about the economy and everyone being annoyed that it wasn't getting better, or if it was, it was happening too slowly. A lot of the things that used to help our business didn't seem to work anymore, and wrestling pay-per-views used to bring in big crowds but that had fallen off dramatically. I remember seeing a pay-per-view and I didn't go out of my way to learn who was who, it was for the Championship and it was two guys that I remembered being bad guys. I asked one of the bartenders about it and he said, "Yeah, it's a heel program, two bad guys fighting it out."

I said, "So who are you supposed to cheer for?"

He shrugged, "I guess you cheer for somebody good to win the Royal Rumble later."

So, that conversation somehow stuck in my head, but what really stuck was the term and meaning of "heel program."

Not as many people were coming out to the bar for the Super Bowl either, and a bunch of people would simply watch it at home with a big crowd on some big screen TV. I was struggling to come up with ways to turn things around and I was more and more afraid that if we didn't do something drastic, the bar wasn't going to survive the year.

It was still hard getting players from various sports teams to show up, but it was starting to get easier because the bad press that surrounded us in 2008 was beginning to fade away. Unfortunately, so was the small boost we had received from having the buffet added later last year. I was running out of ideas and fast, if the players returned soon maybe we could do something but that would be a struggle.

That was when Connor came through with a great idea. "Hey Charles, what if we could install a wall, a big table and some comfortable chairs and create a private room that people could rent. I already spoke to some local high school coaches that really liked the idea."

Of course, there was one problem, we would have to shut the place down for at least two weeks and it might cost as much as $10,000 for the materials and labour. I didn't know if we could really risk that.

He then added, "I also spoke to a corporate client out of Detroit, who is willing to rent it during the day for lunch visits, and he's willing to put $5,000 down so that he can look like a big shot in front of his clients. However, we have to have that done by April."

I then asked him, "What about being closed for two weeks? Because we can't afford that lack of cash flow because we are struggling as it is."

He said, "Charles, I didn't tell you the best part." He paused and said, "Okay, I also spoke to the people at the Mayor's office, one of my friends from school is a counsellor, and he can get us a $3,000 loan and we can repay it by letting them rent the room for credits of that amount."

Reluctantly I said, "Wow, you've been busy. Okay let's go for it." So we went through with the construction, to make it look like a private room. Once again it was a long shot, but Connor was determined to save this business and wasn't giving up without a hell of a fight.

The bookings went well, and that spring we got a lot of extra business from people wanting to meet in a private room. What you may be wondering is, did this get us out of our cash crunch, and the answer is, part way. Unfortunately, we still needed something else, something to draw in people and I kept trying to figure out what it should be but to no avail. Connor spent so much time looking for new business that I was just stunned, because for him this wasn't just some job, this was his legacy and he wasn't giving up on it. I was so proud of how he had grown into an ambitious manager determined to put in his all.

While all of this was playing out, I had tried on a few occasions to contact my kids and it was very slow going, as I might get five minutes here or ten minutes there. I knew I was making progress when I had a twenty-minute call with Randy about the trip he and his wife were taking in the summer. It was so hard to get Jackie to trust me, and Chantel was also being very protective and was warning me repeatedly not to hurt Jackie again. Melina and I were on great terms and Cathy's other kids and I seemed to be getting along.

I began to get impatient about how my relationships with my family were progressing, so I finally asked Billy about it and he e-mailed me back and told me that it takes a long time to undo over twenty years of problems. He told me I had to be patient and that they would open up to me when they were ready. I remember thinking that I wished I could have found a way to speed it up, but I was too busy trying to keep Game Night up and running.

2010 continued to be a struggle, but in some ways it was comforting to know that it wasn't just me as everyone was mad, and I began to see the mass polarization of the American public. The right had the Tea Party and the left had the Occupy Wall Street movement. For the most part, that was the way it was for the rest of 2010, with me trying to keep the bar open slowly but surely, getting my kids to trust me again, and watching an angry country get angrier and angrier. Something else was happening at this time, and I began to see more and more extremism and outright racism towards President Obama. The entire birther movement was nothing short of preposterous, because if he really wasn't born in the United States, it wouldn't have taken long to prove it. It was so childish and stupid, it was hard to take it seriously and I began to wonder about how many more people had started looking at and embracing those Nazi websites like Caleb had done.

By the end of 2010, our numbers were really returning at Game Night and that was partially due to a new neighbourhood being built across town. We saved up some money and Connor must have spent all night putting door tags on the doorknobs that said, "Welcome to Town, now that you have spent days moving in, it's time to celebrate at Game Night."

The campaign worked and business continued to pick up again.

During 2011, the news kept going with its coverage of the Occupy movement, the Tea Party kept claiming that Barack Obama was going to bankrupt the country, and the birthers were still trying to convince everyone that Obama was a Kenyan. While no president was above criticism, this was just ridiculous and that year Obama released his official long form birth certificate, yet it still wasn't good enough for some people.

Also during that year Marco was dating an amazing girl who was sweet, thoughtful, and seemed to care so much. Melina was starting to date a guy who was a lawyer, and he seemed to be ambitious hoping to one day become a partner of his firm.

The bar was beginning to come back together, all of those small decisions had begun to add up and Game Night was once again beginning to take off. It was slow, but little by little, it began to fill up again and the money began to flow again. We still had debts but we were paying them down and now starting to have money at the end of the day.

Over the course of that year, I discovered that somehow Connor still missed his father, despite everything that had happened. Apparently, he saw how I reconnected with my own kids and was baffled as to why he couldn't do likewise with his father. It was at this point, that I remembered the threat I had made a few years earlier and realized that if there were any chance of him coming home, it was gone now. I didn't hear that so much from anyone else, but I guess Connor still saw some good in him even though he was probably alone in that vision of

Jason. Part of me wanted to tell Connor not to bother waiting for him and that he was never coming home, but somehow I just couldn't tell him. Sure he was in his thirties, but still how do I tell him Jason's never coming home because I pointed a gun at him and said don't come back? For me, at that time, the easiest, albeit uncomfortable, answer to myself was, "Don't tell him, just add that to the list of secrets you will take with you to the grave."

Somehow I still wasn't drinking, even though I worked in a bar where I knew it was always within arm's reach but I was somehow able to keep away from it. I kept telling myself that I shouldn't take any stock for personal use or that I had to drive, which was almost always true. I told myself how disappointed Melina would be, and came up with every excuse I could think of to keep myself from starting again.

I remember one particular conversation I had with Matthew about his new girlfriend Jan, whom he apparently thought was great, even though no one else did. As I began to hear the description, I came to understand why; she wasn't unemployed because she had trouble finding a job, she was unemployed because she was painfully lazy, and Matthew for some reason couldn't see it, so I began to fear what his future would be if he stayed with her. I didn't know how to play this, of course, but I wanted to help him. At the same time, I didn't want to recreate the problems that happened with Marco when I tried to get him on the right track. So for the next little while I kept silent, and I also remember having a phone call from Billy and him telling me to give it time. They had only been together a few months, so I waited patiently before the year was over when he saw the light and broke up with her.

The bar was finally getting busier, there were five different debts when we started and now we were down to three, one of them was going to be paid off by 2012 and the others a few years after that. By the time 2011 came to an end, I felt like I had put together a few good years and I was able to look in the mirror as a sixty-two-year-old man who had loads of regret, but also hope.

We had another Christmas at Cathy's house in 2011 just like two years before and it went much better, because there was a lot less awkwardness and I began to feel like we were turning a corner on our relationship. This was also when we got a surprise when Randy and his wife Dorothy stood up, and they said they had an announcement, "We're seven weeks pregnant."

Randy let out a loud, "Woo!"

Everyone rushed to congratulate them, and suddenly I stopped for a moment looking around at this room, and it was amazing, because

I got to be there to hear about my first grandchild. It was almost overwhelming and I remember giving them a big hug and saying, "I'm so proud of the two of you."

In some ways, this was a piece of what I had missed all these years and I finally got to be there for it.

CHAPTER 65

★

NOT THIS TIME

2012 seemed to be starting well and there was another election on the horizon, with everyone wondering who was going to challenge President Obama. They were also wondering whether anything would come of the December 21, 2012 end of the world prediction.

However, I remembered 2012 for something very different, as the bar was continuing to improve its fortunes and everyone else seemed to be doing better. It was around March, when I called Matthew and I noticed that something was wrong, and everything in his voice said nervousness, concern, and evasion. I was worried maybe he had got back together with his ex-girlfriend Jan, so with some reluctance I called Veronica and that was when I found out what was really happening.

I still remember that conversation, "Charles, there's no easy way to say this, his kidney function has been in decline for some time now, and if we can't find a donor, he's going to be on dialysis. I'm worried about how he is going to function, and it's going to be so hard for him."

I began to get upset, "Why didn't you tell me?"

She said, "I'm the only one he told, Jackie and Randy don't even know yet."

I immediately wanted to jump into action, "I'll give him a kidney."

She responded, "Charles, it's not that simple, you have to be a match."

I then responded, "Fine, I'll fly down there, take whatever tests I have to and if I'm a match, I'm doing it."

She said, "Charles, don't get your hopes up."

I said, "Look, I am giving you my word that if I am a match, I am doing this, no questions asked. I will fly out there as soon as I can get my plane ticket."

She responded, "Charles, the dialysis doesn't even start for three weeks."

I didn't care if it didn't start for three months, "Look I'm coming, he's my son."

She interrupted me, "Our son."

I relented, "Okay, our son needs me and I'm going to be there."

I knew that I was going there to find out if I could donate my kidney to him, but what I didn't count on was that Randy was determined to do the same thing. Before I knew it, it turned into an argument, Randy told Matthew that he would give him his kidney but I said, "No, I'm doing it."

He said, "No he's my brother."

I responded, "No he's my son and so are you. You're still young, you need yours, I'm doing this."

He responded, "He needs a fully functioning one not an old one."

I responded, "I had a doctor's check-up six months ago, and I'm healthy as a horse, my son needs me."

Finally, Matthew had heard enough, "Stop it. We don't even know if either of you will be compatible matches, if not, the waiting list is over six months."

Just then Jackie and Chantel walked in and they were surprised. Jackie immediately said, "Dad, you really came?"

I responded, "Of course I did, your brother needs a kidney and I'm going to give him mine."

Then Randy chimed in again, "He needs one from someone his own age that's why he's getting mine."

He and I began to argue again, when Jackie came between us, "Look I know this is a bad situation but everyone just calm down. It's not your decision anyway, and like Matthew told me on the phone, we need to go through the tests and find out."

Chantel then came forward herself and said, "This is no time for the two of you to start arguing about whose is better, but I'm glad you're both here because it brings us up to four possibilities."

I asked her what she was talking about, and apparently Jackie and Veronica were both going for tests as well. Jackie responded, "Look, put your damn egos aside, and at the end of the day we have to do what's best for Matthew. So what matters is who is the best candidate, okay?"

He and I both looked at each other and nodded, although I believed he was making a mistake, well intentioned but still a mistake.

The next day, we all hopped in Jackie's faded orange mini-van and headed to the hospital for the tests. I remember asking Matthew what was entailed in dialysis, if he did have to go through with it. His response that sent chills through me was, "It's a long process that takes hours and just drains you of all your energy, you need days to recover."

I suddenly had flashes of Anita's chemotherapy and how it drained her of so much of the life that used to just radiate from her. I looked out the window and I remember thinking to myself, "Please let me be a compatible match, so I can spare him from that nightmare."

As it turned out, there were two tests for kidney donations. They had to test for blood and tissue. I just remember getting up after the tissue sample, hoping against hope that I could save my son.

Those few days were as tense as any in my life, because I knew that I couldn't drink, so I had to do everything in my power to not give in, and to keep my mind off of that temptation. I forget whether it was three or four days but it felt like an eternity, the pressure was starting to get to everyone. Everyone's nerves got on edge the day before we were supposed to go in for the results, and Randy and I got into an argument again and at a key moment, Dorothy was telling us to calm down and he said, "I'm thinking about the future."

I responded, "So am I, you have a child on the way. Thirty or forty years from now, you may need to do what I won't be able to because I will be gone. I'm sixty-two years old, I may have fifteen or maybe twenty more years if I'm lucky, but I would sacrifice every damn one of them to save you, your brother, or your sister."

I remember that night, looking out the window of the guest bedroom in Veronica's house, the moon hung overhead and I remember doing an informal prayer. "God, six years ago, I thought I had no reason to go on, but I continued on. Maybe this is the reason why, so please let Matthew be okay, even if I have to die on the operating table to make sure he has a good life, I'll do it, please let him be okay."

I went to bed that night hoping that I wouldn't have to carry yet another casket into another early grave.

We all walked into that doctor's office, the doctor's glasses showed a mild glare from the lights above us and he gave us the news, "As you all know, organ transplants are not easy and can have a lot of complications, and obviously the fewer, the better."

I began to get tense, it didn't seem like hopeless news, but what was it?

He continued, "In order to do this we need as much compatibility as possible in both blood type and tissue type. Veronica, you and Jackie did not have the right blood types, O types need other O types and Veronica's is B and Jackie's is an A."

He then shifted his gaze, "Charles and Randy both of you have O type blood."

My heart raced as I wondered whether I would be able to save my son. The Doctor continued, "Regarding tissue samples, Randy we calculate a sixty-one percent possibility of a successful transplant. Charles your compatibility is greater, your probability is eighty-four percent."

I suddenly became hopeful, "Wait, are you saying that I am the best candidate?"

He responded, "Yes, your blood type matches and while one hundred percent is the ideal, eighty-four percent is still very good odds, and combined with various medications, we think you have the highest probability of success."

I was so relieved, Matthew blurted out, "So, I'm not going to have to go through dialysis for six months?"

The doctor said, "Yes, but we will have to do the surgery very soon, and the earliest date available is Wednesday, March 28th."

He was thrilled, "Yes, Dad, does that work for you?"

I responded, "Yes, if your mother will have me."

She was so happy, she just jokingly said, "Of course."

So the date was set for a week from then and I was thrilled that my prayer had been answered. I remember calling Melina and telling her how proud I was and that if something went wrong, she was a second daughter and a wonderful woman. She started to explain that while kidney surgery and heart surgery had certain minor differences, she assured me that most hospitals were very careful. I was hoping she wasn't just saying that to make me feel better.

I remember writing down an "if I don't make it off the table" note. There I told my family that I was sorry for what had happened and hoped that this would be one big step towards making things right at long last. The line that I closed with was, "It has been one of the great joys of my life to see how all of you have grown up. If my last act on this planet is giving you a better life, then it will be worth it. I love you all! Sincerely Charles Melvoy, March 28, 2012."

I laid down on the operating table as I slowly drifted away, despite what I had been assured by Melina, I genuinely didn't know if I was going to survive this. I didn't have any vivid dreams, just strange colours and the odd voice. I woke up in the hospital still hazy and I saw Jackie standing over me with Chantel behind her and I said something and she said something like, "I read your note and Dad I love you too!"

She began to hug me and despite how lethargic I felt, I found the strength to hug her back. I asked how her brother was and she said, "The surgery went perfectly."

They discharged me from the hospital a week later. I was never fond of Jell-O but by then I had had enough of it to last me for the rest of my life.

The doctor wanted to do follow up tests on Matthew about three days later and then have another meeting with us two days after that. That was fine with me because I was in no shape to fly back to Michigan yet. We walked in and the doctor told Matthew and I the news that would make me regret so much. "Charles, your kidney, while compatible, was not in the best of shape."

I looked at him confused, "Because I'm sixty-two?"

He said, "No, the damage that we saw was not simply a matter of age, but a matter of lifestyle. During your testing we clearly asked you how often you drank and you said not at all."

I responded, "I haven't had a drink in over two years."

The doctor looked at the paper with the results, with his eyebrows raised dramatically, "Well then you must have been hitting those bottles hard before then and if you had kept going at that rate, the operation might not have worked at all."

Matthew looked at me with a look that mixed disgust with disbelief, "You were a drunk?"

I responded, "I haven't had a drink in over two years. I swear."

Matthew then turned to the doctor, "So what does that mean for the transplant?"

The doctor responded, "Well for Charles, it means if he goes back to his old lifestyle, he won't be around much longer. For you, it means we are going to have to prescribe additional medication and I'm sorry to say that there is a strong possibility that the kidney, even if you're careful, will end up requiring another replacement surgery in about fifteen years. I am sorry to have to tell you that, but given the facts of this case, I would recommend getting specific kidney function tests every six months. If we begin to see the same issue occur, you will need to put yourself on another waiting list. Hopefully though, you will be in otherwise robust health between now and then."

The doctor sensed the tension, "I will leave you alone for a few minutes, it appears that you have a lot to talk about."

I could sense Matthew's anger, as if everything he had hoped for had just been ripped away from him. "I can't believe I have to go through this all over again in fifteen years."

I responded, "Son I'm sorry, I had no idea that my kidneys were in that shape."

He unfortunately was hearing none of this and said, "Oh well, while you're learning basic health, cigarettes aren't good for your lungs."

He got up in disgust as I pursued him, we had come in the same car and that car ride was twenty of the longest minutes of my life.

We finally got back to Veronica's house and she said, "So what did the follow up tests say?"

Matthew with sarcasm said, "Why don't you ask Jack Daniels here?"

I suddenly remembered the night I confronted my father about his drinking when I said to him, "You've gone from being Mr. Barry Melvoy to Mr. Jack Daniels."

Veronica interrupted that sudden flashback, looking at me with a type of rage, "Charles, what did you do?"

I was trying to think of the best answer and finally I came up with this, "Years ago, I had a drinking problem but I haven't had a drink in two years and apparently I did more damage than I would have ever thought."

Matthew responded, "To put it lightly! His kidney is going to give out in fifteen years and all the hell I have gone through this past year, now I'm going to have to do it all over again because he couldn't control himself."

He marched out in a rage and I stood there with Veronica staring at me with that look of judgment that she had given me so many times after our marriage ended.

She turned away from me with her face in her hand, as I stood there waiting for her wrath, and waiting for her to bang her gavel. She turned around and stared at me and she said, "You know Charles, I will admit that you have changed, I read through your 'if I don't make it' note and I know you are trying to make things right. I guess the question that I've been afraid to ask is, what did you do that made you so guilty that you're now putting in this much effort? What horrible things did you do that finally made you change your ways? I don't know and I'm not even sure I want to know, but I'll tell you this, if any more of those things are going to come back and ruin anyone else's life, I am going to throw you out and this time there will be no coming back. I will throw you out that door and God himself won't be able to talk you back in. Do you understand me?"

I responded, "Yes."

She said, "The only reason why I'm not even angrier is because what happened is probably still better than any of the other the alternatives we had, which should tell you how desperate the situation was."

I went upstairs, not even knowing what to say and decided to go home before things got worse. I did get a text from Jackie who said, "I can understand you having vices, I don't understand why you never told us, and I can't help but wonder what else are you hiding? What other skeletons are in your closet?"

I flew home and I felt not only tired from the surgery but I felt awful because a couple of my mistakes had caught up with me. I feared that the reconciliation that I had longed for was beginning to collapse all over again. It wasn't the apocalypse but for me this felt like a disaster.

CHAPTER 66

★

A NEW HOPE

Once again, the bar continued to recover and we were finally getting the professional athletes to come by, even though we couldn't offer the money we used to, but as long as they could sell some autographs, we were able to make it work. Another thing that also happened was that we started to notice certain staples of the area were closing, like department stores, and Blockbuster was having a liquidation sale, so one day before work I stopped and looked around. Somehow, I found my way to the documentary section and saw a few different things and bought a couple of others for everyone in my attempt to be nice. The two that I bought for myself were the DVD of that documentary I saw in the theatres *The Fog of War* and the other was called *Why We Fight*. Over the course of that week, I watched them both and in both I saw so much. People who were part of the Cold War, people who were full of regret, and in the case of *Why We Fight*, a clear examination of the famous term "military industrial complex" and how it had become real and I had been a clear part of it.

During *Why We Fight* they had Eisenhower's son and granddaughter interviewed and it was amazing to hear them talk about how Eisenhower had tried to rein in some of the military spending. Eisenhower was a five-star General in World War II and he was worried about the country putting too much emphasis on the military. It was hard not to be stunned by that because I had grown up seeing him on the TV and when people think of the 1950s, one of the people they thought of was Eisenhower. The question that eventually crept its way into my mind was if someone did a documentary about my legacy, what would my children or other people say? I guess they wouldn't be able to say too much and I began to think that was what was best. The remainder of 2012 consisted of trying to guarantee the future of Game Night, although it seemed like Connor and Cynthia were gradually doing more and I was doing less.

As the summer of 2012 approached, I was still on shaky terms with my kids and Veronica because they felt like I had pulled something of a fast one on Matthew, although that wasn't my intention at all. I still flew out to California because my first grandchild was going to be born and I stayed out there, although this time I had to stay in a motel in order to not raise tensions with Veronica. I remember having a couple of discussions with all of the kids about it and they were all tense but of course Randy was on the edge of his seat, but how could he not be, he was about to become a father.

It was shortly before the baby was born that he and I had about as close to a heart to heart talk as we had ever had. I asked him how he was doing, he responded, "She was due five days ago, so I know that it is literally any time now. I'm tired, I'm having a hard time sleeping because I keep waiting for it to happen."

I then said, "Well, it will be any time now, but I want to tell you something. We had our go around with Matthew's transplant but the fact is, I was so worried that I didn't see what was right in front of me."

I put my hand on his shoulder, as I began to swell with pride, "You were there for your brother and you were ready to put yourself on that operating table to save your brother. You're a man, and if you want to be a better one than I was, put your family first and I have no doubt that you will be a great father."

We embraced and I saw a little bit of the man I wish I had been and hoped that he was readier than I was when I became a father. The good news was that not long after that on August 10, 2012, my first granddaughter was born. I never heard the reason why but they decided to name her Hope and we also got a mild chuckle that she was born on 8-10-12.

I remember holding that little girl in my arms, seeing such promise, such innocence, and it reminded me of when I first held Jackie, when I felt such pride, and such joy. I remember whispering to that little baby, "I love you and I want you to have the best life possible."

Of course, there was no way she could understand a word I had said, but I still meant every bit of it. It just brought back all those parental instincts, and at that moment I would have fought a bear for that little baby.

I also went to California to make things right, especially with Matthew because it seemed like it had been slow going in our limited phone conversations. He asked me what happened and I told him roughly what had happened with Anita, "I watched her slowly die from breast cancer and it tore me up. When I heard that you were facing something that seemed similar, I just couldn't let it happen again."

He then asked, "I understand that, but when did you become a drunk?"

I reluctantly responded, "When I lost Anita, I came home to nothing and it was hell. A hell I don't wish on anyone and I ended up using that as a crutch."

He paused and said, "What made you finally quit?"

I told him that I had been controlling it more and more, but what made me put it down was the realization that if I put it down, I could get my family back, which was true. He then paused and said, "So, that's what happened?"

I told him, "Yes, it is, I have been living with that for a long time and every March 7th since then is brutal for me."

He then began to understand, "I guess I understand; it was my best chance and it did save me from having to go through dialysis. I also found out that they are making some great progress with stem cells, so who knows, kidneys might be easy to get in 15 years."

Amazingly he forgave me, and once he did everyone else seemed to accept it and by the end of that year I felt good about things, but of course that doesn't last forever.

The polarization of the American people that I was noticing in 2010 wasn't really going away, and if anything, it was getting worse and unfortunately Obama's re-election didn't help anything. Truth be told, I couldn't help but wonder how deep this divide was going to get, would any President be able to bring it together?

As 2013 got going, it seemed like things were going along fine, dare I say even great, and Jackie and Chantel had started the process of adopting and I was amazed that things were going that well. I was stunned when I found out how long the process was, because I heard it was long but I had no idea it was close to two years. I knew they were being careful but even I thought that was absurd.

What I didn't know was that they were several months into the process and that Jackie had been a little bit nervous about telling me. She was surprised that I was still being so supportive. When she asked me why I was okay with it I responded, "Well, Jason and Cathy weren't around much, and they made Melina an amazing girl. So if your grandmother and Cathy part-time could do that, then as long as you guys have your priorities straight, I'm sure you can raise an amazing child or children too."

Hearing me say that made Jackie so happy and knowing that things were going so well was so refreshing and such a relief. However if you have read this far I'm sure you know that when things seem like they are going well, there is always another storm and another battle on the horizon and this one came right after Labour Day, 2013.

CHAPTER 67

★

BACK FROM PRISON

In order to tell you this part correctly, I have to go back a few years and then tell it straight through. When Caleb was sentenced in the fall of 2008 for the hate crime he and his friends had committed, I didn't even want to think about him or look at him. Over those five years he was in prison, I wanted to focus on all sorts of other things, and the few times something reminded me of him, I told myself that those years serving hard time would fix him up.

I had never been to prison and I didn't go out of my way to learn how things worked in there, but apparently Cynthia visited him once in a while and when she tried to tell me about it, the first couple of times I told her that I didn't want to hear about him. At one point, I had overheard her say that he had gotten beat up but I didn't think much else of it. So the day came when he was getting out of prison with everyone wondering what was going to happen. I was trying not to think about it and trying not to let my disgust towards him turn into a desire to beat the hell out of him.

I came home from managing the bar and I went upstairs to change and when I came back down he was watching TV. He was skinny with a shaved head, a healed scar on his left cheek, tattoos on his arms, and wearing a white tank top. I was trying to think of what to say when he beat me to it.

He dismissively said, "Oh, hey old man."

I didn't appreciate that and responded, "Oh, hey jailbird."

He looked back at me and then got up, "You know what, let me make this real simple for you. I'm leaving real soon and when I do, you won't have to worry about it, but until then, shut up before something happens to you."

I responded, "Something happening to me? I have a better question. What are you going to do, do you even have any money, and where are you going to stay?"

He responded, "I'm staying with my brothers, that's where."

He then showed me his tattoo. In jail he had joined a gang called the "Aryan Brotherhood." I was quickly losing my patience, "Did you learn nothing after five years in prison? Are you really that dumb?"

He got right in my face, "Yeah I learned a lot of things, and for starters I learned that the war is coming and prison got me ready for it."

I was baffled, "What war?"

He said, "The war against the people trying to destroy white people. You used to fight for white people and then you gave up."

I responded, "I fought for America and skin colour didn't mean anything."

He responded, "Back then America was a white country but now we got all these other people taking over and now I'm not the scared little boy I was. I'm a soldier for the white army and when the race war begins, me and my brothers are going to win."

I didn't back down one bit and looked him right in the face and said "Caleb, they aren't your brothers, they aren't your family, your family is right here in this house."

He said, "Really? Because I haven't seen them in years. When I was fighting in jail where were you? When I was getting beat down by a gang of nig–"

I interrupted him, "Don't, just don't."

He then said, "You weren't there, you wanted to keep living in your fake world pretending oh, everyone is doing fine. Well we can't, they're coming and if we aren't ready to fight, they will take this country from us. One of them is already the President and we have stop them and take back our society."

I responded, "While you were fighting in prison, I was fighting to keep the family business from going under while you were giving yourself to that gang, I gave a kidney to save my son. I knew a guy like you back in Vietnam, his name was Mark, and he hated everyone who was different. He got a lot of people killed, including the man who saved my life, and they sent him home with stumps for arms. If you go looking for war, you'll find it, but you won't find any glory, trust me there is none to be had."

He got in my face until his nose was up against mine, "I used to think you were a hero, but now I see you are a coward who is ready to surrender our country to the immigrants and the faggots and dykes like your daughter."

I was at the very edge of my restraint, "You think you're a soldier? I actually am one, and if you want to fight me, give one minute notice and you'll find out how hard reality is."

He said, "You're an old man and I would take you apart."

I responded, "Are you sure about that?"

He nodded, my eyes lit up with intensity as I challenged him, "Okay tell you what, tomorrow night you and me in the backyard, I win and you get those damn tattoos removed, get your head out of your ass and you get to work. If you win, you can run off with your gang of hoodlums."

He backed up a bit and said, "I'll call your bluff old man."

I responded, "Who said it was a bluff?"

That was when Connor walked in and said, "What's going on here?"

Caleb walked away and Connor pulled me aside, "Charles, he is a lot younger than you and I don't like him being here, and if he is going to be like this, then I want him out ASAP."

I responded, "If he leaves with them he may never come back, and this is my chance to teach him some respect because he badly needs it."

Connor responded, "If you go through with this, Cynthia is going to be livid and she may never forgive you."

I responded, "Well, if it keeps him from throwing his life away, I think it'll be worth it."

I watched everything very closely for the next twenty-four hours. I barricaded my door while I was asleep, and I moved my car and parked it in a neighbour's garage in exchange for a few free drinks. I wasn't letting Caleb get anything on me until the fight because I thought I could stop this. I had been told by Melina that hitting kids didn't work, but he wasn't a kid anymore. I also began to think about what my strategy would be, how much of my CIA training I would use, and what if I am more out of practice than I realized? What if he tries to use a weapon, like a knife? All of these questions went through my head as I thought about what I would do, and I knew he would be waiting for me. I would be getting home around 8:00 pm that night with Cynthia managing the late shift. I thought back to the other fights I had with Mark, my father, and Marco, but this one felt different, and I couldn't put my finger on how.

One of the reasons why I insisted on the fight being in the backyard was the privacy, high fences and full trees would help block any outside people from viewing the fight and calling the police. I got in the house and then Caleb walked up to me, "We doing this thing?"

I responded, "Fifteen minutes."

He nodded and walked away and I was hoping I could humble him. I went outside and that was when Connor and Marco showed up and then four guys from Caleb's gang showed up.

I accused Caleb, "You need them to help you now?"

He responded, "They aren't going to do nothing."

I rolled my eyes, "Then why are they here?"

He responded, "Because I told them what you said about them not being family and I told them that they are my family and I'll fight for 'em."

I then looked at them, with their similar look, a bald head, tattoos, dirty white shirts, jeans, and scowling unpleasant faces. "When I win, he leaves your gang and then you get off my property and never return, got it?"

I looked back at Caleb, "Okay then."

Caleb began circling me, out of the corner of my eye I had to watch them now just in case they had talked him into ambushing me. He knew I was in the military but had no idea about my CIA training. I wasn't the man I was twenty-five years ago, but I was sure that I was still good enough to handle this situation. As the circling continued, he got closer and closer, he threw a fist and I evaded, then he threw a kick that I blocked and he went for another punch but I grabbed his wrist and flipped him over me. I did it well but I definitely didn't feel the flexibility or power that I would have had twenty-five years ago.

He got back up and charged at me again, but this time I had backed up to evade his strikes, and shoved him so he went face first into one of the bigger trees. He held his face, and as he moved his hand, I could see his rage. He hadn't landed a shot on me yet and he was starting to look bad in front of his gang. I heard one of them yell from the sidelines, "Stop taking it easy on that geezer and take him out."

He then charged at me and I had to flip him over, and as I flipped him the edge of his fist caught me in the head. He got back up and then went for a jumping kick and as I went to deflect, he thrust out his other leg and knocked me over. I fell down immediately, he then said, "I got you now old man."

As he went after me, I rolled backwards but he caught me with a punch to the face. As I fell back down, he tried to mount me and I pushed him back and kicked him with my left leg and he went head first into the wooden fence. As I got back up, he threw another punch but I ducked and hit him in the back with my knee, and as his body contorted and his head leaned backwards, I wrapped my arm around his neck so his head was behind me. I took him down and wrapped my legs around his body with my left arm holding his left arm and began to choke him out.

I felt him struggle and because of how much younger he was, I knew that I had to knock him out here or I would risk losing my advantage. Finally, as I pulled and pulled, he got weaker and weaker, until he finally passed out. As I pushed him off of me, the members of his gang came over and I stood up, "The fight is over, I won, he's staying with this family, get off my property."

One of them said, "There's four of us and only one of you, old man. You really think you can throw all of us off your property?"

I responded, "If you attack me I won't be throwing you off my property, the coroner and the medics will be doing that."

Before that could escalate any further, Connor exclaimed while holding his cell phone, "I'm calling the police now."

They looked at each other and one of them said, "Alright, we're leaving, but he is going to come with us anyway because we're his family, he's one of us."

They all walked out as I watched carefully to make sure they weren't going to double back and cause problems.

About a minute or so later, Caleb began to come to, so I picked up his feet, while Connor and Marco picked him up and carried him the rest of the way. Marco insisted on doing the talking so we took him into the living room and set him down on the couch, as he began to say, "Get off me."

He looked up seeing the three of us and looked around, "Where's the guys."

I blurted out, "They left; it's over."

Marco then told me to be quiet as he sat on the edge of the coffee table trying to talk some sense into Caleb. "Caleb, while I don't approve of violence, there is something to be said for what Charles did, because he was willing to risk his personal safety to get you back into this family. He was willing to fight off all four of them by himself, if necessary. This is tough love, because he was trying to stop you, not hurt you, and if he wanted to knock you out, he would have. I found that out the hard way."

Caleb looked at us confused, as Marco went on. "I know that for the last few years, you've been in a place where being with them felt comfortable and maybe even felt like family. But if you go back to them, it's only going to cause more pain and suffering to everyone, us, you and whoever their next victims are. Caleb, as your Uncle, I am asking you, please don't go back to them, stay here and turn your life around."

It almost seemed like it was sinking in, then he looked at me, looked around at everyone else and stood up, saying, "I'm not quitting my army, no, there is a war going on out there and I need to be a better soldier, and if I don't leave, I'm going to lose my family."

I pushed him back down onto the couch, "Get this through your thick skull, we are your family, and if you follow them you are throwing your life away."

He unfortunately had a response, "Charles, a fighter like you could do a lot to drive those people back where they came from, so join us and stop playing nice with these weak people who haven't woke up yet."

I responded, "I have been part of wars, I have told you that over and over, I already have blood on my hands and I don't want to do it again unless I have to, and you're asking me to fight against some enemy that doesn't exist. The real enemy is them, they have brainwashed you and whoever is at the top of their organization, they won't give a damn if you die, they won't visit your grave, they won't shed a tear, but all of us will. For the last damn time, we are your family, not them!"

Unfortunately despite being clearly torn and clearly split, he wasn't inclined enough our way because he went upstairs, packed his things and charged out the door to join them. When Cynthia came home that night she was devastated, Connor told her everything and she began to blame me for supposedly driving him away. Even though I tried to tell her my side of things, she was too upset and didn't want to hear any of it.

I didn't think it was my fault but it was hard not to wonder, and it seemed like we were close to getting through to him. If only I could have found the right thing to say, maybe he could have turned it around, but unfortunately those words didn't come and because of that he was gone.

I ended up having a huge argument with Cynthia who was convinced that he was gone and he was as good as dead. Worst of all, she blamed me for the whole thing, and in the process of this whole mess, I ended up calling Billy. I remember him telling me that the mistakes began before Caleb ever went to jail, he wasn't taught well enough, and he also became convinced in prison that the Aryan Brotherhood was more there for him than we were.

I asked him, "I thought prisons were supposed to straighten people out, what the hell are they doing in there?"

He then let out a resigned sigh, "Charles, I looked it up when Cynthia and I talked about it when it happened, it's a private prison."

I was confused, "So what?"

He then said, "Charles, they don't rehabilitate, private prisons turn recidivism into a business model."

I began to get even more upset, "So you're telling me they didn't lift a finger to help turn that kid around?"

Billy said, "I hate to say it, but probably not."

It was heartbreaking to think that he might truly be beyond hope. All I could do was cross my fingers and hope, that like Billy, he would find his way home. But then again, Billy didn't run away to fight a war that didn't exist.

CHAPTER 68

MORE TROUBLE ON THE HORIZON

Cynthia became depressed, but while she denied it at first, Marco could see it as clear as day and began to worry that if we weren't careful she might fall into it as badly as Cathy did back in the 1990s. We finally reached the point where by the time December came around, Marco suggested an intervention to try to help her. He remarked that the time from Thanksgiving to Christmas is often the worst for suicides because of how it reminds people of the way life "should be" but if it isn't so good, it can push people over the edge. When you combine that with darker colder weather it can be too much, so we had to act quickly.

It was suggested by Melina, who had apparently spoken to Cynthia previously, that I say as little as possible as she still harboured resentment towards me over the whole situation with Caleb. Marco led the whole conversation and while I don't remember all of it, what I do remember is how cool and calm he was as he slowly got her to open up about the situation. The one part I clearly remember her saying was, "That judge sentenced him to five years in that jail, and I hoped and prayed that he would get out sooner, but he didn't. I waited and waited and crossed off days on a calendar, then when he is finally out, I find out he's leaving and good old Uncle Charles drove him away."

Marco said, "Charles wasn't diplomatic, but how did Caleb decide to become a white supremacist in the first place?"

She responded, "He got lured in by those websites."

He then asked, "Why were those websites so appealing to him?"

She didn't know what to say, but then got defensive, "I don't know, are you trying to say this is my fault? Well you have got some nerve; I had to raise that child without a father and with a grandmother who lost her mind and a great-grandmother who couldn't keep up. I did everything I could."

Marco said, "Did you? What did you tell him about people who are different?"

Her jaw trembled, "Well, uh, I…"

She looked around at the room not knowing what to say and then she grabbed her purse and ran off.

I shook my head in a disappointed way, maybe it wasn't just my fault, or the prison's fault, or the websites fault, maybe in some ways we all failed him and Cynthia just couldn't accept it.

Marco turned to everyone and said, "I think that given some time she will be okay."

Eventually she did come around and began talking with Marco about what she was feeling and she began to accept and move on from what had happened. As horrible as it was, as bad as the odds were, we had hope that he would return and we could all reunite with him, although it still hasn't happened as of this writing in 2022.

During 2014, a few other big things happened. For starters, the bar was having the best year it had had in ten years and it seemed like business was growing and we began to look into once again expanding to another location. We had to carefully consider where, and also we decided after the burden that had been levied on us by loans, that before we did, we would get our current debts paid off first.

The second big thing that happened was something that I didn't think would happen and dreaded the thought of, now Russia was beginning to become aggressive. They had decided to launch an incursion into Ukraine, which resulted in sanctions. I couldn't believe it, the Russians were beginning to once again try and show off their military power. I began to wonder if we were about to start Cold War II, after all Mr. Putin was a former KGB. I also remember wondering what actions against Russia, or against us, were in the works. I began to fear where this might end if the wrong people gained the reins of power in either country. Putin was no saint but I feared what might happen if we began a race to the bottom. Of course, I couldn't let on how much I knew about the situation, how much it bothered me, and most of all I couldn't let on about my involvement in Operation Railroad.

Two more big things happened in 2014, with Jackie and Chantel finally adopting their four-year-old son, whose name was Clayton, and not too long after, I got the chance to meet the little guy. He seemed a little bit shy around new people, and it was amazing to meet my second grandchild. I remember one day visiting and asking him questions and he was surprisingly withdrawn. I began asking Jackie what was happening and why he seemed so scared, and she responded, "It takes time for him to adapt to people, he will develop his social skills with time."

I then said something stupid, "Most kids at that age are running around and talking a million miles an hour, there's something weird here."

Finally, Jackie walked away throwing up her hands and I looked at Chantel and asked what I had said. "Yes Charles, he is different, he has

Asperger's Syndrome, his version of it means he is socially awkward and quiet. It will take time and patience, not judgment!"

I responded, "I'm sorry, I didn't know."

She said, "Watch what you say next time."

I flew back to California, after I saw Hope who was doing very well, and thankfully Matthew was also doing well. Although we both knew without saying it that, his robust health was only temporary.

That fall, Melina's boyfriend Marty proposed, she was thrilled and accepted it with absolute joy. I told her we could have the reception at the bar and she looked at me like I had suggested that we hire a clown to perform the service. She did say, "There are a few things we will have to think about."

I responded, "Like what?"

She said, "Where will we have the wedding? How much should we spend?"

She then began to stumble over her words as she said, "Who will give… me away."

My heart broke a little bit because I knew exactly what she was talking about and without more than three seconds of thought I said, "I will."

She turned to me confused, "Really?"

I said, "Yes, I will. The fact is you aren't just a niece to me, you are in many ways like a daughter and I am so proud of the bright accomplished woman you are, that I would be happy to."

She gave me a big hug and then I said, "The father-daughter dance will need some practice though."

She gave me another big hug along with a bright smile and a bit of a laugh after that line, and once again I was trying to make things right.

That year I turned sixty-five years old and the truth was I only had enough money to retire, if I assumed that I would be dead before seventy. I asked myself about whether or not I should retire, after all I had worked almost my whole life. But I then asked myself a tough question, if I didn't have work, what would I do? Suddenly I realized that if I was just sitting around doing nothing, I was risking diving head first into the bottle again and with one kidney and at my age, that might be the end of me and I had too many good things going on in my life now. I had grandchildren to see grow up; I had a wedding to attend and basically be the father for. I also thought that Matthew might get married one day, and because I had been too stupid to attend my first two children's weddings, I didn't want to strike out a third time. I made a difficult decision, that I would keep working as long as I could, whether it be until seventy, seventy-two, seventy-five or whatever. The day that I sat down and had nothing to do might be the beginning of the end and I had too much to look forward to.

New Year's of 2015 ended with one of the news channels doing a recap of the major headlines of 2014, and of course they covered the celebrity stuff and the odd major storm. But then they mentioned Russia and the host of the show closed with, "There is a big question mark surrounding U.S./Russia relations and what that will mean in the years ahead." That was more than just a question mark; it was something that frightened me at my core because I had grandchildren, and a niece who was basically a daughter who was about to get married. I told myself they deserved better than the fear I grew up with, and I didn't want Hope, in the first grade, being told that any moment they could be attacked so they have to practice duck and cover every week. It also didn't help that on wrestling, the bad guy was being treated like a big, evil Russian straight out of the eighties. It was concerning and made me wonder if the people running our country could handle this difficult situation in the best way for everyone. There was just too much at stake as the people making the decisions now had to have incredible judgment, so I had to ask myself, "Did they have such judgment?"

CHAPTER 69

★

STOP THE FUTURE, I WANT TO GET OFF!

2015 was one of those years that was a reminder not so much to me, but to a lot of other people, about where we were and that it wasn't what we had hoped for. Climate change and terrorism certainly weren't in the brochure, as they say. I kept hearing about the *Back to the Future* trilogy, and whenever I mentioned that I had never seen the movies, people would look at me like I had three heads. I finally asked Melina to find these movies on Netflix so I could see what all the buzz was about because I didn't know what to expect, but they were very enjoyable and I could see why people liked them. The part that's relevant here was the early part of *Back to the Future Part II* when Marty went to the future, which happened to be the year 2015. It looked like such a great place and I remember thinking, "That was 1989's vision of the future and since then we have really fallen short."

We also saw a dark version of 1985 with Hill Valley as a corrupt wasteland ruled by Biff Tannen, which they had to correct. Of course, the third one had the happy ending of Doc Brown telling Marty and his girlfriend, "Your future hasn't been written yet, no one's has, so make it a good one both of you."

I felt this strange guilt, as crazy as this may sound, almost generational guilt. Had we really done our best for the next generation? Based on the news, various statistics about student debt, unemployment, and even these concerns about climate change, it seemed like we almost certainly hadn't.

I tried not to think about politics during the first half of 2015, I wanted to keep my focus on the bar, my kids, Melina's wedding, and with the wedding in June, it took up most of the first half of that year. We booked the church and a banquet hall, thankfully both Melina and her fiancé were making great money so they could afford it, although when I saw what they were paying I was wondering how everyone else afforded it. Everything else seemed to be going along fine, although of course Melina was nervous about finally getting married.

I remember saying to her, "You are an amazing woman and I have no doubt that you will do great as a wife, a mother, or anything else you want to be."

The wedding was beautiful, I remember walking her up the aisle and hoping everything would go well and to my personal surprise it did. When the minister said, "I now pronounce you husband and wife, you may kiss the bride," I sat there in amazement and it was another one of those moments in life when I would have been happy to stop time right there.

The day after the wedding I started to really look on the horizon and began to really dislike what I saw because one of those people who had perpetuated the birther stupidity was now running for President, Donald Trump. It seemed like he was everywhere and the news media couldn't stop talking about him and the things that he wanted to do as President. As someone who had seen the Berlin Wall in person all those years ago, I was bothered by the fact that he wanted to build his own wall between us and Mexico.

As a veteran, I was disgusted when he claimed that John McCain wasn't a war hero because he was captured, although he gave this half-hearted rephrasing after the TV host tried to correct him. The campaign was still early so I was hoping that this was just a fad and it would pass, and when it came time for the votes, the American people would speak and say, "We deserve better than this."

Meanwhile on the Democrat side, Hillary Clinton seemed to be the pre-determined choice, and the only other person who anyone had interest in was Bernie Sanders. Those primaries on both sides became brutal, and it was hard not to sense a general anger in the air, and it seemed like that divide I had noticed a few years earlier was almost cutting the country in half. While Russia was now getting involved in Syria, our country seemed to be at war with itself; the north/south, conservative/liberal divide hadn't been this wide in over one hundred years. I began to repeatedly overhear people saying that they would never vote for Trump or they would never vote for Hillary. I was amazed at how many people my age seemed to like Trump, even though it was hard for me to like the things he was saying.

We came into 2016, and with each passing week Trump's momentum didn't stop and neither did Hillary's. Bernie Sanders did win the odd state, just like Ted Cruz for the Republicans, but it became increasingly obvious that it was turning into Hillary vs Donald. Billy had no interest in Trump and it became obvious that Billy despised him and it was hard not to wonder if he was right or whether the partisan divide had reached him as well. As it turned out, Cynthia and Connor were starting to lean towards Trump in the election while Marco and Melina were vehemently against them. I began to lean towards Trump when

I heard that Hillary and the DNC were rigging the election against Bernie Sanders. I didn't want a crook for President, but then that summer after everything else Trump said that made everyone upset, what finally made me realize that Trump was not a viable option was when he asked, "Why don't we use nukes?"

I knew right then I was not casting my vote for him, because anyone that took nuclear weapons lightly was not the person to be trusted with them. I began to lean back towards Hillary until she said she would set up a no-fly zone over Aleppo, which was just the type of thing that could escalate war with Russia.

My family was split and the arguments began to emerge every time it came up, and I couldn't wait for this election to end. Business at the bar was good, but it seemed like nothing else was. I had seen a lot of elections in my time, but never one as divisive, angry, and downright depressing as this one. Somehow I was reminded of that wrestling match from six years earlier and this election was without question a "heel program." There was no one to cheer for and if there was a better challenger on the horizon, it would be a very long four years until they emerged.

I remember saying to Connor, "I'm calling it right now, whoever wins this election is a one term President."

Connor had become convinced that Donald Trump, as a successful businessman, knew what he was doing and would make a better business environment. He was excited for that, believing it would make things better for small businesses, which would in turn make running Game Night much easier.

Melina on the other hand, was worried about gay rights since Trump's running mate Mike Pence didn't have a good record on that and then she told me about his support of gay aversion therapy, which included electric shocks. The thought of that happening to Jackie made my blood boil. As much as I now saw Reagan in a different light than I did three decades earlier, he always seemed to carry himself with a level of dignity as did most of the other Presidents I had lived under. That was something I had a hard time with, to say the least. With Trump being so undignified, I could never have imagined any of the previous Presidents being so blatantly vulgar. For the very first time, I didn't know who to vote for and I didn't see it as making a difference, so that night I would watch, but not vote. Since Trump's "grab them by the pussy" incident, the polls had been down for Donald Trump and it seemed that Hillary was an almost certain victor.

That night all of us were over at Cathy's house and everyone was over by 8:00 pm, the early poll closings began and piece by piece, things began to fall into a different place. Florida and North Carolina began to go the other way and it became harder and harder to fathom that this man really was becoming President. The next day enough of the numbers came in that established Donald Trump as the forty-fifth President of the United States.

In the weeks that followed, I saw protests, anger, despair, and it was hard not to feel bad for people, especially Melina who was disappointed that this person who seemed to have no respect for women, had been elected. One of the things that really stunned me was the online clips she showed me of white nationalist Neo-Nazis hailing Donald Trump. It was a painful reminder of what Caleb had been pulled into and it began to scare me that armies of these people could be running around. What was even more disturbing was the idea of the President of the United States being sympathetic to their cause. This wasn't part of the brochure, this was not what I fought for, but most of all, it was so much less than what future generations deserved.

CHAPTER 70

THE MANCHURIAN CANDIDATE

Donald Trump was sworn in on January 20, 2017, that day some people were celebrating and others were weeping, I was becoming depressed by the fact that this man was the President. I was really slow to get onto Facebook, but I added all of the kids, mine and Cathy's, as Facebook friends and I ended up seeing one article after another and one video after another, about what was happening with Donald Trump and his administration.

By the beginning of 2017, the accusations of Donald Trump's close ties with Russia began to become commonplace and the question of what degree he was associated with them, was one of the biggest stories in the news. Pretty soon the different intelligence agencies began to come through with information about it, and his travel bans and problems with TrumpCare were just the beginning.

At this point, Jackie and Chantel were deeply scared and Clayton was now going to school and they were scared about what the Trump administration was going to do to education, and not to mention, gay people like themselves. I tried to tell them that they didn't have anything to worry about because they lived in California, which was the most liberal pro-gay state there is. That was only a mild comfort to their concerns, not just for themselves, but for their son, and as it turned out, he was a smart kid but quiet and awkward.

Meanwhile Randy was worried about what education would look like for his daughter, Hope, and his wife Dorothy was convinced that they shouldn't have any more kids if this was how it was going to be. Matthew was now even more worried about the operation he would need when the kidney he got from me finally gave way, and would he even be able to get insurance? There was very little comfort I could offer them at that point and it was so disappointing that at sixty-seven, my children who were now in their late thirties and early forties, were worried about their children's future.

I remember that summer it was around my sixty-eighth birthday, when I promised Matthew that no matter what happened, I would find a way for him to pay for the surgery. The thought crossed my mind that maybe Melina would have a contact who did kidney transplants who could give us a discount.

Trump began to ramp up even more military spending and he kept talking about how great everything was going to be. He was almost looking for a fight, whether it was the bombs he dropped, or the threats he was making to North Korea, but he was determined to show everyone how tough he was. Whether he was firing person after person from his administration, or picking fights with NFL players, he was determined to show everyone how petty he could be while pretending to be a tough guy.

One group of people he wasn't tough on were the white racists who came out of the woodwork, and increasing talk of race wars began to come up from white supremacists. With Trump's election, they were now as emboldened as they had been in decades to do terrible things. These racists made my own father's racism sound enlightened by comparison.

The hardest thing to see was another horrifying incident that happened in a small town in Alabama in 2018, when some local townspeople literally lynched three black men. They posted it all over the Internet next to an older picture of the same kind of lynching from the early 1930s. The caption that they put next to this horrible comparison was, "The return of an American Tradition."

As I am sure you can guess, this story spread like wildfire and it was hard for me not to become so enraged that I wanted to go after those murderers myself with a sawed-off shotgun.

I remember talking with Billy, and he and Hashani were becoming genuinely afraid of what was going to happen. He didn't want them to have a flaming cross put on their lawn or worse yet, have a home invasion by more people taking WSS (White Supremacist Selfies) trying to match or top each other's evil.

I jokingly said to him, "Well if you want I can help you move to Canada; in Canada you're safe everywhere except the hockey rink."

Billy was in no mood for humour, because he was genuinely worried for his safety and quite frankly I was a little bit too.

One thing that I didn't tell a soul about was how disturbed I was by one of the other pictures that came out and one of the guys in the picture looked like Caleb. It wasn't him because his eyes were closer together and the guy in the picture had bigger ears and a smaller forehead. But it looked enough like him that I feared that one day his name would be on the list of people committing these horrible acts. Perhaps even worse, I began to fear that he might return to town some day and try to get revenge for me beating him in that fight in front of

Melvoy's Railroad

the other thugs. All I could do was wonder, what the hell was happening to this country? What the hell were these people thinking? But most of all, what the hell were we going to do?

CHAPTER 71

★

MAKING NIXON LOOK GOOD

I am sure that some of you are wondering, "How did this go on for so long?" Well the simplest answer is that the Republicans had the House, the Senate and so on, so getting the President impeached was not something they were interested in. Talk of the 25th Amendment was thrown around but until the Republicans got interested in it, it wasn't going to happen. Donald Trump and his family, among others, were all under investigation and everyone was trying to make it seem like it was either the biggest scandal of all time or an unpatriotic attack on the President.

Later in 2017 the first charges were laid out and during 2018 more information came out declaring that Trump and other top officials had committed treason and Trump had a long history of money laundering for Russian interests. Trump came out and signed a pardon for himself and his crew and Tweeted, "There, I'm the President, I pardon myself and other great people, that's the end of this foolishness. #BacktoBusiness"

Trump genuinely thought he could simply pardon himself and his crew of the charges and it would magically end. This became a matter for the Supreme Court with the entire world watching and Trump's approval ratings sinking to about twenty percent. By this point the terrorist group ISIS had been largely militarily defeated in Iraq by us and the Iraqi government, and in Syria by the Russians and Syrian governments.

While a handful of Republicans were calling for Trump's resignation, he was having none of it. I had never seen anything like this, with Trump trying to push for war with North Korea and insulting the Chinese for not "holding up their end of the bargain."

While some people were saying they should go to war, a lot of other people said it was clearly unnecessary. It didn't help when one of the White House spokespeople said, "They have weapons of mass destruction, they actually have them this time."

With the 2018 mid-term elections on the horizon, it didn't look good for the Republicans, some of whom were still towing the party line saying, "Mr. Trump was elected to a four-year term by the American people and he should be allowed to complete that term as per the constitution."

If I didn't know any better, I would have thought they were trying to piss everyone off, because when Trump first got elected he had signed an order to end the Environmental Protection Agency by December 31, 2018. So now that the actual end of their agency was on the horizon, people were angry about that too. Every ad against this measure featured footage of adorable animals struggling to survive and they did a great job making them tug on your heartstrings.

What made the Democrats' job easy was when they came out in September stating that if they won the mid-term election, they would guarantee Donald Trump's impeachment. Even some Republicans began to change their tune rather than staying on the sinking ship. The last straw for the Republicans came in October 2018, when the Supreme Court came out and declared that Donald Trump would be prosecuted and Mr. Trump's pardon of himself would not stand. The Democrats won that mid-term election with relative ease and suddenly the race to 2020 was on.

With Trump's Presidency in serious doubt, the Democrats couldn't wait to get him impeached and in January, the bill to impeach Donald Trump was passed and the Senate passed it quickly as well. The big question emerged asking how would Mike Pence be as the new President? On March 25, 2019 Donald Trump resigned as the President. They tried to say it was because he was tired of being in a "no-win situation." Some people suggested that he might have had early onset Alzheimer's. Trump famously Tweeted, "This impeachment is pure persecution #badgovernment #Terrible."

While all of this insanity was going on, a few other unfortunate things had occurred. A lot of local areas had been attacked by this far-right group, who were now livid that "their guy" had been forced out. Certain Democrat politicians were issued death threats and one of the ones from Wisconsin was actually shot and died in the hospital hours later.

Around the beginning of 2019, the economy began to fall through with early April, 2019 being particularly bad, but Donald Trump famously Tweeted that big tumble was because he was no longer President. At this point his egotism was not only a joke, but people were beginning to replace the term Narcissist and Narcissism, with Trumpist and Trumpism. Of course, this terminology wasn't being used by professionals but it became a layman's term.

During 2018 and 2019, Russia began going into other areas, and stories began to come out about Russia supposedly trying to push for a greater deterioration of the European Union. However with these headlines coming through, some people said they needed to impose more sanctions on Russia and find other ways to stop Russia's continued aggression. They were, region by region, beginning to annex Ukraine, as other countries began to band together. When Russia finally seized the capital, the President of Ukraine ended up signing a document declaring Ukraine to be the newest member of the Russian Federation. The Ukrainian President made a half-hearted speech declaring that it was in the best interest of Ukrainians to stop fighting and to be part of a bright new future as part of the Russian Federation.

Poland in particular was deeply worried by what they saw as Russia trying once again to become an empire and feared once again being under their control. They were especially concerned because now they were the next former Soviet State, just one country over from Ukraine. Surprisingly many Republicans said that they should not be worried about Russia, that they should be worried about Iran and other "terrorist countries." Those years became years of inaction, and President Mike Pence became the President that vetoed everything he could. Whether it involved cutting defense spending, raising taxes or adding any other programs that were supposed to help anyone, besides corporations and the wealthy.

Bernie Sanders, despite being wildly popular among leftists, was having health problems and began telling everyone to support Elizabeth Warren. She was now becoming an icon of someone who constantly chased after the Republicans, and was becoming so popular that Jackie dressed up as her for Halloween 2019.

Many people considered one speech she gave a speech that changed the political landscape in America and it was a speech that some people claim made her the front running candidate. Copies of it were all over YouTube and I re-watched it over and over again. She came up to the podium with her papers and looked at the senate:

"Make no mistake, we are in a second Cold War, we have a powerful country with nuclear weapons and imperial intentions. Vladimir Putin is slowly pushing the envelope to see what he can get away with, Poland is no match for Russia, but we are. We need to tell Mr. Putin that we are not going to play his game. We are not going to let him wreak havoc with international law, but we are also not going to respond with military force. If we didn't spend all those years trying to keep up with the Soviet Union, we could have paid for so many things that would have helped American families. We could have paid for universal health care, universal post-secondary education, universal childcare, and major investments in clean energy many times over. We need to sit down with Mr. Putin and the United Nations and say that enough is enough because we don't want the conflicts of the twentieth century to be repeated and surpassed. It's time to break the cycle of conflict, and if I am elected on November 3rd, I will do exactly that."

So as the 2020 election progressed, there were certain information leaks that occurred including one that said that the Democratic National Committee was planning to block Elizabeth Warren's bigger changes, in order to maintain their corporate donors. Of course, the questions of Russian involvement went right to the top of the debate. Now it seemed pretty obvious right-wing, unpopular President versus popular candidate, and a President who seems fine with Russia versus one that says she would stand up to them.

Well there were a couple of things that were going on that might surprise you. First, the extremists were still fighting for Mike Pence and one even threw a brick at Elizabeth Warren. Thankfully it didn't hit her but if she had stepped two feet further forward, it would have hit her right in the head. Secondly, the two conventions that summer were full of angry, scared people preparing for a war, preparing for a brutal election, one where victory and defeat wasn't a matter of simply having different policies, but where it had become a matter of life and death; a matter of life and death for millions and millions of people across the world.

CHAPTER 72

THE COLD WAR BECOMES HOT

This election not only frightened me as much as any election there had ever been but it scared me to think it would probably be my last. My father had died when he was 61 years old and my mother had died when she was 71 years old. 2020 was the year that I turned 71 and this made me not only fear for my country but also my own life. How much time did I have left? If the wrong people were in charge, how much time did the country have left?

As you might guess, this powder keg could only be kept down for so long, and finally in August there were a few major leaks showing that Putin had coerced certain elected officials in Europe. He was supposedly laying down the plans to invade Poland in December, once the Republicans got re-elected in the United States.

As soon as this leaked out, there was absolutely no way back. The Republicans and Mike Pence in particular, did a complete one-hundred-and-eighty-degree turn. He declared that he now had no choice but to draw a line in the sand. If Russia invaded Poland, the United States was prepared to do whatever it took to drive them back and if this continued, even change their regime. Immediately the rhetoric flew and Putin famously said, "America, you know better than that, we are even more powerful than you and we have China on our side, there is nothing you can do."

Suddenly Elizabeth Warren went from being the person who was tough on Russia to being perceived as the one who was soft. She was calling for sanctions and a U.N. mediated meeting, whereas Mike Pence was basically threatening war.

All sorts of world leaders spoke up saying that Pence and Putin were being extremely irresponsible with their rhetoric. However, neither of them had any interest in backing down, and despite this red-hot issue, Mike Pence was still down in the polls because many people were convinced that he wasn't serious.

To the shock of everyone, on October 14th, 2020, Russia marched 60,000 troops into eastern Poland. Mike Pence, with only twenty days until the election, sent the fighter jets and they actually dropped

Melvoy's Railroad

bombs on the soldiers. Those planes were in turn attacked by Russian jets, which quickly turned into a massacre for the Polish civilians in that area. While Mike Pence's poll numbers edged up in some areas, they dropped dramatically in others and when the day came on November 3rd everyone wondered what was going to happen next.

People were confused when Mike Pence was re-elected and it was only later on that they found out why. As it turned out, the state level Republicans in various states had come up with a series of tricks to try to suppress opposition voting. The biggest part of this was their rule, which was called the "fake ID check." It was designed to stop people who "appeared to be under thirty" which of course was targeting young people. These new laws said that people who appeared to be under thirty "had to have multiple pieces of photo ID and they had to bring at least three verified adults to the voting station to say that they were indeed themselves. Be extra careful of people of colour as they tend to appear young in general." As you might guess this was kept quiet so that young people and people of colour would show up on election day to vote and were caught by surprise in several states.

So the Poland issue quickly escalated with Russia telling America to get out of Poland as they were recklessly killing civilians, so America told Russia to get out first. While I don't know what went on behind closed doors, somebody double-crossed somebody else and everyone was paying the price because of it. The situation had become so severe that Billy finally made good on his plan to move to Canada, specifically Prince George, British Columbia. At this point, America and Russia were both seen very poorly in the eyes of the world. I remember seeing something on Facebook that said, "In this case: America = Godzilla, Russia = Rhodan, and Poland = Japan."

People began referring to this as World War III; the old quote from Albert Einstein was dragged out, posted and re-posted over and over. I am referring to the one that said, "I do not know the weapons with which World War III would be fought, but World War IV will be fought with sticks and stones."

The conflict began to spread to neighbouring countries and suddenly laws were passed regarding new Internet surveillance laws to make sure that Russian spies were not in the country or were not spying on us, or at least that was their story. By April 30th, 2021, America sent more soldiers and warships to Europe as everyone feared what was to come. That summer the soldier deaths began to pile up and the ground troops from both countries arrived and the entire world was either taking sides or begging everyone to stop before it was too late.

Mike Pence had a rally late in August 2021 and he told the American

Chapter 72 : The Cold War Becomes Hot

people, "I tried to give Mr. Putin the benefit of the doubt but he had other plans. So mark my words, this is going to end very soon. America will see victory in Poland!"

Although the people at that rally cheered, everyone else began to dread what was to come, were we going to launch an attack on their soil? Were we going to attack their satellites? Everyone was so caught up with this war that the hundreds of people in rural Iowa who died from polluted drinking water attracted barely any attention, and any mention of it was so easily forgotten by this larger issue.

Finally, as if Pence had a truly sick sense of humor, on September 11th of all days they did it, the maniacs really did it; they launched the nuclear weapons and Russia was unable to counterattack... almost. As it turned out, Russia had a few missiles planted in Venezuela so we launched a few missiles back at them. Every square inch of Russian soil was either hit or was in the heavily irradiated zone so the neighbouring countries were hit as well. For all countries surrounding Russia, including China, many of them were about to come face to face with the nuclear winter effect.

As for the Venezuelan missiles, they hit us; specifically they hit us along the southern half of Florida. This strike on our shores resulted in the deaths of over ten million Americans with Tampa being one of the places that was all but destroyed. Thankfully none of my family (unless Caleb happened to be there) died but it was horrifying to think that I could never visit Anita's grave again. It was hard to imagine what I would have said to her if she had found out what had happened. It was astonishing seeing news coverage of incoming missiles and people in the state of Florida being told to evacuate. Of course if you only have twenty minutes and you are anywhere near the touch down points, you wouldn't get very far even if you drove like a race car driver in the best direction.

That day just seemed unbelievable, it literally didn't feel real, I was waiting for an alarm clock to go off, or some other noise to wake me up. But there was no escape, this nightmare wasn't in my head, it was reality and when I actually went to bed that night, I couldn't even imagine what sort of world I was going to wake up to the next morning.

CHAPTER 73

★

WHAT IS & NEVER SHOULD HAVE BEEN

The next day everyone was speechless trying to make sense of what had happened. It was announced that at noon President Mike Pence was going to come out and officially address the American people. I remember watching it while having a burger and fries:

"Ladies and gentlemen, yesterday was a difficult day but a day of tremendous victory. Some people believe that we and the Russian Federation were in the early stages of World War III; well I am proud to say that we have officially won that war and no country needs to ever fear Russian aggression ever again. The losses faced by our people were enormous, however the losses on the other side were far, far greater. There is nothing left of Russia, and what little remains is uninhabitable, and North Korea was badly damaged in the process. Ladies and gentlemen, with every great victory comes a great sacrifice and unfortunately due to unforeseen circumstances we paid a heavy price, however we are victorious. This tremendous but difficult victory was thanks to a plan that has been in the works for some time called Operation Railroad that allowed us to minimize Russian counterattack in our tactical strike. The war is over, feel joy, feel relief, but most of all look up at that flag and feel pride in your country. God Bless You and God Bless America."

When he said "Operation Railroad" I dropped my burger and it landed awkwardly on my plate splitting apart. A few of the people in the bar having lunch looked on in disbelief, and I could barely even think. It was my worst nightmare come to life and it was something I had created that was responsible for incredible destruction. The news reports revealed that the estimated death toll was over one hundred and thirty-five million people, not including people in neighbouring countries. The presumed death toll in Russia was expected to reach virtually one hundred percent of Russians in the country, or one hundred and fifty-two million people within the week, due to radiation sickness. I was in such shock that I could barely speak; I just sat there slowly eating what remained of my food, as all of this was going to unfold and even if I wasn't discovered, I had to live with what I had created.

The guilt was overwhelming and the events that followed only added to it, with millions of other people in the surrounding areas in the affected states either sick or dying of radiation poisoning. It was stated that those areas that had been struck would be completely uninhabitable for decades. Many other countries were now facing food shortages because of the nuclear winter effect and it was expected that it would take years or possibly decades to get the debris back down to the ground. They had people with radiation suits and cameras or drones going over the sites, and they showed the neighbourhoods of thriving cities that were now desolate and in some cases charred wastelands.

The Venezuelan counter-attack led to over twenty million of their own citizens dead and the remaining either sick, dying, or fleeing for their lives. This caused neighbouring countries to wonder how they would handle this disaster that had been done to them and their people.

The footage of what was happening overseas was even worse. The nuclear winter effect made the sun nearly invisible to much of China and portions of Japan. I began to wonder what Mr. Sugimori from all those years ago, would say if he knew the whole thing was my idea. The other countries didn't have it much better, and they were hit in their border areas. Added to that, millions were also dying from radiation poisoning and with these and other factors, the death toll was expected to reach half a billion in the months to come.

As if all of that wasn't horrible enough, it somehow got even worse. The people who lived in northern Florida, Georgia, and other states, that couldn't stay in those areas, were effectively refugees looking for help. Places like Virginia and North Carolina were among the places some of the people fled to. Shockingly some of the people and even the state government of South Carolina tried to turn the tens of thousands of now homeless people away declaring, "We have to look after the people of our own state first."

The fleeing people's pleas fell on deaf ears: "We are your own, we're Americans."

Some of these incidents resulted in a few of them being arrested, and even greater spending on state border security. A handful of incidents with people from militant North Carolina turning away struggling people from Georgia, and in some cases doing so violently. The phrase that came up that broke my heart was, "You ain't our problem."

My initial thought was to show my shock and sadness but never tell a soul about my involvement, but unfortunately that plan didn't go so well, and the nightmares returned with a vengeance. A few of them were things like me walking through a graveyard, and ones where

I myself, was already dead. Even a few where people found out and chased after me, and more than once, they would gain on me and gain on me, no matter how fast I ran. One of the dreams I woke up when I was about to get bashed by a baseball bat. In another, the mob caught up to me and was about to plunge a knife into my chest. It was hard for everyone not to talk about this all the time, but the worst part was that there was so much I wanted to say, but I had a harder and harder time keeping quiet.

Part of the reason why was that in the months that followed, one by one, country after country, decided that they were not going to trade with the United States, both out of outrage or to quell their citizens' outrage. U.S. embassies were attacked and the ambassadors fled for their lives, and because of this, so many of the things that our country was so used to importing stopped coming and many people lost their jobs because they couldn't export their goods. Anti-Americanism was now the worst it had ever been. Some countries were trying to decide how to deal with America and what everyone was calling the ultimate war crime and a genocide that surpassed the Holocaust.

By 2022, there were only about fifteen countries still trading with us and even they were on thin ice. On March 31, 2022, Canada stopped all trade with the United States, so they wouldn't lose the international market that had now offered them an ultimatum. Not to mention many countries were now in such great need, that they decided it was more profitable to sell to the rest of the world. Saudi Arabia began to cave to similar pressures and many of the corporations that were based out of the United States, began shifting their wealth overseas so that they could stay where the action was.

As I'm sure you can guess, with the unemployment rate shooting up from eight percent to seventeen in a period of six months, crime drastically rose as well. This led to a harder clampdown by police and by the time May came around, there was a mandatory curfew in Detroit and some of the other cities that were known for being heavy on crime. Riots, especially political ones, became more common and it actually reached the point where they proposed a new law, which stated that the police should have a "shoot to kill" policy with protestors. Astonishingly this actually passed the House and somehow the Senate, which led to the Supreme Court finally striking it down. The fact that such a bill even made it that far should tell you how insane the situation had become.

Maybe because of all of this guilt and stress, I semi-retired in early 2022, only working about ten to twenty hours a week. It took every single bit of determination I had, to not just crack open a bottle and drink until it was all over, and my one kidney gave out and the pain would finally stop.

As it turned out, as scared as Billy was he decided to return to the United States when he found out about the embargo. He didn't want to be prevented from seeing his family so he ended up returning to a small community in Michigan. He and I had a few conversations and I think he knew something was bothering me, so he asked me what was wrong and I told him I didn't want to talk about it. He knew it had to be something big, so at the beginning of July he and Hashani, who were now retired, actually drove to Cathy's house where I was still living to visit me and see how I was doing.

It was going to be July 4th the next day, and America was going to be celebrating its two hundred and forty-sixth birthday in the worst situation it had ever been in. I think he knew it would take a few days, but at one point he asked me to play a game of chess. I said to him, "Sure."

He then said, "Tell you what Charles, if I win you tell me what's really bothering you."

I said, "Okay," after he tried to wrestle it out of me for a few minutes.

I underestimated how rusty I was at this game and how well he played it. He took a few pawns, I took a knight, he took one of my rooks, and I took one of his bishops. Slowly but surely, he cornered me and eventually after about forty-five minutes, it was checkmate. I stared at that king, that old wooden piece with the little cross at the top of it and I grabbed it with the edges of my fingers and laid it down. I actually began to feel a tiny weight be lifted off my shoulders because I finally had an excuse to finally let it out. I then got up and laid down on the couch, and he looked at me a little confused, "Charles what are you doing?"

I responded, "Well doc, I lost, I'm going to tell you everything."

He was still a bit confused, "You know you don't have to lie down on the couch, right?"

I responded, "I'm going to need to."

That was when I finally, after all this time, was going to break my silence. "Billy, I never managed a chain of grocery stores, it was a lie to cover for the fact that all of those years I was working for the CIA."

He looked at me with shock and said, "Okay, go on."

I took a deep breath and proceeded, "In 1992 after the Soviet Union collapsed, I was afraid that they would return, so I thought of this idea to shut down the Russian missile defense system so that they couldn't launch a strike against us… and we could strike them without counterattack."

Billy looked at me and he was stunned silent by what I was saying.

I continued, "It was called Operation Railroad, which started as a way to control the Russians and then we tried to expand it to the Chinese in the first half of the 2000s. I don't know how many hours I spent setting all of that up before I left in 2006, but we got the Russian one because we started at the right time, but the Chinese one didn't work out."

By this point I had begun wiping away tears and my jaw began to tremble and I felt the familiar lump in my throat. "I thought I was insuring our nation's survival, but by the time I realized that the people in charge had other ideas, the Operation was so far along that people I never knew or met had started taking it over. After I got out of there I began to realize why it was such a bad idea, and I always hoped that after I left it would get shut down, phased out or something. But they did it, they pulled the damn trigger, and now it's all gone to shit."

I sat up and put my face in my hand, as Billy also sat there stunned speechless. Billy regained his composure after a moment of complete silence and asked me, "Charles, why are you telling me now? You returned to Michigan fifteen years ago, why didn't you say anything then?"

I responded, "I wanted to keep everyone happy and I didn't want them to know about the things I've done; I've killed people, I've arranged the deaths of people. There was a guy who molested children in China and we blackmailed him. How do you tell people that? Your children, your nieces and nephews, your family, the people who you love and want to help? They never would have taken me back after that, and they would never want to see me again for the rest of my life."

He had made a few notes and said, "So you've been carrying these secret sins around with you for years and decades?"

I said, "Yes, every day I have to keep my mouth shut because now our country is in awful shape with twenty-two percent unemployment, major crime, livid people, over half a billion dead around the world and counting. I don't know how to keep going, I... I can't carry this anymore, but I don't want to lose everyone I love and care about."

I held up my hand with a small space between my thumb and index finger, "I'm this close to drinking again, I don't even know how I held on this long."

Billy held his hand against his chin and we sat there in silence for another moment. He stared at the floor, and no doubt weighing whatever words he was thinking about carefully. "Charles, I have two things to tell you, the first is the easy answer and the second is the hard answer. I'll give you the easy one first, the easy answer is you built a horrible weapon, or system or whatever it was, but you didn't pull the trigger, so there are several people at fault, not just you. The hard answer is this, you have to get this off your chest and I don't just mean to me, I mean everyone, the family, the public, everyone."

My recurring nightmare of the mob chasing me down raced through my mind, and I looked at him and said, "Somebody will kill me."

He responded saying, "Charles, you can't live like this. You went over twelve years without drinking and this is weighing on you so much you're about to collapse. Charles, I'm not a religious man at all, but when they say confession is good for the soul, they're onto something. So here's what I think you need to do. Take everything you've done, everything you've told me and anything else that is weighing on you and I want you to write it out and then I want you to send what you've written to whoever you have to send it to. Tell whoever you have to tell because quite frankly Charles, you're about to turn seventy-three and with this much stress, I don't know how many years you have left. But whatever they are, don't you want to get that weight off your shoulders as soon as you can, so you can look at yourself in the mirror?"

I knew he was right, I got up and gave him a big hug and I told him, "I'm sorry Billy. Thank you, thank you for being my brother even when I didn't deserve it, like, well, now."

He then said, "Charles, thank you for finally telling me that. I used to wonder if you would ever let me be on your level."

I jokingly said, "I guess it took me long enough."

We watched one of his favourite movies *The Shawshank Redemption*, I watched everything that Andy Dufresne went through and then I watched him come out of that storm drain embracing freedom. After hearing Billy finally tell me what I needed to do and hearing Andy Dufresne from the movie say, "Get busy living or get busy dying," I knew that I had to start writing so I could finally feel that same freedom at long last. I figured what better day to start than on my seventy-third birthday?

So day-by-day I told my whole story because I didn't just want it to be a list. I wanted people to understand why I did it even if my reasons were wrong, which they usually were. I saw a picture on Facebook of Hope, who was celebrating her tenth birthday and saw the smile on her face looking at her chocolate cake with ten candles on it. It was wonderful seeing that even in the pit of this despair, even in this horrible time in history, joy could still be found by the innocent people who deserved it the most.

Also over these months I have been trying to figure out what the moral of this story is, there has to be more to it than "don't blow up countries."

I have pondered this long and hard, and wondered what lesson can my confession pass on? After all, those that fail to learn from history are doomed to repeat it. An event that kills hundreds of millions on its way to a billion, that takes the richest country in the world and kills almost twenty million of its people and leaves the rest in a depression, is something that must not happen again to anyone.

I would like to start with a quote from former President Woodrow Wilson, when he was speaking about the aftermath of World War I:

"You are betrayed, you fought for something you did not get, and the glories of the armies and navies of the United States is gone like a dream in the night. And there ensues upon it a nightmare of dread and there will come sometime, in the vengeful providence of God another war in which not a few hundred thousand will have to die but many millions."

What is frightening about those words were how many wars they applied to, fighting for reasons that were not what you were told. Promising outcomes that never came, resulting in the nightmare of dread of bigger and more horrifying wars in the future. The only part he got wrong was the part about the vengeful providence of God, because it wasn't God's vengeance, it was ours. Our leaders failed us, we failed to do better for our children, and too many times we failed or refused to find a way out of warring conflict. We failed to learn from history and we failed to learn that a country is not just an entity, some land mass far away. It is a land mass yes, but it holds the lives of millions of people who are no less human than ourselves, and forgetting that is never acceptable. We made poor allies and focused on the wrong enemies and went about it the wrong way and with the wrong goals at the forefront.

We put helicopters over health care, we put intelligence agencies over education, we put bigotry over our brothers and sisters, and we put fortunes over futures. As I sit here in my room in the late days of 2022, I still feel that dread of the wars to come. You may wonder who we will be fighting if the Russians were destroyed? Well with all of that death, we have countries with millions of angry people and some undoubtedly wanting revenge. We have angry people in our own country wanting revenge and after all of this time, I finally realized that a gun kills people but it doesn't kill problems. Spilled blood nourishes the seeds of conflict, so with over seven hundred million dead and counting, not to mention the millions before, that the seeds of conflict will have no shortage of nourishment. For this reason, I fear for the twenty-first century. I am left to wonder why we left power in the hands of people who have not learned the harsh lessons of history and don't realize the responsibilities they hold. If I could go back in time and tell people something, I would tell them not to follow anger, not to follow fear because too many followed those feelings into their grave, or into the regret I must live with for the rest of my life.

Finally, if you have not been moved by my words, if like Caleb you still think we need to kill or throw out minorities, if like Mark you think that the enemy isn't worthy of any human dignity, if like me at one time you think that we must cling to the past, remember how many things in the past were hideously inhumane. Remember how we need to pursue the most peaceful future possible and how much our ancestor's failure to do this cost us dearly in one form or another. Melvoy's Railroad made it to its destination and left hundreds of millions of people dead in the process, because we knew we wanted victory but forgot to truly ask "for what purpose?"

If we sink to or below the level of our enemies, why do we deserve to win? Shouldn't we take the high road, as much as we possibly can? If we throw away our principles at the first sign of trouble, what did we stand for? Hopefully those who go on will learn from our mistakes and begin to forge a truly better world. If we fail to learn from history, if in the wake of this endless parade of death we repeat these mistakes, then this confession and all of those dead will be in vain and that will be the greatest tragedy of all.

ABOUT THE AUTHOR

Peter Howe was born outside of Toronto, Ontario, Canada in 1988. He graduated from the University of Guelph-Humber with a bachelor's degree in business administration. Ultimately, he decided to branch out beyond bookkeeping and accounting to incorporate more of his interests into his life. His broad knowledge and passions contribute to his desire to write books of a variety of subjects, genres, and formats.

Made in the USA
Columbia, SC
11 November 2018